THE PEELING

& Other Terrifying Tales

IAIN ROB WRIGHT

SalGad Publishing Group

The Peeling

AN AUTHOR'S WORD

The Peeling was one of the first stories I ever published. It was a novella set in a world where a flesh eating virus was on the loose. Readers liked it. They found it disturbing. And because people liked it, I wrote several more novellas about The Peeling. Each book featured a different character and a different story that added to an overall narrative. The problem was, that after the first book, I didn't have any idea where to take the story. I was writing for market rather than writing for myself, and as a consequence it has never been a series I am happy with. I think the final book 'The Lights' reveals that I had run out of ideas.

Despite my initial visit to the world of The Peeling being one of regret, I always loved the idea. One of the most frightening films, for me, is Outbreak with Dustin Hoffman. It really gets under my skin, excuse the pun. The Peeling is my attempt to capture that squirming horror, and it was great to have a chance to return to the story. The version of The Peeling contained within this book is a completely new story. It is the version told by a fulltime writer of seven years versus the young author just starting out who wrote the original. The older books are also contained in this collection, so you will have an opportunity to compare the Iain Rob Wright then and the Iain Rob Wright now. You will also see the evolution of the greatest plague ever to infect mankind… THE PEELING.

Dedicated to my Patrons

SOME OF MY BEST FRIENDS...

Deb Bergevin, Paula Davis, Ann Nguessan, Celeste Schmitt, Richard Ounsworth, Miss Jacqueline Tew, Rebecca Brock, Melissa Ramsay, Larry J. Field, Leeanne Cavanough, Ruby Marion, G.W. Cheney, Paige Vallee, Minnis Hendricks, Sophie Hall, Lauren Brigham, Darlene Taylor, Tim Feely, Claire Arnott, Adrian Johns, Patricia Wadley, Jonathan D Sergotick, Colleen B Cassidy, Matthew Wilson, Ken Howell, Lisa Forlow, Anna M. Garcia-Centner, Carrie Murphy, Margaret Powers, Patty Jamison, Matthew Stevens, Mary Patterson, Nate S Gian Spadone, Gilly Adam, Barbara Haynes, Kim Tomsett, Claire Armstrong-Brealey, Carolyne Lain, Lynn Delmont, Lynn Neering, Terence Pike, Alyssa Chafe, Janice Ryberg, Jaki Flowers, Julie Parker, John Grathwol, Sharon Hornes, Michelle Shimp, Catherine Manders Eylott, Tom G.H. Adams, Leslie Gil, Janet Carter. Alex Reid, John Heaney, Melissa Kazas, Carla A Snook, Leanne Pert, Susan Hunsinger, Lady Aliehs, Wendy Wagner, Hank Rhoden, Helen M Helton, Carl Saxon, Jennifer Tooker, T Cotchaleovitch, Karen Danvers, Eric Lee, William Skubinna, Annie West Ellzey, Amanda Lundquist, Robert Nickerson, Diane Collier, Philippa Willis, Bob Jefferson+, Karen Oâ€™Neill, Aimee VanCleve, JoAnn Pine, Felicity O'Keeffe, Randy Eberle, Harry Price, Gina, Jonathan Ridgeway, Angela Gear, Tami Franzel, John Watson, Ila Turner, Jason Gardner, Rob Voss, John R. Conant, Kathleen, Eileen Jenkins, Rob White, Andre N, Jackie Davis, Lee Smart, SiÃ¢n Mackie, Claire Whitlingum, Gary Holland, Rachel Mayfield, Chris Hicks, Christine Brown, Cassandra Richards, Julie Christie, Tracy Guinther, Kristie Stailey, Deirdre Stuart, Dinshaw Dotivala, Elizabeth Bryson, Kimberly Sanborn

"Sickness is mankind's greatest defect."

Georg C. Lichtenberg

"The way most doctors practice medicine right now isn't working."

Mark Hyman

"There's some kids in a cabin. They got a disease."

Tommy, Cabin Fever (2002), Lionsgate Film

THE PEELING (2018)

Chapter 1

"It's bitter kaut today, ay?"

Devey studied Mr Opperman's wizened face, then glanced up at the ominous grey sky. "Certainly is, Mr Opperman. Bet you miss South Africa on days like this, huh?"

The old man spat on the small patch of lawn outside his bungalow. "No way, *boet*! I never miss that shit hole. Do you miss Pakistan?"

Devey chuckled. "I was born in Northfield, man, but my parents say India is nice, which is where *they* are from. I'm sure every place has its good and bad."

"Like people," said Mr Opperman, sounding grumpy—but then everything the South African said sounded grumpy. Sometimes he bordered on offensive, too, but he always greeted Devey with a smile, so he liked the old man overall. "Any post for me today, boy?"

Devey slid a letter from his postbag and handed it over. "Just the one, and it looks like a bill, I'm afraid."

The old man spat again and deposited the letter inside his faded green cardigan. "I suppose you're only doing your job, boy. Take care today, ay? It's gunna rain, and you ain't dressed for it."

Devey smoothed his hands over his dark blue shorts. He wore them because he had run out of clean trousers, and groaned internally at the thought of having to do laundry tonight. "And here was me thinking it would be mild today," he said. "You take care, Mr Opperman. See you tomorrow." He waved the old man goodbye and continued to the next bungalow. Right on time, Mrs Partridge emerged from her front door and wheeled her bin up the path. Devey trotted over and took it from her as he always did on a Thursday morning.

"Oh, you're a dear," she said—the same thing she said every week. Devey hated watching the pensioners on Blackstitch Lane struggle with their wheely bins, so it had become routine he would lend a hand during his rounds. He even looked forward to it.

"No problem, Mrs Partridge," he said with a smile. "Here's your post. Someone's popular today!"

The old dear's face lit up at the bundle of letters. Usually she got nothing. "Oh, how wonderful," she said. "I turned eighty today. These must be cards from my family."

Devey gave a thumbs up. "Oh, wow. Happy birthday, Mrs Patridge. Many happy returns. Are you doing anything nice today?"

She shook her head and a melancholy whistle escaped her dry lips. "You stop making a fuss at my age. What I'd give to still be a sprog like you."

"I'm twenty-four!" Devey objected playfully.

"Aye! A babby. Enjoy your youth while you have it because it's gone before you know and you never know which day will be your last."

"Enjoy your birthday, Mrs Partridge," he said, not wanting to depress himself with talk of old age and infirmity. He strolled to the next bungalow, but Miss Mallon didn't come out to greet him like she usually did. The pensioners treated their weekly bin run like a social event, an opportunity to wave and check in with one another. Miss Mallon was usually out with the rest of them. But not today.

"Suppose I'll have to do it the old fashioned way," Devey mumbled as he pulled the woman's post from his bag and headed down her path. The front curtains were closed, which was another unusual sight as Miss Mallon was active for her age—an avid Bingo player and a regular at the swimming baths according to their chats—and she took pride in her house's appearance.

The front door was open. Just a little.

"Miss Mallon?" he called out. "Mary? It's Devey, I have your post."

No answer. His empty stomach growled, but it wasn't in hunger. He stood on the doorstep, unsure whether to go in. He called out again, but still he got no answer. Knocking bought no response either. Mary's hallway was dim and unlit. Why was she not answering?

He could lose his job for walking into an addressee's property he reminded himself, but he couldn't just drop off Mary's post and leave, right? What if she was hurt? "Come on, man," he chided himself. "She might have fallen and broken a hip. What's to think about?"

Mind made up, he prodded the front door with his trainer. The smell hit him like an open palm—a sickly-sweet odour like curdled milk. "Mary? Are you here? It's Devey, the postman. You've got me worried." He peered down the hallway, then took one cautious step after another. "Your front door was open," he said. "I hope you don't mind me checking on you."

He passed by the lounge and peered inside. An embroidered couch faced a small flat screen television, but there was no Mary. Further down the hallway, a doorway opened onto what he assumed was the kitchen. The room was lit and, as he walked towards it, the odour increased. He called out again. This time a reply met him.

A whimper.

Carpet covered the hallway, but Devey had been unaware of it until it changed texture beneath his feet. His trainer left the bristly fibres and came down on something tacky—a substance not quite wet but not quite solid. He lowered his gaze and saw blood, a slick trail leading into the kitchen. All at once, the walls tilted either side of him. His vision spun. The slim tendrils of fear that had been clutching him since he'd left the doorstep now swelled into monstrous tentacles wrapped around his guts. "Mary? Mary, if you're okay now is the time to say so. Mary? Mary, please answer me!"

Another whimper. A low moan.

Devey swallowed a gelatinous lump in his throat and stepped into the kitchen, fighting the urge to run away.

Blood smeared the cream linoleum. A cat fussed over something in the centre of the room and flinched when Devey entered. It didn't abandon its prize, though, and even let out a low growl to warn him off. The animal was not his concern, and he glanced around for Mary. A flimsy wooden table and chairs blocked his view of the far side of the kitchen and left him with no choice but to go further inside. He'd now lost all hope of there being a simple reason for Mary not putting her bin out.

Man, do I really want to do this? Still time to turn around and leave. Pretend this never happened and go back to my rounds.

How would I sleep at night?

Goddamn it!

He took a step forward.

And found Mary.

Although it could have been anyone.

The stench which had been a mild annoyance up until now, became a noxious wave that doubled him over. His balance deserted him and he fought to keep from tumbling to the blood-streaked floor. Mary's wide eyes stared up at him, and her teeth clacked together trying to speak—but she had no lips or tongue. Tendons stretched back and forth across her face, ending at her hairline in sticky clumps. Barely a scrap of healthy skin remained. She was a ghoul.

Mary lifted an arm to him, just an inch, but Devey understood she was asking him for help. He reached down to take her hand, but recoiled in horror when he saw finger bones bursting through the pads of her fingertips. "I-I'm sorry," he said, stepping back. "I-I'll get help."

Mary's arm collapsed to the ground. The light faded from her lidless eyes.

Devey kept backing away, legs like rubber, until his heel struck something. He turned around and saw the cat. It hissed at him and scurried away, leaving behind its prize—one of Mary's ears.

Devey vomited again before fleeing the kitchen.

MR OPPERMAN WAITED with Devey on the front lawn until the ambulance came. The wrinkled South African was smoking a cigarette on his front step when Devey had spilled out of Mary's home screaming for help. The old man did his best to calm him down, rubbing his back and chatting, but it didn't work. Devey was still shaking by the time the police arrived ten minutes after a pair of paramedics in an ambulance. Devey didn't even remember if it was him who had called 999. His phone was still in his pocket.

"You say the front door was open when you arrived, Mr Singh?" asked one of the two police officers, a lanky man with coppery sideburns to his chin. His partner remained in the car, talking on the radio. Both officers were as freaked out as him—the horror was written all over their faces—and they'd come rushing out of Mary's house one minute after going in. Blackstitch Lane was busier than ever with an ambulance, police car, and several gawking neighbours. Mr Opperman had waved a hand at them to go back inside several times, but none of them obeyed. Devey tried to speak. That gelatinous lump choked him again, and he struggled to swallow it down. Mr Opperman rubbed at his back, which helped. "There, there, boy. You're out of it now. Just tell the policeman what you saw, *ja*?"

Devey nodded. "Y-yes, the door was open."

The police officer frowned. "But you found her in the kitchen? Why did you go in?"

"I was worried. Mary is—*was*—a strong lady, but she's still old. I thought maybe she'd fallen."

"Mary? You knew her personally?"

"No, I just… I know most of the people on this road. I watch out for them."

The police officer tilted his head like a curious puppy. His long side-burns added to the effect. "Why?"

"Because he's a decent boy," said Mr Opperman snippily. He didn't seem to like authority and glared at the officer every time the man asked a question.

The police officer shrugged. "Okay, fine. So Mrs Mallon's front door was open, and you found her in the kitchen?"

"Miss Mallon," Devey grunted. "She never married. There was blood on the hallway carpet, like maybe she'd dragged herself into the kitchen. She might have got ill in the night but couldn't make it outside, or changed her mind about going outside to get help and went back in. I think she collapsed in the hallway."

The police officer studied his notepad before putting it away. "We found a mobile phone on the floor next to Miss Mallon's body. It's possible she was about to leave her house but couldn't manage it, so went back inside to call for help instead." He pinched the bridge of his nose and took a deep breath. "What a wretched way for an old lady to end up."

Devey agreed wholeheartedly. The pain Mary must have gone through... He could not imagine it. "Officer? What was wrong with her? There was barely anything left of her. What can do that to a person?"

The officer appeared just north of thirty, but right then he looked like a scared little boy. "Mr Singh, I wish I had the slightest idea, but I don't. Perhaps the paramedics will know more."

Devey glanced down the path to where the ambulance was parked on the curb. Both paramedics spoke on their radios, animated and fidgety.

From first impressions, it didn't seem like they had a clue what had happened to Mary either. In fact they looked downright scared. A car door slammed and the police officer's partner got out of their car. She looked anxious about something. The male officer excused himself and went off to speak with her.

Devey clutched himself to keep from shaking. Mr Opperman trembled too, pulling his cardigan around himself. "You should go inside," Devey told him. "You were right, I think it's going to rain."

"Don't you worry about me, boy. You wanna tell me what you saw in poor Mary's house? Everyone who goes in there comes out looking like they met the devil."

The image of Mary's decaying body flashed through Devey's mind, and he screwed his eyes shut hoping to make it go away. He rubbed at his forehead and wondered how he would ever sleep again. That sickly-sweet odour might never leave him. "You don't want to know, Mr Opperman. Her skin… Her skin had peeled away in a hundred places. There were pools of blood all over the floor. It…"

Mr Opperman waved a hand. "*Ja, ja*, okay. You tell quite the picture, boet. Is there anyone who can come get you? You can have a *dop* of whiskey at my house if you need to gather yourself first." He frowned. "Do you people drink?"

Devey chuckled, surprised he could still manage it. "I'm Sikh."

Mr Opperman shrugged and raised his eyebrows.

"So yes," Devey explained, "I can drink."

"You brownies all look the same to me."

Devey chuckled again. "And during my first year on this route I thought your accent was Australian."

"Ha!" The old man slapped his back. "You wouldn't be the first."

The two police officers came hurrying back. Devey wasn't sure what had changed, but they seemed hostile, like they would have shot him if they'd been carrying guns. Mr Opperman moved in front of Devey and put up a liver-spotted hand. "Whoa, whoa, where is the fire?"

"Mr Singh?" The male police officer spoke only to Devey, ignoring Mr Opperman. "Did you touch the body?"

Devey struggled to understand. "You mean Mary? She reached out to me before she died."

"Did you touch her?" The officer took a step forward, but his partner seemed hesitant to follow.

Devey stepped back, feeling threatened. "What? No, I never touched her! I bolted just like the rest of you did."

"What are you doing? This man has done nothing wrong." One of the paramedics hurried over from the ambulance. She glared at the two officers, her pretty face contorting with ugly anger. "Is there something we should know about?"

"Mr Singh needs to be isolated immediately. You should get instructions any minute."

The paramedic's tough expression withered, and she glanced at Devey nervously—maybe even fearfully—before taking a half-step back towards the ambulance. Mr Opperman took a step back too, removing his hand from Devey's back. "Eh, boy, perhaps you better do as they tell you, ja?"

Devey shook his head and licked his lips. "What's going on? You don't need to-"

The police officer pulled something from his belt and held it in front of him. "Mr Singh, this is CS gas. If I am forced to spray you, the effects will be extremely unpleasant. Please don't make me."

Devey turned his face and splayed his fingers out in front of him. "Hold on, man! I don't understand what's happening here." A squawk from a radio and the two paramedics hurried back to take a call from the ambulance. Their eyes never left Devey as they stood talking into the receiver. In fact, all eyes were on Devey. He felt like an animal at the zoo. The police officer with the CS gas lowered the cannister. "Look, Mr Singh. Devey, isn't it? I'm not sure what's happening myself. All I know is that I reported in the scene as normal, but then we got a call back from HQ saying to use any means necessary to keep you from leaving the scene. That usually means you're dangerous, but we also got orders to see you into the custody of the Ambulance Service who are to isolate you immediately. I think you know what that means."

The female paramedic who had stuck up for Devey now shouted over from the ambulance. "We need to take you in, Mr Singh." She looked at the police officers apologetically. "You both need to present yourselves, too, at Quest Lane Hospital. That's where we're heading."

The male police officer nodded that he understood, then turned a scowl on Devey like somehow this was all his fault. He felt like telling the guy to go shag himself. He'd done nothing wrong. Instead, though, he asked a question—a question he had asked already. "What was wrong with Mary?"

The police officer shook his head. "No one has a fucking clue, but if it's contagious... Look, please just get in the back of the ambulance."

If it's contagious... Devey shuffled his feet like a zombie, so utterly terrified he would do whatever he was told if it meant not having to process what was happening. The paramedics kept their distance as he stepped into the road and rounded the ambulance. They slammed the doors the second he was inside. The engine rumbled almost immediately. As they drove away, Devey peered out the ambulance's rear window at the residents of Blackstitch Lane. The pensioners stood in a line at the end of their paths, watching silently. He wondered if he would ever see any of them again.

Chapter 2

"Are you lightheaded or nauseous, Mr Singh?"

Devey grimaced. "Yes! Because I watched a woman die of some horrible disease and then got arrested for no reason."

The doctor—a well-spoken black man, surnamed 'Zantoko' according to his name badge—had a kindly manner, despite his face mask and latex gloves. "I understand, and I am sorry for keeping you here like this. You are in no way 'under arrest,' but you may have encountered something rather nasty. I want to make sure you are okay, Mr Singh. That is all."

Devey felt his heart thudding in his ears. "What is it I might have? Nobody will tell me why Mary died."

"I haven't seen the deceased," the doctor admitted, "but I understand my colleagues at Public Health are yet to identify the cause of death. With any luck, it won't be a contagious disease, but I'm afraid I need you to stay here until we know for sure."

"I really need to finish my route," said Devey pathetically. He knew it didn't matter, but it was nagging him all the same. He had never missed his rounds before. His postbag lay on the trolley bed beside him. "It would be a criminal offence if anything happens to this post, and I would be responsible."

"I shall lock it away for you, if you wish, Mr Singh?"

"Call me Devey. And yes, that would be helpful, Doctor. My biggest worry is my bosses. I haven't called them, and they'll see from their trackers that my van hasn't moved from Blackstitch Lane in over two hours."

"If you have a mobile phone, you're free to make a call. If you need, I shall talk to your bosses and explain."

Devey huffed. "They probably wouldn't believe you. The Royal Mail does not make excuses. Sure I don't need to tell you how it is as a fellow employee of the government. Is the NHS any better these days?"

"No," said the doctor, then turned and retrieved something from a cart he had wheeled in with him. The penlight hurt as he shone it in Devey's eyes. "All of your tests so far seem to be fine." He moved slowly from one pupil to the next. "I am confident you are okay, but I must ask a nurse to take blood and urine to run further examinations."

"What if I just walked out?"

The doctor lowered his penlight and took a step back as if Devey might try to dodge past him. "As I said, you are not under arrest, but I have strict orders to inform the police if you leave this room. The two officers you spoke to this morning are right next door, having the same tests as you. So are the paramedics. This is not personal, Devey. It is in the interest of public health. Would you want to leave if you could infect people with something dangerous? I do not think you are that man."

Devey studied his hands and rubbed them together. "No. I'm a decent guy, but that's what got me into this mess. If I hadn't bothered to check on Mary… Man, why didn't I mind my own business?"

"You did the right thing, Devey. I would have done the same in your position."

"Thank you, Doctor. That almost makes me feel better."

"You are most welcome. Please excuse me." The doctor left to get the nurse, and Devey sat alone again. He needed to call work, but wanted to put it off for a few more minutes—he wasn't calm enough to speak to his bosses yet. Willis was on today, and Willis was a twat. A strange urge came over Devey as he thought about making the call—he wanted to call his father. It had been three years since their last conversation—a shouting match really—and he'd been too angry to consider ever talking to him again. What was happening now eroded those feelings of anger and instead left him with a sickening fear that made him want to be with family. Even if that family consisted only of his father.

Would Dad even come if I call him?

Only one way to find out.

Devey reached into his pocket for his phone, but then the door opened and a nurse entered. She was pretty—fair-featured and blue-eyed. He couldn't see her mouth behind her mask, but he imagined it was smiling. Also, she was heavily pregnant—the bump rising beneath the plastic apron she wore. He left his phone in his pocket and stood up. "Should you come near me in your current... state?"

"It's okay," she said cheerfully. "It's actually very easy to avoid infection with the proper precautions. I'll just take some bloods and then we should hopefully be able to find out what the score is. My name is Sonja. You're Devey, right?"

"Yes. My actual name is Dayabir, but nobody calls me that. Or they try and get it wrong. Just easier to call me Devey. I like that more anyway." Why was he babbling? He felt embarrassed in front of the nurse for some reason. There was a chance he might have a disease, and it made him feel dirty.

The nurse beamed at him. "Oh, how lovely. It's nice to hear a name a little different. Dayabir? Did I get it right?"

"Yes, you did! Feel free to name your baby after me."

"I'm having a girl. Would that still work?"

He thought about it. "No, it's a boy's name, I think. So when are you due?"

"Six weeks. I'm off the job in two. Can't wait." She prepared a syringe on a tray she'd wheeled in, taking it from a plastic packet. "You have any kids?"

"No," said Devey with a firm shake of his head. "I'm only twenty-four. It's the single life for a few more years yet."

Sonja gasped behind her mask. "How can a handsome man like you still be single?"

He puffed out his chest as he gave an answer, then felt silly. "Just never found anyone to be close to like that. I'm too used to being on my own, I guess. Always figured I'd meet someone and settle down later, so what's the rush? How about you? Have you been with your husband a long time?"

She had the needle assembled now and held it out in front of him, almost like a threat. "I'm not married."

"Oh, sorry. I shouldn't have assumed."

"That's okay." She pointed to her belly. "What you're looking at is the result of a one-night stand." She pulled a face, but only ended up looking cuter. "Not my finest achievement, admittedly, but I can't wait to meet my daughter. I grew up without a father in my life, so I know what she'll need. Me and her will be a team."

Devey enjoyed learning about people—the part of his job as a postman he liked the most—but he felt uncomfortable to hear so many personal details, especially when they reminded him so much of his own. Sonja was clearly a person who hid nothing of herself, and he supposed it might be a defence mechanism. By being upfront about the things people might knock her for, she diffused their power to hurt her. He did the opposite and showed as little of himself as possible. "So is this where you stab me in the arm with your needle?" he asked.

"Afraid so. Don't worry, I'll be gentle."

He held his breath and looked away, focusing on a poster on the wall. CATCH IT. BIN IT. KILL IT. It was an info sheet about sneezing into tissues and washing your hands afterwards. Basic stuff, and it surprised him that people even needed to be reminded of such basic hygiene. Then he wondered how Mary had caught whatever had killed her. Had someone sneezed on her? Was it contagious? He shuddered as he remembered almost taking her hand. Those skeletal fingers.

Mary's last moment was asking him for help, and him recoiling in horror. "Do you know if Mary had any family?" he asked as the needle went into the crook of his arm. He winced, and kept his eyes locked on the inane hygiene poster, reading each word earnestly.

"The poor lady who died?" said Sonja. "I haven't been told much about her. She's being dealt with by Public Health."

"Who's that?"

She adjusted the needle in his arm, making clinking sounds as she changed the cartridge. Devey glimpsed his own blood leaking out and went woozy, chiding himself for not keeping his eyes on the poster. "Public Health," she explained, "deal with any health threats to the public, like when we get cases of bird flu or someone gets Mad Cow Disease. They also get involved if something infectious or unidentifiable shows up. It sounds like Mary had a flesh-eating disease, which is uncommon, so they've taken ownership of her case."

The needle withdrew from Devey's arm and he sighed with relief. "Believe me, that works out better for you," he said. "Mary was a real mess. I doubt your squeamish, being a nurse, but it was a nightmare."

She tilted her head and gave him a lopsided smile that he realised was pity. "I spoke to Lucy, one of the paramedics who attended, and she told me how bad it was. And trust me, paramedics are used to dealing with everything."

"What's the worst you've ever seen?" Devey asked, then felt embarrassed for being so morbid. He let the question stand though.

To his surprise, Sonja seemed happy to answer it, and did so without hesitation. "They brought in an elderly man once who hadn't washed or changed his clothes in years. His toenails had fused with his slippers and they tore off when we removed them. The smell was the worst thing imaginable."

Devey groaned as he imagined it. Could it have been worse than what he had smelt in Mary's kitchen? Both were smells of rotting human flesh, so perhaps they were the same. "I don't know how you do this job."

"It's not all bad," she said, pulling a plastic stick from a clear packet. "Open wide. I need to take a swab from inside your cheek." He did as he was told and the swab darted in and out of his mouth before he knew it. Without even watching what she was doing, Sonja had popped it back into the packet and pulled a zip. Bodily fluids were mundane to her. Maybe that was how nurses and doctors coped. "Okay, then!" she said. "Last thing we need is a urine sample. I'll leave you this plastic pot here. There's a toilet behind you, so I'll pop back in a bit to see how you're getting on."

"The blood results…" Devey nodded to the three tubes of his blood on the cart. "Will they take long?"

"We're not entirely sure what we're looking for, so they'll probably need to run several tests. Just sit tight and I'll try to keep you updated. Can I get you a cup of tea?"

Devey almost gushed with joy. He hadn't realised how thirsty he was, or how wonderful a cup of tea sounded. "God yes! White, two sugars, please. Man, that would be great."

Sonja patted his shoulder then left him alone. Not wanting to sit and think, he took his plastic beaker into the toilet. A mirror caught his eye, and he took a moment to study himself, pulling at his eyelids and staring into his own pupils. He didn't know what he expected to find—black threads of poison or swirling parasites creeping around, he supposed—but he seemed to be okay. He was pale, and oddly weary for what could only have been early afternoon, but he was still himself. Not sick.

Satisfied, he turned to the toilet bowl, which was flanked by handlebars and various pull cords. He prepared to take a leak, prompting his mind to conjure images of him pissing bucketfuls of blood, so he undid his fly apprehensively. It was a relief when a bright yellow stream appeared, and he got a majority of it in the beaker and only a slight amount on his fingers. The chance to wash his hands at the sink was welcome, and he soaped them up for a good ten minutes. He wished he could scrub his insides too.

What if he had what Mary had? Would his skin start peeling away? Would his organs melt? Would he end up a pile of cat food on the kitchen floor? No, he would die here in this hospital while doctors ran an endless battery of tests, his final moments consisting of suffering heaped upon suffering.

Come on, man. You're going to send yourself crazy.

To calm himself, he had to give himself some positive possibilities to offset the bad. Number one, he felt fine. Two, even if he wasn't fine, they could treat him right away. Most things could be treated if you caught them early enough, right? Mary might have only needed antibiotics, but she'd been an old lady not wanting to make a fuss. Maybe the fact she was old had led to her death. He was a healthy young man, his body would fight off whatever Mary had caught. Thirdly, he told himself that she might not even have had an infection. She might have been tortured by a skin-flaying psychopath, or victim to a nasty blood disorder. A virus was only one possibility out of many, and all he should be thinking of right now was how poor Mary must have suffered. He'd liked the old lady, and it was a tragedy what had happened to her. Once, when it had been raining, she'd invited him in for a biscuit.

What the hell happened to her?

Devey decided, that if nothing else, he would at least find out that.

SONJA RETURNED ten minutes later for Devey's urine sample. She switched on the television and handed him a cup of piping hot tea. Then she left again. For a while, he'd sat and watched a *Friends* episode—one where Ross still had Marcel the monkey—but he was now surfing for something else. He'd been in the hospital for over three hours now, and he was still yet to call his bosses at work. He'd now left it so long, he decided to wait until he left the hospital. At least then he could get into a long—potentially loud—conversation. The trauma of the morning had worn off, and he no longer felt so worried. Instead, he was simply bored. He wanted out of this room. He flicked through the Hospital's limited

TV channels, hoping to find something to get him through the next bout of waiting, but everything was old or out of date. *Jeremy Kyle* had gotten stale years ago, and *Morecambe and Wise* were only acceptable at Christmas. They even ran repeats of *Porridge* on BBC Two. Didn't they make new programmes anymore?

Then he caught the end of the news.

The main report concerned a rumoured sex tape featuring Meghan Markle, and how it would shame the Royal Family if true, but the ticker across the bottom of the screen featured a public health warning. It read:

Bengali Flu Strain to hit Britain. People advised to wash hands and stay indoors.

Not the most alarming news he'd ever read, but ill timed considering the morning he'd had. Was that what Mary had caught—Bengali Flu? What the hell was 'Bengali Flu' anyway? Flu from India, he supposed, but what was the difference? Swine Flu, Spanish Flu, Bird Flu, Australian Flu… Wasn't the flu just the flu?

Did Bengali Flu make your flesh rot away like Mary's had?

A ridiculous theory, and he knew whatever killed Mary had been something truly awful. A flesh-eating disease, the nurse had said. Like something out of a horror movie.

The door rattled, making him jump out of his skin, but he settled down in time to be sitting calmly by the time Doctor Zantoko entered the room. The man was smiling, which he hoped was a good sign. "Devey, you're looking much better. Have you recovered from the shock of such a terrible morning?"

Devey smiled. "I'm beginning to, but I imagine it will have a lot to do with what you are about to tell me."

"All your tests came back normal. We will need to monitor you for the next few months, or until we find out more about what killed Miss Mallon, but as of now you are perfectly healthy."

Devey wasn't sure if he heard bad news or not. "So I might still have something? What do you mean, you need to monitor me?"

The doctor perched on the bed beside him. "Sorry, let me explain. Many viruses have incubation periods, so we will need to see you every couple of days to run more tests, but in the meantime we will give you a course of antibiotics and a mild steroid to amp up your immune system."

"I thought antibiotics didn't affect viruses. They create superbugs or something, right?"

"That is entirely correct, but there could be a bacterial infection or parasite at play, in which case we should treat you accordingly. The steroids will help your immune system fight off any potential viruses and the antibiotics will fight most everything else. But understand, Devy, we are just being overly cautious. You had no physical contact with Miss Mallon, and I believe you to be healthy. Come back in if you feel unwell, but today you may leave and go about your day."

Devey sighed, overwhelmed and teary. He cleared his throat and steeled himself before he stood up and shook the doctor firmly by the hand. "Thank you so much for looking after me, doctor." Before he left, a question found its way to his lips, and it made him stop before he reached the door. "The paramedics? Are they okay?"

Zantoko nodded. "It appears so. The police officers too. I shall pass on the same good news to them in a moment."

A crash sounded next door. It startled both men. Devey looked at the doctor. "What was that?"

"I…" He looked concerned. "I do not know."

He disappeared out the door in a hurry, white coat billowing behind him. Devey stood alone in the room, fidgeting. He'd got the all clear, so could he leave? No, he should wait for Zantoko to come back and discharge him. There must be paperwork involved, there always was. He decided to fill the time by making that call he'd been putting off. Pulling out his phone, he dialled work. Odd, that he felt so guilty, as he'd done nothing wrong, but he reminded himself he'd gone into a private residence uninvited. Royal Mail was very clear about trespassing. The front porch was as far as a postman should ever go. He'd seen guys get chewed up and spat out for dropping a parcel into someone's hallway, or even a lounge in one case. If the homeowner complained it was a serious matter—an actual crime being reported.

Ring-ring. Ring-ring. Ring-ring.

Devey pressed the phone to his ear for over a minute, but it kept on ringing. Kept on ringing past the point where he expected voicemail to kick in. It seemed no one had turned the service on. If they were busy at dispatch, his absence would be appreciated even less.

Ring-ring.

Devey waited a few more seconds then put the phone away. The telling off would have to wait. Maybe he'd go get his van and finish his round before facing the music. It would help his case. Better late than never.

Another crash sounded next door.

"Enough of this shit!" He needed out of this room, out of this hospital. The more he knocked around here, the more his head filled with things better left unremembered. At first, he'd been preoccupied by the possibility he might have a flesh eating disease, but now he was hanging around and waiting. Thinking.

Time to leave.

He headed for the door, trying to ignore the ruckus coming from the next room. Who was in there? The paramedics? The police officers? Or some drug addict having a fit? The corridor outside became a rushing river of people and equipment. Something was happening. He hurried, but couldn't help looking into the room next door as he passed it. What he saw turned his stomach.

Chapter 3

The door hung wide open, allowing Devey to see inside the next examination room. Doctor Zantoko stood with the nurse, Sonja, and two orderlies flanking him left and right. They were all trying to calm the female paramedic who was shouting at them hysterically. The woman had shed her jacket and now wore only green trousers and a white vest. Sweat drenched her chest. She looked terrified.

She looked ill.

Devey wanted to rush for the exit, but his feet disobeyed and took him into the room. His mind failed to provide a full understanding of what was happening, but his gut told him it was something bad. Something he needed to know about.

"Get away from me," the paramedic shouted, clutching at herself like she was hiding something. At the back of the room, her partner told her to sit down. There were tears on his cheeks.

Dr Zantoko saw Devey and pointed at him. "Stay back. Do not come into this room."

Devey groaned. "She's sick, isn't she? Does she have it?"

The frightened paramedic reacted to his voice, and her eyes homed in on him. "You! You need to help me!"

"Me?" Devey pointed to himself. "What can I do?"

She thrust out her wrist and revealed the blistered flesh oozing beneath her palm. "You said you knew that woman. What did she have? What the hell did she infect me with?"

"I… I don't know. I'm just the postman. She was fine when I saw her last week. How… How did you…?"

"I fucking touched her!" The woman put her hand against her forehead in despair, speaking in sobs. "I checked her neck pulse. That's all! Two fingers against her throat." She stared desperately at him. "Did she travel anywhere lately? Did she… did she have anything wrong with her? Did she say anything before she died?"

Devey shook his head, not knowing what to say to the woman. Seeing her panic made *him* panic. If she had it, he might too. Dr Zantoko took over, trying to calm things down. "Claudia, we will figure this out, but we need to get you some place secure. Something this infectious—something this *fast*—must be isolated. We shall find out what's wrong with you, but you know what needs to happen. You're a danger, Claudia."

Her shoulders dropped and some defiance left her. "Julien, I don't want to die."

"You won't!"

Tears streamed down the woman's face, and Devey covered his mouth with revulsion when he saw one of her eyes weep blood. She glanced his way again, but this time he averted his eyes and looked down at the floor. There was nothing he could do or say to help her. He was just a terrified and confused postman.

So he turned and walked away.

Dr Zantoko shouted after him. "Mr Singh, you cannot leave!"

Devey walked faster.

"Don't let him leave!"

The two orderlies hurried after him.

He ran.

"Stop right now!"

But that was the last thing Devey was going to do. Zantoko had said he was healthy, so he was getting as far away from this virus as he could. He'd hide under a goddamn bridge if he had to. They could arrest him later if they liked, but only once this thing was under control. The orderlies yelled at Devey as he picked up speed, which caused other members of staff to try and block him, forcing him to dodge and change directions so many times he ended up disorientated and lost. He risked a glance back over his shoulder, pleased to see he'd already put twenty metres between himself and his pursuers. They were a pair of paunched, middle-aged men chasing a twenty-four-year-old who visited the gym twice a week. He could do this.

Just find the exit and I'm out of here.

He entered a new corridor, and at the far end he saw two more orderlies coming his way. They were speaking into a radio. The other two were still behind him. "Shit!" He searched for a way out, racing over to a window and pulling at its lower lip. The thing was stuck solid. No escape there. "Shit! Shit! Shit!" There was only one door between him and the two orderlies ahead, so that was what he went for next. He prayed for it to be unlocked, because if not, the jig was up. They'd throw him right back in that room next to the paramedic. Next to the infection.

Claudia. She has a name.

She has what Mary had.

The orderlies in front saw Devey and shouted at him to stop. He rattled the door handle desperately and shoved his shoulder against the wood. It swung open, and he fell through. Shaking with adrenaline, he smiled at a little girl with curly blonde locks who was getting a chocolate bar from a nearby snack machine. Obviously, she knew something was up because she grabbed her *Snickers* bar and hurried off to mummy who sat on a long plastic bench along with a dozen other people.

A waiting room.

He'd entered the hospital's main waiting area, an expansive space with numerous seating, a newsagent, and a coffee shop. The main entrance and exit lay ahead. Salvation.

"Can I help you?" asked a woman from a long desk a few feet to his left. She had tight skin and short hair, more like a librarian than a receptionist.

"No, thank you." He smiled politely and tried to walk away. But he couldn't contain himself, and soon he was running again, colliding with the thick handlebars of an old man's wheelchair. The old man's daughter swore at Devey and even took a swipe at him, but there was no time to apologise. He ignored the pain in his hip and raced through the waiting room, startling both patients and staff in his path. Devey hated drama, and the memory of this would make him cringe later, but the sunlight flooding through the large glass doors ahead was too glorious to resist. It rained outside, just like Mr Opperman had predicted, but that only made the sunlight more miraculous. The rain and sun combined would cleanse him, rinsing his every pore free of corruption.

The orderlies crashed through the door next to the reception desk and shouted after him, but no way could they stop him now. The exit lay right ahead. He felt shame for running, but not enough to slow him down. "Mr Singh, stop!"

"Leave me alone," he shouted back. "I'm going!"

He made it out the waiting room and funnelled into the wide hallway leading to the exit. The glass doors opened automatically, but it couldn't have been him that had activated them. Not yet. He wasn't close enough. Flashing lights and sirens flooded the courtyard outside, distorting the rain in multi-coloured shafts. Several ambulances backed up against the entrance, tyres screeching. Paramedics raced about in a panic, yanking trolley-beds onto the pavement and rushing them into the hospital. A flood of bodies filled the entrance, all of them shouting.

"No! No! No!" Devey skidded on his heels, wondering how he would ever dodge past the moving obstacles choking off the entrance.

"Sir, out of the way, please!"

Devey wailed. "No! No, I need to get out."

A trolley-bed rolled right towards him, no sign of stopping. "Sir, move now!"

Devey dodged aside before he was crushed, and that's when he saw the casualty's blistered face—lips rotting away and nostrils peeling back. He stumbled in shock, and it cost him. Two orderlies raced up behind him and got him by both arms, dragging him away from the exit. He didn't fight them. He was frozen.

Frozen stiff.

"THEY ALL HAD IT!" Devey screamed at anyone who would listen. "I saw them coming in. They were blistered and peeling. They had what Mary had. Let me out of here!"

Sonja grabbed his shoulders and forced him to look at her. "This is a hospital. It's full of sick people every day. You are perfectly fine in this room, Devey, but you have to stay calm."

He tried to blink but couldn't, staring at the nurse like a wide-eyed lunatic. "I was in the kitchen with Mary. What if I have it? What if I'm going to die?"

Someone strode into the room. "Because if you had it, you would be showing signs by now like Claudia."

The male paramedic strode into the centre of the room like he wanted to punch someone. Devey shook his head at the man. "What?"

"Two years." The paramedic grunted, clenching his fists and shifting from foot to foot. "Two years I worked with Claudia. It might not sound like a long time, but it is. It's long enough to know everything about a person. Long enough to know how great a person is. She's the one who needs help here, not you! So be quiet and stop taking up these people's time."

Devey realised then that the room was full of staff—three orderlies, Sonja, and Dr Zantoko. The hospital buzzed with activity, but all these people were having to try to calm him down. He was an asshole. "I'm sorry," he said. "You're right, I'll be fine."

Sonja let go of him. "Are you calm? Will you stay in this room and not move?"

He nodded.

"Thank you, nurse," said Dr Zantoko, putting a hand on her back. "Could you please report to triage?"

Sonja tottered off with her hands on her swollen belly. Two orderlies accompanied her, but the paramedic had slipped out as soon as he'd said his piece. That left Devey, Dr Zantoko, and the remaining orderly. "Mr Singh," Dr Zantoko tugged at the lapels of his doctor's coat as if to regain his authority, "I cannot leave this room until I'm sure you understand what is happening here. There is an outbreak occurring, and you were exposed to it. Now, my earlier assessment of you being fine still stands, but we cannot—I repeat, we *cannot*—take any risks with this sort of thing. You must remain here until the situation is under control. Do you understand?"

Devey nodded. He was ready to shit in his shorts, but he understood. Despite having wanted to escape this room more than anything, it suddenly felt like a cocoon. In the hallways outside, the infection festered, but in this room he would be alone and safe. "Doctor? Have you ever seen anything like this? There were half a dozen patients rolling out of ambulances when I tried to leave—maybe more."

"Eight!" Zantoko folded his arms and let out a nervous sigh. "Eight cases all at once. All from a nearby old people's home."

That struck a chord with Devey. "Did any of them play Bingo?"

Dr Zantoko frowned. "I'm sorry?"

"Mary played a lot of Bingo. I know because she won £5,000 once and gave me a twenty pound Christmas tip because of it. She was…" his eyes brimmed unexpectedly with tears, "a nice lady."

"I don't know if they were Bingo players, but thank you the information, it could prove helpful. Finding out where the outbreak began will be vital to containing it. I'll pass on your theory to Public Health."

Devey lifted his chin and felt proud of himself. If they stopped some terrible outbreak because of him, he might get called a hero. He'd be in the paper. Then he considered how much grief he would get at work and the thought became less attractive. The lads would make all kinds of fun.

Dr Zantoko left him with the orderly who was a towering, heavy-set man. He stared at the floor in a trance, and Devey asked him if he was okay. He looked up as if surprised. "What's that, mate?"

"Are you okay? Looks like you checked out for a minute there."

"I'm a bit freaked out, to tell you the truth. I've worked here long enough to know when the doctors are worried."

"Shit, man," said Devey. "Don't say that! Aren't you all supposed to keep calm and carry on, or something?"

The large man tutted. "I'm a soddin' orderly, mate. My job is to move equipment around the hospital and wheel patients here and there. If there's something nasty in this hospital, I want no part of it. I might knock off and go down the pub, job be damned."

Not the noblest attitude Devey had ever heard, but he couldn't help but understand the man's fears. Doctors and nurses probably considered their jobs a calling, but this guy was just picking up a pay packet. He didn't sign on for this. "You think things are bad, huh?"

He huffed. "Didn't think I'd need to convince you of all people. Weren't you were the one who found patient zero?"

"Mary? She was an old lady on my round. I never touched her though. Dr Zantoko said I'm fine."

"Yeah, I heard him talking with Sonja. They don't think you have anything to worry about, but they've been getting orders from above. The big wigs have got their knickers in a twist."

It was good to hear from yet another person he would likely be fine. It made him instinctively like the orderly. "What's your name?"

"Ken."

"Pleased to meet you, Ken. I'm Devey. Feel free to hide out with me if you want, but keep me updated if not."

"I'll be ordered off somewhere else any minute, mark my words. No harm staying out of the way until then though."

Devey walked over to the bed and perched himself on the edge. He considered switching the TV back on, but decided it would be rude with company.

"Turn the telly on," said Ken.

"Oh! Yeah, okay." Devey picked up the remote and pointed it at the TV. The news came on again.

The reporter, a Chinese woman with a slight lisp contorting her privately educated accent, looked incapable of emotion. Only her mouth moved. "*Mr Trump was quoted as saying, 'When I win a second term, I will shut Amazon down completely, and send a warning shot to all the other companies that think they are bigger than America. Thank you and covfefe.'*"

Ken tutted. "Nothing on the news. Suppose that's a good sign."

Devey shook his head. "No, look at the bottom."

Across the lower edge of the screen, the red ticker displayed text in capitals: **BENGALI FLU CASES HIGHER THAN FIRST FEARED. PUBLIC ADVISED TO AVOID UNNECESSARY TRIPS AND STAY INDOORS.**

Ken shrugged. "So?"

"Don't you get it? There's no such thing as Bengali Flu. The Government knows what's happening and is trying to keep it under control without panicking people."

"You're paranoid, mate. The news would be all over it. They don't work for the government."

"Maybe there's a law that let's the Prime Minister restrict the media in a health crisis or something, I don't know. This feels like too much of a coincidence. You work in a hospital, ever heard of Bengali Flu?"

"I've heard of a lot of things I can't remember, mate. You're just panicking. The doctors here are good. You'll be okay."

Devey huffed. "You've changed your tune. I thought you were hiding out in here because you were worried."

"If you go into another panic, I'll get the blame. Seriously, though, you're the safest guy in the hospital right now. That's why I'm in here with you." There was a crackle and Ken looked down at his belt. "Ah, bollocks. Told you!" He spoke into his radio and hurried out of the room. The voice squawking at him sounded angry—or stressed. Devey chuckled and surprised himself. The fact he was a prisoner at a hospital in the middle of an outbreak was absurd. So absurd it was funny. At the very least, it would give him something to tell the grandkids one day.

Just so long as I don't end up like Mary.

He had no intention of leaving the room again, but neither did he want to sit alone watching news reports he didn't trust. The best solution, he decided, was to peek out the door and try to stay informed. He'd keep out the way, but would see what was happening.

What was happening didn't look good.

Doctors and nurses zipped back and forth, spilling out of rooms and racing in all directions. Every receptionist had a phone glued to their ear, and anyone not in uniform stood around confused and upset. One man in particular was making his temper known. A large man with short brown hair and tattoos on both forearms, he shouted angrily. "What the hell is going on? I came here to see my mum, so where the fuck is she?"

"Your mother is being brought down to us now," said the receptionist in a trembling voice. "She's on her way."

"I've been here twenty minutes and you keep saying that. I want to see her right now or I'm going to fuckin' kick off."

"Just calm down, mate," said Ken, exiting a side room and approaching quickly. The angry man snarled like a whipped dog. "I ain't your mate. This place is a disgrace. My old lady is sick and you people won't let me see her. Take me to her this second before I lose my bloody rag."

"Sir, I'm not sure exactly where she is right this second," the receptionist chimed in, "but if you take a seat and—"

Devey yelped from the doorway when the man suddenly lashed out. He shoved Ken to the ground and kicked him. Ken was a big bloke, but the attack had come without warning. Now the angry man stood over him. "Fuckin' NHS. Will someone do their bloody job around here for once?" He noticed Devey staring at him from the doorway. "The fuck you looking at, Paki?"

Devey felt his stomach go awash, a horrible flood of emptiness. The brute marched towards him, looking in no way like he wanted to chat. Was he going to hit him? Devey couldn't quite believe it. As if his day could get any worse.

"Get back in your hole, you nosey shit, before I knock your block off."

Devey froze, unable to take his eyes off the human tank rolling towards him. Why weren't his feet moving? Ken floundered on the floor, his large belly making him resemble a tipped turtle. The receptionist shrieked behind her desk. It was just Devey and the brute.

"Sir, sit down right this second before I call the police." Sonja tottered down the corridor with the hard expression of a woman far uglier and older than she was. Her face was bright red and sweating, but she showed no fear, only extreme irritation and weariness. Whether from the situation or her pregnancy was unclear.

"Piss off out my way!" The man lashed out again, this time swiping Sonja aside like a fly. She bounced against the reception desk with a yelp and toppled sideways to the ground.

"What the hell are you doing?" Devey howled. "She's pregnant, you idiot."

The man's face fell in horror and he half-turned to look at Sonja who clutched her swollen tummy and moaned. "Jesus Christ, shite, shite, shite. Look sweetheart, you shouldn't have got in my way. I just want to see my mum. Why won't anybody let me see her?"

Devey raced over to help Sonja. She winced in pain, but looked more worried than hurt. To his utter surprise, she got up and tottered back over to her attacker without the slightest expression of ill will. She still wore a face mask, but she pulled it down now to speak. "If you refuse to calm down," she said, looking him in the eye, "I shall call the police and press charges. What is your mother's name?"

"Elizabeth Summers."

"Okay, take a seat over there and I'll see what I can find out for you. Last I heard, she was on her way down here, but I'm sure you can see things are a little hectic."

The man apologised for his behaviour and scampered off like a beaten bear.

Ken climbed up and put his arm around Sonja. "Jesus, Sonja, what were you thinking?"

She still clutched her tummy, but she didn't seem too anxious about it. "The worst thing to throw at a violent man is another man. It would have got nasty."

Ken grunted as if he knew she was right. "It already was nasty. Are you okay? The baby?"

"My baby is fine. I hit the desk with my elbows. I only clutched my stomach to guilt the son of a bitch into calming down. If he acts up again, call the police. He doesn't get a second chance."

Ken nodded, and Devey thought he would have saluted if it was protocol. Sonja was an impressive and frightening woman. And she was glaring at Devey. "Mr Singh, why are you out of your room?"

"I came to help."

"Thank you, but everything is under control. Let's get you back inside."

Devey rolled his eyes. "Okay, okay."

Back inside the room, Sonja went over to a water dispenser above the sink and filled a plastic cup. She gulped it down and stayed there a few moments to catch her breath. Devey asked if she was okay.

"Yes, sorry. I don't like violence, that's all."

"You dealt with it well."

"I did my job."

He grunted. "Your job is hard. I don't envy you."

She turned away from the sink and smiled at him weakly. Some exhaustion had left her face, but it wasn't completely gone. "How are you feeling, Devey?"

He shrugged. "So far so good. How's Claudia?"

"She's been moved to the end of this ward. She's calmed down a lot. In fact, she hooked herself up to her own monitoring equipment to keep anyone from touching her, bless her."

"Will she be okay?"

Sonja nodded forcefully as if she intended to impose her will on reality. "Dr Zantoko has put her on a course of the strongest antibiotics we have. She'll feel pretty rubbish, but as long as she fights off whatever we're dealing with she'll be thankful."

Devey was glad at her confidence, but he couldn't help but feel she was putting on an act. "What about the other patients? The old people?"

"Devey, I really don't know. The hospital has closed off this ward and one other to treat the infected, but I'm just a nurse. There're specialists from a dozen different hospitals on their way here, and even a couple guys from the CDC."

"Isn't the CDC an American thing?"

"Yes, but they have a team working in the UK that helps out during times like these."

"Times like these? Things are bad, aren't they?"

She glanced towards the door, then back at him. "I shouldn't tell you this, but yes. Things are bad. The severity of the infection, along with it being so contagious… It'll make the news tonight, let's put it that way."

"It hasn't yet," said Devey. "The only report is about Bengali Flu."

She scrunched up her face. "Bengali Flu? I've never heard of it."

And there you have it, thought Devey. His paranoia was vindicated, but it didn't bring him much relief. He looked down at Sonja's pregnant belly and worried. "You need to be careful. Don't end up like Claudia."

It was a heartless thing to say, but she nodded at the comment and took it how he meant it. She held up her hands for him to see. "I'm wearing two pairs of gloves, and anyone in contact with Claudia or the patients upstairs are wearing oxygen filters. Don't worry about me."

"I am worried about you."

She tilted her head and frowned. "Why?"

"Because you seem like a nice girl, I suppose. And because I feel responsible. If I hadn't found Mary-"

"Then somebody else would have!" She put a hand on his arm and rubbed. "Just stay put and things will be under control before you know it. This is the whole reason hospitals exist—to treat sick people and prevent illness from spreading. Let us do our jobs and everything will be fine."

Devey nodded. "Okay."

She turned to leave, but doubled over and moaned. "Ow! Ow! Ow!"

Devey grabbed her to keep her from falling. "What? What's wrong?"

She straightened up, brow furrowed, eyebrows meeting in a V. "I... I had a twinge there for a moment, but it's fine n—" She doubled over again and this time she yelled in pain. "Ahhh!"

"Shit! Is it the baby?"

"I-I don't know! Get help. Call for help."

Devey raced for the door and threw it open. "Help. We need help in here!"

The only person out in the hallway was the animal who had attacked Sonja. He was sitting down, but flinched when Devey screamed in his direction. "What the hell are you shouting about?"

"I need a doctor!"

The man stood up, turned a useless circle, then held his hands out. "They all rushed off, mate. Something is going on."

"No shit! You need to find someone right now. I think Sonja's baby is in trouble."

The man's face dropped. "Because of what I did?"

"Yes, probably, you jackass. Go find a doctor."

He nodded and rushed off.

Devey hurried back into the room. Sonja bent over the trolley bed, panting and puffing. "The baby's coming," she bellowed. "It's on its way."

"Bloody hell," said Devey. "Oh, bloody hell."

SONJA SEEMED to get better for a while, but then she went through the pain all over again. Contractions. Devey rubbed her back and wished he knew what to do. "Where is that jackass?" he said. "He should've found a doctor by now."

Sonja blew air out of her cheeks and produced a guttural moan. Once it expired, she looked at Devey. "I need to get to Obstetrics."

"Is that where people have babies?"

She nodded. Her face was an impossible shade of red.

"Okay, just… wait here a sec." He rushed out the door and shouted for help again.

The man who had pushed Sonja and appeared around the corner. "I can't find anybody. Is she okay?"

"No! No, she's not. We need to help her."

"Okay, tell me what to do."

Devey sneered. "You've done enough."

He lowered his head in shame. "Look, mate. My name's Lee, and I'm sorry. My mum is somewhere in this hospital and I'm worried as shit about her. I lost my head and-

"You lost your temper!"

He sighed. "Just let me make up for it, please."

Devey didn't like the man, but he wanted his help enough to agree. "Okay! She needs to get to the obstetrics ward. Grab a wheelchair and meet me in this room."

Lee nodded and rushed off. Sonja had another contraction and Devey fell right into the routine of rubbing her back, not knowing if it was helping or not. She didn't tell him to stop. "What's happening?" she said. "Where's Dr Zantoko?"

"I don't know. Lee is getting a wheelchair and we're taking you up ourselves."

"Who?"

"The guy who shoved you."

Sonja groaned. "No way. Keep that idiot away from me."

The door bashed open, shunted by a wheelchair. Lee wore a grim expression. "You're right, I am an idiot. But this is my fault, so let me get you where you need to go."

Sonja rolled her eyes and moved towards the wheelchair. "Just try not to shove anyone else."

Lee kept his head down like a scolded puppy as he spun the chair around behind her and put her in it.

"I'll get the door," said Devey, and Lee wheeled Sonja out into the hallway.

"Where is everyone?" Sonja asked, looking left and right.

"They all hurried off," said Lee.

Devey had a bad feeling. In fact, he'd had a bad feeling since the moment he'd first walked down Mary Mallon's path—and it was only growing worse. Right now, though, Sonja had to come before his concerns. No way was he letting her drop her baby in a corridor.

They hurried for the lifts, and Devey jabbed at the call button. Sonja filled the silence while they waited, moaning and panting. Lee and Devey exchanged worried glances.

Ping!

The lift on the right opened. Lee wheeled Sonja inside. "Which floor?" asked Devey.

"G-Ground floor," said Sonja. "Obstetrics is on the ground floor."

Devey pressed the button. The doors closed and the lift whipped them upwards. His tummy fluttered, and he wondered what the baby would think of the sudden, odd sensation.

The doors reopened. Chaos met them.

Doctors, nurses, and other staff rushed back and forth like branded chickens. Members of the public argued amongst themselves. A full blown panic was underway, and nobody could get control of it.

Devey stepped out of the lift. "What the hell is happening?"

"Who cares?" said Lee. "Let's get our girl where she needs to go."

Ken passed by and Devey called out to him. The large orderly turned, confused. At first he didn't know where to look, but then he saw them huddled over by the lifts. "Sonja? Are you okay?"

"The baby's coming," she groaned.

"Shit! We need to get you to Dr Robbins." He shoved Lee out of the way and grabbed the wheelchair. "I'll take it from here. I suggest you both get back to the ward. It's a war zone up here."

Although he didn't want to delay Sonja, Devey grabbed Ken's arm to keep him from leaving with her. "What's happening?"

Sweat covered the orderly's face. He looked ready to drop, so when he spoke he did so quickly. "More cases keep flooding in," he said.

"Most are coming in the back of the hospital now, but the cat's out the bag. People know something nasty is in the hospital and they want their loved ones out of here. The doctors are expecting a quarantine order to come through any minute, which means we'll be forced to keep people here."

Devey observed the tipped over chairs and strewn litter. People were combusting, and it would only get worse if they were told they could not leave.

Sonja moaned louder, another contraction. "Get moving!"

Ken hurried off with the wheelchair while Devey and Lee stood in awe of what was happening.

"My mum is somewhere in this hospital," said Lee. "I need to find her."

"Then you should go. Get her out of here if you can."

"What caused this?"

"An infection," said Devey. "Or a virus. Whatever. I've seen it, and you want no part of it. Get your mother and go." *Unless she's one of the cases Ken was talking about*, thought Devey. *In which case, Lee, you should get the hell away from her.*

Although many people stuck around in the waiting room to shout and cause trouble, others spilled out of the hospital's front entrance and ran for the car park. If Devey wanted out of this place, now was the time. No one would stop him?

But what if I'm infected?

He checked himself over, looking for the slightest blister. The paramedic had shown symptoms within a few hours, and he was well beyond that now. He didn't think he was sick, but that might not remain true if he stayed in this place any longer.

"I'm leaving," said Devey. "Good luck finding your mother."

Lee nodded. "Thanks, and, um, sorry, about earlier. What I called you."

"No worries." Lee raced off, and Devey put one foot in front of the other, heading towards the exit. What he was doing was irresponsible, but he didn't care. He had to get out. Needed to be where the fresh air was.

He jolted forward as someone barged him from behind. His foot came down on an ownerless handbag and his ankle turned. He hissed in pain. Then swore.

"That's a naughty word," said the same little girl he'd spooked at the vending machines earlier. She looked up at him, alone in the chaos—a tiny stone in the centre of a stream. Her ruffled blonde locks fell all over her face.

"Sorry," he told her. "I hurt myself. Are you okay?"

She shook her head. "I lost my mummy."

"Oh?" He glanced over at the entrance, freedom right in front of him. "W-would you like me to help you find her?"

"Yes, please."

Devey wanted to leave, but he took the girl's hand. "Where did you see your mother last?"

"Jessica. My name is Jessica."

"My name is Devey."

"I like that name."

"Thank you. So, your mummy? Where was she last?"

"She went the toilet, then everybody got mad. I think something scary is happening."

Devey tried to give her a reassuring smile. "I think you're right. Let's find the toilets."

Tip-toeing to look over the crowd, he spotted the icon for the toilets. That was where he headed, but halfway there, he and Jessica encountered an old man kneeling on the ground. At first, Devey thought he'd been knocked down, but then he saw the man was cradling an old lady. He looked up at them with watery grey eyes. "Help me, please."

Devey searched for a doctor, but they were being bombarded on all sides by angry members of the public. "I'm sorry. I can't do anything for you."

The old man said nothing else, just shook his head and sobbed. It felt wrong leaving him, but Devey had a child to take care of. He took Jessica to the far side of the room where the toilets were located. Going inside the ladies wasn't something he felt comfortable doing, but he didn't want to send the little girl in alone, so he put his hand against the door and pushed. But the door was stuck. Something blocked it from the other side. He knocked. "Hello?"

No answer.

"She might be inside," said Jessica hopefully.

Devey placed his leg against the door and shunted it with his hip. It moved slightly, shifting whatever was in its way. With no one objecting, he shoved again, harder. The obstruction slid aside and the door banged against the wall.

"Mummy!"

Devey gasped at the woman lying on the floor. Her head rested on the tiles and blood covered her face. She looked bad—maybe even dead. He grabbed Jessica and pulled her close—an instinctive action. "This is your mummy?" Jessica broke free and threw herself on top of the woman, making the answer to his question clear. "I think you should come away from her, Jessica. We'll go find help."

"No! Mummy, wake up!" She shook her mother over and over.

The woman opened her eyes. Her mouth released a moan and she bolted upright, clutching her head. "Sh-*sugar*, is that you?"

"Yes, Mummy."

The woman pulled the little girl into a tight embrace and held her tight. "Sweetheart, I'm so sorry."

"Mummy, what happened to your face?"

"Someone hit me with the door. It's just a nosebleed."

Devey winced. It was a hell of a nose bleed. "Can I get you anything?"

The woman didn't know Devey, but she seemed easy with the fact he was there. "No, I'll be fine. What on earth is happening? People have gone nuts."

"There's been an outbreak. I think you should take your daughter and leave."

She climbed up off the floor, keeping Jessica against her hip and using the wall to help her. Once she was up, she brushed herself off. "That sounds like a good idea."

"I'm leaving too," said Devey. "We'll go together, but you might want to wash your face first."

"Oh, yes!" She headed over to the sinks and soaked her face until the blood rinsed away. Then the three of them got going.

The chaos in the waiting room had lulled, but not because people had calmed down. It was because a horde of people had fled the hospital rather than stick around. The entranceway was still writhing with bodies wanting to leave, but it was all one way traffic heading in the direction Devey wanted. He could still get out.

"As soon as you get home," he told the mother and daughter, "lock up and stay there. I've seen the virus and it's bad."

The mother blinked at him. "What virus?"

He wasn't about to call it Bengali Flu, so he gave it his own name. "The Peeling," he said. "Best way I can describe it."

"I don't like the sound of that. I hope I don't have to see it."

"I hope so t-" Devey stopped in his tracks and threw his arm out to keep his companions back. A man crouched in front of them, holding his face in both hands. A group of people had spread out around him as though he were a bomb. It sounded like he was crying, but the sound came out in an odd whistling sound.

"What is he doing, Mummy?"

"Just stay back, sweetheart. I think he's upset."

The man stood and turned around, letting out a garbled scream. Others around him screamed too, including Devey. He didn't seem real, more like a man in a Halloween mask. His lower lip dangled from the bottom of his chin like a turkey's bright red snood.

Jessica buried her face in her mummy's tummy. Devey wished he could do the same.

The man shambled towards them. "Help me! Please… help me."

"Get back!" Devey shouted. "Stay away. You're sick!"

The people in the entranceway redoubled their efforts to shove their way to the front. Doctors and nurses tried to regain control, but stopped as soon as they saw the sick man in the middle of the waiting area. Devey felt ashamed for backing away--even worse when he shouted at Jessica and her mother to run. They cut a wide berth around the infected man and sprinted for the exit. Ahead, a dozen people spilled out into the rainy afternoon.

Clap-tssh. Clap-tssh!

Two young men fell side-by-side in the courtyard, falling onto their fronts and not getting back up again.

Clap-clap-clap-clap-tssssssh!

Half-a-dozen more people fell. A few cried out, others were silent. A trail of blood trickled down the glass panels of the entrance.

"People are shooting," Devey cried. "People are shooting guns!" He grabbed Jessica and her mother and threw them both to the ground, covering them with his body and keeping his head low. The mob turned tail and ran the other way, fleeing back into the hospital. Their fear reached a crescendo as they pushed, trampled, and threw one another aside in sheer panic. A heavyset woman trod on Devey's sore ankle and aggravated the sprain he'd given himself tripping over the abandoned handbag. Those stuck at the rear of the rout caught bullets in their backs and fell down dead, adding to a growing carpet of bodies. Blood rose in a murky mist, making it hard to see what was happening outside. Nothing moved in the courtyard, that Devey could see, and nobody shouted any warnings. Yet bullets continued zipping through the entrance and hitting people in the back.

"This is all wrong!" It was the infected man shouting, his flapping lower lip distorting every consonant he attempted. "You can't do this!" He shambled towards the entrance, screaming his garbled words at whoever was out there. Panic had turned his fear to anger, and he cut an imposing figure amongst the bodies at his feet—a wraith amongst the corpses. "You can't do this!" he bellowed again at the top of his lungs.

Clap-tssh!

The infected man stopped walking and went statue still. No more words came out his ruined mouth. He fell in stages, first down onto his knees, head dropping to one side, then onto his hip. Finally, he rolled onto his front and went still. Seconds passed, and it became clear the man was dead. Any doubts were dispelled by the spreading petals of blood at the back of his shirt.

"This can't be happening," said Devey, looking up from where he lay. "This just can't be happening."

Two black squares appeared either side of the courtyard, getting larger as they came closer. The large sheets of metal blocked the entrance, extinguishing the sunlight as they slapped up against the cracked glass doors.

They were being locked in.

Devey tried clambering to his feet, but couldn't remove himself from the tangle of Jessica and her mother. He reached out and screamed, begging the people outside not to do this. But they weren't listening. The sound of power tools ripped the air, and soon even the narrow tendrils of light around the edges of the metal sheets disappeared as they locked into place.

"They're trapping us inside," he said, barely believing his own words. "They're trapping us in here to die."

Chapter 4

People threw themselves against the steel barricades, banging their fists and pleading. Devey sat against the wall with Jessica and her mother watching it all transpire.

"Mummy, I'm scared."

"I know, honey. Mummy is too." She turned to Devey. "Thanks for protecting us."

"No problem. I'm Devey."

"Barbara."

He reached over and shook her hand. His were clammy, but hers were dry and firm. When he'd found her, she'd been confused and disorientated, but now she seemed focused and alert—even despite her swollen nose. "Pleased to meet you, Barbara. I wish it were under better circumstances."

"You can say that again."

"I wish it were under better circumstances."

Barbara moaned at the awful joke, but Jessica found it hilarious. Her laughter was a wonderful thing to hear against the backdrop of terrified shouting. Barbara stroked her daughter's curls until they were once again under control and then looked at Devey again. "What do we do?"

"I have no clue. I can't even fathom who was shooting people, surely not the police. It would be all over the news." He remembered the earlier report, and the lies about 'Bengali Flu'. Suddenly he felt unsure. Were the media being controlled by the Government? Was some kind of emergency decree in place? If so, then this sickness must be a lot worse than he'd feared.

Barbara chewed her lip, then said, "Maybe it's a madman with a rifle, like that guy in Washington a few years ago."

Devey frowned. "Who?"

She shrugged. "I don't really remember. Some guy was sniping people at a petrol station in America. Innocent people. It was horrible."

"That kind of thing doesn't happen here. The only people with guns are the Police and the Army—and a few gangs who shoot mostly at each other."

"You said you didn't think it was the police."

Devey sighed. "Maybe what I meant to say was that I *hope* it's not the police."

Two men threw punches at one another nearby, over by the vending machines, but it was now so commonplace they ignored it. Jessica watched them as if they were acting out a play. A girl with greasy hair and an oversized Black Sabbath t-shirt shuffled casually by them to get to the machines and bought herself a bottle of water. Then she rejoined the crowd. Devey spotted someone he recognised and leapt up, startling Barbara and Jessica. "Wait here," he told them. "I'll be back." He cut through the crowd, losing sight of his target briefly, but then re-locating the man over by the reception desk. Devey hurried over. "Officer?"

The police officer didn't hear Devey. He snatched at one of the phones on the desk and held it tightly against his ear. Eventually, he slammed the phone back on its cradle and swore loudly. "Damn it, they've cut the phones."

Devey raised his voice. "Officer!"

"Not now!" He turned with a scowl on his face, but then saw it was Devey and frowned instead. His thick, coppery sideburns were damp with sweat. "Oh, Mr Singh. Hello."

"What's going on?"

"We've been quarantined." He stated it as if it were an ordinary thing to say. "They've disconnected the phones. Mobiles aren't working either."

"What?" Devey leant against the desk for support, his knees swaying. "They can't do that!"

The officer shrugged. "You're right. But they did it anyway."

"Why? Why are they doing this?"

"You know why."

Devey didn't want to say it, didn't want to admit that he was a part of this whole thing, but the officer was right—he did know. "This is because of Mary."

The officer leant back against the desk and cricked his neck. Before he spoke, he let out a long and weary breath. "Mary, yes, and the other eighty-odd people infected with this ungodly disease."

Devey blanched. "What? No, Dr Zantoko told me it was less than a dozen."

"It was less than a dozen, until it was more. Until about twenty minutes ago, my radio was working, and a colleague of mine on the Emergency switchboard told me there were cases flagging up all over the city, and several more as far south as Gloucester. They rated it a Class 9 Health Risk."

Devey grunted. "What the hell is that?"

"If I told you there isn't a Class 10, would you get the idea? Whatever your friend, Mary, had is about as bad as things get. Probably a weaponised strain of something already deadly enough."

Devey slumped further onto the desk and knocked a pot of pens with his elbow. The unexpected racket made him flinch. "This is terrorism?"

The officer looked at Devey like he was an idiot. "Something this fast and this lethal? What else could it be? I'll tell you one thing though—this didn't come out the Middle East, they don't have the resources. It will be China or North Korea or Russia. Some shitfuck country with a bunch of scientists locked up in a basement somewhere. We all knew it was coming."

"I don't believe that."

The officer sighed and pinched the bridge of his nose, squinting. "Yeah, well, maybe I don't either. Someone did this though. I'm sure enough about that."

"Why were they shooting people outside?" Devey pictured the bloodshed at the entrance and felt dizzy. "Was it the police?"

"No! None of the people I work with would ever shoot unarmed members of the public."

"Then who?"

The officer went around the back of the reception desk and sat down. He leant forward and put his head and arms on the desk, staying there. Devey realised the man was finished with words, and that it would be best to leave him alone. So Devey headed back to Barbara and Jessica, but when he reached the spot where he'd left them, they weren't there. "Great! The only two sane people and I've lost them."

There was a scream, louder than all the others, and it spun Devey to face the centre of the waiting area. Things swirled in slow motion, people tussling and fighting, some slipping and clambering on their hands and knees, others bulldozing their way through. A girl stood pleading for help, blood sputtering from her lips. It was the girl in the Black Sabbath t-shirt. Her jet-black hair, leather bangles, and purple nail varnish created a heavy metal look, but what pushed her towards death metal was the blood pouring out of her eyes. Her windpipe glistened through the tissue-paper skin of her neck.

"Get the fuck away from us!" someone shouted.

"Stay back!"

The girl screamed for help, clutching at her face and pulling slithers of gluey flesh with her fingernails, turning her purple nail varnish red. Somebody tossed something, and it struck her cheek. An impressive shot, but its effect was sickening. The blow sloughed away a massive clump of flesh and exposed the girl's cheekbone. More projectiles launched, and the girl crouched down and tried to shield herself.

"They're going to kill her!" said Devey, but no one was listening. People were either running away or joining in throwing things—cowardice or cruelty, the only two options in play. He had to do something.

But what?

He spotted Barbara and Jessica standing over by the newsagent. Jessica was clutching a pile of comic books—the reason Barbara must have moved from where he'd left them—and when she saw Devey, the little girl waved a hand at him. He raced over to join them, but it was something behind them that caught his interest.

The fire extinguisher was heavy with a huge nozzle, but once he yanked it off its hook, it wasn't too unwieldy. He hoisted it against his hip and yanked the pin out the nozzle's handle. It seemed easy to operate, and that was probably the point, but he still paused before heading off, asking himself if he was sure he really wanted to do what he was about to do. Then he saw another piece of debris hit the poor Black Sabbath fan in the head and told himself there was no choice.

I won't be a part of this shit show.

He ran to the edge of the baying crowd and squeezed the fire extinguisher's handle. The large nozzle bucked in his hand like a python until he took a firmer grip. That a jet of slippery foam came spurting out instead of water surprised him, but it worked out for the better as the people caught in the blast started coughing and spluttering. Devey kept his hand clamped on the handle and crept forwards, fanning the foamy spray from side-to-side, dispersing the mob as best he could. It worked like a charm, and within one minute the crowd had broken. They hissed and growled at him like vampires, but he had a crucifix to keep them at bay. He released the nozzle and the foamy spray ceased, but he remained on guard for anyone who tried any funny business. The Black Sabbath fan huddled on the floor, trembling like a mouse. "It's okay," he told her. "Everything will be okay."

A sobbing voice answered him. "No, it's not. I've seen what happens."

"What do you mean?"

The girl lifted her head to look at him, and it took all he had not to flinch in horror. The flesh of her ruined cheek slid down her face—a waxwork figure beside a fire—but her eyes were vibrant and alive. If there was any mercy to this virus, it would cause a fever and offer its victims the bare respite of delirium. But that was not the case. This girl was rotting alive while fully aware of the fact.

"I was supposed to take my nanna shopping this morning," the girl sobbed, "but when I called round she didn't answer her door. I have a key so I went inside. She was still in bed when I found her, still breathing, but she didn't know what was happening. She was making this sound like-like a baby crying, you know? That pitiful sound that gets you right here." She clutched her chest. Her hands were bleeding. "She couldn't see me because her eyes were gone. I could see inside her sockets. The ambulance took an hour. I held her the entire time. They brought us here." She looked at the crowd, at the frightened faces gawping at her from all corners. Her short speech must have been enough to humanise her because they made no more moves to attack. She seemed to realise this because she kept on talking. "A couple hours ago I started itching down below. I went to the toilets to see what was going on and my knickers were soaked with blood. My neck and face started itching about an hour ago, and by then I could already guess what was happening to me, but I didn't want to admit it. I have it, whatever took my nanna."

Devey sighed. "Your nanna is…?"

"Dead. About twenty minutes ago. They wouldn't let me see her, and

I was about to tell them I had it too, but then all this happened." She looked at the crowd again. "I don't blame them."

"She'll infect us all!" someone yelled.

"She needs to go!"

The girl turned to the crowd and yelled. "Where? Where am I supposed to go? They've locked us in here, so fuck off and just let me die in peace." Someone threw a plastic coffee cup and it only just missed her. Things were about to ignite all over again. Devey didn't know if he could hold them off a second time. He studied the various faces in the crowd and saw nothing but fear. Somehow that seemed worse than anger.

"EVERYBODY STAY EXACTLY WHERE YOU ARE AND LISTEN!" Dr Zantoko appeared, barking into the mouthpiece of a large green microphone. A sticker on the side marked it as NHS property. Once he had the crowd's attention, he handed the microphone to a nurse and climbed up onto a bench so that everyone could see him. Even without the amplification, his voice was booming. "We need to remain calm," he said in his educated tone. "And yes, yes, I know that is easier said than done, but I promise you, if we descend into madness there is no hope for any of us. There is a virus in this hospital as I am sure you all know by now. Our labs are studying it as we speak, and so far we are in agreement that it is transmitted through direct contact and bodily fluids. It is not—I repeat NOT airborne. Therefore, if you remain calm and follow the instruction of this hospital's staff, you will all remain healthy. We will divide the hospital in two. The infected shall assemble in the lower wards where they will be treated with everything we have available. The uninfected will be moved to a different part of the hospital to reduce the risk of exposure. We will work together. We shall be brave."

"What about the people keeping us inside?" someone shouted, but it was not aggressive. The arrival of a doctor with a posh accent had turned the panicked mob into an attentive audience. "Why did they trap us in here?"

"We are not yet informed of who is encircling this hospital, or why they felt it necessary to barricade all the exits and windows, but it changes nothing. The only thing we need focus on right now is behaving rationally and helping those in need."

In need? Devey studied the Black Sabbath fan's ruin of a face and thought the phrase absurd, but he understood that Zantoko was trying to play down the infection. It seemed to work because nobody put up a fight as orderlies and nurses appeared in force and began herding people into groups.

The situation was under control.

For now.

DEVEY GRABBED Dr Zantoko as he tried to head inside an office. "Doctor! Can I do anything to help?"

Zantoko seemed different now, like a coiled spring, but in a good way—ready to react, ready to leap. For a second, it looked like he would dismiss Devey, but then he recognised him. "Ah, Mr Singh. Are you still symptom free?"

Devey patted himself down theatrically. "So far so good."

"If you have any strange sensations, you must report to staff immediately. From what I gather, itching is an early sign."

"I feel itchy all over, but that's because you've put the thought in my head. I get how dangerous this thing is—if I get it, I'll come clean, I promise."

Zantoko put his hands on his hips and nodded. "Good man."

"Have you learnt anything about what it is?"

"It's a virus. We've had it under a microscope and confirmed that much, at least."

So it really was a virus—an invisible monster clawing its way through people's bloodstreams, rotting them from within. Devey shuddered. "But it's not airborne?"

"We don't know."

"But you said-"

"I know what I said," Zantoko cut him off. "I was trying to stem a riot. Thank you for your help with that, by the way. I can't believe, out of all these people, you were the only one acting against violence."

Devey watched the people form up into groups, unspeaking, unmoving. "People are scared," he said. "Not everyone was violent. Some ran."

"But only you tried to help."

"The girl in the Black Sabbath t-shirt. Is she okay?"

Zantoko frowned, and Devey realised it had been a stupid question. So he asked another. "Is there anything you can do for her?"

His question hung in the air for several moments before the doctor answered it. "The virus kills in less than 48 hours, and symptoms usually present within 2. It moves so fast it's like coming into contact with acid. The organism attaches itself to the flesh and breaks it down rapidly with enzymes. There isn't anything this lethal recorded in all of medical science. I fear the worst for us all if we do not contain it."

Devey's mouth went dry. He'd watched a movie about Ebola once, and few things had filled him with more dread than that—but this was actually happening. "Did you… was it… the people outside… did you call them?"

Zantoko nodded. "Yes, but I didn't realise they would do this. Eighteen months ago, Public Health set up a weaponised disease team. All medical personnel are instructed to contact them if suspicious of a biological attack. Myself and the other consultants agreed that this situation more than qualifies. The Public Health team took charge of the body you found this morning and promised to send a team to help us."

"It wasn't a body when I got there," said Devey. "Mary was still alive. And as for their team, it appears they had no plans beyond barricading us all in here."

Zantoko ground his teeth for a moment, a stew of anger and confusion on his face. "You're lucky you didn't touch Mary," he said. "The virus membrane has hooks. It latches onto whatever it comes into contact with. If you want to help, keep an eye out for the infection. I don't trust people enough for them all to come forward. Seven people have fallen ill since we received the first cases, and I suspect there are more."

"I'll watch out for anybody itching," said Devey, glad to have something to do. It wasn't like he wouldn't be checking out every single person who stepped in his direction anyway.

Someone called Zantoko, and the doctor had to leave. "If you'll excuse me, Mr Singh."

"Devey, and yes, of course. Thank you, Doctor."

Zantoko disappeared into the office and, as the door opened, Devey saw other doctors gathered inside. What were they talking about, he wondered? Not wanting to stand there alone, he went and rejoined Jessica and Barbara. Jessica was cross-legged on the floor, reading her comics, while her mother leant up against the wall. Barbara looked a little pale and washed out, but despite that she smiled at his approach. "That was pretty amazing what you did back there," she said.

"What are you talking about?"

"With the fire extinguisher. You helped that poor girl."

"Maybe it's because I was almost in her situation this morning. I found one of the first cases. Anyway, I doubt I did much to help her."

Barabara went to pat his arm, but he dodged away. She pulled her hand back and folded her arms, embarrassed. "Sorry, I just... You're right, we shouldn't touch each other."

Devey gave a weak smile. What Barbara didn't realise is that he'd not even been thinking about the virus. He didn't like strangers touching him. Why was it only now he realised that about himself? When did it start? He remembered sharing cuddles with his mum all the time as a kid, but after that... after she died? When was the last time he had let another human being hold him?

No time for self-reflection, Devey shook himself back to the present. He knelt down beside Jessica. "Hey, what you reading?"

The little girl looked up and beamed at him. The near riot from earlier had seemingly not left a lasting impression on her. "My Little Pony," she answered. "Mummy got me lots of comics for being good."

"You are good, aren't you! All this scary stuff going on, and you're not causing any fuss at all. I have a niece your age, and she plays up something rotten."

"Doesn't her mummy tell her off?"

Devey laughed. "Her mummy should tell her off a lot more than she does, believe me. So what is your comic ab-" He stopped mid-sentence, jolted by something Jessica did. She scratched behind her ear.

Barbara noticed him staring and questioned him about it. Her tone was suddenly defensive. "What are you looking at?"

He blinked, as if he'd simply been daydreaming. "Oh, um, no reason, just lost my train of thought. How you both doing, anyway? You holding together?"

She studied his face, and he forced himself to smile. The disguise held up because she relaxed at the shoulders and sighed. "We're doing as well as can be expected. I keep trying to call my husband, but I'm not getting any joy."

"I think whoever is outside is blocking our phones. Mine doesn't work either. Your husband will be worried."

She looked at Jessica. "Not as worried as I am. This is a nightmare."

"The absolute worst," he admitted, "but you heard the doctor—stay calm and we'll see it through. It's spread by contact, so keep your distance from anyone who looks *unwell—especially people scratching themselves*." In the corner of his eye, Jessica scratched behind her ear again. He didn't dare stare at her for fear of upsetting her mother. Did the girl just have an itch?

Please just let it be an itch.

"Okay, I'll keep my eyes open," said Barbara.

"You don't feel any symptoms yourself, do you?" Devey asked, still forcing himself not to look at Jessica who was still scratching away behind her ear.

Barbara shook her head. "I feel fine."

"Good! Okay, well, if you get any odd sensations, the best thing to do—"

Shouts erupted, cutting him off. A scuffle had broken out and Ken the orderly was caught right in the middle. A young woman in jogging bottoms, three layers of cheap makeup, and two ounces of gold chains was thrusting her finger in his face. To Ken's credit, he didn't react, merely stood there motionless as she shouted at him. A nurse stood nearby in gloves and a mask.

"You ain't fucking touching me, you piece of shit. None of you is laying a hand on me, yeah!"

"Calm down, miss," said Ken. "We're doing this to everyone."

"Well, I ain't no mug like the rest of these people. You got no right to touch me. You need my permission, innit?"

"To be honest, miss, the normal rules don't apply right now. This is a serious situation, and we need to assess everyone here. If you're okay, you have nothing to worry about."

"I'm worried about you touching my tits, you perv."

Ken rolled his eyes, starting to lose his patience. "A nurse will conduct the examination," he explained. "I'm just here to help."

"Help yourself to this!" The woman stuck up her middle finger and stuck it in his face.

Ken let out a long breath. Devey noticed he was clenching his fists. "If you won't submit to an examination," he said, "we must assume you are an infection risk. We'll have no choice but to isolate you, miss."

The woman sneered, and it was obvious Ken was close to losing his shit. Who could blame him? Every person here was on the edge of losing their marbles. "You ain't doing nuffin, you fat fuck. Touch me and I'll break your nose."

Ken finally took a step, closing the distance between them and escalating things physically. "Now look here!"

Devey took his cue and hurried over to help. He stood in front of the woman and tried to match her tone. "Just let 'em get on with it. They're just doing their job, innit?"

The woman raised a painted eyebrow at him and snarled. "Who asked you to stick your nose in?"

Devey put his hands up. "I'm trying to keep the peace. The only way we can make sure nobody is infected is by working with the doctors and nurses. Nobody else here has a problem with it."

She scratched at her hip without seeming to realise she was doing it. Her eyes locked on Devey. "Fuck everybody else. I have a problem with it."

"Because you're infected," said Devey, and he heard the low-level bustle of the crowd disappear into silence.

"The fuck you talking about?"

Devey spoke softly, trying to let her know he wasn't her enemy. Nobody was enemies here. Circumstance was the only adversary they all faced. "Did you touch anyone with the infection?"

"What? No, I…" she trailed off, her eyes settling on the ground.

Devey stepped closer, trying to make it him and her and nobody else. "What do you want to say?"

All at once, the aggression melted away and a nervous wreck took the woman's place. "I-I… the girl with the greasy hair, the rocker… She was outside smoking and I… I asked to bum a smoke. She only had the one, so we shared it. Is she dead now?"

Devey shook his head although he didn't know. "She's getting treatment, which is what you need. You have it, don't you?"

She reached towards her hip, hands shaking, and peeled down the waistband of her jogging bottoms, revealing a grape-sized sore. It wasn't horrific, considering the state of the other victims, but Devey knew it was only the beginning. The woman knew it too. She was damned.

"We're all in this situation together," Ken chimed in. "We want to help you."

The woman nodded. Tears dropped off her chin as Ken led her away. Devey noticed others being led away too. The infected were being drawn out like blackheads. "If anybody else is infected," a doctor, not Zantoko, said loudly, "or if you are with someone who is, please come talk to us. We will do all we can to help you and your loved ones, but if you don't come forward, you will continue to get sicker and sicker." Three people came forward, shellshocked and stumbling, and the nurses took them away.

"Good," said the doctor. "Anyone else?"

No one came forward.

"Then I ask the rest of you to remain vigilant. If you experience any kind of discomfort, come forward. If you see anyone acting suspiciously, report them so that we may help them. Thank you, that's all."

Devey took a moment to check himself over. His entire body squirmed and itched, but it was likely all in his head. He checked his arms and wrists, shins and tummy. No sores. No blood. He was fine. For now.

"Where do you think they're taking them?" Barbara asked. Without realising, he had drifted back towards her and her daughter. Jessica was still reading comics, but looked ready to doze off. Barbara was watching the exodus with interest, a congregation led by masked nurses and doctors. "I'm not sure I trust the doctors."

Devey frowned. "Why not?"

"Because they seem to be working with the people outside. Why aren't they demanding answers, or trying to find a way out?"

Devey folded his arms and thought about his conversation with Zantoko. "They're focusing on the things that matter, which right now is ensuring every person in this hospital doesn't get sick. I spoke with a doctor earlier. He didn't expect to get shut in any more than we did."

She nodded. "I saw you talking. Do they know how to treat this thing?" The way she said it, her voice cracking slightly, made him suspicious.

"I don't know, but if we avoid getting sick in the first place, it won't matter."

She nodded, a little too eagerly, and gave her daughter the briefest of side glances. "It's all so frightening, that's all."

Devey watched the little girl reading her comics. Her head swayed like she was having trouble keeping it up. She scratched behind her ear again. "Still reading My little Pony?" he asked her.

"I'm reading a princess magazine now. It's a bit boring, but it has stickers."

"How are you feeling?"

Barbara grunted. "What are you doing?"

He ignored the mother, cringing at his own rudeness, but knowing she would try to distract him. "Jessica, can you turn your head that way for me, please, sweetheart?"

The little girl frowned, but she did as he asked, lifting her chin and turning her head sideways. A patch of skull poked through behind her ear, slithers of skin peeling back around the edges.

"Get away from her!" Barbara grabbed his shirt and shoved him away. Jessica flinched, her eyes growing wide. "Mummy, what's wrong?"

"Everything is fine, sweetheart. Just stay there."

Devey stepped away and kept his voice low as he spoke Barbara. "Everything is not fine!" he hissed. "Your daughter is sick. Very sick."

"No, she's not. She's got... *eczema*."

Devey would have laughed if it wasn't so sad. "Not eczema. You know it's not eczema. We need to tell the doctors."

"No!" She snarled at him. "I'm not letting my daughter out of my sight. I'm not letting them take her away to shove her with all those other sick people."

"She is one of those sick people. They will let you go with her." A death sentence for Barbara if she wasn't already sick, but he supposed she wouldn't care. "You won't be apart."

Barbara shook her head, but it was desperation now rather than defiance. "She's young. She'll fight it off. All the others were old people."

"The girl in the Black Sabbath t-shirt wasn't old. She was barely twenty."

"Still, Jessica could be fine. She might—"

Devey cut her off. "We need to tell the doctors."

"Not yet! Just..." Her eyes welled up with tears. "Give her a little more time before they start sticking needles in her and scaring her. Please."

As he watched Jessica innocently reading her comics, he couldn't imagine what she was about to go through. He barely knew the child, but his heart ached to think of her suffering. And if that was how he felt, how must her mother feel? He saw then, the utter, absolute dread behind Barbara's eyes. She was keeping it together for one reason only—her daughter.

"Okay," he relented. "I won't say anything yet, but you can't let her near anybody. How did she get it, anyway?"

Barbara shook her head. "I don't know! Jessica is so friendly. Before everything went crazy, she was running around playing. She could have touched anyone."

"The woman with the funny eyebrows gave me a sweetie," said Jessica, not bothering to glance up from her comics. "You were talking to her earlier. You made her swear lots."

Devey frowned. "You mean the woman I spoke to? The one they took away? The woman in jogging bottoms?"

Jessica nodded. "She pulled her trousers down."

"Yeah, she did a little bit. She had a… rash. I think you have it too, Jessica."

She closed her comic and looked up at him. Her eyes were puffy and red. "Behind my ear?"

Devey felt woozy. Barbara put a hand on his chest and whispered in his ear. "Just give her a little more time, please! I'll keep her away from other people."

The girl needed help now, not later, but was it his call? He sighed. "Fine."

It was too hard to watch Jessica anymore, so he took a break and headed away from them, towards the vending machines to get a bottle of water. He swigged down the entire bottle, not having realised how thirsty he was. He got himself a chocolate bar too and wolfed it down equally fast. It put a little strength back into him, but as soon as his eyes drifted to the entrance, and the imposing metal barricades there, he deflated. How the hell had he stayed so calm throughout all this?

Was there something wrong with him? A gaping hole inside of him that kept him losing his head like everybody else? Barbara and Jessica moved away from the wall and started moving towards the lifts. Devey knew in an instant that the mother intended to make a run for it, but what good would it do her? She couldn't keep her daughter safe from something already in her bloodstream. But where was the harm in letting her take Jessica somewhere to hide? Maybe they could isolate themselves somewhere and die in peace.

But what if not? What if they jeopardised healthy people? Devey looked around and studied the frightened faces of the men and women, huddled together in shock, wishing they were anywhere but here. And then he saw other children. Children who were not yet infected. Children who still had a chance.

"Stop!" he shouted, pointing his finger at Barbara and Jessica. "That little girl is infected!"

The low-level bustle ceased again, and the crowd looked first to Devey and then to Barbara and Jessica. Mother and daughter stopped in their tracks. Barbara's eyes sought out Devey, and when they settled on him, there was so much hatred in her stare that he actually recoiled.

Had he done the right thing? It didn't feel like it.

Dr Zantoko appeared beside Devey. "Who is infected?"

Devey pointed again, the taste of acid in his mouth. "The little girl over there has it behind her ear. Her name is Jessica. Her mother is probably sick too by now even if she doesn't know it."

Jessica looked up at her mother and muttered something. Barbara got down on her knees and hugged her. Both started to cry. Then the nurses took them away and Devey cried too.

Chapter 5

Devey stood alone for several drawn-out minutes, his stomach wrenching itself in knots. He'd just betrayed a woman he knew nothing about, and owed nothing to, yet he'd never felt so ashamed. The look on little Jessica's face as they'd dragged her away… The utter hatred Barbara had displayed towards him…

"Mr Singh?"

He turned to see Dr Zantoko with Ken. "Devey, please."

Zantoko nodded. "Devey then. You have been making good use of yourself and I would like to thank you for your calm head."

"I don't want things to get any worse than they already are."

Zantoko clasped his hands together like a sage. "It is hard to think of others when you are yourself endangered—it is something doctors train many years for—yet it seems to come to you naturally."

Devey tugged at his postal uniform. "Well, as you can see, I'm no doctor."

"You're one of us though," said Ken, one hand on his belly like he had stitch. "You're dealing with this crisis instead of being a part of it."

Zantoko waved a hand as if he didn't want his orderly to do the talking. "Kenneth, there is no them and us. There is only a great deal of frightened people to whom we have a duty." He turned back to Devey. "But the sentiment is more or less correct. You have a cool head, Devey, and you have helped tremendously already. That is why I would like to ask you to now work with the staff directly."

Devey didn't understand what was being asked of him. "What do you mean?"

"I mean," the doctor spoke slowly, "it would be most useful to have a member of the public act as a go between. We need to impose order on this hospital before things get beyond our control. The more bodies working towards that end, the better."

"So I'm like a prisoner with special privileges?"

Zantoko tittered. "Yes, I suppose so. Are you interested in helping?"

Devey huffed. "What kind of question is that? Who wouldn't want to help if they could? I'll do whatever you need."

Zantoko clapped his hands. "Fantastic! We're about to have a meeting in the nurse's station. Join us, please."

So Devey followed Ken and Zantoko into the staff area behind the reception desk. The police officer from before had gone, but the room behind was busy with people. It was a small lounge, littered with paperwork and dirty coffee cups. When Devey saw a group of weary nurses off to one side, he remembered a past worry and turned to Ken to address it. "Is Sonja okay?"

"In labour, mate. What a time to have a baby, huh?"

"Yeah, I hope everything goes okay."

"She's in the best hands."

Zantoko moved in front of a whiteboard and tapped it to get everyone's attention. A scruffy circle drawn in marker pen took up the centre of the board, and it featured multiple L-shaped bristles coming off of it. Zantoko pointed to the drawing with his index finger. "This is what we are dealing with," he said, and let the statement linger for a few seconds before continuing. "While it presents in a similar fashion to necrotising faciitis, in reality it is entirely dissimilar in both structure and function. From our initial studies, we can surmise the infection is not airborne. Therefore, identification and isolation is sufficient to stop transmission. You have all worked extremely hard, but we must continue to remain vigilant. Onset of symptoms is as little as two hours, so if we can go beyond that with no new cases, we may just be able to keep this thing contained. Needless to say, full-preventative measures are in place. I don't want to see anyone handling a patient with less than two sets of gloves. Any questions?"

A doctor put his hand up, a younger man with floppy Hugh Grant hair. Zantoko acknowledged him and let him ask his question. "Are we treating the infection?"

"In triage no, but the supervising doctors in Wards 3 and 6 are administering *penicillin* and *vancomycin*. We don't yet know if it's having any effect."

"What about the lock-in procedures? Who barricaded us in here? Are we in contact?"

Zantoko couldn't maintain eye-contact for this question, and he answered it with his eyes on the ground. "I believe Public Health are in charge of the hospital quarantine, but we are yet to receive any directives. In fact, to my knowledge, all lines out of the hospital are blocked."

"They're going to get us all killed," a nurse muttered.

Zantoko eyeballed her. "What happens to the people in this hospital is down to us. We shall deal with the greater scope of things later. All I shall say is that someone outside must feel it prudent to seal this entire building."

"Which means they know what this is," said Devey, surprising himself with the sound of his own voice. "Someone outside is taking extreme measures. No government official would risk the public backlash from this unless the greater good were at stake."

A smattering of nodding heads told him he was right. Zantoko sighed. It was a statement he obviously wished had not been made publically. "Ladies and gentlemen. This is Devey Singh, who has been a great help during this morning's events." He eyeballed Devey for a moment, then said. "And unfortunately I agree with him. The only situation in which I can envisage these kinds of absolute measures is to prevent an outbreak of something so deadly that it would threaten society as a whole. The only way the public would forgive actions like these is if the alternative is even worse."

"Oh God," said Dr Hugh Grant. "Then we really are screwed. What chance do we have?"

"We have every chance," said Zantoko. "We already know transmission can be avoided. All in this room are healthy, despite being around sick people all day. This hospital is big enough to keep everyone apart, so we work to that end. Keep the healthy away from the sick."

"Where are you putting the sick?" asked Devey.

"Sub-basement 1. The oncology department and rheumatology take up most the floor, but there's also a pair of high-risk wards. Devey, that was where you were placed when you first got here."

"And the paramedics and the police officers with me?"

Zantoko nodded. "Let's focus forward. Devey, let people know the virus is contained--that the only thing that could jeopardise us now is people trying to hide an infection. You did the right thing telling us about the child."

Devey's cheeks grew hot, and he looked away. "Didn't feel like it."

"The right thing is rarely the easy thing." Zantoko said it in a tone suggesting he knew from experience. "You saved lives by doing the right thing, Devey, I promise you. We have this thing contained."

"Is that true?" He didn't get the impression anything was contained at all. A huddled mass of frightened people was not containment, and in the last hour he'd seen people funnel off into a dozen stairwells and corridors. Infected people could be everywhere. "Is it really under control?"

Zantoko folded his arms and exhaled. "The infection will be contained so long as the situation is. Twenty-eight people handed themselves into our care, and in the last hour only four new patients have displayed symptoms. Once people know the new cases are lessening in number, they might remain calm until real help arrives."

"And what is the real help?" Dr Hugh Grant asked.

"Whoever removes the barricades and tells us they'll take it from here," said Zantoko. "We won't be expected to deal with this indefinitely, I'm certain. Someone with greater authority will come."

Devey felt a shiver down his spine at that. Whoever was outside didn't care about the people inside this hospital. If the barricades came down, he wasn't sure he would like what came next. But Zantoko seemed hopeful, so he held onto that.

After more brief discussion, the doctors and nurses went on their way, all with their own specific set of instructions to carry out. Zantoko was clearly the man in charge, but Devey wondered why that was—so he asked the man while he was getting a cup of water from the cooler. "Are you in charge of the hospital, Dr Zantoko?"

"Ha! Heaven's no. I'm head of A&E, which makes me the obvious candidate to man the front lines. The administrators are in charge of the hospital but they work in a building down the road. There are other consultants and surgeons with the same seniority as me, but they are all holding the fort in other areas—we still have a hospital full of ordinary patients to attend to. All hands on deck, I'm sure you can understand."

Devey nodded. "What do you want me to do?"

"Just what you have been already. Keep your ear to the ground and help where needed. Get others involved, too, if you can. People behave better if you empower them."

Noise erupted outside, and the door sprung open and crashed against the wall. A nurse staggered back into the room with her forehead bleeding. "Help! Help me!"

Zantoko ran to her, catching her before she fell. He asked her what happened, but she wouldn't focus on him enough to answer, too dazed, too confused. He helped her over to a small couch and then marched out the door into the waiting area. Devey was right behind him.

The waiting area played scene to yet another riot, but this one was worse than the others. Blood ran everywhere as people kicked and punched one another like spooked mules. It was obvious to see why. Devey spotted a dozen people with bleeding, festering wounds. Many bled from their faces, but others tried to hide their shame. They weren't fooling anybody.

Zantoko didn't react for a moment. He stood there with his jaw hanging open. "No, no, no. This is wrong. I don't understand."

Someone with half their face missing like Phantom of the Opera saw Dr Zantoko and came racing towards him. Devey shoved the doctor back into the office and closed the door. "Stay inside and lock the door!"

The infected man turned his focus on Devey, angry at him getting in the way. He reached out with his infected hands, seeming to understand that his touch was a death sentence. Devey dodged out from behind the nurse's station, dragging a chair with him. He shoved it into the speeding man's path and sent him tumbling like a skittle. His arms went out to break his fall, which caused the skin to slough off from his elbow to his wrist. He came to rest on his side, bleeding. "I'm so sorry!" Devey said before rushing off into the fray.

It was all over. All chance of keeping the infection isolated had evaporated. A third of the crowd bled from infection, and their blood coated everything. The crowd succumbed to mass panic. The infected clawed and begged the healthy to help them—spreading the infection further. It was over. They were all going to die.

Despite that realisation, Devey still fought to keep his distance. He backed away until he hit something, and when he turned around, he saw the vending machines. A slash of blood ran the width of their glass fronts, and finally he understood what had doomed everyone—himself included.

The Black Sabbath fan had been heading to the vending machines when he'd first seen her. She'd bought a bottle of water, prodding the buttons with her infected fingers—the same buttons he had later pressed. As he now looked down at his fingertips, he saw clusters of tiny blisters, so small it was no wonder he hadn't noticed them until now. He pressed his thumb and forefingers together and felt the blisters pop like bubble wrap beneath his skin. A trickle of blood appeared on his left thumb. That was the reason so many people had wounds on their faces—they used the vending machine and then touched their face.

Just like he had. *He was going to die.*

The screams intensified as people scattered, seeking clean air to breathe. The infected clutched at anyone within reach, murdering with their touch. Children screamed for their mummies. Mummies screamed for their children. Nurses lay on the floor, knocked out and powerless.

Ken appeared amidst the chaos. "Devey! The infection is everywhere. We need to get out of here." Devey dodged back before the orderly could touch him. "I have it!" he said. "The infection is all over the vending machines—probably a dozen other places too. Don't touch me. Just… go somewhere and hide. Maybe you don't have it."

Ken looked Devey up and down, searching for wounds, and it seemed to take him a while to understand. "I… I'll head to the maternity wards. They have extra security and it's been locked tight since this whole thing began. Join us there if things turn out okay. If not, I'm sorry, mate."

Devey nodded. "Just go! Dr Zantoko is in the nurse's lounge. Take him with you." "Okay, good luck." Ken sprinted away and just like that, Devey was alone in Hell, surrounded by demons bleeding death upon the earth.

DEVEY WATCHED the world end with a strange sense of detachment. The blood and carnage should have been enough to double him over in revulsion, but since finding Mary on her kitchen floor he had encountered one horror after another. Could a person become desensitised so quickly?

The waiting area was no longer bustling as people fled into the bowels of the hospital. Now it resembled a film set—the Haunted Hospital--and rubbish and flesh littered the rows of benches. The floor was awash with coffee cups, handbags, shoes, and blood. Half a dozen bodies lay mangled, trampled to death or brained by one panicking brute or another.

Besides the dead, there were living too. Several frightened faces peered from behind desks and other cover. No one spoke. No one tried to help. The only person not hiding was an old man, the same one from earlier who had been cradling an old woman. Devey had refused to help him then, but perhaps he could do something now. He took a seat beside the old man. "Are you hurt?"

The old man didn't react to Devey's presence at first. He stared into space, exhaling slowly. Blood streaked his craggy cheek, but it didn't seem to be his. "We like to think ourselves civilised," he eventually muttered, "but we are animals. Put a flame to our feet and we will always leap into the trees."

"People are trying to save themselves," said Devey.

The old man continued staring into space, blinking once or twice. "Yet they succeed only in doing the opposite. I'm ashamed to be human today. I'm ashamed this is what we are."

Devey didn't know what to say, so he said nothing. His eyes couldn't help but search the room, scanning every morbid detail. What looked like an obliterated eyeball lay squished on the tiles near his feet, and his eyes followed a slick trail to the body of an old woman ten feet away. Devey realised then that the old man wasn't staring into space, he was staring at this body. It was the old woman he'd been cradling before. Her head had been stomped to mush, and the only part of her recognisable was her bloodstained cardigan. "I'm sorry," said Devey. "I should have helped you earlier."

"No," the old man said. "You were helping a little girl."

"Still…"

The old man looked at him with watery, grey eyes. "My name is Derek. My wife's name was Stella. She's only here because she wanted to come with me to get my blood taken. I've always hated needles, you see. She was supposed to outlive me. We both knew I would never cope on my own."

Devey rubbed his hands together in his lap and saw blood smears on his palms. It didn't seem to matter. "What happened to Stella?"

"Heart attack, I think. When all the commotion started, she got anxious. It was too much for her. Eighty-six, she was."

"Wow! And how old are you, Derek?"

"Eighty-two. Not a bad age to end on, I suppose."

It felt like a point to argue—to say something like: *you could live another ten years yet!*—but they would have been empty words. No room for platitudes when you were surrounded by the dead. "Can I do anything for you," Devey asked. "Not everyone is infected. There might still be a way out for some of us."

"No, I think I'll just stay here with my Stella. She was always afraid of being alone."

Devey stood and wiped blood from his palms onto his postal uniform. The crimson matched the Royal Mail insignia on his breast. "You sit tight. I'll come back later."

Derek stared at his wife in silence.

Someone rose from behind a bench and bolted for a nearby corridor. Devey paid them no attention and wondered why they were even running. No one was trying to stop them. What would happen next, he wondered, now that things had reached their climax? Before things had deteriorated, the infected were being led to the sub-basement. Would that be the best place for him? Zantoko said patients were being treated with drugs. Might those drugs work?

He raised his hands and inspected them. His right palm had split open in a bloody chasm and several fingers on both hands were blistered and peeling. The patch of skin beneath his nostrils was also itching fiercely, but he dared not find a mirror and look. He couldn't stay in this waiting room though, surrounded by flesh and filth. So he headed to the lifts. Like everything else, they were covered in blood. He reached out to press the call button.

The lights went out.

His finger jabbed the call button, but it was dead. The corridor fell to pitch-blackness. Without his sight to navigate by, his other senses increased. The coppery twang of blood grew stronger in his nostrils.

He stumbled away from the lifts, squinting to see the green and white signs hanging from the ceiling. He knew the stairwell was nearby, so he felt his way along, seeking the next doorway he could find. Somewhere in the depths, voices shouted and argued, but he was all alone in this particular piece of darkness. Despite being in his twenties, Devey still kept the hallway light on in his flat while he slept. Ever since he was little, total darkness had always provoked his imagination to run wild. The memories of his father closing his bedroom door and demanding him to grow up and go to sleep were still fresh in his mind. The feeling of laying there trembling all night, missing the light. Missing his mum.

Devey's groping hands slipped from the wall and clutched thin air. Some kind of alcove. Stepping into it, he found a door, and when he opened it he saw the hazy shape of a staircase. He'd found what he was looking for.

He held onto a handrail on the wall as he descended, taking each step carefully as he felt his way with his feet. The lower he went, the more he worried about what he was sinking himself into. The lower floor was where the infected were, which meant he would likely encounter a whole lot of sick people. In the dark, he wouldn't even see them coming. He had little choice but to keep going, but what he wouldn't do to get the lights back on.

The stairwell lit up, a glowing blast hitting him in the face. He cried out.

"Who's there?" a voice barked at him from a few steps below.

Devey shielded his face, trying to see through the blinding corona. "I-I'm Devey."

"Devey Singh?"

"Yes! Who is that?"

The light lowered and Devey blinked away his blindness. In front of him stood the police officer with coppery sideburns. He looked glad to see him. "It's me, Officer Mitchell, but you may as well call me Mike. Seems our paths are destined to keep crossing."

"I'm glad to see you, Mike, but don't get too close. I'm infected."

The officer took a step lower. "Ah, sorry to hear that. I've been waiting for them to cut the power."

"Waiting? Why?"

"Let's go downstairs. We don't have long."

Devey followed the officer to the bottom of the stairs, and they entered one of the wards of the lower floor. Devey recognised it as the one he'd been kept in. Doctors and nurses rushed back and forth, lighting candles and switching on torches.

"Who cut the power?" Devey asked as he continued walking with Mike. "And why?"

The officer stopped walking and faced him. "Them outside. They cut the power."

"Why?"

"Because they're planning to come in, guns blazing. It's textbook. Secure the perimeter, cut the power, storm the gates. We're about to get slaughtered. Not that it's a bad thing. A mercy at this point."

In the growing candlelight, Devey glanced inside the various side rooms at patients lined up in beds. Doctors and nurses moved between them. He looked again at Mike. Mike who seemed to know everything, so long as it was bad news. "How long have you been down here? Is the treatment working?"

"Not that I can see, and certainly not fast enough if it is. My partner has it—that's what I'm doing down here. Both paramedics too. Guess I'm the only one with any luck out of the four of us from this morning."

"I wouldn't call any of us lucky. Still, you should get out of here. The healthy have made their way to the maternity ward. Go there."

He headed for one of the open doorways. "It won't matter where any of us are soon. I'll stick around here, thanks."

Devey was struck by a smell as he entered the room alongside Mike. Six beds took up the space, each surrounded by curtains. A nurse supervised, but she looked ready to drop. Her left arm was wrapped in a bloody bandage, and a sore had opened on her cheek. Her own dying didn't stop her from visiting each bed with medicines though. From where Devey stood, only the first patient was visible—an unconscious young man. His lower jawbone was exposed. "What does this?" said Devey, his tongue thick with saliva. "Natural or man-made, this is wrong. No one deserves this." He looked at his bloody hands. "I don't deserve this."

Mike gave a small shrug. "If I were a philosopher, I might have answers for you. All I can say is tough luck. Tough luck for us all."

Devey needed air, so he hurried out of the ward and into the corridor. Sickness floated thickly in the air, a revolting wet smell that made every breath a feat of endurance. Human beings reduced to rotting meat. Never had he felt so insignificant, so worthless. His death had arrived from nowhere, and there was nothing *he could do to prevent it.*

He'd woken this morning the same as always, groping around for his phone beneath his pillow before stumbling into a shower at a time when most people were still asleep. He wished he'd stayed in bed.

But things might not be any better outside the hospital. Would a virus like this be contained to a single hospital? It may have started with a game of Bingo, but how many other people could the blue-rinse brigade have passed it on to? Mike said earlier that reported cases went as far south as Gloucester—and that had been several hours ago. What now? Had the virus reached London? Europe? Suddenly he had visions of the world ending.

This is insane. I don't know anything for sure.

Devey hadn't even tried to help himself yet. His sickness was in its early stages. He needed treatment. He had to at least try to beat this.

The door to the next room was open like all the others. He stepped inside, hoping to find a doctor, but instead he found the male paramedic from this morning. He sat silently in a chair, a candle on the windowsill behind him. Even though they were in the sub-basement, the floor seemed to be only partially below ground, being sited along the rise of a hill. Whoever was outside, had not forgotten to barricade the windows of the hospital's lower section, and the glass panes looked out onto featureless steel. In the resulting gloominess, it was hard to tell whether the paramedic was looking at Devey as he entered.

"Hi. Sorry to disturb you. Do you know where any of the doctors are?"

The paramedic shifted in his seat. "They're about somewhere, but don't expect them to help you."

"Why not?"

The paramedic reached behind him and took the candle. He bought it onto his lap and rendered himself visible. No doubts remained about whether he was sick because both his eyelids had liquefied and slid away —it gave him the odd expression of a startled ghoul. "They can't help you because all the doctors and nurses down are sick too. None of us are going to get better. Best we can do is ration the morphine."

Devey noticed then, the patient lying in a bed to his left. They lay so still he'd been unaware of their presence until the paramedic gave a subtle glance in their direction. Despite the power being off, there was equipment still running, taking measurements and slowly spitting out a never ending stream of paper. Devey sighed. "Is… is that your partner?"

"She doesn't have long left," said the paramedic. "Suppose she must've been one of the first."

"You have it too," Devey motioned to his eyelids. "How did you catch it?"

The paramedic leant towards the bed and clutched his partner's blistered hand. "I caught it the moment she did. I wasn't going to leave her alone to rot. I've been holding her the whole time, and I'll keep doing it until there's nothing left."

If not for the printouts coming out of the machine, Devey would have assumed the woman was already gone. He couldn't hear her breathing. "I'm sorry."

"Sorry? If not for you, Claudia wouldn't be here."

Devey wobbled, knocked off-balance by the accusation. "What?"

The paramedic bolted to his feet, and Devey thought he was going to attack him, but instead he grabbed for something else. His fingers clamped on the corner of Claudia's bedsheet and he yanked it like a magician uncovering his latest trick. Unleashed, the stench of human decay washed over Devey and made him gag. Claudia looked up at him, her eyes the only thing left of her face. She was a slick, gristle-covered skeleton. Her lungs pumped in her chest, lifting the soft veil of rotting skin with each breath. Her breasts had fallen away, given her the look of a mannequin. Her blood dyed the bedsheets red.

"See what you did?" The paramedic shoved Devey in the chest, knocking him back three steps. "See what you did?"

"Hey!" Devey put his hands up in front of himself. "Wait a minute."

But the paramedic kept on coming. "Get out of here! Leave us alone." He shoved Devey again, knocking him into an unused drip stand. He had to struggle to keep from falling over it, and the delay allowed the paramedic to get in another shove.

Devey retreated to the doorway. "Okay, I'm going. I'm… I'm sorry."

The door slammed behind him, and he stood in the hallway alone. A nurse walked down the corridor in his direction, only a slight blemish on her cheek, and enough strength left to smile at him. Maybe she could help—give him the drugs he needed to finally accept his fate—that he was dying.

But before he could talk with the nurse, an almighty racket broke out in the corridor behind him. He turned to see a window rattling in its frame. The sound of power tools pierced the air.

The people outside were coming in.

Chapter 6

The nurse stopped, staring in confusion. Devey, on the other hand, knew he needed to move right now. The sound of heavy bolts being removed was a herald of an approaching threat. It wouldn't be long before the people outside came in.

He bolted into a side room, aware that people were watching him with confusion. He warned them to be ready, but most were too far gone to care. A few took the warning to heart, and got up out of their chairs, but they still didn't look like they understood what was coming.

The sound of power tools continued, roaring beasts, and Devey sprinted down the corridor back towards the stairwell. Before he got there, the glass panes of a window shattered ahead of him. He skidded on his heels as a monster appeared at the window. The soldier, donning a nightmarish gas mask over his entire head, climbed through the broken window and landed in the corridor in front of Devey. He lifted a stubbed-nose machine gun at him and bellowed. "Get down! Get down now or I'll shoot."

Devey put his hands up and backed away. A side room lay off to his left, but he dared not look inside for fear of tipping off the gunmen, so he continued backing away slowly until the right moment presented itself.

"I said get down!" "Screw you!" Devey bolted to his left, dodging through the doorway. Gunfire broke out. *Rat tat tat.* People screamed. Everybody screamed.

Devey searched desperately a lifeline. There were no weapons in the room, or anybody to protect him—only frighten people who were looking at him like he might have an idea what to do. He was going to die amongst strangers.

"Everybody down on the ground!" The gunman entered the doorway gas mask distorting his voice and giving it a ghostly quality. With no other choice, Devey put his hands up.

"Please," he said. "These people are sick. They're afraid. Please."

"Shut up!" The gun shook, and the soldier's finger twitched and tightened. "Just… shut up!"

The gun went off, spraying bullets into the floor. The soldier slumped to the ground, and in the place where he'd stood, Mike snarled and brandished a steel bedpan. "I ain't going to make this easy for you assholes!"

Devey flinched. "Mike? What are you doing?"

Mike tossed the heavy bedpan and picked up the gun. He examined it expertly before holding it against his chest. "I might be a dead man," he said, "but that doesn't mean I'm about to lie down and let these sons of bitches kill me."

"Why are they coming in?" Devey asked. "They could just leave us trapped in here."

"Leave us in here too long and we'll try to make an escape. They can't risk someone getting loose."

The people in the room had remained silent until now, but the sound of more gunfire outside caused them to start sobbing. Devey wanted to turn and shout at them to be quiet, but he knew it was just the stress. He kept his attention on Mike. "You're not helping by fighting back. Put the gun down."

Mike laughed. "Do you hear yourself?"

More gunfire. Screams of people dying.

"There might still be healthy people in this hospital," said Mike. "People with a chance. You think it's okay for these fascists to come in and gun them down?"

Devey glanced around the room at the frightened faces. He spotted a nurse, herself infected, but not as badly as some. Until the gunfire had started, she would have been administering drugs and care to those worse off, giving comfort and dignity. Not shooting the sick like diseased dogs. "Okay…" Devey nodded. "Let's go down fighting."

Mike smiled and clapped him on the back. "Into the fire then."

With the stubby machine gun against his shoulder, Mike raced out into the corridor, whooping like a cowboy.

Ratatatat.

He flipflopped in front of Devey, limbs thrashing in all directions. The gun dropped out of his hands and skittered across the tiles, hitting Devey's trainer. He picked it up without thinking, surprised by how heavy it was. It was an alien thing in his hands, industrial. Dangerous. Mike crumpled in the corridor, dead and bullet-riddled.

Another soldier in a gas mask appeared, moving in view of the doorway and staring down at Mike's corpse. He raised a gun and put a bullet in his head. The ferocity of the act made Devey yelp, which tipped the man off that he was stood there watching him.

The soldier pointed his gun at Devey.

Devey's entire body clenched, including his finger around the trigger of the gun he had picked up off the floor. The weapon bucked in his hands, and he had to fight to keep it from flying off. The soldier jerked backwards before falling down dead. The people in the room screamed. Screamed because they had just seen two men die.

Something grabbed the back of Devey's leg and he realised the people in the room had been screaming to warn him. The solider Mike had hit with the bedpan was climbing to his feet, trying to grab Devey and pull him down. This time, Devey acted with purpose. He bought the gun around and placed it against the soldier's forehead.

"No, please," begged the soldier, but Devey had already pulled the trigger.

Housed inside a balaclava and gas mask, the soldier's head didn't explode, it crumpled—his body flopped sideways onto the floor where he bled slowly onto the tiles. Devey looked back at the nurses and patients. "Hide." Then he crept out into the hallway, avoiding Mike's fatal mistake by checking the coast was clear first. At the end of the corridor, he saw shapes—soldiers stepping slowly through the shadows. It was dark outside, night having fallen without him realising. Moonlight leaked in through the windows. Gunfire continued, but was less sporadic now, more of a methodical *pop-pop* as patients were exterminated like rats. Devey pressed himself flat against the wall as a woman spilled out of a side room and went crashing into a trolley cart. She begged for her life, but one of the soldiers at the end of the corridor turned in her direction and gunned her down.

No way Devey could take down every soldier on the floor—he wasn't even sure how many bullets he had left in his gun—but he would try to avoid his death for as long as possible.

"No! No! Leave my little girl! Plea-"

Ratatata.

Devey recognised the voice coming from the next room and winced when it was interrupted gunfire. He sprinted inside and opened fire as soon as he spotted the soldier's black body armour. This time his shots were precise and measured—all three rounds struck the man in the centre of his back. A woman lay in the centre of the room, but she was still alive, clutching her bloody stomach and moaning. Her eyes went from confused to surprised. "D-Devey?"

"Barbara? Shit, are you okay?"

She shook her head. "He shot me. I… Please, help Jessica."

There was a bed behind her, and Devey moved towards it slowly. Jessica lay asleep, hooked up to a machine like the paramedic had been. Her pretty little face had peeled away, revealing a sticky, pink mask. She didn't have long left. The sickness had moved fast.

"Help her!" Barbara cried. "Just… please… help… her."

Devey heard the strength fade from the woman's voice, and when he looked back from the bed, he saw she had passed on. She lay peacefully on her back, arms resting at her sides. Was she dead because of him? Would her fate have been different if he hadn't shopped her in to the doctors?

Jessica shifted in bed, her head rolling on the pillow. Her hair stuck to the fabric in clumps, and a bloody tear spilled from her left eye. Mercifully, she remained unconscious.

Devey realised his cheeks were wet and wiped them with the back of his sleeve. His uniform was spattered with blood, but it didn't matter. He turned to a vacant bed beside the one Jessica slept in and took its pillow. Then he placed it over the little girl's face. He bore down, expecting a struggle, then stayed there for over a minute. Eventually, the machine next to her bed sent out a high-pitched alarm. The little girl was gone.

Devey turned away, leaving the dead child and stepping over the dead mother. On his way out, he exchanged his gun for the one the soldier in the room had been carrying. He hoped it had more ammunition, but even if it did, he doubted he would get to use it all. He was already playing a losing hand, having survived an encounter with three trained soldiers, all of whom he had killed. Three men dead because of him. And now a little girl. He was about to head back out into the corridor, ready to face his own death, when he heard a voice in the room. He took a moment to realise it, but it was coming from the radio attached to the dead soldier's shoulder. "*Secure your areas and regroup at the main entrance.*"

"*Roger that,*" said another voice from somewhere in the building. "*Requesting det charges on ground floor west,*" said another. "*Targets holding out inside Maternity Ward. Need to blow the doors.*"

Devey froze. The maternity ward was where he'd told Ken to go. It was where Sonja was, and maybe others too. Mothers and babies. The man on the radio called them *targets*.

"Screw this!" Devey rushed into the corridor and headed for the stairs.

"Hey! Stop!"

Gunshots.

Devey felt the air move, and the plasterboard exploded to his right. He zigzagged, picking up speed and keeping his head low. More bullets whizzed by, hitting the wall on both sides, floor, and ceiling, yet miraculously he was unharmed.

"Stop!"

Or what? You'll shoot me?

Devey made it to the stairs, and raced up the steps, praying he didn't trip in the dark. The soldiers yelled after him and let off more shots. Evey second, he expected to feel a sting between his shoulder blades, followed by a suffocating death, but the bullets continued to chip at the masonry either side of him. When he eventually made it to the top of the stairs, he didn't know what to do. He had been so sure he was about to die.

The stairwell was closed off by a single door which he slammed shut, not daring to glance down the stairs at the soldiers pursuing him. Acting fast, he grabbed a trolley bed from a nearby alcove and wheeled it in front of the door. Then, more by luck than planning, he located a brake over the rear wheels and stamped on it, locking the trolley in place. The thing was heavy.

"Open up!" Fists banged on the other side of the door. "Open up right now!"

Devey shook his head in despair. "Did they really expect him to just give himself up to be shot? To put some doubt into his pursuers, he fired his gun at the door. He didn't know if the bullets passed through the wood, but the banging stopped at least. He used the distraction to make a run for it, heading for the maternity ward. He just had to find it.

Devey found the old man still sitting in the waiting area, except now he was dead. A line of bullet wounds crossed his brittle chest. He had refused to move as the soldiers came and shot him.

A radio chirped and Devey ducked down behind the benches. He peered over the top and spotted two soldiers in the entranceway. The steel barricades were still in place, but a fire entrance hung open nearby. The soldiers spoke casually into a radio, guns hanging from their hips. Devey thought it best not to interrupt them, so he kept low to the ground and scurried away. According to the signs overhead, maternity services was housed with A&E, X-Ray, and Out-Patients. A busy section of the hospital, but would it be busy now? His gut churned with the worry that he would find nothing but a lot of corpses. The gun trembled in his hands, feeling heavier by the second.

The ground floor was as dark as the sub-basement had been, and most of the windows were barricaded still. It made sense that the soldiers would want to keep most exits locked down, avoid people escaping. The only good thing was that Devey didn't have to worry about someone grabbing him through an open fire exit or window. In fact, the corridor he walked down was deserted. Where were the soldiers? The staff?

A sign overhead read Maternity Services and pointed to a set of double doors on the right. An intercom sat on the wall, but there was no reason to buzz for permission—the doors were chipped and splintered in the middle where they met, the locks snapped. Was he too late? Was everyone dead?

He heard shouting.

Instead of running the other way, he slipped in through the broken doors and hurried down the proceeding corridor towards movement he spotted at the far end.

"Open up," someone barked—a soldier. There were two of them. "We don't want to hurt you."

"Leave this hospital," came a well spoken, yet defiant reply from Dr Zantoko.

Devey slowed down to a creep. He held his gun ready, disgusted at how easily he contemplated killing. These soldiers had it coming though. They were the ones bringing guns into a hospital full of sick people. Innocent people.

The space at the end of the hallway was lit by a pair of floor lamps, the industrial kind you found at construction sites. Thick cables disappeared into a large square box that must have been some kind of giant battery. The light made it easy to see what was happening, but difficult to stay hidden. Dr Zantoko and a dozen other people huddled inside the neo-natal ward. They had barricaded the doors and windows with beds and equipment, and Zantoko peeked through the glass the pair of soldiers outside.

"Doctor?" One of the soldiers banged on the glass. Like the other soldiers, his voice was distorted by his gas mask. "Someone is bringing an explosive to blow this room open, which is a very messy way of dealing with things. Come out voluntarily and we will lead you out the hospital to safety."

"Like you did all the others?" Zantoko spat. "Not likely."

"Those people were sick. You people inside are well. We don't want to hurt you."

"Then leave!"

The soldier pulled his gas mask up over his head and sighed. "I can't do that, Doctor. Please, just work with me here."

Zantoko pressed his glaring face up against the glass. "There are babies in here, sirs. Are you going to kill babies?"

The soldier groaned and turned to his colleague. "Jesus, where the hell is Chris? Sooner we get this over, the sooner we can get back out in the fresh air. I swear I can't breath properly." He pulled his mask back down. "I don't care if the people in there are healthy or not--I'm ready to burn this place to the ground." Zantoko and the others were uninfected. They still had a chance. Devey raised his gun and pulled the trigger. The stream of bullets struck the soldier on the left, reducing his head to pulp. The gun was still a bucking mule, so as he tried to rake the bullet stream towards the other soldier, but his aim went high. The soldier collided with the wall and let out a cry, but he didn't go down. He raised his gun at Devey and pulled the trigger.

Devey felt a wasp sting his collarbone and he bit a chunk of his tongue to keep from screaming. He thought he was dead, about to be torn apart by gunfire, but the soldier who had just shot him dropped his gun and slumped to the ground, clutching his neck and coughing. He fought to remove his gas mask.. "Ah fuck! Y-You shot me!"

Devey stumbled over to the wounded soldier, ignoring the agony in his entire right shoulder. "Serves you bloody right," he grunted. "The people inside that room are healthy. Leave them alone."

The soldier sighed, wincing as he pressed against his neck. "It… It's not my call."

Devey aimed his gun at the man's face. "Whose call is it?"

"PH3," he muttered.

"Who the hell is that?"

"The... the people who cut off a hand to save an arm. The virus is... it's everywhere. We need to contain it or we're..." he gritted againt the pain in his neck, "finished."

Devey lowered his gun. "The virus is everywhere?"

"It came out of nowhere. Started at a bingo hall in the city, but now it's spread all over the country in less than a day. The fact it presents so fast is the only reason we have any chance at all. If we euthanize the infected, we can cut off the hand before it takes the arm."

Devey raised his gun and used it to point to the neo-natal ward. "The people in that room are healthy."

"Orders. No one leaves the hospital."

"That's insane." He aimed the gun at the man's face again.

The soldier tried to lift his hand away from his neck, but he couldn't. "Please, it's not my choice. It's my orders."

"I'm giving you new orders." Devey scowled at the soldier bleeding to death at his feet, then shoved his hand against the bullet wound in his shoulder. He brought his fingertips back bloody and thrust them inches away from the soldier's face. "I assume you know the infection is spread via contact."

The soldier nodded eagerly, terrified. He tried to shuffle back, but there was nowhere to move.

Devey growled. "You do anything to hurt the people in that room and I'll fist you with my bloody hand. Leave this ward and don't come back."

The soldier groaned. "I can't go until I have dealt with this entire floor."

"You don't have a choice," Devey snapped. "Because I'll kill you before you get a chance. So go."

The soldier's radio buzzed, and a voice came out. "Daniels, we're ten minutes out on the det charges. We didn't bring any in the initial load out."

Devey thrust held his bloody hand next to the soldier's face. The soldier shuddered and turned to face the radio on his shoulder. When he did so, he revealed the flesh wound on his neck. It was bleeding steadily.

He pressed a button on the radio and gave a reply. "Negative. Cancel det charges All targets eliminated. Stevens didn't make it. Some asshole with one of our guns."

"Roger that. Someone took out one of our guys and managed to arm himself. Must have been some kind of ex-special forces. Made a right mess of Charlie Team. Well done for getting the bastard. Are you standing down?"

The soldier grunted. "Roger that. Mission accomplished. I'm hurt though. I need Thompson to take a look at me."

"Regroup at the main entrance. We're pulling out in five."

"Roger that."

Devey let out a breath, not realising how tense the radio call had made him. The soldier, for his part, had lied convincingly. "Your men are leaving?" he asked.

"Not my men, but yes, we're pulling out. The hospital has neutralised." He side-eyed the neo-natal ward behind him. "Almost."

"Not a word," said Devey. "I'm letting you leave here with your life. Thank me for it."

The soldier fought his way back up to his feet and went to retrieve his gun. Devey kicked it away. "Nice try. Your machine gun stays with me."
"It's a sub-machine gun," the soldier replied pettily.

Devey frowned. "What's the dif—actually, it doesn't matter. Just get out of here, asshole."

The soldier stumbled away, but before he exited, he stopped and turned around. "It's bad out there," he said. "Best thing you can do for the people inside is put a bullet in their heads. If you don't, you'll infect them all anyway." The soldier tapped at his own forehead which prompted Devey to feel his face. He felt the raw, bleeding skin and wondered what he must look like. The soldier left, and after a few minutes, Devey decided the coast was clear. With the muzzle of his gun, he tapped on the glass window of the neo-natal ward.

Zantoko appeared, glaring, but then he saw Devey and frowned. "Mr Singh?"

"Hello, Doctor. Everything is okay now. The soldiers have gone."

"How?"

"It…" He puffed out his cheeks out, too tired to explain. "It doesn't matter. Is everyone inside okay?"

"Yes! We are all healthy. I'm afraid you must stay away, Mr Singh."

Devey nodded. "I understand. I won't try to come in, but you need to stay in there until it's safe. How long can you hold out in there?"

There was a pause while Zantoko thought about it. "Two days perhaps. There is food in the nurse's fridge and we have milk formula and access to clean water. You think we should remain inside?"

"The sickness is passed by touch, right? The fact you're all okay means it must be clean in there. Maybe in a couple days the infection will die off and it will be safe to come out, but right now you are best off staying put."

"But we need help," said Zantoko. "There are newborn babies here."

Devey's fear doubled at the thought of infecting babies with his sickness. "The virus has spread everywhere. It's a mess. The longer you stay safe in there the better. You're a doctor—you can look after the babies." Zantoko nodded slowly behind the glass. "Okay. I think you may be right. You should leave though, Mr Singh. Find someone who can help you."

Always a doctor, Devey thought, as he saw the compassion on the weary doctor's face. He smiled warmly, but then considered that he might look more nightmarish than friendly. "There's no one left to treat me, Doctor. I'll be outside in the corridor, watching out for you all."

Zantoko sighed. "Thank you, Mr Singh—Devey. I'm sorry things turned out this way. I feel responsible."

"You're not, but thank you." He looked past Zantoko and saw Ken and some other staff he recognised. He also saw a mother cradling a tiny baby. Seeing that hurt more than the rotting flesh on his face. It forced him to turn around and leave. Out in the corridor, Devey heard engines starting and equipment being loaded. The soldiers were pulling out, but would the one he'd released keep his word? Or would a team of gunmen appear any minute to finish the job? The longer Devey waited, the more things seemed to be okay. Eventually it was silent, the middle of the night, and he was sitting all alone.

He must have fallen asleep because he jolted when he heard a noise. It was a voice, distorted but understandable. "Hello? Devey? Devey, can you hear this?"

Devey got up in a fluster and raced over to where the voice was coming from. He realised it was the intercom next to the broken doors. Blinking himself awake, he gave a reply. "Yes! I'm here. Who is this?"

"Sonja."

"The nurse who took care of me?"

"Actually, you took care of me. Ken is here too. We both made it here in one piece. I had a little girl, just like I told you. Her name is Lauren."

Devey grinned. "That's a beautiful name."

"She's got a set of lungs on her. I just woke up to feed her and Dr Zantoko told me about what you did. You made the soldiers leave."

Devey smiled, even though she wouldn't see it. "I helped. They were leaving anyway."

There was a sigh on the other end of the call, then Sonja said, "I heard you were sick. Is there anything I can do?"

"Yes! Keep away from me so you can tell Lauren what a handsome and brave man I was."

Giggling. "I will tell her all about you, Devey. Do you need me to call anyone for you? Our mobile phones are working again, off and on."

Devey fingered his own phone in the pocket of his shorts. "That's okay. I don't need to call anyone yet. Is everyone still okay in there?"

"A couple of sore ladies, but yes, we're fine. The infection would have shown by now. We're all lucky. How is the rest of the hospital? Did anyone else make it?"

"I don't think so, I'm sorry. I keep meaning to check things out, but I… I must have fallen asleep."

A baby cried in the background. "Don't worry about us, Devey. Go find some drugs and a bed. You need to rest."

"I'll be dead soon, Sonja. Rest is not the best use of my time."

"I'm so sorry."

He thought he was crying, but when he rubbed his face, he saw blood. "Me too. I hope we speak again before… well, you know."

"I'm here, Devey."

"Me too," came Ken's voice, sounding thick and emotional. Devey smiled again. "Thanks."

HE COULDN'T RELAX until he knew the hospital was truly empty, so Devey headed back to the main waiting area. It was the same as he'd left it, except now the blood was dry. The main entrance was still barricaded, but the fire exit hung wide open, held in place by a bin. He could finally walk right out of there, but what would be the point? He would die wherever he went. The vending machines were shattered from gunfire, and a doctor lay dead in front of them. His white coat was stained red. Thirsty and hungry, Devey stepped over the corpse and helped himself to snacks, propping his gun against the wall so that he could fill both hands. No one would mind his theft, he was sure. And he wouldn't need to worry about the calories.

He took his haul over to the long reception desk and sat down on a roller chair. As he tucked himself in, his knees knocked against something soft.

"Fuck! Watch it!"

Devey threw himself back in his chair and yelled. When he saw the man hiding under the table, he almost laughed. "Lee? Shit, man, what are you doing here?"

"People were fucking shooting up the place. Are they gone?"

Devey nodded. "Did you… find your mum?"

He cleared his throat and then got out from beneath the desk with a grim expression on his face. "She went in her sleep," he said. "They told me she didn't suffer for the last part."

"I'm sorry. Was she… did she have?"

"Yeah, she was a rotting mess at the end. The smell was foul. So where is everyone else?"

"The maternity ward. Dr Zantoko, Ken, Sonja, and others."

Lee beamed with delight, and it was then that Devey saw his gums were bloody. Several of his teeth were gone too. From his grinning expression, he didn't seem too concerned. "That's great," he said. "Come on then, what the hell are we doing here?"

Devey reached out and held the Lee's forearm. "We can't, we're sick."

Lee shrugged free of his grasp. "Which is why I want to see the doctors."

"They can't help you."

"The fuck do you know?"

Devey grabbed the man again, this time hard around his wrist. "Look at my face, Lee. Do you think if the doctors could help, I would be stood here talking to you. All that will happen if you go to see them is you'll infect them. We're dead men walking. It sucks, but there's no changing it."

Lee tried to break free again, but this time Devey held firm. "Let go of me. Now!"

"I can't do that. I have put up with as much as I will take today. You're not going there and infecting everyone."

Lee grit his teeth, but then sighed and relaxed, finally seeming to understand. Then he showed otherwise by smashing his fist into Devey's nose. The pain was immense, not just from his nose breaking, but from his infected flesh tearing away from his cheekbones. He crumpled to the ground, clutching his bleeding face, and sure he was going to choke on his own blood.

"Fuckin' Paki!" Lee growled and kicked Devey in the ribs, sending him rolling in agony. Then Lee stormed off. Devey reached out to stop him, tried to yell, but all that came from his beaten lungs was an endless moan. He collapsed onto his back, trying desperately to breathe. He went so long without air he started blacking out. His vision curled at the edges and his stomach turned flips. If he didn't get a hold of himself, Lee would reach the maternity ward and kill everyone. Including Sonja and her baby.

Lauren.

Devey gritted his teeth and focused the pain inwards, into his centre. Then, all at once, he was sucking in air like a jet engine. He lost his breath again momentarily, but after several erratic gasps, he was inhaling and exhaling again in the regular rhythm. He wiped blood from his face and stumbled back to his feet, using the desk for support. He took off after Lee, but not before first revisiting the vending machines.

The sub-machine gun was a part of him now, and he enjoyed its ability to deal with problems so efficiently. With all the innocent death he had witnessed this day, shooting dead a few bad guys did not disgust him. He just hoped he wouldn't pay for the sins in the next life. He hoisted the weapon and took off down the corridor as fast as he could, hoping he knew the way better than Lee did.

Devey caught up to Lee scant moments before he was about to enter the maternity ward. The thug strolled casually as if he had all the time in the world. Did he not realise that no doctor could help him now? Did he think Zantoko would present him with a handful of pills to make his sickness go away?

The man was insane.

"Lee! Stop! I can't let you go in there."

Lee spun with his fists clenched, ready to fight, but when he saw the gun in Devey's hands his snarl turned to a tight-lipped frown. "Where the fuck you get that?"

"From a man I killed, and you'll be next if you don't back away from those doors. You're not going in there."

"I need help," he said, softly like he might get down on his knees and beg. "Let the doctors tell me themselves if they can't help, but I have to try."

"They can't help you, Lee! Now step aside before I shoot you."

Lee gave a lopsided grin that was bordering on a snarl. "You ain't going to shoot me."

Devey took a slow breath, enjoying it as something so simple and yet so numbered. In addition to Lee's bloody gums, he now noticed a soreness to the man's eyelids and nostrils. It could have resembled a simple cold, but Devey knew Lee's flesh was only minutes away from peeling away. The guy had no chance. Neither of them did. "I can't murder a dead man," said Devey before pulling the trigger.

The surprise on Lee's face betrayed the fact he had truly thought Devey bluffing. In the split-second he realised he was about to be shot, Lee bolted forward to tackle him. He took a bullet, but was still able to make contact. The two of them went down in a heap with Lee on top. They fought and punched at one another. Lee was the bigger man, and less sick, so he clattered Devey across the face with lefts and rights. All this he did despite bleeding from a bullet wound in his chest. Devey was reminded that he had been shot too. His whole body screamed in pain.

He was in danger of blacking out again, and as he threw his hands out desperately, he wished he had managed to keep hold of his gun. Lee swatted his hands aside easily, and Devey grew more and more desperate.

"Devey? Is that you? What's going on out there?"

Lee looked around confused, not understand that the disembodied voice had come from the intercom on the wall. It bought Devey enough time to jab his fingers into the bloody bullet wound on Lee's chest. The bigger man wailed and fell away, allowing Devey to roll free. The gun lay on the floor nearby, and he snatched at it urgently. He made it up to his knees by the time Lee charged at him again. "I'll kill you, you fuckin' Paki!"

Devey lifted the gun. "I'm not Pakistani. I'm Sikh." Then he squeezed the trigger and punched Lee back against the opposite wall. He slid down onto his rump, leaving a slick trail of blood behind him on the plaster. The gun *click-click-clicked,* finally empty.

It was over.

"Devey? Are you there? Is everything all right?"

Devey dragged himself over to the intercom and pressed his back against the wall. "Everything is fine, Sonja. How's that little baby of mine?"

Sonja giggled. "She's fine. Did I hear gunshots?"

"There won't be any more," he said. "All of you get some rest. Tomorrow will be a long day."

Chapter 7

Devey struggled to the roof of the hospital as he had told Dr Zantoko he would do. The building was only two levels above the hill, so he couldn't get a view for miles, but he could see the town, and the edges of the city beyond.

Things were bad.

A dozen fires burned, and sirens blared all over. Chaos reigned in the city, but death had not yet won. Chaos meant people. Even more positive, the area surrounding the hospital was deserted, which meant Zantoko and the others could leave without being accosted. The plan was for them to go to the large country home of a colleague of Zantoko's—a heart surgeon from an old money background. Zantoko had taken the man's keys from a locker, expressing sadness that his colleague was likely dead, but recalling visiting his large home on several occasions. It would be a safe place to hide out until the chaos died down, and Zantoko pledged to make it there if only to inform his colleague's family of what had befallen him.

It was a plan.

But not one which involved Devey.

By now, almost two whole days since this thing began, he was barely human. His hands, resting in his lap, were skeletal and sore. His breast fell away in long, slippery strands—like unravelling a jumper by a pair of threads. He coughed up blood, and felt something come loose each time, and he could not blink for his eyelids had deserted his face. Still, as he perched on the rooftop watching Zantoko and the others pile into a hospital mini-van, he was not feel entirely without hope. These people were alive because of him. He had kept them safe, protected them. He watched Sonja now with her little girl and told himself that Lauren would live a life because of him. It made his death a little less wretched.

He counted fourteen people in total and winced as they crammed themselves into a mini-bus built for ten. Still, after being shut inside the hospital's deathly atmosphere, it probably felt great being outside again. What would happen to them all now was anybody's guess, and something he would hold no influence over. Maybe things were okay beyond the city, but as he watched another fire leap up in the distance, he wasn't so sure. Whatever happened from now, the country would never be the same as it was. Lauren would live a hard life.

The world was infected, sick and dying.

It might take a long time for it to be well again.

Before the mini-bus pulled away from the courtyard, Dr Zantoko looked up towards the roof. He spotted Devey there and waved. Devey waved right back. Then they were gone, travelling down the road into town. Eventually, they turned a corner and he no longer saw them. That was how hospitals had always gone for Devey. People he cared about always left him in these horrible places. His mother had left him alone in a hospital room, clutching her hand and sobbing. That his father had not been there as she passed was something that had driven a wedge between them. Devey had been a boy, yet it had been him who had done the man's duty. He had taken it away from his father.

Devey reached into his pocket, wincing as the last scraps of flesh tore from his fingers, and pulled out his phone. He had switched it off last night to keep the battery from dying, but now he turned it back on. As Sonja had said, the mobile service had returned, but it was poor, unreliable. No harm in trying to make a call though, and this would be the only chance he got. He coughed another mouthful of blood and understood that it was only a matter of minutes before he would tear something vital inside of himself. Each cough might be the one to kill him. With shaking, senseless fingers, he prodded commands into his phone, struggling to see through the bloody smears he left on the touchscreen. To his surprise, the call connected and started ringing. Now all he needed was for his father to pick up. He could finally say he was sorry.

If his dad answered.
If...
"Hello?"
Devey smiled. "Hi, Dad. It's me."

<<<<>>>>

The Peeling Omnibus

THE ORIGINAL NOVELLAS

To follow are the 5 original novellas set within The Peeling universe (and a prequel short). They were written during 2012 and 2013.

THE PEELING OF SAMUEL LLOYD COLLINS

THURSDAY

My big toenail fell off today. That leaves three on my right foot and two on my left. It stung at first, but now my toe just feels…hot. I'm keeping the nail in an ashtray in the kitchen.

My name is Samuel Lloyd Collins and I suppose, in a way, this is my last will and testament, except I don't have anybody to leave anything to, so I guess this is really just my last testament. Or maybe writing this is merely the closest thing I have to company.

I don't have to be alone. I could go next door and take part in one of their endless political debates that echo through the walls and keep me awake at night. Sometimes I think about yelling at them to 'keep it down', but what would be the use? Politics are high on everybody's agenda right now. One would expect them to be.

Everyone has their own theory on how 'The Peeling' started, but I personally think it was the Arabs. It's always the Arabs, isn't it? Saddam is dead and the Yanks finally got Osama. So what choice did they have left but to go for broke? Everyone assumed their master plan would culminate with a nuclear attack on a major city, but in many ways this virus is worse. We may have snuffed out the leaders, but their passion for killing, it seems, will never die. You cut the head off a chicken and it runs around like a maniac, spraying anyone nearby with blood. That's what 'The Peeling' is: arterial chicken blood spraying us all with its infectious filth. I guess the Arabs won in the end…

I came down with the sickness on Tuesday. Two days ago. I've already lost a bit of hair and some skin off my testicles, and you already know about the toenails. Funnily enough, my fingernails are currently unaffected, probably the only reason I'm able to write this. I thought about typing this on the computer, but somehow it felt like a man's final words should be in ink, don't you think? Maybe when it comes right down to it, paper is more permanent than a collection of cheap circuits.

My future is laid out for me now. I'll be dead within a week, give or take a day. The beauty of the Peeling is that it leaves no room for hypothesising. No room for hope. It kills every time, no exceptions. In a way that certainty has allowed me to come to terms and accept my fate. This time next week I will be a bubbling oil-slick of rancid, dissolving flesh. Somehow I'm fine with that.

But I need to know who is responsible for the pain I'm in. I already told you I think it's the Arabs, but unless I know for sure…Well let's just say that knowing for definite would bring a certain degree of closure to the situation. Of course, the honourable men and women of the Government's various agencies are urgently investigating the origin of this disease and those responsible, but as each second passes, Great Britain withers and dies beneath its second great plague. I just hope to be alive when they determine the guilty party.

Already know it was the Arabs, just need to know for sure…

FRIDAY

I woke up this morning stuck to my pillow. Not because I had been drooling in my sleep, but because the skin below my left eye had rotted and fused with the cotton. I had to rip the pillow away and half of my face with it. The resulting meld of infected flesh and sickly white cotton reminded me of a surrealist painting, beautiful in a way. Maybe I'll have it framed before I die.

What an odd thing to muse upon! It would not surprise me if I have gone quite mad. I'm already starting to feel delightfully delirious (or maybe that's just the throbbing and burning where my face used to be).

Such good bone structure I was blessed with, but did not know of, until I was today faced with it in the mirror. The bone of my cheek now shows right through, covered only by several, thin slivers of sinewy gristle. I look like the Phantom of the Opera (albeit a grizzlier version). I wonder what part of me will dissolve tomorrow. That's the fun part of this sickness, I suppose, not knowing which chunk of skin will decompose next. It isn't like typical flesh-eating diseases; they have a point of infection and usually spread systematically. But The Peeling strikes the body at random, necrotising a man's feet before popping up a day later and doing the same to his ears. I've seen hundreds of case photographs and no two victims follow the same path of infection. The only non-variable: it's always fatal. No one understands this disease at all…

…and no one can stop it.

I think it's starting on my chest…

SATURDAY

I can see my ribs. Two of them, glistening at me like curved piano keys. It's amusing, in some morbidly fascinating way, to see one's inner workings. The pain is starting to subside, and thankfully only throbbed for a few hours in the morning, but the cloying odour inside the house is repugnant. Ideally, I would open the curtains and windows, but I don't wish to be disturbed by the outside world. I would only become resentful of those who still have all of their skin. Besides, it was being around other people that infected me in the first place, sealing my fate, and I hate them for that! But retaining my humanity is all I have left to focus on for now and resentment will only make that task harder. I have decisions ahead of me that should not be made in temper…

I have been corresponding all day with a trusted associate that is supplying me with up-to-date information on the current pandemic, along with the progress of the on-going Government investigations into the crisis. So far it seems clear that this was a premeditated and focused attack on the western world. The Peeling has, so far, hit 90% of Europe and is seeping its way into the East. USA and South America are also stricken, worse than we are in fact, but it is unsurprising to me that, as yet, the Arab world is unaffected. I am eager to see just how far into the East the disease spreads before ceasing its journey of human pestilence. I'm guessing that it will be shortly after it runs out of Christian nations to infect.

SUNDAY

I lost a hand today. Thank God it was my left and that I can still continue writing this. I now have a withered stump that drips periodically with a viscous yellow discharge. It looks similar to the contents of a Cadbury Cream Egg but smells worse than anything I could ever hope to describe to you now. I suppose it's the aroma of lingering death.

Next door are still at it. Talking incessantly at all hours. I need peace and quiet right now. Time to think. I already informed my colleagues that I would be working from home for the next week and am not to be disturbed under any circumstances. They were not happy, but I'm the Boss, so they'll have to cope. They don't know that I have the sickness, of course, probably too wrapped up in their own fear of it to even consider the possibility. People only worry about themselves nowadays.

My associate emailed today and told me that the infection was definitely engineered – *Wow. What a revelation!* – and that it was unleashed upon the world at strategic locations: Major cities, along coastal areas so that the disease would work inwards from all directions, eating around the edges of England as though it were a Jaffa Cake with a chewy orange centre…

God what I would do for a box of Jaffa Cakes right now! The stump of my wrist is itching just thinking about it. Perhaps it's excitement?

Anyway, I have sent a reply email asking what is currently known about WHO engineered the disease. That is what I have to know.

Then maybe I can do something about it.

MONDAY

I have lost an eye today. It is indeed unfortunate, but in a way I am blessed to have persevered this long anyway. Many do not, and at least I have the other eye. My left one just dribbled out of its socket today like an under-boiled egg with its top sliced off: all foamy white and custardy-yellow. I almost laughed when I looked in the mirror. I look like a zombie-pirate.

At least it doesn't hurt. Not physically.

I suspect I have little time left now and I am anxiously awaiting news from my associate. I can feel the illness seizing my internal organs in its corrosive grip and it's only a matter of time before they start to decay completely. I have already taken to soiling myself involuntarily, so I assume that my intestines are already rotten. I would take a shower to get clean, but the pressure would only shred what remaining skin I have left. For now I will sit and wait for my associate to provide me the information I so desire…

Who is responsible? Who turned me, and most of the free world, into a quivering mass of mutilated flesh?

I wonder if there's any Jaffa Cakes in the pantry.

TUESDAY

It has now been one week since I first noticed the skin under my armpit was peeling away in pus-filled chunks. One week since I realised I was a dead man walking.

Dead man peeling! Ha!

But I am still alive, devoid of nearly all my skin, granted, but alive nonetheless. Moist splatters of pungent flesh litter my home now, whilst foul scabs fall from my body constantly. The only merciful thing about this disease is that I feel nothing.

Nothing except for the soft scraping of insanity inside my fleshless skull.

WEDNESDAY

Today will be my last. I can feel it. My lower legs snapped today when I got out of bed, too rotten and malformed to bear what little weight my frail body has left. It is of no importance however, as I awakened to something wonderful: *You have mail.*

I am about to drag my withered limbs over to the computer right now, to see what my trusted associate has for me. I will record the email, and my response, for you right here, as I feel it will be important.

Dear Prime Minister.

I sincerely hope that you are keeping well in this time of dire need. Great Britain is within the talons of great turmoil and despair, but I trust that your inspired leadership will see us through as ever. This shall not be the end of our endless empire and the good people of this nation will go on stronger than before. That is our way and always will be. May Angels sit on our shoulders as God guides our souls through the times ahead. Long live Great Britain.

But without further ado, Prime Minister, I will provide you with the Intel you require. It was discovered at 0300 GMT today that the disease is not contained to western nations as first assumed. In fact we now have reliable information that the infection, commonly referred to as 'The Peeling', was contracted in Turkey and has quickly spread as far east as Japan. I'm sure you can appreciate, that with the USA also affected, it effectively means the disease has travelled the entire circumference of the world… Yet there is one country that has shown no effects of the illness, despite being surrounded by it on all borders. We have tried to contact that nation's Government but they have declined all opportunities to reply. It now seems a reasonable assumption that the country in question is responsible for this worldwide plague.

That country is North Korea.

As always, I await you orders on how to proceed, but I implore you to act wisely.

Yours,

General Harvey Whitehead

Dear Harvey

I was certain it was the Arabs! Guess we can all be wrong sometimes…

Regardless, since my dear Martha and the children were taken from me by this wretched sickness, I have had no time to mourn them, so I regret to inform you that this will be my final act as leader of this nation. I hope that you and your family are well, and remain so. I wish the same for Great Britain.

Without continued procrastination, my orders, in regards to the Godless entity of North Korea, are as follows:

Send the Nukes.

Send them all…
They will not take this world as their own.

Yours regretfully,

Prime Minister Samuel Lloyd Collins

THE PEELING: BOOK 1

JEREMY'S CHOICE

The *Never Stop News* Studio was cramped with bodies. The typical skeleton crew of six or seven had swelled to at least four times that amount, people cramming together in front of the studio's news desk while the two young anchors prepared to go live with the evening's stories. The overcrowding had made Jeremy's job very difficult.

Jeremy was a security guard for Never Stop News, responsible for keeping out anyone not invited to be there. With the news studio and its roaming reporters providing content twenty-four hours a day live, there was always a risk that some anarchic member of the public, with a grudge and a message, would try to sneak in front of the cameras and interrupt the feed. With current events, and the public being so frightened, the risk of a security breach skyrocketed. People wanted answers, and when people wanted answers they came after the Government first and the media a close second. With so many people filling up the claustrophobic studio, it was impossible for Jeremy to keep his eyes on everybody.

There was just one more hour to go before he would be relieved from his post by the night guard, Greg – just one more hour. He could not deny that he dreaded being there even another *minute* longer, though. Bad things were happening in the world, that had started almost a week ago, and the situation didn't seem to be getting any better. Jeremy didn't want to be there anymore. He didn't want to hear another goddamn thing about *The Peeling.*

The studio was silent and the lights went down as the countdown till live began. The network was currently running a pre-recorded football report on its dedicated satellite channel and on its website, but would turn back to its studio anchors in seven-seconds.

Six seconds.

Five.

"Okay, guys," one of the production assistants shouted over the crowd. "You're live in three…two…"

Sarah Lane, one of the anchors, cleared her throat and said, "Good evening, UK. Things are still pretty scary right now, but rest assured Tom and I will be bringing all of the latest news for the next four hours. Get yourself a nice hot cuppa and snuggle up on that sofa because Never Stop News will be looking after you tonight."

Jeremy still struggled to accept such a casual approach to the news. Sarah and Tom were only mid-twenties, and were dressed and spoke as such. Never Stop News's entire premise was to provide the day's events with a laid-back and youthful approach. Their slogan was: *All the truth. None of the nonsense.* Jeremy found it even more surprising that such an approach had been successful. Never Stop's hip approach to the news had gained them a younger audience unattainable to the traditional networks. It had even started to eat into the more mature demographics as well. It seemed that people were tired of the byzantine stuffiness of days gone by and were happy getting the news from a bunch of plucky youngsters. As a consequence, the Never Stop News Corporation was one of the fastest growing media companies in the world. Jeremy imagined that the lovely Sarah Lane had at least a small part to play in that success. Her shapely legs and curved figure, always on display beneath the glass news desk, were a constant feature of trashy celeb magazines and trashy websites.

The equally attractive and immaculately-groomed, Tom, took the lead from Sarah and got started with the programme. "We've been reporting all week the current crisis in the UK and – it now appears – many other parts of the world have also been affected. Reports suggest upwards of four-million people have been affected throughout the UK alone and over ten times that amount worldwide. The numbers have been rising, hour-by hour, and with no end in sight, there is great fear that the current number of casualties is just a small percentage of what will be the final number."

Sarah Lane took over again. "While both Private and Public sectors are working tirelessly to find both a cause and a solution, it is clear that the world is suffering under what can only be described as – a global pandemic. Commonly referred to as *The Peeling*, the unknown virus has spread throughout our nation and others with a virulence never before seen. Affecting young and old alike, there are no clear vectors for contraction. Government officials admit to knowing nothing about its origin and very little about its pathology. As previously stated, all members of the public are advised to remain inside their homes and avoid all contact with anyone besides their immediate family. The military are permitted to use force where necessary, to ensure the spread of infection is contained."

Jeremy swallowed back a mouthful of acidy saliva. His reflux was bad, but his pills were at home. It was unlike him to suffer heartburn in the day. If he'd a job someplace else, he'd be home right now like most other people, but news was an essential service. Jeremy's job, in many ways, was a matter of national security – his job to make sure the anchors were safe to give their reports. Unfortunately for England Jeremy was just a middle-aged man with bad acid.

At fifty-two, Jeremy's limbs were stiffer than they used to be, and his arthritic bones ached more often than not. He was certainly willing to take a stand against anyone looking for trouble, but he couldn't claim truthfully that he was the best man for the job. Most days he just hung around the corridors, half-asleep, until he returned home to his wife. That was why all of these people in the studio were such a thorn in his side – they forced him to concentrate and stay focused despite his weary mind's desire to shut off. Most of the people didn't even need to be there – they were just clerks and office assistants from other floors or departments – but no one wanted to leave while news was still coming in. Everyone wanted to know more about the disease. Their fear and panic was palpable and Jeremy could sense it hanging over the dimly-lit room like a soiled blanket.

"As we have little fresh news to report from official sources," Tom told the audience at home. "We will be turning the air over to you – the public. For the next two hours we want to hear from *you*, Great Britain. We want you to tell us what you've seen, and what are your thoughts about The Peeling? Do you have it? Does someone you love have it? Is there any advice you can give to help others out there? We want to hear from you now."

Jeremy didn't know what they expected to get from the public that they didn't know already. It was well-documented that The Peeling started with a tingling sensation in the hands and feet – sometimes the nose and ears – before moving on to a streaming cold and flu-like symptoms. After a day-or-so of runny nostrils and messy sneezing, the virus really started its magic. Jeremy shuddered thinking about what The Peeling did to the human body.

"Okay, we have our first caller," Sarah reported. "We have Keith on line-1. Hello, Keith."

"Hiya, Sarah. Hiya, Tom. I just want to say that you've been a constant comfort during these last few days. I don't have any family, and not being able to leave the house has been really hard on me."

"It's been hard on a lot of people," Tom said. "But right now the only way to stay safe is to lock yourself away."

"Do you have The Peeling, Keith?" Sarah asked in her typical caring manner. Although, Jeremy noticed, that the young girl wasn't as calm and collected as she usually was. She fidgeted a lot and her hair was out of place

There was a pause on the other end of the line, followed by a muffled sound that could only have been sobbing. Eventually, Keith came back on. "Yes…I have it," he whispered down the line. "I've had it three days…since Wednesday."

"I'm really sorry to hear that, Keith," Tom said. "It's truly terrible what this virus is doing to people. Absolutely horrifying." The reporter took a deep breath and suddenly seemed very tired, as though he'd dropped a mask that had been hiding his true face all along. Jeremy sympathised from over by the studio's door. Tom wasn't much more than a lad, really, and he had suddenly found himself responsible for consoling an entire nation.

Sarah sat forward on her chair and clasped her hands together on top of the desk. "Keith? If it's not too hard for you, could you tell our viewers what it's been like since you got ill? Could you tell us about your symptoms?"

After another short pause, Keith replied that he would. "I got home from work at about six on the night – I'm a mig-welder. Anyway, Man U were playing Chelsea and I wanted to see them get their arses hammered, so I got some beers in and plonked myself down in front of the telly. I was happy, you know?"

"We know," Sarah confirmed understandingly.

"Well, I'd been feeling a bit under the weather all day and my nose had been running like a tap, but I thought it was just a cold. I mean, no one really knew what was going on then – it was all just rumours." He trailed off and begun to sob.

"Just go on when you're ready, Keith," Sarah told the man. "We're here for you."

"Right, sorry, anyway," Keith gathered himself, "I was sat watching the game, but I couldn't help but scratch at my feet the whole time. Was a bit like pins and needles, but no matter how much I itched or walked around the living room, it just wouldn't go away. Thankfully it got a bit better after a couple beers and I managed to ignore it."

"What happened next?" asked Tom, filling a brief moment of dead air.

"Then I fell asleep on the sofa. Do most evenings if I have a drink. I woke up later, in the middle of the night. I knew it was late because the shopping channel had come on, selling their usual junk. So I sit there for a few minutes, trying to wake up a bit so I can get myself up and go to bed, but soon as I lean forward, I feel this sharp stab of pain."

Jeremy rubbed at his eyes in the doorway. He'd heard enough reports to know what was coming next. He'd even seen what was coming next first hand.

"I look down at my feet," said Keith, fighting back sobs, "and I can hardly…I can hardly believe what I'm seeing."

"Tell us, Keith."

"My feet they were…oh God…they were like raw steak. They had no skin. I could see all the gristle and bone and blood. They looked like those anatomical dummy things they have in school, you know? Anyway, like a fool I grab down at them, like I needed to make sure my eyes weren't still half-asleep and seeing nonsense. When I touched my feet it was agony. I almost passed out it was so bad. Worst pain I'd ever felt…but I would give anything to feel that way now – it was heaven compared to the pain I feel now. The skin from my ankles started peeling away the next morning, blistering up and peppering the floor like dandruff. Then it moved further up my legs. Then it….then it…." Keith finally allowed himself to sob openly down the line. "My dick is gone! It fell onto the carpet like a goddamn sausage."

The man began to wail inhumanely and the phone line went dead. Jeremy didn't know if it was the caller or the studio that had cut the conversation short. Probably the studio. They had a duty not to cause the public any more distress then they were already in.

Sarah smiled awkwardly into the main camera. "We seem to have lost Keith, there, but I'm sure we're all united in our prayers that his condition gets better."

"Absolutely," Tom added. "I think we should just move on and take the next call."

"That would be Angela Thomas on line-4."

"We're all going to die. God is punishing us for letting the queers and the-"

The line went dead. This time Jeremy was certain it had been the studio's doing. There was nothing like a crisis to bring out the hate-filled vipers from their pits. Britain liked to act like all the whackos lived abroad in less civilised countries, but working in a news studio made it quite clear that there were as many nutjobs here as there were anywhere else.

Jeremy checked his watch. There were only forty minutes till he could leave, but it seemed like an eternity. At home, his wife was sick – like so many other people – and it felt like a betrayal not to be with her now, looking after her. He'd betrayed her for most of their twenty-year marriage, with various other women and his hidden gambling habit, but failing her now was enough to make his guilt muscle finally take notice. He was a hypocrite, that much was true, but he knew there were times when a man needed to step up and be selfless for the woman he loved; this was one of those times. The entire nation lived in hope that The Peeling would soon be dominated by a cure – that man would triumph over nature once again as it had always done. But Jeremy knew better. He knew that the virus wasn't just bird-flu on steroids. This was the end. Even if the virus was destroyed, the amount of death it had already caused would be monumental. Millions. The world would never be the same again. Perhaps that meant Jeremy would get the chance to be a decent man again, to be a good husband – even if it was only for the handful of days his wife had left. She could get better, but something in his gut told him not to hold onto that hope. He had to get home.

The next call came from line-2. A cantankerous old man, named Bob. "It's them bloody Koreans, I'm tellin' ya. I'd blame the Arabs if I could, but they don't have the smarts for this. North Korea has been closed off to the rest of the word for decades. We don't know what they've been up to, do we? But I tell you one thing for nought; they've obviously been plotting the downfall of the world this whole time. Kim Jong Il arranged for it to happen before he died and, surprise surprise, a virus the likes of which the world has never seen, has come out of a country no one knows anything about. Prime Minister Lloyd-Collins knew about it; tried to do something about it before he died."

Sarah butted in while she had chance. "Now, Bob, it's already been confirmed that North Korea has been affected like everywhere else. Early reports that they were the instigators of this pandemic turned out to be false. Prime Minister Lloyd-Collins's directive to bomb their country was just the paranoid actions of a dying man. General Harvey Whitehead was right to do what he did by holding emergency cabinet hustings and taking command of the Government."

"All so he could get in power," Bob asserted.

"Come on," said Sarah. "Do you really believe that? General Whitehead was only made Deputy-Prime Minister temporarily because his military background is exactly the skillset needed to help manage the nation through this crisis. His decision to ignore Lloyd Collins' directives – God rest his soul – averted a nuclear war."

"And also let the bloody Koreans get away scot-free. You bloody watch what happen. This time next year we'll all be slaves to a bunch of slitty-eyed-"

The line went dead. Jeremy had heard enough of this. Holding a public phone-in was just morbid and macabre. There would be no hope gained from talking with them, for they were the most hopeless and lost of all. The men and woman of the United Kingdom were floundering helplessly in the dark, rotting away slowly in both body and mind. Their sad stories would do nothing but spread more suffering, infecting people's thoughts in the same way The Peeling infected their flesh.

Jeremy was just about to abandon his post when a ruckus erupted in the corner of the studio. A handful of people had begun to scuffle with one another while others backed away fearfully. Angry voices filled the air and bounced off the narrow walls, interrupting the on-going news report.

"We seem to be having a few problems here in the studio," Sarah told the audience. "I think we should cut to a commercial break briefly, but don't go anywhere, guys. We'll be right back."

Sarah and Tom stood up from their desk and headed away from the violence, whilst Jeremy shoved past them and headed for the centre of the squabbling crowd. As he got nearer, he realised that it was not a fight that had broken out, but an attack on a single individual. A pair of men and one woman were kicking hatefully at a downed body.

"Everybody, back away, now," Jeremy hollered at the group with great force in his voice. While he may not have been a physically imposing man, he had a voice that commanded attention. The group of people immediately stopped what they were doing and backed away from him. The victim remained on the floor, huddled and whimpering: a blonde woman, a girl really.

"She has it," said a woman in a grey power suit. Her face dripping with anger. "The bitch has it and tried to hide it."

Jeremy looked down at the girl shaking on the floor and saw no signs of The Peeling. He looked up at the power-suit woman who had spoken. "What?"

"It's true," said a tall, Black man standing next to her. "She's been sneezing non-stop for the last hour."

Jeremy raised an eyebrow. "Sneezing? A young girl sneezes and you all think you have the right to attack her? A big strong man like you?"

"She deserves it. We could all be infected because of her. I have a family."

"Then you should be with them, instead of here acting like a thug. Now help her up off the floor."

The man shook his head. "You pick her up. I'm not touching her."

Jeremy took a step forwards and stared the man hard in the face. "You just did touch her, with your fists. Help her up now. I won't ask you again."

The taller, larger man just laughed at Jeremy, then shoved out with both arms. Jeremy acted quickly, grabbing one of the man's thick wrists and pulling him forwards, off balance. Then he kicked out and took the man's legs from under him, sending him to the floor with a *thump*. Jeremy was just about to follow him down to deliver a knockout punch when Sarah called out to him.

"Jeremy, don't! I'll help the girl up and we'll take her somewhere to lie down."

Jeremy looked up at the young news anchor, confused. "Sarah, you have the news to be getting on with."

"We're on a break, and Tom can handle it for ten minutes." She glared at the nearby crowd and shook her. "You people should be ashamed of yourselves."

Sarah went over to the fallen girl and knelt down beside her. Jeremy knelt the other side and together they gathered the woozy young woman to her feet and walked her away from the baying crowd. There were a whole host of angry mutterings that followed after them, but no one had the guts to act out after what had happened to their ring leader.

Jeremy and Sarah took the girl out into the corridor, soothing her all the way.

"We can take her to my dressing room," Sarah said.

Jeremy nodded. It was a kind offer, and that was why he had always liked Sarah. She was as friendly as anybody else, despite being a national sex symbol. Her ego had every right to be much larger than it was, but she was surprisingly down to earth.

They half-carried, half-dragged, the girl into the dressing room and set her down on a plush sofa filling one side. She was weak and upset, but seemed coherent.

"Are you okay?" Jeremy asked her.

Her eyes had filled with tears, but she nodded. "I don't think they would have stopped."

"Animals," Sarah said. "They should be arrested."

The girl waved her hand. "It's okay. I'm just going to go home and forget about it. Can I just rest here for a while first?"

"Of course you can, sweetheart. Take as long as you need."

"Is it true what they said," Jeremy asked the girl. "Do you have it?"

"I...don't know. I have the sniffles, but I've been sneezing for a few days now and nothing else has happened."

"You just have a cold," said Sarah. "If you've been sneezing that long and haven't come down with other symptoms then you're probably fine."

Jeremy nodded and let out sigh. Despite millions of people being sick, it was still a relief to know that this one young girl was going to be okay – for now.

The girl laughed pitifully. "I think people forget that The Peeling didn't make all of the other, regular illnesses go away. Not every sneeze means you have the plague."

"Exactly," Sarah said. "Now you just relax here until you feel better. There's water in the fridge and some cookies. Help yourself."

"Thank you, Miss Lane. You're really kind – kinder than I would have expected you to be."

"Yeah," Jeremy agreed. "A big celebrity like you, mixing with the common people like us."

Sarah bopped him on the arm playfully. "Don't be silly. I'm C-List at best. Anyway, I have a feeling that the world will have little need for celebrities soon."

"You shouldn't think the worst. The world will get through this, one way or another. Not everyone is getting sick." As Jeremy said it he didn't believe it, but it felt like the correct thing to say.

Sarah took Jeremy by the arm and led him back out into the corridor. It seemed like she wanted to tell him something, something that couldn't be anything good.

"Is everything alright?" Jeremy asked her, noticing the tears that were brimming in her eyes.

"No, it's not alright. Things are definitely not alright, Jeremy. You don't know the half of it."

"What do you mean?"

Sarah leant back against the wall of the corridor and for a moment it looked like she might collapse completely. "I have the producers in my ear, nonstop, telling me facts, figures, things to say – and what *not* to say. We're not telling the public anything close to the truth."

"They know the truth. It's right in front of their faces."

Sarah shook her head. "They're all locked up inside while police and military patrol the roads. All they see is what's out their windows."

Jeremy wasn't following. "So what *is* the truth?"

"That there's thirty-million dead in the UK, not four-million. The worldwide estimates are over half a billion. The USA and most of Europe have been decimated three-times over."

Jeremy's stomach swelled against his ribcage. Vomit rose in his throat. "You're telling me that half of the UK is infected, in less than a week?"

"The NHS has estimated that the virus affects one-in-two people. Everyone has a fifty-fifty chance. They've also put the chance of death at 100%. Anyone who catches The Peeling will die. No exceptions."

"But you haven't been telling people that. You've been reporting the numbers of infections, but you haven't said people are dying. You've even implied that there's a chance of recovery."

"I don't make the decisions about what to report, Jeremy. The Peeling doesn't kill people instantly. They suffer for days. The death toll has only just begun, as the first people to catch it have had it for almost a week now. We didn't know the virus would kill in all cases, at first, but with the data coming through today, it's clear that no one is surviving it. The Government are trying to make the decision on whether to go public with the information or not."

"The Government? What right do they have to dictate to the news outlets?"

"They can control information in a national crisis. They always have."

Jeremy stood wearily in the corridor, shocked and sickened. He had known The Peeling was a plague beyond anything ever witnessed, but he hadn't thought it powerful enough to wipe out half of the world – 50/50. There would be no containing it now, no cure – just unimaginable death and suffering that would linger in the consciousness of mankind for centuries.

He looked at Sarah and could not imagine the burden she was forced to carry – to have such information, but unable to share it.

"What are you going to do?" he asked her.

"I'm going to finish up tonight and then go home. I'm finished after tonight."

"You're quitting?"

"Not exactly."

"What then?"

Sarah took in a deep breath and let it out slowly through her slender nose. She stared at Jeremy for a moment, then put her left hand to her right sleeve. She rolled up her cuff and exposed her wrist."

Jeremy shook his head in disgust. "No. You can't have it…"

The wound on her arm was puckered and wet, the skin gone and exposing the flesh of her muscle beneath. A tangy odour filled the room like spoiled bananas.

"I've been hiding a cold the last couple days, but I didn't know I had it for sure until this morning. Noticed it in the shower. It's already spread twice as much since then."

Jeremy rubbed both hands down his face and imagined his cheeks peeling off beneath his fingernails. He was one of the lucky ones so far; the right side of 50/50. "You're sure there're absolutely no survivors?" he asked. "There's nothing the NHS can do?"

Sarah shook her head, seemed resigned to her fate. Maybe she felt luckier to be one of the infected than one of the healthy – at least for the infected the nightmare had an end in sight.

"I'm already dead," she said. "I don't know if I'm infectious, but I don't want to take the risk anymore. I'm going home tonight and staying there. It's where I'd rather be. I need to feed my cat."

"I'm sorry," Jeremy said and truly meant it. "I wish there was something I could do or say."

Sarah rolled her sleeve back down, covering her wound. "I'm just glad you don't have it as well. As long as some of us get through, then I guess things aren't completely doomed."

"My wife has it. She came down with it three days ago now."

Sarah put her hand on his shoulder and squeezed. "Then you should go home and take care of her."

Jeremy glanced at his watch. "My shift isn't-"

"It doesn't matter. I don't think anything matters anymore. This is just the calm before the storm. Things are about to fall to pieces and the only thing we can do is look after the people we love. Go home, Jeremy. Look after your wife."

Jeremy watched Sarah return to the studio and knew that it would be the last time he ever saw her in person again. He hoped her passing would be peaceful, but that was a luxury The Peeling gave to no one. She would feel pain beyond anything she had previously imagined, and then she'd die – adding to the statistics that she'd been reporting for the last week.

It was time to go home. Sarah had been right about nothing mattering anymore. If those people in the studio wanted to start fights then let them. Jeremy wasn't about to waste another minute watching over a bunch of unruly strangers turn on each other.

The news studio was on the second floor so he had to take the stairs downwards to reach the building's exit. The reception area was empty, its staff all sick and dying at home. Jeremy knew most of them, but not well enough to grieve for them. He headed for the heavy glass doors that led outside to the parking lot.

Outside were several vehicles, belonging to the people inside. Sarah's Jeep Cherokee was parked next to Tom's more audacious Jaguar XK; beyond them both was Jeremy's Ford Focus. He took out his keys as he headed over to it, pressing the fob to unlock it. The lights flashed twice and the doors unlocked. He opened the driver's side door and slid in behind the wheel.

Turning the ignition, Jeremy started the engine. The needle on the fuel gauge headed towards empty and stopped a little ways off. He laughed. Some things would never change, no matter what happened to the world; cars would always run out of fuel, and fuel would always cost a bomb – especially now that the military had commandeered it all.

The military were everywhere, as were the police. It was to be expected, Jeremy supposed, but it was still disconcerting to watch olive green, 3-tonne trucks patrolling every main road. With the UK's history of riots, the Government was taking no chances. There was even a sentry posted at the news station's car park, controlling the bright-red automatic barrier instead of the usual civilians that had done so before. Jeremy pulled the car into gear and drove towards that barrier now. The armed soldier stepped up to meet his car as it approached and Jeremy lowered the electric window and leant out with his security ID. It wasn't his usual station ID, but a new state-issued ID that allowed him to leave his home and travel to work. They called it a Vital Services Identity Card – pronounced V-SIC. It was a privilege to have one in many ways, but a burden too. Being outside was a constant danger for many reasons – number one being exposure to The Peeling. Still, if Jeremy was going to come down with the sickness, he surely would have caught it by now.

"Everything okay in there?" the soldier asked him, motioning to the news studio with his head.

"There was a bit of trouble earlier. People are getting scared. Might be a good idea to post a man inside."

"No can do," said the soldier. "Orders are to remain outside at all times, unless absolutely necessary."

Jeremy understood and nodded. "Can't have people thinking that the military are controlling the press." *Even though they are*, he thought secretly.

The soldier gave no reaction, his expression implacable. "Drive safely, sir. Go straight home."

Jeremy nodded and crept the car forwards as the metal barrier rose in front of him. Once past it, he pulled into third-gear and increased his speed. It was easy to drive fast because the roads were all empty. Travel had been restricted to prevent the spread of infection and only certain vehicles were allowed on the road. Jeremy's Ford Focus qualified and had a luminous green circle on both the front and back. It told any passing military that he was allowed to be out – for the most part they left him alone. In fact, a convoy of trucks was heading toward him right now and seemed unconcerned by his presence on the highway. The driver of the lead truck nodded to him as it passed, and it was only a few moments before Jeremy was the only car on the road again, driving along the withered husk of the nation's once-heaving infrastructure.

He lived almost forty-miles away from the news station, but with the roads wide open, he would get there in thirty minutes. He turned on the radio but quickly switched to CD mode. The last thing he wanted was more news – or uninformed hypotheses masquerading as news, more accurately. The sound of Blue Oyster Cult's *Don't Fear The Reaper* came on from a mix-disc he'd filled full of rock songs. It seemed pretty apt for the mood he was in and he let it play to its conclusion.

AFTER TAKING the dual-carriageway most of the way home, Jeremy took a slip road into Stratford. As he crossed over the bridge into the centre of town, he could see that the police were patrolling the River Avon in modified barges. Every single day the police and military presence seemed to increase, and it now seemed that Britain's waterways were just as restricted as its roads.

Much of the routes through town were cordoned off and Jeremy was forced to manoeuvre his car along the riverbank, passing in front of the Globe theatre. The historic, thatched-roof building lay abandoned and mournful now, its function to entertain no longer required. Jeremy suddenly regretted never having been inside before to experience the lively works of Shakespeare. There would probably be a lot of things he'd never experience now.

Something flew out from behind the theatre and stumbled into the road. Jeremy hit the brakes.

Standing in the centre of the narrow side-street was a peeler – a victim of the plague. Whether it was woman or a man was unclear now, but the long, matted hair suggested the former. Jeremy gawped in horror as the figure approached with the shambling gait of a zombie, but this thing – this human being – was worse than a zombie. This thing was living agony, stumbling towards Jeremy like a nightmare made flesh. It was the worst case of the infection he had yet seen and the woman had not a single inch of skin left intact. Her muscle – and even bones – were exposed from head to feet. Eyeballs bulged from her glistening skull like gelatinous orbs of pus and focused on Jeremy intently. Her bleeding arms stretched out pleadingly, but she made no sound, perhaps incapable of doing so. Behind her was a trail of viscous fluids and spoiled meat. It was a miracle the woman was still alive, let alone able to walk.

Jeremy put the car into reverse, planning to flee. He couldn't help this person. Even if a cure was found, this woman was beyond the point of salvation. "I'm sorry," he said out loud, then lifted up the clutch. The car began rolling backwards, away from the woman.

She followed after him for a few more steps, seeming to lose more flesh and blood with every movement. So transfixed was Jeremy on the horrible sight that he almost didn't see what was in his rear view mirror. He slammed on the brakes again. "Shit!"

Behind him a military truck blocked the road where he had come from. A single soldier hopped out from the elevated cabin and landed on the cement with his heavy jackboots. The man had a scruffy beard and his sleeves rolled up past the elbows. The standards of appearance for the British Army had obviously been forgotten in the last week. It was hardly surprising.

The infected woman was still coming closer, still reaching out her arms pleadingly. The soldier moved in front of Jeremy's car and faced down the woman. He pulled out his sidearm, a mean-looking pistol, and pointed it forward casually. Then he let off a shot. A single bullet did the job, hitting the woman in her cheek and passing through her skull. Gore and grey matter painted the road, adding to the mess that was already there.

Jeremy's breath caught in his throat and he could actually feel his heart beating against his chest. He was not used to the sight of guns and he'd never before seen one used to kill another human being. Numbness washed over him that was probably the beginnings of shock.

The soldier holstered his weapon and marched over to Jeremy's window. Jeremy unwound it and quickly grabbed his ID card from where it lay on the dashboard. His hands were shaking.

"Thank you, sir. Everything seems to be in order. Are you on your way home?"

Jeremy stared out at the dead woman on the road and found himself unable to blink.

"Sir?"

"Huh? Oh, yes. I'm going straight home now."

The soldier seemed to notice Jeremy's concern and knelt down to match his eyelevel. "It was for the best, sir. Like putting down a sick dog."

"A…a dog?"

"It may seem cruel, but when the infection gets that bad, it's kinder to just end it. A lot of them have started to lose their minds – who can blame them – but they're becoming dangerous. If you see any more of them I advise you keep on going."

Jeremy swallowed. The soldier spoke about the infected like they were *things* not people, but was that really so surprising? Anyone with The Peeling was insane with agony and doomed to die – had any humanity still existed inside the woman now dead in the road?

"You go on now, sir? Get moving."

Jeremy pulled the car back into first and headed forward, steering around the mutilated corpse of the woman. The soldier remained standing in the road and watched until Jeremy was out of sight.

STRATFORD HAD BECOME a military outpost like many other small towns with open areas. Further downriver, the waters teemed with gunboats, and the roads led to checkpoints in all directions. Cars and houses lay abandoned, while large fires raged in many open areas. Jeremy had a morbid realisation that the soldiers were building pyres and stacking them with the bodies of infected. The movement amongst the flames made it clear that not all the bodies were dead.

What the hell was happening? In only the nine or ten hours since Jeremy had travelled to work, things had deteriorated to frightening levels. A police state was in effect and sick people were being quarantined and burned alive. Even the healthy were being caged inside their homes without compassion. Jeremy turned a corner, heading away from town, and saw a squad of Royal Fusiliers boarding up a house while frightened people tried to escape through the windows. A small boy actually managed to get free of the house and made a run for it down the road. A moment later the boy was dead, a rifle round between his shoulder blades. Jeremy couldn't even tell if he'd been infected.

Jeremy thought about his wife. Would he return home to find that she had been rounded up, too? Rotted away and thrown on a fire? The thought made his foot stamp down harder on the accelerator. Once he was home he would stay there until the very end, until it was over. What he would do then, he did not know. His life would go on whilst his wife's would end. In many ways he envied her. The world going on around him was not one he wanted to be a part of anymore. In less than twenty-four hours things had gotten so bad that he dreaded to think about what just one more day would bring.

THE MILITARY PRESENCE reduced as he left the town centre and headed into the residential areas. By the time he reached his own house, it'd been almost ten minutes without seeing another soul. His home was dark, the windows shaded by closed curtains. The light had started to hurt his wife's eyes and the lamps had all been left off since the night before. Her condition had been in the early stages then – he worried what she would be like now. The virus worked so fast, a destructive force akin to an invading army. The body's skin and muscle cells got obliterated, one by one, helplessly succumbing to infection until they were nothing more than soup.

Jeremy parked the car up on the curb and turned off the engine. He stepped out and pressed the key fob, locking the car. Then he started up his path and headed for his front door. Before he got there, though, it opened from the other side.

"Hey, honey. I've been waiting for you to get home. It's been lonely without you."

Kara hopped off of the doorstep and took Jeremy by surprise, planting a kiss on his mouth and slipping in her tongue. He pushed her away.

"What's wrong?" she asked.

"Everything," he said, stepping through into the house while she followed. "Have you looked outside the window lately?"

"No. I don't want to know what's going on out there. It's too frightening. Is it bad?"

Jeremy stared at her. "You have no idea."

Kara approached him and put her arms around his shoulder and planted another kiss on his cheek. "Well, as long as we still have each other."

Jeremy pushed her away again and sighed. "Kara, what are you doing here? Where's your sister?"

"In bed. She wasn't feeling good so she went to sleep."

Jeremy thought about his wife, alone upstairs and suffering. He felt outraged at Kara. Did she not care? It was her sister, for Christ's sake. He took a deep breath and fought to remain calm. "How is she?" he asked. "Is it bad?"

"What do you think? Hasn't that news station of yours found a cure yet?"

Jeremy huffed. "They're journalists, not doctors. And to answer your question, no. There is no cure. It's killing everyone who has it."

Kara slumped down on the sofa and finally seemed to get a little more serious as concern etched itself across her face. Perhaps she did care about her sister after all. "There's really nothing anyone can do?" she asked.

Jeremy shook his head. "That's why we need to look after your sister – my wife. Carol needs our love and support. We can't fool around behind her back anymore. I'm done behaving like that."

Kara didn't reply. She stared at the blank television screen as though the glass were a portal to another, more interesting life. Jeremy didn't care to console her. He'd had enough of his wife's younger sister. Once Carol passed on, she could leave, go back to her own place, and they should never speak again. If he was honest with himself, his wife was the only woman he had ever truly loved, and once she was gone, he was giving up on women for good.

Jeremy didn't want to waste any more time. The value of a second had increased exponentially since The Peeling had found its first victim – whoever that might have been. He placed his foot on the first step of the staircase and looked up. The second floor seemed miles away – another world, filled with horrors and regret. He began to climb, dreading what he would find upstairs. What pain would Carol be in? Would she cry out when he entered, or would she remain silent like the woman gunned down in the road? He was about to find out.

Reaching the top of the stairs, he headed across the landing to the master bedroom, where he placed an ear against the door and listened. Silence. Without even realising it, his hand went to the handle and began turning it. A moment later, his legs carried him through into the bedroom.

Carol was asleep in their double bed, the duvet kicked down to the bottom of the mattress. She was hot and the heat of her fever filled the room with a sweaty aroma. Her body was pale and smooth, but still healthy. Her face however…

Jesus Christ!

…her face was little more than a sinewy skull. Her jaw and teeth were utterly exposed, making it seem like she was grinning constantly. Her cheeks had worn away, leaving her eyeballs sunken beneath the thin, translucent scraps of her eyelids. Beautiful brunette hair lay disembodied on the pillow, no longer attached to her head. She looked like a corpse. Yet she breathed.

"Sweetheart?" Jeremy approached cautiously, not wanting to startle her. If she was in pain, then it was probably cruel of him to bother her at all. But he needed to talk to her. It was time to confess his sins.

Slowly, the tissue-like skin of her eyelids rose. Beneath them, his her eyes were as they'd always been: green and full of life.

"J-Jerry?"

"Yes, sweetheart. It's me. How are you feeling?"

Despite the mess that was her face, Carol managed a weak laugh. "My face felt like it was on fire earlier, but now I can't feel anything at all. It's...nice."

Jeremy placed himself down on the bed. The sheets were damp and bloody. He noticed that a patch of skin the size of a hockey puck had begun to rot away on her side. The smell was sweet and odious.

"I'm going to be here for you now, my love. I'm not going back to work."

"I...I thought you'd been ordered to?"

"Screw their orders. Besides, I don't think they'll be any orders left this time tomorrow."

Carol's eyelids fluttered and it seemed like she was going back to sleep. Jeremy was prepared to let her, but was surprised when her eyes opened wide again and seemed completely awake.

"My...sister was here."

"Kara? She's downstairs. Did you want to speak with her?"

She shook her head gently. "No. No. Just tell her...I forgive the both of you. I don't want to die angry."

Jeremy's throat clammed up, and for a second he thought he might choke. She had known all along? About him and her sister? Would she know that he had been planning to tell her everything? Had the absolution of confession been taken away from him now? Would it have even counted anyway? To tell somebody something on their deathbed was not brave. In fact, it was downright cowardly.

"How did you know?"

"She's not exactly subtle, my sister – always here, sniffing around you. Doesn't matter now. You can be together."

"That's not what I want. I don't care about her, or anyone else. The only woman I love is you."

She patted him on the hand. Her skin was soft, fragile. "I know. I know none of those women were anything other than sex to you. You disgusted me for years, but eventually I accepted that it was just your nature to be so...weak. I...I had my own fun in the end."

Jeremy stood up from the bed. "What?"

Carol smiled. "I've probably fucked around more than you…these last few years."

"You goddamn whore!"

"I'm not ashamed of it, Jerry. It was fun. You should know."

Jeremy backed away, towards the door. He could barely believe the grinning skull on the bed was the woman he'd been married to for twenty years. "W-why are you telling me all this?"

"Because I don't want to die with secrets, and…and despite everything I've always loved you. None of it really matters anymore, other than the fact we loved each other in our own way."

Jeremy lowered his shoulders and took a few breaths while he digested what he'd just heard. His stomach ached and he felt sick – but Carol was right. None of it mattered. He loved this woman and he wanted to be with her. He sat back down on the bed.

"Can I do anything to help?"

Carol took a long, laboured breath, and a sliver of skin fell from her neck, sliding away onto the bed sheets. "I don't want to die…"

"I know that, sweetheart. I know."

"…later. I want to die…now."

Jeremy looked at his wife, deep into her eyes – the only part of her that was still the same as when he'd married her. "What?"

"I don't want to lie here rotting away. I don't want to feel the pain when my body begins to bleed. I've said all I needed to say. I'm ready."

"You can't ask me to-"

"You owe me." She said the words forcefully, suddenly full of vitality – but it only lasted a minute before she seemed to deflate again.

She was right, Jeremy told himself. He owed her many things. Their whole marriage had been marred by him abusing her integrity and violating her trust. What she was asking for now was dignity – a simple thing. The dignity of refusing to let the virus defile her body in the same ways that he had defiled their marriage. But he couldn't kill her. No way.

"I'm sorry. I won't."

Carol stared at him. He couldn't tell if she was angry. The facial muscles that would usually form expressions were all gone from her face now.

"I understand," she whispered. "Leave me alone."

"What do you mean?"

"If I have to go through this, I want to do it alone. I don't want anyone watching while I die. If you won't help me, then give me some privacy."

The last thing Jeremy wanted was to leave her alone. To die with no one around was be a lonely, helpless demise, but it was Carol's choice, not his. He stood up from the bed.

"I'll check on you later," he said.

"No, don't. There's nothing you can do for me."

Jeremy's heart felt like a weight in his chest and it was difficult to drag his body away from his wife's bedside. They may never talk again. This was goodbye.

He left the room without another word. Anything he'd said wouldn't have been enough. Downstairs, Kara was still sitting on the living room sofa. She had switched on the television and was watching it intently. She showed no interest in his presence and did not ask about the state of her sister.

"Carol is in a bad way, in case you were wondering."

Kara turned her head away from the television and looked at him. "Should I go see her?"

Jeremy sat down on the sofa beside her, making sure to stay as far away on the cushions as possible. "She wants to be left alone."

"Okay." Kara went back to watching the television.

"Do you even care?"

"Of course I do. She's my sister. But there's nothing I can do. I don't want to watch while she rots away."

"Then why are you even here?"

She stared at him again and this time seemed very sad. "To be with you. I thought you cared about me."

Jeremy sighed. "I…I do. You know I do. But Carol is dying and it's not right anymore. I'm sick of hating myself."

"She's dying. We can be together."

"I'm sorry, but I don't want that. The world is a mess. The last thing I can concentrate on right now is a relationship."

Kara stood up from the sofa and shook her head. She'd suddenly become very emotional. "You really want to be alone while the world dies around you? We need to look after each other. You need to look after me."

"What do you mean? You can look after yourself."

Kara wouldn't look at him. She averted her eyes and stared at the wall.

"Kara? What is it?"

"What do you care? You've made your feelings clear enough."

Jeremy sighed and lifted himself off the coach. He went over and put his palm against her back. "Tell me what's really wrong. You're not this upset because of me."

She broke down in tears and buried her head against his chest. It was then that he smelt the same sweet odour that had come from Carol's rotting flesh. He eased her away so that he could look at her. "You have it, don't you?"

It looked as though Kara wanted to speak, but was unable to. Instead she nodded solemnly and reached a hand up to her long, brown hair. She scooped it away from her neck and exposed the skin. Beneath her right ear was a blistering patch of skin.

Jeremy bit at his bottom lip and almost drew blood. "How long?"

"I noticed this morning. I came straight here to wait for you. I was hoping you'd know how to help me, that you would have gotten answers at the news station."

"How did you even get here? The military have the roads blocked up."

"I walked. I kept away from the main roads."

"You walked four miles through that hell out there?"

"It was better than being alone. I thought if I came here, you'd look after me."

"I will," Jeremy said. "Of course I will."

"You've changed your tune."

Jeremy huffed. It suddenly felt like he hadn't slept in weeks. "I care about you, Kara. You're Carol's sister."

"*Carol's sister.* Is that all I am to you now? A fucking obligation?"

Jeremy sat back down on the sofa and rubbed at his face. "Kara, if you want me to look after you, I will, but that's all. I'm not going to argue with you, not now."

"You mean *now that I'm dying?*"

Jeremy wasn't going to lie, so he nodded.

"There's really not going to be a cure?" she asked.

"No. I don't think so. The Government haven't even worked out how it spreads, let alone how to beat it."

Kara slumped down on the sofa beside him and seemed defeated, all the energy had gone from her voice. "How did I get it? When you came over to warn me that people were getting sick, I stayed away, kept indoors. I never went near anyone infected, but I still got it. How does that make sense?"

"I don't know. It doesn't. Truth is nobody really knows anything about The Peeling."

"But it's bad isn't it? I mean, really really bad."

Jeremy nodded. "At the rate it's going, half the world is going to die. Half the people get it while the other half don't."

"Guess you're one of the lucky ones."

Jeremy laughed, but didn't find anything funny. "Doesn't feel that way."

Kara pulled her legs onto the sofa and laid herself across his lap. He let her. Together they watched the television in silence, trying to clear their minds of horror. Ironically, Never Stop News was on. Sarah and Tom were continuing to give the news with as much pluck as they could muster, but Jeremy could tell the toll was becoming too much for them. Sarah's face was pasty and wiry strands of hair clumped against her damp forehead.

"They look as lost as everyone else," Kara said.

Jeremy stroked her hair and was shocked by the heat coming off her head. "That's because they are. They're as frightened and as lost as we are. They're just trying to help by making us think that things are still normal. The news and weather make people feel like there's still someone in charge."

"And is there?"

"I guess so. The military are everywhere, ever since General Whitehead took over after Lloyd Collins died.

"Jerry?"

"Yeah?"

"I'm scared."

"Me too."

Six hours later and The Peeling had taken all of the skin from Kara's neck, so much so that her windpipe was now exposed. Jeremy wasn't repulsed. The sight of rotting flesh had become commonplace.

On the television, Sarah and Tom were still reporting about The Peeling, refusing to wrap things up while the cameras were still running. They would both have usually left the station by now. By the weary looks on their faces, Jeremy had a grim feeling that, behind the cameras, the military had become the directors. Their promises of staying out of the station may have been overridden as things continued to deteriorate.

"While we are yet to receive confirmation, rumours have begun to circulate that researchers at the National Institute for Medical Research in London have made a breakthrough concerning the transmission method of the virus. We are persistent in our attempts to get more information on this matter, so please bear with us."

"What difference doessss it make?" Kara's voice had taken on a serpentine hiss as her throat rotted away. "Unless it's a cure, it's no good to anyone."

Jeremy sucked in a breath and listened to it whistle between his teeth. His stomach felt empty, nauseous. While Kara was correct in her pessimism, it was still welcome news to hear that somebody had possibly discovered something about the nature of the virus. Knowledge made the virus seem more natural, more beatable, and less like an unstoppable flesh-consuming monster. If people knew how it was passed on, the fight to contain it could finally begin. Not that Jeremy would have anything left in his life to fight *for* if mankind succeeded in destroying the beast.

"How do you feel?" he asked Kara.

She tried to laugh, but her tattered vocal chords seemed to lack the ability now. "I feel like my head's going to fall off into my lap any minute. My neck feels numb, like it's not even there anymore."

JEREMY WAS ABOUT to tell her he was sorry, but then decided it would be a pointless gesture. Apologies provided no solace. Besides, Kara seemed to be growing angrier rather than brooding.

"This is probably what I deserve, you know?" she asked him.

"What do you mean?"

"I mean, I've been fucking my sister's husband – among my many other sins – and this is probably my punishment."

Jeremy shook his head. "She forgives us."

"What? She knows?"

"Yes. She told me earlier. She loves us both and forgives us."

Kara hitched forward and tears were instant in their arrival. As they fell down her face, they gathered flakes of skin and a film of blood from her cheeks, so fragile was her flesh. "I'll go to hell for what I've done.

Carol can forgive – she's a better person than us – but I doubt God will be so compassionate."

"Don't talk nonsense, Kara. We all do things we regret. Carol isn't holding it against you, so you shouldn't hold it against yourself."

"Fuck you!" The outburst was sudden and vicious. "You're the one who should be melting away, not my sister. You're the one that's spent your whole marriage fucking around. What did you ever do for her? Nothing! Yet she's the one dying while you're perfectly fine."

Jeremy sighed and tried to keep his focus on the television. He had a feeling that she would strike at him if he made eye contact. "If I could take her place, I would."

"You're a liar. They have a cure at that news station. Look at them. They're fine, just like you."

Jeremy looked at Sarah's tired face on the screen and shook his head. "Actually, one of the reporters has the virus. She showed me earlier."

"Bullshit!" Kara sprung up from the couch. You have a cure, but you won't share it. With me and Carol out of the way, you can carry on screwing around. Probably already got a new fancy-woman."

Jeremy stood up and backed away. He could sense violence inside Kara and he wasn't interested in stoking that particular fire. Nonetheless, she came at him, withered fingers outstretched like talons.

He stepped aside and shoved out, sending her sprawling sideways onto the couch. As she fell, her legs shot forward and upended the coffee table. Immediately her ankle began to bleed. She clutched at it and sobbed.

"I'm fucking melting," she wailed. "What did I do to deserve this? I'm not a bad woman – not really. I don't deserve this. I don't. I don't."

Jeremy left while she was distracted. A madness seemed to have overtaken her and his presence seemed to make it worse. He felt endangered, an enemy inside his own home. He wanted to see Carol. He wanted to be with his wife.

At the top of the stairs, the noise of the television faded away and Jeremy was again met with the eerie silence of the landing. There was every chance that Carol was dead already – part of him wanted that peace for her. If she had passed on, he would sit with her for awhile and hope that, somewhere, someplace, she was still with him. But when he opened the door, he saw that the mercy of death had not yet visited his wife.

Carol lay on the bed, looking more like a puddle than a human being.

Her skin clung to her now only in patches and in many places her bones were showing clearly. But her eyes…her eyes were still flawless. Beautiful.

He sat down on the bed and went to touch her, but then realised there was nowhere he could do so without causing her pain. "I love you, Carol. I wanted to tell you that one more time."

It was an obvious effort for Carol to form words, but she seemed eager to do so all the same. Her voice was a crackling wheeze. "I… love…you…too."

"I wish I had more time with you. I wish there was time to make it all okay. I'm going to miss you every minute till the time I join you. I just hope that when I get there, you'll be waiting for me. If not…I'd understand."

Carol's eyes flickered as if fighting away sleep – or death. Jeremy wasn't sure if she'd heard the words he'd just spoken, but he hoped so. Eventually she came back to him and managed to speak again. "Please, Jerry…please."

"What, sweetheart? What do you want?" But she didn't need to answer. He knew what she was asking for. He nodded, felt tears well up behind his eyes. "Okay."

He leant forward and kissed his wife's forehead. His lips came away moist and sticky, but he did not care. Trying to be as gentle as possible, he pulled loose one of the pillows beneath his wife's head. Her eyes stared at him intently and he knew that if she could, she would have been smiling. By doing what he was about to do, Jeremy could show his wife the kindness in death that he could not give her in life. Jeremy put the pillow to his wife's face and pressed down. It took only a minute for her to die.

Jeremy sat with Carol for almost a full hour before he left her. He knew that once he exited the bedroom, she would truly be gone forever. Part of him had also been curious to see whether her body would continue to rot away after death. It had not. If he'd obeyed her requests earlier, then her body would have been more intact as it was lying there now. It was just one more regret to add to his list.

Downstairs, Kara was missing. The television was still switched on and, if he wasn't mistaken, the volume had increased. Sarah and Tom were still reporting and there was an urgency about them now that he'd never seen before. He looked around the living room, but found only shadows.

"It has now been categorically proven," Sarah said on the television, "that the virus is passed on through carriers. While only fifty-percent of those exposed to the infection become symptomatic, it has been discovered that the other fifty-percent are not immune as originally thought. The seemingly unaffected are in fact passing on the virus by becoming highly-infectious carriers. While half of the population is dying, it is the other half who are infecting them. It is for this reason that a nationwide quarantine is now has now been put in effect. Healthy or infected – all will be restrained if found outside their homes at any times. Lethal force will be used if necessary. Through isolation, it is hoped that the infection will reach a saturation point and that non-symptomatic sufferers will remain healthy. There is still hope for a great deal of us, Great Britain, but we must stay calm, and we must stay indoors. Never Stop News is now the official channel for the British Government, along with the BBC, so please leave your television on at all times for further updates. We will be interspersing our regular newsfeed with episodes of *Friends* and *The Simpsons,* so sit back and enjoy that as it's coming up next."

"You did this."

Jeremy turned his head away from the television and saw Kara moving out from one of the room's shadowy corners. Her face had peeled away from her skull and her snarling mouth made her look like a vengeful demon.

"I did what?" Jeremy asked her.

"You infected Carol and you infected me. You are the one who should be dead."

"You don't know that I have it. You don't know anything."

"Yes, I do. I haven't been around anyone since this whole thing started – no one, except for you. You fucked me last week."

Jeremy thought about earlier in the week when he'd popped round to see Kara at her home – popped round for his weekly booty call and to warn her about the virus. "I'm sorry," he said, worrying that she could be right, that he could be the one responsible for his wife's death, and others.

"Quiet!" Kara stepped further out of the shadows. She was holding a large carving knife from the kitchen. "I don't want to hear you anymore."

Jeremy nodded. "Okay." He made no move to get away, unsure whether Kara even had it in her to do him harm. In normal circumstances, he thought not, but these were not normal circumstances and she was most certainly not her usual self.

"You've been fucking us both for a long time, but now it seems like you really got the job done. You're a murderer, Jerry. If Carol and I had never let you near us then we would be okay. We would be healthy."

"Half the world has The Peeling, Kara. You would have gotten it anyway, one way or another. Carol is my wife; you really think I would infect her purposefully?"

Kara came closer with the knife. Still Jeremy did not move. She growled at him, blood spilling from her lips and covering the exposed bone of her lower jaw. "Men like you have been a sickness on women since time began. Women have always suffered because of misogynistic perverts like you."

"You're talking nonsense. The Peeling is killing as many men as women. It's just luck of the draw who gets infected."

Kara came at him with the knife. "Lies! You did this. You killed us!"

Jeremy was about to dodge the knife attack, but at the last second he decided to remain in place. He thought about seeing Carol again as the knife entered his chest and forced him back like a punch. He fell backwards onto the sofa, blade jutting out from between his ribs, and ended up facing the television. Joey and Chandler were playing foosball in a world that knew not of such horrors as The Peeling. It was a nice way to go, and by the time Jeremy bled out, he almost managed to kid himself that the world still had a chance.

THE PEELING: BOOK 2

(THE STADIUM)

Brett rummaged through the defrosting contents of the grimy industrial freezer and frowned. The police or the army, or whoever, had finally cut the power in the area and the stacked supplies of cheap burger patties and hotdogs were now starting to thaw. They would go bad in a matter of days. The French fries would fare a while longer, but they wouldn't last forever either. It made Brett realise that, at some point, the situation would have to change. Birmingham's BR Football Stadium wouldn't provide them refuge forever. Eventually he and all the others would have to face the outside world again.

When The Peeling first hit, people had been content to lock themselves away inside their homes to wait it out. You could see a person with the infection a mile off – rotting skin and blistering flesh pulling back to reveal bone. People assumed that so long as they kept themselves isolated, they would be okay. When news came out that the victims of the plague – those suffering with the rot – were not the contagious ones, things changed. It quickly became public knowledge that the infection was transmitted via random carriers – from among those who displayed no outward symptoms but carried the disease all the same. The healthy population were the ones to be afraid of.

Brett hadn't paid much attention to the news back then. He'd decided there were more constructive things to do then to wallow in the misery on television. A local action-group had formed amongst the residents of

Smethwick, the Birmingham district where Brett lived, and he had been only too happy to join with them. With the blessing of the local authorities, the group of concerned citizens had been granted permission to temporarily leave the quarantines of their homes and congregate in a public area. The leader of the committee, Reverend Long, had chosen the BR Stadium – home of the local lower-division football team. The elderly vicar was a big football fan.

A military escort had accompanied the Reverend whilst he visited the homes of the nearby parish, collecting Christians, Muslims, and atheists alike. Many did not open their doors, for fear of allowing the pestilence inside, but many others did and were relieved at the opportunity to leave. Brett had been one of those people. He'd joined up eagerly with the growing group, glad to once again have company after his parents had died. But even back then, he had been questioning himself about whether it was the right thing to do, leaving his home.

Along the way to the stadium, the military had been rough with the group of civilians and those seeking to join them. Brett had seen soldiers exercise lethal force several times, especially against any infected people trying to run towards the group. Brett had panicked at the sight of the already-bleeding bodies being ripped apart by automatic rifle-fire, and so had most others in the group, but Reverend Long had raised his hands to address the crowd and endeavoured to keep them calm. He told them their focus needed to be on helping those still within helping. There would be time to mourn the dead and the atrocities committed on them later. Brett had been uneasy around the military ever since.

"How we doing, Brett?"

Brett turned around to see Emily, with her bright ginger hair and dorky spectacles. He shrugged at the girl and told her the truth. No point in lying. "The food is all defrosting," he said. "It'll go bad eventually. Luckily it's all processed rubbish and not fresh stuff, or we'd have even less time to eat it. Can't believe those assholes cut the power. What are they trying to do?"

Emily adjusted her spectacles and glanced into the freezer behind him. "Perhaps you should shut the door then and keep in the cold as long as we can then. I'm sure everything will work out okay. They'll probably give us back the power soon."

Brett sighed. Emily, like many other people in the group, had not yet grasped the seriousness of their situation. They still thought the squads of riflemen surrounding the stadium were there to keep everybody safe, and that the power cut was due to some sort of technical hiccup. Brett knew the truth, though. The stadium had been quarantined, and any attempt to leave would be met with a bullet. They were just ants now, stuck inside a bottle hoping somebody would take off the lid.

When the news had broken that the infection passed via the healthy and not the infected, the world's dynamic had changed. Suddenly, the brief freedom Brett and the others in the group had been granted was eliminated. Suddenly, they were the ones who were dangerous, not the sickly-skinned lunatics rotting away in their homes. An Army officer had informed Reverend Long that his group were to remain inside the stadium until further notice, and make no attempt to leave. It was made clear that the consequences would be severe if anyone made a run for it.

That had been three days ago. Now, after another horrible night's sleep on the cement floor of the East Stand kitchen, Brett had been placed in charge of the food reserves. Luckily, the stadium had several snack bars that all backed onto the same kitchen and staff areas. The supplies were allocated to provide for the twenty-thousand football fans that used to fill the stadium every weekend, which meant there was plenty of food for now, but a great part of it was perishable. What made Brett so mad was how people were tearing into chocolate bars and crisp packets like they were having a party. Something about being able to help themselves to bottles of pop and cans of cider made them feel unadulterated. It was the mob mentality of looting, and it seemed to make them happy, but what they didn't seem to realise was that every mouthful of snack food they ate was a mouthful they wouldn't have later when they really needed it. They were eating the non-perishable items first and that had to stop. It would have to be cold burgers all around for the next few days.

"So what you up to today?" Emily asked him as if they were buddies.

"I don't know," he answered testily. The girl irritated him. "Guess I'll see if the Reverend needs anything done."

Emily giggled at him and bopped him on the arm. "Are you always so work work work? You should let others worry about things for a day. You and me are just teenagers. We should leave it to the adults."

"I'm twenty-two, Emily, and this isn't a game. Things are bad. Those soldiers outside will shoot anyone who tries to leave, which eventually we *will* be forced to do. Half the country is dead or dying, and we might be infected with the thing that killed them. We're fucked."

Emily winced at his language and adjusted her spectacles. Her freckled cheeks went a shade redder. "No need to speak to me like that.

I'm just being friendly." The girl walked away and, if Brett was honest, he didn't care. Emily was a pest as far as he was concerned. She needed to get her head in the game. So did everybody else.

Reverend Long would probably be at his usual place at the centre circle of the football pitch, so Brett headed there now. The football pitch was outside, with the stadium built around it on all sides, comprised of four stands. The snack bar and kitchen was in the East Stand, which also housed a bank of televisions that had kept everyone informed about the ongoing situation until the power had ceased that morning. Last anybody had heard was that the UK's quarantine procedures had been increased indefinitely until a screening process was put into place.

Brett took one of the several flights of cement steps leading up to the pitch and the stadium seating. The dull sunshine hit him as he rose to the outside. Birds chirped from the rafters as if all was right with the world. How wrong they were. In the centre of the pitch, Reverend Long conducted one of his regular sermons that were as much about organisation and survival as they were religion. People looked to the holy man as their leader by default, but Brett had his suspicions that the man was out of his depth. People were scared and Reverend Long was doing his best to comfort them, but he wasn't trained to deal with a situation like this.

"Ah, young Brett. How are things in the pantry?"

Brett took the final few steps across the football pitch and placed himself in front of the Reverend so that their conversation was private from the other people gathered around. "We have plenty of food, Reverend, but most of it will go bad in only a few days. The freezer's still pretty cold at the moment, but with the power off..."

Reverend Long placed a hand on Brett's shoulder and gave him a warm smile. "The lord will provide, young Brett. Do not fret."

Brett sighed. "So what's next? Any news from outside?"

"I spoke with Captain Lewis this morning. His men still won't allow us to leave – in fact they wouldn't even let me near the turnstiles. I had to shout out through the entrance like a hooligan."

"They can't keep us in here forever. It's not right."

"I agree. Fortunately, so does Captain Lewis. He has assured me that he is doing everything he can to move things along and get us out of here. We just need to be patient."

"Bullshit," said someone from behind Brett. It was Ethan. Ethan was a pudgy businessman and local property developer. He was well known in the West Midlands and Brett hadn't liked the man from the moment they'd met.

"There's little need for such language, Ethan," said Reverend Long.

"Like hell there isn't. Do you honestly believe that professional thug and his band of mercenaries are ever going to let us out of here? They've got every exit covered. Our choices are to starve in here or face a bullet in the chest."

"Young Brett here has just assured me that we are perfectly okay, food-wise."

Brett frowned. That wasn't strictly true.

"For now," said Ethan. "But we can't live on dodgy hamburgers forever. We need to get out of here, back to our homes."

More like your cushy mansion, thought Brett, understanding why the man wanted out, but he couldn't deny that the businessman's concerns were on par with his own. It was almost as if Reverend Long had chosen to interpret the food report how he'd wanted.

"What do you suggest, Ethan?" Brett asked. "If you have a solution, I'd love to hear it."

"We fight our way out. There could only be a dozen soldiers out there. There're almost fifty of us."

Brett shook his head and laughed. "That's ridiculous. They'll rip us to shreds before we even make it ten feet. And it's not just the army out there anyway; there's a load of police as well."

"The police aren't armed. It's only the soldiers we need to worry about. We can take them, I'm telling you. I'm not the only one who thinks so."

Reverend Long placed a hand between them and halted the conversation. "Please, Ethan. Violence will accomplish nothing. We are all men here, inside the stadium and out. We must not fight one another during these trying times."

"Oh, stick a sock in it, old man. Jesus isn't going to save us. Everything is an utter mess and those men outside are only interested in their own wellbeing. We can all die for all they care. There's been so much death recently that we'd be just another statistic. It's them or us, Reverend. You can keep your useless God for yourself."

"Calm down," said Brett. "If it's them or us, then perhaps you should stop turning people against each other. I agree with the Reverend: the time for violence is a long way off yet."

"Perhaps, but believe me, before we know it, it will be the only option left." With that Ethan walked away and reintegrated with the throng of people that covered the halfway point of the pitch.

"Asshole!"

"Forgive him, young Brett," Reverend Long soothed. "Worry makes men mask their fear with anger."

Brett shrugged. "Maybe, but we don't need people like him right now. Things are bad enough. We all need to stick together."

"You're wise beyond your years, boy. Perhaps you could do me a favour?"

"Of course. What's up?"

"Captain Lewis has made a request that we make a list of everybody here – names and addresses. He wishes to inform people's families and also wants to know how many of us there are in here. I'm assuming it may well have to do with them getting us some supplies."

It's also a great way to keep tabs on us, Brett mused.

"Okay, Reverend," he said. "I'll go get started."

THE ATTEMPT TO take down people's names and addresses was met with hostility. The men and women inside the stadium still did not really know one another and the thought of giving away their personal details to a stranger was something they were wary of, regardless of the fact that they no longer had homes, possessions, or bank accounts to even worry about. But with a little bit of perseverance, and a shedload of patience, Brett managed to overcome most people's objections and get their details. His list was now over fifty names long. Things had been going pretty smoothly – that was until it was Ethan's turn.

"Go screw yourself, kid."

Brett sighed and decided to hold out the pen and paper anyway. "Ethan, I'm done arguing with you today. Can you just help me out, please? I just need your address and surname."

Ethan shoved the paper back at him. "You know how I feel about those thugs outside. I'm not telling you a thing. You know who else used to take lists? Nazis."

A bout of concerned whispering broke out amongst the people gathered nearby. They were all huddled together, as if for protection.

"This isn't Hitler's Germany, dude. This is England, so stop trying to scare everyone. They just want people's names so that they know how much supplies we need."

"Then just give them a number. Tell them that there's one-hundred men and woman here to be fed."

Brett frowned. "There's not that many of us here."

Ethan looked at Brett as if he were a fool. "No shit, Sherlock. They don't need to know that, though, do they? The more people they think are in here, the more food they will give us – and the less likely they are to attack us."

The man had a point, but there was a flaw in his thinking. "Well, wouldn't it be better if we said there were less of us than there are. That way if they do launch an attack they'll underestimate our strength."

Ethan's face contorted for a split second, as if the notion of being second-guessed by a twenty-three year old was tantamount to blasphemy. Then the man cracked a smile and patted Brett on the back. "That's good thinking, kid. You should be using that brain to have more ideas like that, instead of running around after that geriatric preacher. We need to get ourselves ready."

"You make it sound as if we're going to war."

Ethan stared Brett in the eye. "It's about time people realised that we *are*."

Brett sighed and walked away. There was no point trying to force Ethan and his group to give their details. In all honesty there was a chance that Ethan was right. Captain Lewis may have requested the list so that he could strategize an attack on the stadium.

Other than firing off a couple of warning shots to those trying to leave, Lewis's men had not tried to enter the stadium or hurt anyone inside, but they'd made it very clear that no one was to leave. There was no reason to doubt the captain and his men just yet, but Brett would have felt less apprehensive about the situation if he knew their endgame. How long were they planning to keep everyone rounded up inside the stadium? What would they do once people started running out of food? Were the Army still responsible for protecting people, or had it become a different entity entirely? Brett thought about the movies he'd seen about the *Gestapo* rounding up Jews and decided that perhaps the situation wasn't entirely dissimilar from Nazi Germany.

Brett headed over to the turnstiles in the East Stand. They only allowed people inside, not out. The large wooden hatch-door was used to let crowds out after a match, but it had been barricaded by the soldiers outside. The same had been done with all of the stadium's exits, including the delivery bay off the kitchen. The only way to speak to Captain Lewis was to approach him at the turnstiles and talk across them.

When Brett got there, he was met by the steely gaze of a squaddie. Brett didn't know the man's rank but his arm featured two chevrons, which was less than he'd seen on the uniforms of others, but one more than some.

"Halt!"

Seriously? Halt? Why not, "who goes there?"

"I'd like to speak with Captain Lewis. I have the list he requested."

The soldier nodded but did not leave his post. Instead he stuck a dirty finger in his mouth and whistled before performing some bizarre hand gesture to someone unseen.

After a few minutes, Captain Lewis arrived in front of the turnstiles. The officer was fully-kitted in olive-green combat uniform, including helmet. He was taller than his men and his bony face was covered by thick black stubble.

"Where is Father Long?"

"He's busy," Brett replied. "He asked me to gather this list for you."

"Excellent. Good work, chap. Hand it over."

Brett kept a hold of the handful of papers. "What do you want it for?"

The captain glared at him for a moment, but then seemed to soften. "I need to know who we have in there. Their families will want to know. Now, do as you're told, lad, and give me that list. There's a good chap."

"What about supplies? Are you going to get us food? How about some blankets?"

The captain shook his head. "I will make a request to my coordinator, but that's not something I can promise."

"Then what fucking use are you to us?"

"I beg your pardon, young man? I suggest you show a little more respect to my rank."

"I'm a civilian. Your rank doesn't mean shit to me. In fact, I wipe my arse on it. If you're not going to help us then we're not going to help you."

"Go and get Father Long immediately."

Brett stood still.

"Do you hear me?"

"I told you," said Brett. "I don't take orders from you."

Lewis took several steps and closed the distance between them. "You're playing a very dangerous game here, young man. In case you didn't notice, the world is a scary place right now. It's chaps like me that are the only thing protecting you."

"Then tell us what's going on," said Brett. "How long do you plan on keeping us here? People are getting anxious."

"Look," Lewis said, sounding a little more open to reason as he realised that his bluster wasn't working. "I will look into getting you some supplies, but you need to calm down and stay inside. Now, how many of you are there?"

Brett thought about Ethan's theory about being attacked and chose not to answer the question. "You get us some food and blankets, *then* we'll talk."

Brett turned around and took the list of names with him. He didn't know whether to fear Lewis or not, but right now it seemed like it would be best to keep his cards close to his chest. If the captain was just following orders then there would be no way to know what he was planning to do.

As Brett re-entered the East Stand eating area he was met by a commotion. There were people gathered in a group outside one of the burger bars, while a middle-aged man tried to hold them back. The man's name was Steve and Brett had not seen him so worked up before.

"Steve, what's wrong? What's happening?"

"They're trying to get my little girl." He screamed at the crowd surrounding him. "You're all a bunch of monsters."

"She has it," said a brunette in her thirties. "She has The Peeling."

Brett looked at Steve and saw that the man was terrified and sweating. "Is it true? Is she sick?"

Steve nodded. "But she's not contagious. You heard what the news said when we still had the TVs. The infected are not contagious; it's the carriers who pass it on."

"We don't know shit," someone shouted from the crowd. "We don't know what causes it. We need to get the girl out of here before we all end up catching it."

Brett turned to the baying crowd and raised his hands to keep them back. "Steve is right. If his daughter is ill, then she's no danger to us." He turned back to Steve and tried his best to smile reassuringly. "Come on, take me to her and we'll see what we can do for her."

"She's hiding in the back. These animals scared her to death."

Brett followed Steve into the kitchen area of the burger bar, entering through a staff door. The area was cold, and getting colder since the electricity had gone off. It wouldn't be long before the entire building became unbearably frigid as there was no way to close off the entrances to the pitch side and the cold air outside was free to whistle in through the corridors.

At the back of the kitchen area, lying on an aluminium preparation table was Steve's daughter. Brett could not remember the young girl's name, but he'd noticed her a few times over the last few days. She was about eight-years old, thin and gangly like her father. She wore a pink t-shirt that left her bleeding right arm exposed. The flesh on her wrist was peeling away, hanging loose in a great wet flap. There was no doubt that she had The Peeling.

"I noticed a rash on her yesterday afternoon," said Steve. "I can't believe how fast it spreads. Whatever this thing is, it's pure evil."

Brett looked closer at the girl's wound and noticed dozens of thin, red tendrils running beneath the surface of her skin. It was almost as if he could see the virus moving and spreading up her arm, rotting away more healthy cells with every second.

"I don't even think she has a week," Steve sobbed. "My poor, sweet darling."

"I'm sorry," Brett said. "I wish I could do something for her."

"There's nothing you can do for her," said Ethan, strutting into the room. Reverend Long was hurrying up behind him. "She's already dead. We need to think about those who are not."

"Get out of here," Steve pleaded. "Just leave us alone."

"I'm afraid I can't do that. We need to deal with this now."

"For God's sake," said Brett, then noticed the Reverend. "Sorry, Father."

"God forgives you."

"I'm not doing this to be horrible," Ethan said. "I'm just being the pragmatist here because nobody else wants the job. Your daughter could end up killing us all, Steve. We need isolate her, or…"

"If you're about to suggest killing her then I would just shut your mouth," said Steve. "No one is hurting my daughter."

"I was going to suggest having the soldiers outside remove her."

Steve shook his head and leant over his daughter, sobbing and snivelling. "I won't let them have her. You've seen what they do to the infected. You all saw the piles of bodies and the executions in the streets."

"And right now, we're all safe from that," said Ethan. "But your daughter is a threat to us staying here."

"I agree..." said Brett.

Ethan grinned. "Thank you!"

"But we're not going to turn on each other. Steve, you need to take your daughter away from everybody else. I'll help you take her up to the Press Box. Nobody goes there and it's away from everybody else. You can look after her there until...well, until it's over."

"I also think that is for the best, Steven," Reverend Long added. "I will come and check on you as much as I can."

"This is bullshit," said Ethan. "If this thing is airborne then we need her completely out of the stadium. We can't risk breathing within a hundred meters of her."

"Be quiet," the Reverend ordered, more forcefully then his usual manner would allow. "Don't you ever get tired of conflict?"

"Conflict is the world we live in, padre. If you don't all start waking up to reality then there's no hope for any of us."

"It's been decided," said Brett. "Steve is going to take his daughter upstairs and keep her there. There's no danger."

"Fine, but I swear you're only going to get more of us killed." Ethan stomped out of the kitchen.

"Thank you," said Steve. "It doesn't really matter, I suppose, but at least now I can make sure my daughter dies with some dignity."

Brett took Reverend Long to one side and spoke quietly, so that only he could hear. "We need to do something about Ethan. He wants to be in charge of everything like this is one of his businesses."

"If that's what people want then they will follow him. If not then they won't. It is not my place to influence people's opinions."

Brett sighed. "But he's going to make bad decisions. I can feel it."

"Maybe so, but I am not in charge of anybody here. What would you have me do, young Brett?"

"You need to make sure people are busy. Get everyone working together and focused on something. Then people will be too busy to listen to Ethan and will feel too secure to take stupid risks."

"Perhaps you're right. There are lots of things we could be doing. We need to ration food and search for blankets."

"We also need to set up a barricade. I'm not sure I trust Captain Lewis and I don't want to make it easy for his men to get in here."

"I'm not sure I like the sound of that, but if you think it will make everyone feel better…"

"Okay," said Brett. "I'll help Steve get upstairs and then I'll get to work."

DESPITE HAVING BEEN in the stadium for three days, no one had fully searched the grounds. The first thing Brett did was to gather up volunteers and split them into several groups. He made a point to avoid Ethan and the small contingent that followed him around like lost children. He knew the man would just try to take over things.

There was now a group that would search for food, blankets, and first aid kits, and another group that was to look into starting a fire on the centre spot of the pitch. Brett's group was in charge of constructing barricades at all of the exits.

The stadium had four main exits, one for each of the stands. There were also a couple of small staff entrances leading outside from the kitchen and also from the club offices. They blocked those off first – the one in the kitchen was now blocked by a heavy freezer unit. The office exits were blocked with chairs and tables that had not been used for the centre-pitch fire. The group were now in the middle of manoeuvring a ride-on floor buffer to the turnstile entrances in the Clark Stand. The Clark stand was where the Away supporters were usually located and it backed onto an enclosed car park. It was here that the military and a small police force had positioned the majority of their vehicles. Several tents had also been erected, which Brett assumed housed the soldiers while not on duty. It was crazy, but he felt like he was holed up in the middle of Helmand Province, not a rundown district of Birmingham.

Of all people, Emily was the one riding the big floor buffer. She had once been employed as a part-time cleaner at a leisure centre and had driven one of the machines daily. Truth be told, the teenaged girl seemed to know what she was doing and had impressed everybody.

Brett pointed at the turnstiles. "Okay, if you just pull it around here and park it in front of the hatch doors at the centre. They open inwards so the weight of the machine should be enough to stop anyone coming through."

"What about the turnstiles?" someone asked.

"I don't think there's any way to reverse them. Maybe gather up some broom from the Janitor's closets and trap them in the mechanism as a precaution."

The people in the group did as they were told and Brett suddenly realised that he was giving orders to a bunch of strangers. This time three weeks ago, he'd been unemployed, an embarrassment to his parents and hoping to get noticed on *Clipshare* for playing his guitar. Now he didn't even have a guitar, both his parents were dead, and he had found himself in a position of assumed responsibility – as modest as it was. Brett had always felt like he had talent to offer the world, but it turned out that everything had to turn to shit before he actually got off his arse to try and do anything. He felt pretty ashamed of himself now. He'd done nothing with the last twenty years of his life, and his parents had both died of infection without ever having been proud of him. Of all the millions who had died over the last fortnight, Brett didn't feel like he deserved to be one of the ones still healthy.

"Hold it right there! What's going on?"

Brett turned around to see that one of the soldiers outside had walked up to the turnstiles and was looking through at them. He did not look happy and his rifle was slightly raised.

"We're making the place secure," Brett replied matter-of-factly.

"Why? You're perfectly safe."

Brett huffed and took the few strides necessary to take him face to face with the soldier. "Nobody is safe anymore. The rules have changed and you know it. The world has gone fruitloops; you'll have to forgive me if I don't trust you just because you're wearing a uniform."

Much to Brett's surprise the soldier actually smiled and lowered his weapon. "I suppose I can understand that, but I can tell you right now that Captain Lewis is not going to be happy about this. He's going to insist that you move all this stuff away from the doors."

"The captain can bite me. Where is he anyway?"

"He's off duty. I'm second in command. Lieutenant Bristow. Who're you, lad?"

Brett answered, despite himself. "Brett."

"Good to meet you, Brett. You've obviously got a decent melon on your shoulders to organise people like this."

"It would be much better if you and your men helped us. We can't survive here forever."

"Have you asked Lewis for help?"

Brett nodded. "For all the good it did. When are you going to let us go? We don't even know what's happening in the world anymore. Did you cut the power on us?"

"No. The power's out in most places. The stations are undermanned and it's not safe to run them without adequate staff. Things are…pretty bad all over, lad."

"No kidding."

"No, Brett. I mean things are far worse than they were even a few days ago when you came here. There's no order left anymore. Lewis hasn't received commands in almost forty-eight hours now. The men are getting restless."

Brett raised his eyebrow. "Why the hell are you telling me this?"

The Lieutenant shrugged. "I suppose because I don't think there's going to be much difference soon between you and I."

"Then why are you keeping us in here?"

"Believe me, you wouldn't be any happier out here. There's nothing but death and panic on the streets. People with the infection have started wandering around like crazed lunatics. The pavements are red with blood. Way I see it you people have it better than anyone. This stadium is a paradise in comparison."

Just then, Emily returned with armfuls of broomsticks and mop handles. They were as tall as her and it was a comical sight.

"You want some help there, Em?"

"I'm fine, thank you. Did you say you wanted them jammed in the turnstiles?"

Brett took a step back from Lieutenant Barstow and nodded. "Yeah, make sure you jam them up nice and tight. If this is going to be our home, then we're damn well going to protect it. You can tell your captain I said that, Lieutenant."

The officer shrugged his shoulders. "Will do. You all take care of yourselves."

Brett reorganised everyone and prepared to leave. He was even more confused about what to think of the army outside now. Lieutenant Bristow seemed a lot more trustworthy than his superior. In fact it seemed like the man barely considered himself even much of a soldier anymore. T*he rules had apparently changed for them al.*

IT WAS a couple of days later when Brett heard the shots.

Ethan was the first on his feet and alert. Brett could hear the man shouting from somewhere in the grounds. Ethan and those close to him slept in the executive boxes at the top of the ground, while the other small groups of people were dotted around the various stands. Steven and his daughter were alone in the Press Box. The little girl would moan and cry long into the night. Once or twice, her father had joined her.

Brett got up from his bed on the floor of the East Stand staffroom. Emily was lying nearby and quickly sat up. The girl had been bedding down next to him for a couple of days now and had been getting gradually closer each night.

"Did you hear that?" Brett asked her.

"It was gunfire," she said. "Least I think so. Is something going on outside?"

Brett got to his feet. "Those bastards best not be trying to get inside."

Brett ran out of the East Stand and onto the pitch. The cold night air hit him in the face like a slap and he suddenly realised he was without a t-shirt. Reverend Long also stood on the pitch and Brett headed over to him.

"Ah, young Brett. It appears we have some sort of commotion outside. Guns, I believe."

"You're sure it's coming from outside? Are the army trying to get in?"

"I don't know. Ethan just ran off to find out."

"Which way? I'm going after him." Brett headed off in the direction Reverend Long indicated: the Clark Stand.

When he got there, Ethan was squeezed up against the turnstiles and peering through into the darkness. There were more gunshots coming from outside, but they sounded distant.

"What's happening?" Brett asked as he moved up beside Ethan.

"They're shooting at each other. Can you believe that?"

"Who are? The Army?"

Ethan turned around, his eyes wide and white in the dark. "The Army, the Police, I can't even tell, but they're definitely taking shots at one another. I told you they were all dangerous. Well done for putting up the barricades."

"Thanks. Let me have a look what's going on."

Ethan moved aside and allowed Brett up to the turnstiles. It was hard to see anything outside, except the jagged flashes of muzzle fire. The sound of bullets hitting steel and masonry were mixed with the sounds of men dying. Whatever had happened outside had turned lethal, but there would be no way to see what was going on until the sun came back up. There was no way Brett was going to shout out and draw attention to himself.

"I'm going to keep guard," said Brett. "Ethan, can you get some people to watch the other exits? I can't see a thing out there, but we have to be ready if anybody tries to get inside.

"They won't try to get in here. Not tonight."

"We don't know that."

Ethan thought about it and then nodded. "Okay."

ETHAN and a few others headed back into the stadium, while Brett remained behind. It was only a couple minutes before Emily arrived to keep him company.

"WHAT DO you think things will be like?" asked Emily, sitting on the floor beside him. "I mean, once this virus goes away and everything goes back to normal. So many people have died. Not just from the disease either."

Brett's eyelids felt heavy, but he did his best to stay with the conversation. "I don't know. I don't think things will ever be *normal* again. For all we know, half the world could be dead right now. People have lost their families…lost everything."

"What have you lost, Brett?"

"To be honest I had less to lose than most. I didn't have many friends. My only family were my parents and we…we weren't that close. I guess I'm lucky when I think about it."

"Nobody is lucky anymore. This has been hard on all of us. It's not a contest for who has lost the most."

Brett nodded and smiled at her. Emily was annoying, but it seemed like her heart was in the right place. "So what happened to you before we all got together?"

"I was at church with Reverend Long. I'd just lost my mom and I didn't know what to do, so I went there. Couple days later a group of us decided to try and gather people up and come here."

"I reckon if you hadn't done that most of us would be dead. I don't think it's safe out there anymore, not even at home."

"I don't think so either. Still, I miss my bedroom, my bed...and I wish I'd taken my violin when I'd left. Or my piano if I had the strength of ten men to carry it. God I miss my piano."

Brett's eyes widened. "You play music?"

She nodded enthusiastically. "Yeah, I'm...I *was* studying Music Theory at college. I can play violin, clarinet, piano, and a little bit of guitar. I was even in a little band me and some of the other girl's had as a hobby."

"You're shitting me?"

"No, I'm not...pooping you!"

Brett laughed. "I play guitar, too. Music is my life – at least my old life."

"Huh, maybe we can play together one day?"

"Yeah," said Brett. "I'd like that."

Emily smiled and leant her head on his shoulder. Brett was surprised to find out that he didn't mind. In fact, within a few minutes they were both asleep, snoring besides the turnstiles while the gunfire outside continued.

"HEY. Hey, Brett! Brett wake up, son. I need your help."

Brett opened his eyes slowly, not knowing if a dream had woken him, or something else entirely. When the steel turnstiles behind him rattled, he sat bolt upright with fright. So did Emily, who let out a girlish yelp as she scuttled away on her hands and knees.

Lieutenant Bristow was at the gate. He was breathing in short stutters and bleeding from a wound in his shoulder.

Bret headed over to the man to help him, but realised that the turnstiles were jammed up. "Shit, man. What the hell happened out there? Are you okay?"

Bristow shook his head. "I took a bullet. Captain Lewis went and lost his damn mind. Started firing at the police officers who had set up with us when we got here. We haven't had orders in almost a week, so the captain decided he was going it alone. He ordered the police to hand over their vehicles and supplies. When they refused, Lewis started firing on them. They were unarmed and...they didn't stand a chance. That's when I and some of the other men turned on the captain. Our detachment split in two: Captain Lewis versus me. Luckily I came out on top, but most of my men are dead, and I…I need help. You have to let me in. The fighting's not completely over. I don't want any more of my men to get shot. We need to rest."

"Let him in," said Emily.

Brett turned to her and shook his head, then nodded, then shook his head again. "I don't know if that's a good idea."

"You can't leave him out there to die."

"It's not like we have any doctors in here that could even help him anyway."

"Brett," it was the Lieutenant speaking. "I know that you're all scared. I know that the Army has done nothing to make you people feel safe, but trust me when I say that the only chance any of us has is to stick together. I'm not following orders anymore. I'm just a man like you, and I'm asking for your help."

Brett's gut had told him to trust the Lieutenant the last time they had spoken, and it was telling him the same thing now. The bullet wound in the man's shoulder suggested that his story was true enough.

Brett took a step toward the turnstile.

"Don't you dare let that man in," said Ethan, hurrying to get in front of him. "We're not letting a single one of those thugs in here. They were the ones keeping us trapped in here. They made their own bed; they can damn-well lie in it. We owe them nothing."

"The Lieutenant isn't like that," said Brett. "Captain Lewis is the one who wouldn't let us leave."

"That's right," Bristow spoke weakly. "Lewis is dead now. You can all leave if you want to, but please help me first."

Ethan was unwavering. "You can die for all I care. The only people that matter are us in here. We don't need to risk our lives helping you. You and your men are the reason this country has turned to shit as badly as it has. For every person lost to The Peeling, there's been just as many shot by barbarians in the Army. I guarantee you that at the very least he stood by and watched it happen."

"You're right," said Bristow, his words thick with pain. "I did. I'll never forgive myself for following orders so blindly, but that is behind me now. All I can do is try to make up for the past by helping to protect as many people as I can from now on. But I need to rest before I can do that."

Reverend Long appeared and seemed confused by the scene that met him. "What on earth is happening here?"

"Captain Lewis lost control," Brett said. "There's people injured outside and they want in."

"Which isn't going to happen," Ethan added.

Reverend Long looked across at Lieutenant Bristow lying bloody in the turnstiles. "If people need help, it's our obligation as human beings to help them."

"If he gets in here, we're all dead," said Ethan. "Do I have to remind you that they're the reason no one has been able to leave here in a week? And how many innocent people have the army shot since things turned bad? It's been a massacre, and now you want to let one of them in here?"

"I think he's different," said Brett.

"But you can't be sure," Ethan replied.

"No, you're right. I can't."

Lieutenant Bristow let out an anguished sigh. "Please. I'm begging you."

Reverend Long marched over to the turnstiles but Ethan stood in the man's way. "Leave him," he said. "We don't owe him anything."

"We owe him decency at the very least. I will not leave a man to suffer. The world may have changed, but I have not."

Ethan looked at Brett and raised his eyebrow. "You going to let him do this?"

Brett wondered why the hell the decision lay with him. Somehow, in the last few days, the three of them must have formed some unspoken coalition. His vote was the tiebreaker. But what should he do?

"Let him in."

Ethan backed off and let out an angered huff. "Fine. On your head be it. But make sure that we have his rifle."

Reverend Long grabbed the broom handle blocking the mechanism of the turnstile and Brett hurried up to grab a hold of the Lieutenant. Eventually they managed to drag the wounded soldier through the entrance and into the hallway inside. The wound in the Lieutenant's shoulder left a slick red trail on the floor behind him. Brett made sure to grab the rifle off the floor. It was heavier than expected.

"Right," said Brett, pointing the weapon at the floor. "Getting him inside is one thing. Now what do we do to help him?"

Lieutenant Bristow answered the question. He opened a small utility pouch on his belt and said, "I have bandages and disinfectant. I just need someone to dress my wound. I think the round went straight through. I should be okay."

Brett handed the rifle over to Ethan – immediately wondering if that was a good idea – and knelt down beside Bristow. He reached into the man's utility pouch and found gauze, bandage, and a tiny bottle of Iodine. Reverend Long sat the soldier up while Brett removed his clothing. Beneath the olive green t-shirt was a tiny, circular hole that oozed blood. Brett doused the wound with the orange liquid from the Iodine bottle and clamped down a square of gauze before the blood had time to flood the area again. He held it there for a few seconds until the blood fused it in place. A couple of minutes later Brett had Bristow's entire shoulder wrapped up in soft white bandage.

"How's that feel?"

"Better already. I just need to rest."

"I'll get the penthouse ready," Ethan muttered.

"Ethan," Reverend Long scalded him. "Please…"

"It's okay," said Bristow. "He's right to be hostile. I'm grateful to you people for helping me, truly."

"Don't mention it," said Brett. "You think you can stand?"

Bristow nodded and Brett helped him to his feet. He seemed a little shaken but his body was stiff and powerful, trained for survival. Brett felt better having a grizzled soldier in their midst. He felt surer that his decision to let him through the turnstiles was the right one. That didn't mean he was willing to let his men through just yet, though.

"Ethan," get the turnstiles secure. No one else is coming through until we know more about the situation."

Ethan didn't argue, probably because it was an idea he could get behind. He jammed up the mechanism and then decided to stand watch beside the entrance. That probably wasn't a bad idea either.

"People are going to be nervous about you being here," Brett told Bristow. "I think it would be best if we took you up into the stands for tonight."

"Okay," said Bristow, starting to bear more of his own weight with every step. "Anywhere is fine."

Emily appeared in front of them then. Brett hadn't notice her leave earlier but it appeared that she had something important to tell them. Before she had chance, though, people started shouting over at the East Stand.

IT TURNED out to be Stephen causing the panic. When Brett entered the food area of East Stand, he immediately saw the festering sore on the man's face and the fear in his eyes. The Peeling had begun its work. Somehow he had caught it from his daughter.

"Stephen, you're sick." It was stating the obvious, but Brett knew nothing else to say.

"I'm fine," he replied, his voice already weak and slurring from the infection. "You need to help my girl. She's, she's…God help me, there's nothing left of her. Just...bones. Bones and blood." Stephen threw up on the floor, the vomit steaming and thick with blood.

"Get the fuck back," shouted Ethan. "You need to get away from us."

Brett hated to be cruel, but he agreed. "Stephen, go back up into the stands. You're dangerous."

Stephen stepped forward. "I'm fine. There's nothing wrong with me."

"Your face…"

Stephen stopped approaching and put a shaking hand to his cheek. When he pulled it back his fingers were clammy with sticky flesh. He looked at Brett with panic in his eyes. "Help me!" He rushed forward, arms out in desperation.

Lieutenant Bristow pulled the trigger on a handgun he had pulled from nowhere. An explosion of sound was followed by a tiny dot of blood spreading wider on Stephen's forehead. The man fell down dead.

Ethan spun around and pointed the rifle at Bristow and begun shouting. "What the hell are you doing?"

"What needed to be done."

Brett shook his head and had a bad feeling. "You said you were done with this. You said you didn't want to kill anybody else."

Bristow lowered his gun and gave them all a stern look. "He was already dead. I did him a favour."

Reverend Long said, "It is that attitude that has seen this country's military turn into savages and bullies."

Bristow laughed. "You people really don't get it, do you? The world has ended. Things aren't just bad, they're over and done with. Anyone lucky enough to still be alive should be doing everything they can to stay that way. Whatever it takes. Because if we fail it's the end of the goddamn human race."

Ethan aimed the rifle at Bristow's unflinching face. "*We'll* decide what it takes. This is our home you just stepped into. You live by our rules."

Bristow slowly raised his gun again and this time aimed it at Ethan. "You point a rifle at someone, you need to be willing to pull the trigger, mate. You got the stones for it?"

Ethan began to sweat, a bead appearing above his right eyebrow. He clutched the rifle tightly, but he seemed more concerned with the fact that a weapon was pointed at him.

"There are no rules anymore," said Bristow. "It's all about whoever has the biggest bollocks."

"Well, right now, I do," said Ethan. "I have the bigger gun."

Bristow smirked. "But it's not loaded."

Ethan panicked and pulled the trigger. Nothing happened and he flinched as Bristow let off another round from his pistol.

The bullet hit the wall just behind Ethan's head. Then Bristow put the weapon away, shoving it into a holster near the small of his back. "Now, believe me when I say that if I had wanted to hit you, I would have. I'm not here to have war with any of you. I meant it when I said I was done with all the killing. I just want somewhere secure to ride this thing out."

Brett laughed. "So now you want inside the place you've been keeping us prisoner in. Nice."

"I already told you that Lewis was calling the shots. He's dead now. Things are different."

"We'll see," said Brett. "Hand over your gun."

"No."

"Look, if you want us to trust you, you're going to have to give us reason to. Hand over your weapon."

"I'll take it," said Reverend Long. "I think it's best if it's in the hands on someone not willing to use it."

Bristow thought about it for a second, then let out a sigh. "Fine. Here, take it."

Reverend Long took the gun and placed it inside his vest pocket. "There, now let's get Stephen somewhere before anyone else gets sick. I have a feeling it's going to be a long day."

EVERYONE WAS UNDERSTANDABLY upset to learn that one of the soldiers was now inside the stadium. Brett had taken Bristow up into one of the executive boxes at the top of the stands and told him to stay there for the time being. The boxes had locks on them and Bristow secured himself inside as Brett left him.

Now Brett was standing with Reverend Long and Ethan. The three of them addressed the rest about what had happened.

Reverend Long was the first to speak. "It would seem that there has been a civil war, of sorts, between the soldiers and the police. Sides were taken and Captain Lewis is now dead."

There was a brief cheer amongst the group. Most had not met the captain, but they all knew it was him who had been keeping them trapped inside."

"We're now all free to go," said Ethan, "but it's starting to look like that may not be a good idea."

"We can't stay here forever," said Brett, "but for now, we're all safe and we at least have the option of leaving now. That changes things."

"Safe?" said one of the crowd. "How are we safe with that man in here with us? We can't trust the military."

"Not to mention the fact that The Peeling is inside," added another unseen person in the crowd. "Stephen and his daughter are dead."

"How did they even get it? No one else has it. It doesn't make any sense."

"Look," said Brett. "I don't think we understand things as well as we think we do. I know the news reports said that half of us are carriers, which means we won't get the disease itself, but in all honesty who the hell knows the truth? It hit us all so quickly and so hard that I doubt the Government even had half a chance to try and figure it all out. At least for now, no one else seems to be sick, so we shouldn't tempt fate by going outside or changing our behaviours."

"Or letting new people in," said someone in the crowd. "Like a goddamn, bleeding soldier."

"It wasn't my idea," said Ethan. "I think we should turf him out as soon as he's had twenty-four hours rest."

The crowd murmured amongst themselves and seemed to agree.

"No," said Reverend Long. "We must remember the compassion we all once had, before fear perverted our good natures. Lieutenant Bristow handed over his weapons willingly and is a victim of all this, just like us. We should not turn away a stranger in need. In the times ahead of us, there may well be a time where we ourselves need to rely on the compassion of others. Let us not turn into animals. We are men and woman, and the direction of the future will be down to us."

"Very dramatic," said Ethan. "Perhaps you're right, though. Maybe we shouldn't forget how things were before. Let's vote. All in favour of ejecting our unwanted guest tomorrow morning raise your hands."

Over two thirds of the group raised their hands and Reverend Long let out a sigh.

"Democracy. Can't argue with the group," said Ethan. "The will of the many supersedes the will of the few."

The Reverend shook his head and walked away. Brett thought about going after him, but decided not to. Brett couldn't say anything that would change anything. If a majority of the group wanted Bristow gone, then who was he to argue? Maybe things would be different tomorrow. People would have had time to think.

Brett just hoped Bristow didn't put up a fight.

Because nobody else was willing, Brett and Reverend Long took Stephen's body upstairs to rest beside his daughter. The little girl's body had been reduced to mush that hardly resembled human form. In a way, Stephen was lucky to have died before he suffered the same fate. The smell had been overpowering and Brett could still smell it on his clothing. Fortunately, when Emily approached him she didn't seem to notice.

The sun was beginning to go down and Brett had got into one of the stadium's offices. He was looking out of the window across the carpark, and the devastation outside. Dozens of bodies littered the streets; witnesses to the fire-fight that had broken out between the police officers and soldiers. Bullet holes pockmarked the scattered vehicles and blood covered the pavement like spilt paint. There wasn't a single person alive out there; so where were Lieutenant Bristow's men?

"You okay?" asked Emily, moving up beside him at the window. She shook her head when she saw what he did. "You know, it's horrible but it doesn't even bother me anymore, the bodies and stuff. It's normal now. Does that make me bad?"

Brett touched her on the back. "Course not. I think people just adjust to survive. We're all doing it. I've changed too."

"Tell me about it. People really listen to you now."

Brett watched a stray dog appear from between two houses and begin sniffing around the debris of the street. He hoped the dog wasn't far gone enough to start eating the bodies. "People don't listen to me," he said. "They listen to Ethan and the Reverend. I'm just the poor sod caught in the middle most the time."

"Well, doesn't that make you the most powerful of all then? If they keep butting heads and making opposing suggestions, with you being the one deciding on the outcome, then technically you're the one making all the decisions around here."

It was an interesting thought, and perhaps close to the truth, but it was an unwanted truth. "To be honest I'd rather not be making any decisions at all. I'm not cut out for responsibility."

"I disagree," said Emily.

"Really? Well, I can't help feeling that I'm putting people in danger. It was my decision to bring Bristow inside, and he's already killed one of us."

"Stephen was already doomed."

"Yeah, he was, but why was that? Because I let his daughter stay inside with us after she had The Peeling. Then Stephen caught it. Who knows if anyone else will get ill because of my decision?"

Emily put an arm around him and he shuddered with discomfort. It had been so long since he'd had human contact that he was no longer used to it. Emily kept her arm around him regardless. "It's not your fault. So many people have died already that trying to do something about it is almost pointless. We're not in control of anything anymore."

Brett sighed and turned away from the window. Melancholy wasn't in his nature and he was reluctant to allow himself to indulge the feeling now. The only furniture that hadn't been taken from the office to build barricades was a couple of office chairs. Brett sat down on an executive, leather high-back and spun around on it, trying to replace his sadness with dizziness. Emily took a chair for herself and rolled it up opposite him.

Brett looked up at Emily and asked her a question. "So come on, then, tell me. Why do you always seem to be there whenever I look up? Are you following me?"

Emily blushed and seemed a little annoyed. "High opinion of yourself, much? I just like being around you because there's not that many people to choose from anymore."

"Oh, cheers."

Emily cracked a smile. "Plus, there're even less young people, and… you make me feel safe."

Brett raised an eyebrow. "Safe?"

"Yeah. You don't seem to let worry get to you like everyone else. You stay calm and do the right thing. You remind me of how things were before things went bad, calm and normal."

"So what were you like before all this? What did you do for fun?"

"Not a lot," Emily replied. "I was a big saddo, as you can probably tell by my bright ginger hair and spectacles."

"Maybe I thought that about you at first, but you seem pretty cool after getting to know you."

"Nope, I've always been a hopeless case, I'm afraid. My parents sent me for piano lessons and choir when I was ten and my nerdom never looked back. I tried picking up guitar and listening to rock to try and be cooler but it never worked. People still crossed the street to avoid me. Truth be told I'm probably more popular since things went all loopy."

Brett laughed. "Maybe your problem is that you say things like 'loopy'. This situation is a few levels above loopy. Let me hear what you really think."

"What do you mean?"

"I mean that you're being polite and well-behaved, but the time for manners is over. Time to stop being a nerd. Tell me what you really think of the world we're currently stuck in."

"Well…I, I think it's messed up."

"Keep going."

"It's…well, it's *fucked* up is what it is."

"More."

"This situation is totally batshit-crazy, fruitloop-fucking-insane. It's a barrel-full of shitballs."

Brett laughed so hard that his chest hurt and he started choking. When he regained his breath, he said, "Well, those are some ways to put it, I guess. I think I agree with you, though; this situation is certainly a barrel-full of shitballs."

Emily laughed too. "It's fuck-fuck-fucked!"

"There you go. Doesn't it feel better to say what you really mean?"

"Yeah, it does. Thanks for rescuing me from my none-swearing life-style. I feel much happier now."

"Okay, okay," said Brett, trying to keep from another bout of laughter. "Now that you've reinvented yourself, what would you be doing right now if you could?"

"I'd be back at home at my piano. I know it's not cool, but I always preferred it over guitar. Doesn't mean I can't rock out, though. The last CD I brought was by a band called Fozzy. I think I would be listening to them right now. I miss music so bad, you know?"

"Fozzy? Shit, I know them. They're good. Well, I think the music may have stopped for now, so once things settle down it's going to be up to us to bring rock back to the world."

"Deal," said Emily, offering out her hand to shake. Once he shook it, she looked him in the eye and said, "You know what else I would do right now if I had the choice?"

"No," said Brett. "What?"

"This." Emily stood up and climbed onto Brett's lap. Then she kissed him.

BRETT WOKE up in the pitch blackness and for a moment did not know where he was. Sliding off the edge of sleep, Brett's world was once again normal and devoid of the horrors of the last few weeks. The warm body lying beside him made him feel even more that things were normal. But then it all came back to him.

He sat up in the darkness and realised he was sweating. The room had gotten stuffy while he and Emily slept. Being fully-clothed had led to him becoming overheated. Emily felt hot, too, beneath his hand, but had not awoken. She snored softly as sleep continued to embrace her

Brett needed to get some air. He was beginning to feel quite ill and bunged up. He had never been a good sleeper and his sinuses would often constrict throughout the night, waking him up. The world may have been shattered and torn asunder, but some things never changed.

Brett crept to his feet, not wanting to wake Emily and leave her frightened and alone in the dark. He planned on heading over to the East Stand to cool down in the open area beside the pitch. Then he would come right back and lay beside Emily. It was strange to him that the thought of getting back to her was so important, but right now she was the only thing making him still feel human. The bond between the two of them was something he never would have predicted.

He pawed his way through the dark, searching for the wall that would lead him to the door. When he found it, he pulled it open gradually, trying to avoid the squeak of the hinges. The corridor outside was dark, too, but Brett knew that there were no obstacles in his way and that he needed only to head along the wall until he reached a further door at the end.

He stepped out into the moonlit East Stand and was immediately invigorated by the cool air rushing through the cement structure. He sighed as it flowed over his clammy cheeks and lifted up his shirt to allow it to caress his torso. Already he felt his temperature drop.

There was someone else milling about in the area, moving across the walkway at the far end of the stand. It was probably a smoker getting their middle of the night fix. Brett fancied some company while he cooled down, so he headed toward the stranger, but before he got there they disappeared into the turnstile lobby of the stand. Unless they planned on leaving the stadium, Brett didn't know why they would want to head there.

He took hurried steps, somewhere between a run and a walk and reached the turnstile area quickly. He was surprised by who he found there. "Bristow? What are you doing?"

Brett took a step back when the Lieutenant pulled a gun on him. It was a different handgun to the one he'd handed over to the Reverend. He must have hidden it on himself somewhere.

"What are you doing?" Brett repeated.

Bristow said nothing. He turned back towards the turnstiles and started pulling at the debris that had been stuffed into the mechanism to prevent it from turning. The stile wouldn't let the lieutenant out; it would only let people in.

"Step away from there, Lieutenant. No one else is coming in h-"

Brett hit the floor before he even realised that a bullet had been fired at him. Pain exploded throughout his entire body and then settled down to just his midsection. Examining himself frantically, he saw that the bullet had nicked his hip, grazing against his pelvic bone and cutting a furrow into his flesh. The wound spat blood onto the floor, but didn't feel as bad as it looked. Brett was still able to drag himself along the floor and around the corner, shielding himself from any further shots. Although he could no longer see Bristow or the turnstiles, he could hear the man continuing to clear away the debris. Whoever was waiting outside was about to be let in soon.

"Don't do this, Bristow. We can all get along."

"I agree," the Lieutenant shouted back. "But we're in charge now. The Army is in charge."

"Those days are over, man. You said it yourself: the rules don't apply anymore

"Exactly. It's all about power and who has the muscles to take it."

Ethan came running down the corridor and slid down onto the floor beside Brett. He noticed the blood pouring from his hip. "What the hell is going on?"

"It's Bristow. He's opening up the turnstiles. He's trying to let someone in."

"Who? His men?"

"I don't know, but he has a gun."

"Long. Goddamn that bloody self-righteous-"

Brett put a hand on Ethan's wrists to halt his tirade. "It wasn't the Reverend. Bristow has a different gun. He must have still had one on him when we took him in."

"Right. We're not standing for this bullshit. I'm through having a bunch of disbanded soldiers calling the shots." Ethan stood up and marched around the corner. The next thing Brett was aware off was more gunfire, but not, this time, from a handgun. It was automatic rifle-fire.

Ethan fell back into the hallway, bullet-riddled and already dead by the time he hit the floor. The way he fell left him staring at Brett like a soulless puppet with glass eyes.

Brett leapt his feet and almost fell back down again when his vision tilted. He hoped his injuries weren't too bad, because he didn't expect there was much chance of seeing a Doctor anymore. He set off into the stadium, fleeing the turnstiles and Lieutenant Bristow.

Inside the East Stand, people had already begun to gather anxiously. They had heard the gunfire.

"What's happening?" one of the people asked.

"Ethan's dead. Bristow shot him. He's opened up the turnstiles. The Army is coming in."

Everyone panicked.

"We need to get out of here," Brett shouted at them. "We need to get out of here right now. Everyone head for the North Stand. We can get out there."

"Nobody is going anywhere!" Gunfire into the ceiling made everyone hit the floor.

Brett looked up at the man with the rifle and was shocked to see that Captain Lewis was alive and well. Lieutenant Bristow stood beside him with a satisfied smirk on his face. Four riflemen backed them

"Why are you doing this?" Brett demanded.

"Because this stadium is an asset," Captain Lewis replied. "It has several, easily defended exits and a great deal of space. Lieutenant Bristow did well to gain your trust and get inside. It will be perfect as my base of operations."

"For what?"

"For Project Restoration," said Bristow on behalf of his superior. "It's time we regained order and began adjusting to the new world. There is no longer a centralised government, I regret to inform you all, and this is now a militant state. As the most senior officer in this area – perhaps in the entire country – it is Captain Lewis's prerogative to take charge of the local populace. You are now all under his command."

Captain Lewis beamed proudly. "Thank you, Lieutenant Bristow. Now I'd just like to assure everybody that I intend to be firm but fair. You will be given jobs to perform and you will be expected to do them. Any resistance will be dealt with via martial law. Any chance to abandon your place here will result in capital punish-"

A gun shot rang out and the Captain stood silently for a moment, looking at the group with a surprised look on his face. A couple of seconds later, another shot rang out and Lieutenant Bristow hit the floor, dead. A large circle of blood started to spread around Captain Lewis's heart and it became clear that the first bullet had struck him.

All at once, the remaining four soldiers raised their weapons and scanned the area frantically. One of them fell as another gunshot rang out, but then one of the men pointed his rifle off towards the food desks. Brett spun around to see that Reverend Long was standing there, Bristow's pistol smoking in his hand. The man's tolerance for violence had been breached. The soldier that spotted him fired off a hail of automatic fire and Reverend Long jolted backwards behind the serving desk.

Brett screamed in anger and leapt to his feet, rushing at the rifleman. He hit the soldier in the face and yanked the weapon from his arms. He had no clue how to fire a rifle so instead he swung it like a baseball bat, clubbing the soldier in his forehead. Before he knew it, Brett was being faced down by the remaining two riflemen. There was no way he could reach them before they let off a shot at him. Brett was a dead man and he knew it.

Like a mob of highland warriors the others got up off the floor and rushed forward as one, shouting and screaming with violent rage. The two soldiers took their eye of Brett and focused on the approaching gang of men and women. Their eyes went wide with fear and they ran.

Brett watched the two soldiers make it about twenty metres before the mob caught up with them, dragging them roughly to the ground. He decided not to watch what happened; he had somewhere else to be.

He headed back towards the office block of the stadium and made his way through the unlit corridors. When he got back inside the office, Emily was still asleep and snoring soundly. She'd missed the whole thing. Brett sat down beside her and rocked her gently awake.

"Wha…B-Brett?"

"Yeah, Emily. It's me. You need to wake up. We're leaving."

"L-leaving?"

Brett stroked a hand over her forehead, leant forward and kissed her. "Yeah. It's not safe here anymore."

"Where are we going?"

"I don't know. I was thinking we could maybe go back to your house. You can play your piano again. We can stop off and get my guitar first. The world may be over, but that doesn't mean we can't spend whatever time we have rocking out."

Emily laughed and Brett wished he could see her face. "We could form the world's last rock band," she said. "I'd finally be cool."

"You already are," said Brett. "You already are."

They waited until sunrise, before setting off into the world.

THE PEELING: BOOK 3

WARRIORS

Staff Sergeant Matt Parker stood tall on the back of the tank and peered through his binoculars.

"Slow her down," he shouted as he clung onto the Warrior's turret.

The Perkins-Rolls-Royce V8 Condor engine of the British Army Infantry Fighting Vehicle slowed down with a disappointed grumble. Discarded rubbish and human waste crunched beneath the weight of its treads. All around, the city of Birmingham lay in ruins; its humanity abandoned and broken. Paint peeled from every building, but the ever-present bloodstains seemed only to intensify with age. Gradually the city was turning red.

"You spot something?" Corporal Cross asked his sergeant from the gunner's seat. The tank's 30mm cannon was empty, as was its coaxial chain gun, but it still commanded attention from those who did not know. The only ammunition Parker and his men had been able to snatch up when things had gone bad at Tidworth was enough explosives for a single barrage from the tank's eight grenade launchers (positioned in two clusters). Fortunately, they were all equipped with personal arms and each of them carried a L85A2 assault rifle (or SA80) with roughly a magazine of ammunition each.

Parker inched his binoculars to the left, picking up movement amongst the rubble of a firebombed Post Office. "We've got civvies up ahead. Two-hundred metres. Bring us to a halt; let them come to us."

The civilians up ahead were just kids, and they were visibly afraid. Upon seeing the tank, the two teenagers tried to scurry behind a scattered pile of masonry. Parker picked up the megaphone that hung from a lanyard attached to the Warrior's side storage. He raised it to his mouth and moistened his lips.

"Strangers, you have been spotted. Please identify yourselves so that we can categorise you as non-hostile."

The teenagers did not come out.

Parker increased the megaphone's volume. "I am Sergeant Matthew Parker of her Majesty's Armed Forces. I mean you no harm. If you need assistance I will provide it to you. Come out now, please."

Tentatively, the two teenagers reappeared from behind the rubble like frightened mice. It was a boy and a girl. The boy was Black while the girl was pale and ginger-haired. They were an odd pairing, indeed, but then, in the current world, people found companionship wherever they could. Social norms no longer applied.

The teenagers approached the tank; the boy walking protectively in front of the girl. As they got closer, Parker identified them as young adults. He also saw that his early estimation of them being afraid was not entirely accurate. They were not so much afraid of Parker or the tank as they were distrustful.

Parker placed the megaphone down and placed both his palms out to his side, showing that he was unarmed. He also tried to smile but found he had forgotten how to.

"What do you want?" asked the teenage boy defiantly.

Parker shrugged. "Just want to check in with you folks. Everything okay? Are you in need of assistance?"

The lad huffed and shook his head. "We were doing just fine until your boys kicked us out of our home."

Parker didn't understand. "Who kicked you out of your home?"

"Your man, Captain Lewis, and his sidekick, Bristow."

"Captain Lewis? I'm afraid I don't know the man. Are you saying this man is with the Army?"

"*Was,*" the lad corrected. "He took a bullet when he and his men started taking hostages at the football stadium down the road."

Parker sighed. Hearing that one of his colleagues had been shot should have been cause for him to apprehend these two kids, but somehow it seemed unnecessary. There was no longer any law and order to maintain. Even the lines between good and bad had become increasingly murky.

"Is it something we should look into? Are people hurt?"

The lad shook his head. "I don't know. One thing is for sure, though: the last thing the people still at the stadium want to see is another bunch of soldiers."

Suddenly the girl spoke up: "Just because you have guns doesn't give you the right to push people around."

Parker nodded. "I agree, young lady. Right now I think it's important that we all work together. Do you kids have a destination?"

"We're going to my house," the lad answered. "Problem with that?"

"Of course not. Just keep safe and be careful. There're a lot of desperate people in the world right now and nowhere is safe. Not even your homes."

The kids seemed confused for a moment, as if they had expected the situation to go differently. Then they nodded to each other and began walking away, continuing their journey.

"Hey, you two!" Parker shouted after them. They both turned around. Parker managed to smile this time. "What are your names?"

The boy answered. "My name is Brett, and this is Emily."

Parker nodded and reached into his pockets slowly, not wanting to startle the kids. "It was nice meeting you both, he said. "Here, take this." He hurled a pack of chocolate bars through the air and the lad caught them with his left hand.

The lad looked at the package for a moment as if he was stuck in a daydream. Then he looked up and said, "Thanks. It's nice to see that there are still some good guys left. I think if people knew that not all the Army had gone bad they wouldn't all be so afraid."

Parker watched the two kids head off to their unknown destination and thought about what the lad had meant. Obviously something had happened at the nearby football stadium but Parker intended to take heed of the lad's warning about his presence being unwelcome. There was no point forcing his way into a situation that did not want him. The thing that concerned Parker the most was hearing that some of his brothers-in-arms were acting more like tyrants than protectors.

When news of the deadly wasting disease, The Peeling, first broke, the Military and Police forces kept a tight grip on the country's population, cordoning off highways and restricted people to their homes. It was a cruel, but necessary step. Parker had been glad to have been posted at base. Manhandling sick civilians wasn't what he signed up for and he was glad to be occupied with other tasks. Later, however, when the disease penetrated fifty percent of the populace, things had started to become untenable. Key figures in government, military, police, healthcare, and other key services fell ill and died, leaving all departments undermanned and in disarray. The chicken had lost its head. Communities rioted, lashing out at the remaining authorities as they sought to get away from the sick and dying. Fear of contagion had become a crazed, primal instinct that drove people to animalistic behaviours.

Then the news broke that the sick where not infectious; they never had been. Scientists confirmed that it was the seemingly healthy who were the contagious ones. It was *they* who carried the brutal virus which killed all who succumbed to its necrotic effects. Everything fell apart. With one half of the population dying and the other half responsible, society crumbled. No one could trust anybody else and the only way to be safe was to seek absolute isolation – and then defend that isolation if necessary. Battles over rural farmhouses and other sought-after real estate had been constant and bloody.

But things had gone quiet recently. The infection seemed to have plateaued. Those that had caught the sickness were mostly dead or long on their way, and those that were still healthy seemed to be confident of remaining so. Parker himself, along with all of his men, had been exposed to countless civilians but were still entirely healthy, albeit slightly malnourished. Parker made sure that his men ate only what they needed and gave the rest away to whatever civilians they encountered. But, it seemed, eventually he would have to start prioritising the health of his men above those they encountered on the road. The world was becoming increasingly dog-eat-dog and his public duties were diminishing. It seemed that some of his colleagues from other outfits had already gone into business for themselves.

"You want to check the kid's story out?" Cross asked. "If there's a unit out there, we could combine Intel."

Parker shook his head. "If there's anybody left I'm assuming they're not the type to cooperate."

"Another unit gone rogue?" Cross suggested. "Fuck a duck."

"Sounds like it. When things degenerate into chaos there's a lot of temptation on those with guns to take things without asking. We all spent enough time in Afghanistan to know about that."

"Some of the men are wondering why we're not giving in to that temptation ourselves. It's been weeks since we received any orders. We're alone out here."

Parker sighed. He wasn't about to have this conversation. "We're not about to start abusing our authority. It was people doing that which got the country into such a mess in the first place. If people had worked together instead of shunning one another we may be in better shape right now. We're not about to start making things worse by tyrannising a bunch of scared people."

Cross nodded, seemingly satisfied. "So, where next, Sarge?"

"Same as always," Parker replied. "Forward."

THE NORTHERN SUBURBS of Birmingham were deserted, exactly like Wolverhampton had been, and Stoke before that. People still existed in small pockets, but they were unseen like rats during the daytime. They scurried about at night, foraging for things they needed. It didn't help that most people were terrified of the military now; Parker and his men driving around in a tank was a red flag to most survivors. It was hard work trying to help people that didn't want to give you the chance.

The last time they had found a substantial group of people was inside a pub in Wolverhampton city centre. There the men wore replica shirts of the local team and had brought along what was left of their families. The beer and atmosphere had made for a jovial atmosphere and Parker and his men had been welcomed for a round of drinks. It was funny that the only group of like-minded people had been brought together under the banner of a football team, while religion, ethnicity, and political affiliation had all failed to galvanise society. Parker guessed that the old saying that 'football was the new religion was true.'

Since moving on from that pub, Parker had encounter only loose fragments of humanity; some hostile, some friendly, but all afraid. Any attempts to find an organised group of people had been a failure. There was no Government, no emergency services; no order.

The tank's driver, Schumacher (real name Corporal Hollis), fizzed through on the radio. "We're low on fuel," he said. "Should I head for the nearest petrol station?"

"Affirmative," said Parker. "Take us back out to the main road. See if we can locate a supermarket or retail park."

"Roger that."

The tank gathered speed and adjusted its heading down a side-street that would lead them back to the duel carriageway. As they rounded the corner they approached a funeral pyre, stacked ten-deep with scorched bodies. It was not the shocking sight that it should have been, as several weeks back, the entire country had been lit up with similar bonfires of human flesh. When the military and police still had some semblance of control, they had gathered up the dead infected and set light to what was left of their putrid remains, hoping that to do so would be enough to stymie the spread of the virus. When it became known that the dead bodies of the infected were not contagious, it eventually stopped, continuing only in the city centres where the volume of corpses posed health risks regardless of the Peeling. Cholera was the country's second-biggest epidemic.

The Warrior trundled by the bodies without slowing down. Parker closed his eyes and tried not to hear the crunch of human bones beneath the tank's caterpillar tracks. Sometimes it felt like the only sounds left in the world were ones of suffering and death: like the screams that randomly carried on the winds from time to time.

Cross turned around from the gunner's position and frowned at Parker. "Can't believe we've been in England's second city for three days now and the only people we've seen are those two kids we just passed."

Parker sighed. "I figure most people fled for the countryside to get away from the virus."

"Can't blame them," said Cross. "It would certainly smell better there at the very least. I don't remember the last time I took a breath that didn't make me feel like chucking my guts up."

Parker knew what he meant. The tang of death covered everything. The slithers of necrotic flesh coated the landscape like a new species of pungent moss. Bodies continued rotting in every building they had checked.

"Maybe it's time we moved on ourselves," said Cross. "Gather supplies and try to set ourselves up somewhere in the sticks. We might have the wrong idea looking for people in need. It might be better to let them come to us."

Parker thought about it and found himself agreeing. "You might be right. Let's find somewhere to fill up and we'll re-strategize; figure out what's best."

It was just starting to get dark when they came upon the supermarket.

THE SUPERMARKET's abandoned petrol station was just off the main road, accessed by a roundabout. There was a collection of beat-up vehicles blocking the pumps, but they posed no problem for the Warrior's winch. They shifted a tiny Citroen out of the way of a diesel pump and began to fill the tank. Private Michelle Anderson and Private Thomas Carp grabbed the half-dozen Jerry cans from the tank's side storage and headed off towards the other pumps to fill them. The station's petrol supply seemed to be fine and Parker was grateful that the military quarantine early on had included the restriction of vehicle use, and thus the country's need for petrol.

The forecourt's single building, however, was a different story. Parker could see from several metres away that the petrol station's small convenience store had been raided until only dust remained on its shelves. In the final few weeks before the panic had turned to quiet isolation, people had been desperate. Food, water, and perhaps even more importantly, alcohol, had become the world's new currency. An unopened bottle of vodka had become more valuable than gold. Anything that could help a person blot out their pain and misery was the only luxury the world had left.

"You think it's worth checking out the supermarket?" Cross asked.

"We'd be remiss not to," said Parker. "You never know what we may find."

"Okay. The petrol tank is full so we can move out as soon as Carp and Anderson are done.

Parker nodded and dismissed his Corporal. Then he took up his binoculars and pointed them at the Supermarket. It was situated at the far end of a large flat car park. Cars littered the various spaces and many sat unlocked with their doors hanging open.

Parker's eyes were drawn to something else, though. At the front of the supermarket's main entrance was a stalled convoy of lorries and vans. They sat, end-to-end, in front of the building, blocking any way in through the front. It could turn out to be quite a challenge getting inside.

Five minutes later, Carp and Anderson had secured the now-full Jerry cans back against the side of the Warrior, and were now back inside the tank's troop space.

Schumacher started up the engine and they got going, swivelling in the direction of the supermarket.

"WHO DO you think positioned all these lorries here?" asked Cross. "And why?"

Parker thought the answer was obvious. "They were put there by whoever is inside to keep people out."

Cross raised an eyebrow. "You think we got survivors in there?"

Parker shrugged. "Probably not. Probably just a bunch of dead bodies now, but at some point there were people taking refuge here. It was a good idea to park the trucks in front of the entrance."

"Not so good for us," said Cross. "How the hell are we supposed to get inside?"

"Through the back, I'd imagine. Whoever parked the trucks would have had to get back inside somewhere. They probably left a back door clear. It would still be much easier to defend then the massive sets of automatic glass doors behind the trucks

"So, what's the plan?"

Parker looked around and thought about it. There was a single lane access road that went alongside the supermarket; a road meant for deliveries. It would no doubt lead to the cargo area.

"Wait here," Parker said. I'll go check it out. You hear anything, then follow me, but just keep watch here otherwise."

Parker headed off towards the access road, passed by the front of the building, and began a route down the side. It did indeed lead to a cargo area; a large paved area, big enough for an articulated lorry to turn around. Set against the building was a long, stretched-out platform that would line up with the rear bays of those lorries and allow people to roll out the stock directly into the building. The whole area was lined by a wire-mesh fence and backed onto a stretch of woodland. The space was currently empty.

Up ahead, the wire-mesh fence looped around and cut across the access road. It was linked to a wide metal gate that could obviously be opened to allow lorry access or closed and locked to deny entry. Much to Parker's dismay, it was currently closed and secured by an unusually large padlock. Parker considered whether or not the fence would sustain the weight of the Warrior if they attempted to drive through it.

While Parker considered that notion, someone appeared to his left, high up and in the corner of his eyesight.

"Hold it right there, Corporal Cockhead."

Parker looked up at the man on the roof and narrowed his eyes. "I'm a Sergeant actually, but you can call me Parker. Now, what's the problem, friend?"

The man leant further over the ledge of the building's roof and Parker saw that he was holding a gas-powered nail gun. It was pointed right at Parker's head. Parker's own weapon was stowed in the Warrior.

"You're the one with a problem, Sergeant Shit-Stain. You and your men take that tank and just roll on out of here, you hear? This place belongs to us and we're not following any more of your orders."

Parker shook his head. "What orders?"

"Orders from you and your fucked-up outfit. Tell me, when did the British Army become a bunch of bandits and thieves?"

"I'm not following you. My men and I are just looking for those in need. We're still trying to protect the people of this country."

The man huffed, lowered his nail gun a quarter-inch, and said, "Yeah, right. Well, when you see your buddies, tell them that they aren't taking any more of our food. Not after what they did. They'll burn in hell for what they've done to Stella and the others."

Parker sighed and scratched a fingernail against the tip of his nose. "Who's Stella? If I can understand what you are talking about then perhaps I can help."

The man shook the nail gun at Parker and scrunched up his face in anger. "Look, I'm not going to buy any of your bullshit so just get the hell out of here. There're a dozen men inside this supermarket and they're all ready for a fight – including Brad; the husband of the woman your buddies abducted and raped."

Parker put his hands in the air and begun backing away. It was obvious by the man's angry and suspicious demeanour that the conversation could not be steered in a direction other than the one it was already on; and that seemed like a direction that would result in a three-inch nail in Parker's forehead. It was unclear what had happened, but it was obvious the strange man was distrustful of the military – just like the two teenagers had been.

"Okay, we'll leave," said Parker. "We're not looking for any trouble. You and your people just take care of yourselves."

Parker headed back around to the front of the building where his men were waiting patiently. Corporal Cross nodded to him as he approached. "Find anything?"

Parker shrugged. "Just a nervous guy with a nail gun. I figured it was best to just leave him be."

"Are you kidding me? He could have a supermarket full of supplies in there. We should just take him down; it's only one man."

Parker shook his head. "He told me there was another dozen men inside, not to mention the woman and children there may be."

"Bullshit," said Cross. "He's just saying that to scare us off."

"Look," said Parker, a sternness to his voice. "We have no more right to this place than he does, and we have no way to know if there is anyone inside. People are already beginning to fear the military and I'll be damned if I allow my actions to add to that."

Cross sighed and rolled his eyes. "Fine, you're the boss. So what *do* you want to do? You said we'd discuss it."

Parker let out a sigh and craned his neck to look back at the looming monolith of the brick supermarket. "I think the people inside there need our help, but they aren't about to accept it willingly."

"So we should leave them to it, then

Parker shook his head. "No. I think we should set up nearby and keep an eye on things. Maybe we can find out what's going on. Apparently there is another outfit in the area."

Crossly raised an eyebrow. "You think it's Bristow's unit?"

Parker shrugged. "Who knows? I'm guessing it's somebody else, but we won't know unless we hang around."

"Roger that. There's a grass verge at the edge of the car park. We could set up camp there amongst the trees."

"Do it," said Parker. Best do it now while the ground is dry. Could be raining later."

Cross glanced up at the grey sky and nodded. "More than likely."

WITH THE CVRT crew shelter set up (a large four-person tent) Parker lit his gas lamp beneath a mess tin full of beans. Their rations had been affording them perhaps a thousand calories a day and it was starting to show. His men were visibly tired and the barrel chests of the men and the voluptuous bosom of Anderson had shrunk back against their ribcages. He himself must have dropped more than two stone since things began. They would need to find supplies soon – real supplies.

Like what they may have inside that supermarket.

Parker couldn't deny that the thought of storming the building and taking what they needed by force was tempting, and maybe even sensible, but there was still a part of him that would not allow him to use aggression against British citizens. His body may have been wasting away, but his morals were as strong as ever. Parker held on tightly to that fact.

Schumacher took a seat beside him, the man's face overgrown with thick black stubble. "You okay, Sarge? You look like you remembered you just left the oven on."

Parker laughed. "I wish my problems were as simple as that. I miss worrying about the stupid, little things, you know?"

"Sure I do. I even miss having to clean the toilet. Now I don't even own a toilet to keep clean and it makes me sad. I miss the smell of bleach and air freshener and window polish and everything else that makes a home smell like a home. Now all I ever smell is shit and death and fear. I don't even remember what my wife's perfume smells like anymore. Shit, towards the end, no perfume in the world would have been strong enough, anyway, to get rid of the stench of her…well, you know?"

Parker thought about the flesh destroying evil of the Peeling and nodded. He had lost people to it as well. They all had. "We'll get it all back one day, Schumacher. Eventually people will come out of hiding and start working together again. All of this paranoia – looting and stealing and killing one another – it has to stop eventually.

"I hope so, Sarge, because to tell you the truth, I'm beginning to lose sight of what the hell we're fighting for."

Parker shook his head. Schumacher sounded just like Corporal Cross. "We can't abandon people that need us. If we do, then you're absolutely right: there's no point in fighting. But we aren't going to do that. We're going to show people that there are still those of us that have remembered who we are. We're all still human beings."

"That's what worries me," Schumacher said and left it at that.

The two of them sat in silence for a few minutes until the others joined them. Carp and Cross sat opposite, while Anderson worked on constructing a single birth tent to separate her from the men at night while they slept. Parker's men were the perfect gentlemen, but some habits died hard, and somehow it seemed important to Anderson that she kept her female identity intact.

Parker leant back on the grass verge and looked up at the sky. It was getting dark and the clouds were slowly disappearing into the velvet background of a starry night. The thickness of the air suggested rain and perhaps even a storm was approaching. Parker hoped so. Despite the difficulties that bad weather brought, particularly when travelling, it had a cleansing effect on the world. It washed away the blood from the streets and dampened down the rotting stench of bodies. It swept away the rotting humanity and replaced it with the pureness of nature. Yes, Parker enjoyed the rain.

"Want to play a round?" Carp asked.

"Sure," Parker said, knowing the game that Carp was suggesting. Every night they would all name one thing that they wished to find most in the rubble of what was once England.

"Okay," said Carp. "I'll start. I wish I could find a…piano. I really got a hankering for a bit of Elton John. *Don't let the sun go down on me.*"

"You play piano?" said Parker. "I never knew that."

"Guess there's a lot about each other we don't know. Probably never will. Playing the piano now is about as useless a skill as there is."

"I disagree," said Parker. "I think it's more important that you realise. When we come across a piano, you're going to play for us all. All night long."

"Sounds good to me." Carp grinned.

"Okay," said Schumacher, "me next. I want to find…a jar of paprika. God, I miss a bit of spice on my food. I'd mix it right in with Parker's beans and swallow 'em down whole."

Parker felt his mouth water. He'd never thought about seeking out spices and condiments, but now it seemed like such an obvious thing. It was a small luxury that they could still have in the world.

"What about you, Anderson?" Carp shouted across at the female Private as she finished up erecting her tent.

She turned around and wrinkled her face as she thought about it. "Erm…I guess I would like to find…a bodybuilding calendar. I'm tired of looking at your skinny asses all the time."

They all laughed and Cross took his turn. "I would like to find a nice fat bottle of Jack, or maybe even amaretto. Just before shit got messed up I was really into this drink called a *Godfather.* It was a shot of whisky with a shot of amaretto. Was a nice tipple. Would feel good to get wasted again. I think we'd all agree about that?"

Everyone nodded and then focused their attention of Parker. It was his turn.

He sighed. "I don't know… I guess the thing I would like to find most is a nice, freshly made king-sized bed. One where I could just sleep for the next month. Then I would like to wake up to a nice full-English breakfast."

The sound of people's mouth's watering was almost palpable.

"Cheater," said Anderson, sitting down and joining them. "That was two things. I'll let you off this time, though, just because I agree with your choices. A nice juicy sausage would be heaven right now."

After a brief second, they all started snickering. Anderson blushed and put her hands up. "Okay, okay, calm down. I didn't mean it to sound like that. Anyway, I said a nice juicy sausage, not a bunch of chipolatas."

"Ouch," said Carp. "Way to attack a man's pride."

They all continued laughing, long after the sun had disappeared to be replaced by the moon and twinkling star. It was a beautiful night there amongst the trees.

PARKER'S EYES snapped open inside the darkness of the tent. The noise that had woken him was the sound of hushed voices somewhere outside. He rolled onto his side to find that he was alone and that the shadows of his sleeping comrades were absent.

Parker shuffled out of his sleeping bag and crept to the zipped-up entrance of the tent. Then he listened to the voices outside.

"Should we do something?"

"I don't know. What if they're hostile?"

"We can hold our own. I say we act now while they're not expecting us."

Parker unzipped the tent and pushed his way out into the chilly night. Carp and Cross were standing there.

"What the hell is going on," he demanded. "I've already said that we are not going to bother those people."

Carp put a finger to his lips and shushed him. Parker was about to lose his temper when his eyes caught the distant torchlights. He placed a hand over his brow and squinted to see what was going on.

"They turned up about five minutes ago," said Cross. "Carp was just about to relieve my post when they came flooding out from the woods."

Parker crouched down low in the shadows and continued to stare. "It must be the other outfit the guy at the supermarket was talking about."

"Should we engage?" Cross asked. "They could have Intel."

Parker shook his head. "No, not yet. We need to observe what they're up to first. I got the impression that they're hostile."

"Not to other military, surely?" said Carp.

"We can't assume anything anymore. Keep distance and recon whatever you can. I'll wake Anderson up and dig in here; cover you both if things go bad. Go wake Schumacher up and take him with you."

Parker's men nodded and crept away down the embankment. Parker snuck over to Anderson's tent and whispered her name. Eventually she awoke, and was alert and outside her tent within two minutes. She looked weary, but capable.

"We've got unidentified targets in front of the supermarket. Carp, Cross, and Schumacher are checking it out now. You and I are going to keep a cover point.

Anderson nodded and un-shouldered her rifle. She went prone and targeted the group of strangers down her SUSAT scope. Parker went prone himself about six metres away and pulled up his binoculars to his eyes.

The new group consisted of seven men, fully armed. They all carried the same rifles that Parker's men carried – British Army issue. All of them had arrived by foot and they were too far away to make out their insignias, but their black berets identified them as infantry – grunts. Whether or not they were battled-hardened grunts or green recruits was unclear, but they carried themselves with confidence; shouting and laughing as they milled about the front of the supermarket. There was also one woman with them, but she wasn't military. The woman looked to be in her thirties and was wearing a ragged and stained summer dress. It would likely provide little protection against the harsh kiss of the cold night air. The woman was being lead over to the front of the supermarket, in front of where the trucks were lined up. One of the soldiers – a large man wearing a red bandana instead of a beret or Kevlar helmet – was hollering something at the men around him.

In the corner of his binocular's vision, Parker caught movement on the roof. As he repositioned his focus, he saw that it was the man he had met during the day – the one with the nail gun.

While the sound didn't carry far enough across the tarmac to reach Parker's ears, it was clear that a conversation was being had between the soldier on the ground and the man on the roof. *What the hell is going on? Is this the outfit the guy was talking about? The ones he was wary of?*

Parker continued to watch as the scene unfolded in front of him. The woman was brought in front of the soldier with the bandana. Then something bad happened.

A punch to the woman's ribs dropped her to her knees. Parker heard her pained gasp as it left her anguished lungs. She was now kneeling in a position that Parker knew only too well.

Parker had no time to do anything but watch in terror as the woman was executed – a 5.56mm NATO round through her skull the tool responsible. The sound brought back memories of Afghanistan and Iraq to Parker and, for a moment, he was glued in place, unable to move. Human life had become no more important than that of a lowly housefly. Justice and punishment had fled the world.

Beside him, Anderson cursed. "Goddamn motherfucking barbarians. What the fuck!"

Before Parker knew what was happening, more gunfire rang out. He realised quickly that it was Carp, Cross, and Schumacher – the men having made the autonomous decision to engage. Parker did not blame them. He pulled up his own rifle and flipped off the safety. He squeezed the trigger and caught one of the unknown soldiers in the wrist. The man leapt back behind one of the trucks and looked around in a panic as he struggled to keep a grip on his weapon. All around the car park, the hostiles were taking up cover behind abandoned vehicles. Carp and Cross were nowhere to be seen, but the sounds of their rifles could be heard off in the distant treeline of the surrounding woods.

On the roof, the man with the nail gun was screaming and shouting, seemingly madder than he was scared. Luckily for him, the hostile gunmen in the car park were paying him no mind as they searched around frantically for Parker and his men.

Parker lined up another shot, aiming for the soldier in the red bandana – the leader. The bullet whistled across the car park and headed straight for the man's skull. But it missed by a fraction of an inch. The round struck the aluminium of a nearby panel van and left a ragged dent. The near miss was not lost on the soldier in the bandana and the shock was evident on his face. He shouted above the din of battle and waved an arm to his men. Within seconds, the hostile soldiers were gone, fleeing into the cover of the woods. Several moments later, Carp and Cross appeared from the adjacent treeline and scurried up to the supermarket's blockaded entrance.

Parker surveyed the area through his binoculars, checking that the other unit had truly fled the battlefield. It appeared they had, for now, but Parker knew they would just be regrouping. They would come back.

"Come, on," he said to Anderson. "We'll rendezvous up front with Cross and the others."

Parker and Anderson kept low and beat a path between abandoned cars and overturned shopping trolleys until they were at the front of the Supermarket with Cross.

"Status?" Parker asked.

"We're all fine," replied Cross. "Bad news is: so are they. We only downed one of them."

Parker nodded. He had already noticed the dead soldier slumped up against a battered Honda Civic. Its iconic lighting strip above the front bumper was smashed and smeared with blood. Then Parker turned his attention to the dead woman, still lying in the spot where she had been callously executed by the solider wearing the bandana.

"That was Stella," came a voice from above.

Parker spun on his heels and brought his rifle up to his shoulder. It was the man on the roof. The man with the nail gun.

"S'pose you've earned yourself an invitation," the man said. "Hold on. I'll come let you in."

Parker looked at his men and shrugged. "About time something went right for a change."

TWO MINUTES LATER, the man with the nail gun appeared at side access fence where Parker had first met him. He quickly unlocked the thick padlock and dragged the chain-link door open. It scratched a white line into the tarmac as it slid across the ground.

As soon as Parker and his men passed through the gate, their host relocked it again anxiously. His hands were visibly shaking.

"You okay?" Parker asked.

The man fiddled with his hair and sniffed his nose. "Yeah… I-I'm fine. It's just… Well, I think I was about to pretty much give up before you guys showed up. That asshole Mack would have finally finished me off this time."

"Mack?" asked Parker. "The guy in the bandana? Who is he?"

"I figured you'd know better than me. Being soldiers and all."

"Unfortunately, the British Army is a big group – *was* a big group, anyway – most soldiers don't know each other from Adam. I've never met the man before."

The man with the nail gun unlocked a small door on the supermarket's loading bay and allowed everyone to funnel inside. "Well," he said, walking after them. "You can take my word for it that he is a scumbag piece of shit. I wish he'd caught a bullet when you fired on him."

"We'll get the fucker next time," said Cross.

Parker disapproved of bad language in front of civilians, but when he saw what relief the show of bravado caused on their host's face, he decided to let it slide.

"You guys hungry?" the man asked them. "A lot of stuff spoiled early on, which is part of the reason why the whole place stinks so bad, but there is tons of canned food and other stuff that is just fine. Help yourself to anything you see."

"Hell, yes," said Schumacher.

Parker put a hand up to shush his men before they became uncontrollably excited. Food was the world's only important resource nowadays and they had just stumbled upon a goldmine by the sounds of things. They were still soldiers, though, and acting giddy was inappropriate. "We won't take food from your people," Parker said. "We will just take whatever you can spare."

The man with the nail gun stopped and turned to face Parker. He looked beaten and glum. "Yeah, about that...My people consists of just me. Everyone else is dead. I lied to you before to warn you off."

When Parker stepped from the warehouse into the supermarket's public area, all he could see, all he could smell, was death."

AFTER ALMOST PUKING at the sight of so many bodies, Parker and the others had slunk back into the warehouse and had followed their host into a comfy staffroom. It was a disconcerting contrast to the horror outside.

"What the hell happened here, man?" Cross spoke in a tone somewhere between aggression and pleading.

The man put down his nail gun on the table where he sat and shook his head. His body had slumped so much that he seemed inches shorter. "Lots of things happened. First man to die was a guy named Stephen. He tried to rape one of the woman we had here and...well, I guess the rest of us retaliated. Then Mandy went into a diabetic coma and died as soon as she used up all the Pharmacy's insulin. Tom and Annie committed suicide; both their sons died of The Peeling. Talking of which, there was a second outbreak of the disease. Just when we thought everyone left alive was immune, about a dozen of us came down with it. We tried our best to nurse them, but it was useless. It took weeks for them to rot down to the bone. Then Mack came and finished off the rest of us."

"How many were left when Mack came," Parker asked.

"There were nine of us. Four woman, five men. When Mack first came, he wanted food, and we gave it to him. We were glad to see him and his men. We were naïve."

Parker looked around the room and saw empty wrappers and dog-eared magazines. "You've been holing up in this room?"

"Yeah. I figured it would be unhealthy mixing with all the bodies out there. Plus they were my friends, you know? Besides, I'm just one man. I can't move three dozen bodies. Got nowhere to take 'em anyway."

"What's your name?" asked Anderson. There was sympathy in her voice.

The man looked surprised by the question. It was almost as if the notion of having a name was lost on him. Perhaps it had been a while since he had shared it with anybody. "My name is Dennis. I was a carpenter before all this happened. Hence the nail gun." He motioned at the power tool on the table. "Gas powered. Thought about using on myself lately."

Anderson patted the man on the back. She smiled. "There's no need to do that now. We can get you out of here."

"Screw that," said Cross. "We should bunker down here. We got food, security-"

"Security!" Dennis laughed. "Mack and his men have made sure that security is the last thing we have here."

"What happened to the nine of you that were left when Mack arrived?" Parker enquired.

"After we fed him and his men, they came back, but this time they didn't want food."

"They wanted the woman," said Anderson, looking sick to her stomach.

Dennis nodded and looked sick himself. "We wouldn't give them up, of course. So Mack and his men assaulted the supermarket. We were unarmed and were going to kill us all. Once they got inside. My wife offered to go with them as long as they left the supermarket. Then the other woman showed their support and stood beside her. The women sacrificed themselves so that the men would be safe. Mack just laughed about the whole thing, like it was a game or something. He took the woman and they drove off, but, before he left, he told us to be gone by morning; that the supermarket was his.

"But you're still here," said Cross.

Dennis nodded. "When Mack left, we decided to barricade the supermarket. They had taken everything from us and we were damned if we were going to let them take this place."

"So what did you do?" Parker asked.

"Got the trucks up against the entrance, used the hardware supplies in the warehouse to nail the windows and doors shut. Found the biggest padlock we could and secured the access gate. Made some firebombs from whiskey and lighter fluid. It didn't protect us, though. Soon as we put up resistance, Mack brought out the woman. They were tied up like animals, bleeding and crying. I have nightmares about what they must have gone through. When Mack started executing them one after the other, the men I was with surrendered. They went outside to give themselves up. Mack shot them all."

"Why didn't you go out there with them?" Anderson asked.

"Because I was a coward. I was too frightened to go outside, so I locked myself in this staffroom while the other men went outside."

"Well, being a coward is probably the only reason you're still alive," Parker said.

"When I had the guts to come out, I saw the dead woman and the dead men and I realised that there was no way out of this. Mack would kill me eventually, my wife, Stella, too. The only purpose I had left was to make it as hard on him and his barbarians as I could. I decided to keep fighting until a bullet found me. I would have finally given up today if you hadn't been here."

"That woman was your wife," Parker surmised. The woman Mack executed in front of the building was your wife."

Dennis nodded and a tear spilled from his eye. "I thought she was already dead. When I saw her, I thought maybe there was a chance Mack would give her back to me if I just stopped fighting and left. But he shot her before I even had chance to say anything to her. They've had her for weeks. I barely recognised her. Even though she was alive, her eyes…her eyes were dead. I'm glad she passed on. I hate thinking it, but she could never have gotten through what they did to her. I just wanted to be dead too, to go wherever she was. Then you started firing on Mack's men and here we are."

"Where are they based?" Parker asked. "Are they nearby?"

Dennis shrugged. "I couldn't tell you. The nearby woods aren't massive but I figure it a good place to set up camp. It won't be long before they come back."

"You're sure they will come back?" Cross asked.

Dennis nodded adamantly. "Mack won't let this go. He doesn't accept the word, *no*. He'll be irate that you took out one of his men. I guarantee you that he will be back."

Parker nodded and began to think. "Then, we make sure we're ready for him."

PARKER SPENT the next two hours directing Dennis and his men in various tasks designed to increase their tactical advantage should another attack occur. They stockpiled as many food and supplies from the supermarket floor back into the warehouse as they could. Then they undertook the unenviable task of stacking the heavy freezer units, shelving stacks, and till desks up against the front of the building where the plate glass windows could potentially be breached. The task was unenviable due to the rotting, foul-smelling corpses that littered the area. Some were mottled grey skeletons – victims of The Peeling, while others featured gunshot wounds no doubt delivered by Mack's men. The odour of death was something they were all used to by now, but this amount of death so close together was still enough to turn their stomachs. Parker forced a grin onto his face; it was a proven technique to fight off the urge to retch. He just hoped Dennis did not misinterpret it as disrespect.

The current task that occupied them all was the search for viable weaponry. Dennis had his nail gun and Parker's men had their rifles, but their ammunition was low after the previous fire fight. They needed alternative means of arming themselves in case Mack's resources outlasted theirs.

Cross was busy, emptying bottles of bleach and detergent onto the floor of several aisles, while Schumacher and Anderson attempted to block the adjacent aisles with pallets, cardboard boxes, and household stock items. The plan was to create a bottleneck, and funnel Mack's men into one or two individual aisles, creating a kill zone. The cleaning fluids on the floor would hopefully cause one or two of their attackers to slip and fall, and would, at the very least, slow them down as they were forced to step carefully. The fumes coming up off the floor may also have the added benefit of blinding Mack's men.

Dennis was busy super-gluing nails to the floor and shelving units. It seemed absurd, but if he could secure as many nails in an upright position as he could, there was every chance that one of Mack's men would plant a foot down on one of them. Every time Dennis covered a small area with nails, he would drape flat pieces of cardboard over the top, obscuring the hazard. Somehow the supermarket, that would once have been the epitome of mundane, civilised life, was now more akin to the booby-trapped expanses of 60's Vietnam. The world was a battleground and all were warriors.

"Hey, Sarge, take this," Anderson came over and handed him a large chef's knife.

"He frowned. I already have a knife." He pointed to the army-issue blade on his belt.

"I know. But I thought we could use a spare to throw if the fighting goes close-quarters."

Parker laughed. "I think that only works in the movies, but I'll take it just in case." He took the brand-new tungsten blade and slid it into his belt. It wouldn't hurt to have *too many* knives.

It was time to wrap things up, bunker in. "Okay, everyone," said Parker. "Let's fall back to the warehouse. Dennis? How do you get up to the roof? It wouldn't hurt to have someone posted up there on watch."

"There's a ladder at the back of the warehouse," Dennis explained. "Leads up to a walkway and the roof hatch."

"Okay," said Parker, heading through to the back. "Anderson, you take first watch. Cover up with whatever you can and keep your eyes on the treeline."

"Roger that," she said, double-timing it deeper into the warehouse.

"What should the rest of us do?" Dennis asked.

"We wait," said Parker.

Parker was about to fall asleep on the one of the staffroom couches when something caused his mind to snap back to full alertness. He looked around the unlit room and could see the soft shapes of his comrades sleeping. He could hear their gentle snores.

Parker stood up from the sofa and listened out. He was groggy and unsure of what he had heard, but somehow he knew something was up. After years of being in the Armed Services, Parker had a sixth sense for danger.

Parker picked up his rifle from where it was propped up against the wall and wrapped the strap around his neck. Then he slid out of the room and into the pitch-black darkness of the warehouse. There was complete silence in the building, but Parker didn't trust it. He headed for the ladder at the back of the area; the one that led up to Anderson's position on the roof. Parker listened out but could make out no sound from up above.

He placed his hands on the rungs of the ladder and raised his foot onto the first step. He climbed slowly, cautiously. With each rung he rose up, he became more and more certain that things were wrong. Anderson was an alert sentry and should be aware of his approach. She should have called out to him by now.

He pushed open the roof hatch and slowly rose up to see over the top. Anderson's was lying prone against the far edge, covered by cardboard and some old tarpaulin. If he hadn't expected to see her, he may have missed her completely. She was well camouflaged.

"*Anderson!*" He called out in a hush. "Anderson, what's your status?"

No answer.

Goddamn it. Parker shook his head and prayed she was just asleep. He would bollock the shit out of her for neglecting her post but it would be a relief all the same. He hoisted himself up onto the roof and kept low to the ground, shuffling forward on his elbows and knees.

As he got closer, Anderson still did not move. She was like part of the building, completely still.

He reached her and spoke out again. "Anderson, wake the fuck up!"

He clenched his hand around her ankle, expecting her to flinch and wake up with a start. But she did nothing. He shook her leg and was dismayed to find no response. He crawled up closer.

Then he saw that it was not Anderson.

"Jesus *fuck!* Carp?"

Carp's face was a caved-in mess of blood and gristle, but the thick black hair was a dead giveaway. Before Parker could even speculate on what had happened to the Private, a bullet shattered the cement two inched in front of him, sending stabbing shards of masonry into his eyes.

"Shit! Shit! Shit!" Parker rolled away, sliding his body back towards the roof hatch. Mack's men had a hotshot, someone who'd been able to take Carp out without him even seeing them. The attack had begun. It was time for battle stations.

PARKER KICKED OPEN the door to the staffroom and shouted at the top of his lungs. "Hands on socks, off cocks! We're under siege."

His men were immediately on their feet, well-drilled by years of midnight inspections. Dennis was a little slower, but also impressively alert. Parker spotted Anderson grabbing her rifle and approached her. "Anderson, what the fuck happened? Why is Carp up on the roof, dead?"

Her face dropped. Behind her Cross and Schumacher cursed. "Carp is dead?"

"As a fuckin' doornail. Why was he up there?"

"He said he couldn't sleep. Came up to relieve me. I was beat so I saw no reason to argue."

Parker nodded. It didn't really matter. Carp was dead and nothing would change that. He was a good man, but too many good men had been lost to mourn each one.

"Shit, it should have been me up there," said Anderson. "I should be dead, not Carp. It's such a waste."

"Beat yourself up later," said Parker. "Mack's men are out there, right now. We have to take up positions."

Anderson nodded and headed out the room, back in full-on professional mode. Cross and Schumacher followed after her. Dennis looked at Parker with fear in his eyes.

"You ready," Parker asked the man.

He nodded. "Everyone gotta die sometime. I just hope I take as many of Mack's men with us as we can."

Parker put a hand on the man's shoulder and looked him in the eye. "We'll get them all, Dennis. They aren't getting this supermarket. You have my word."

Dennis nodded and ran out of the staffroom.

Two minutes later, everyone had spread out at the back of the store, focusing their fire into the bottleneck they had created in the centre aisles.

Parker currently crouched behind a heavy, glass and steel deli counter. Cross had taken position in the alcove of the supermarket's bakery, aiming his rifle through the bread shelves. Dennis, Anderson, and Schumacher held positions behind a barricade made from plastic-wrapped pallets of tinned goods: beans, spaghetti hoops, and other assorted sundries.

The supermarket was silent as they waited. Mack's men were not hasty or impatient. No help would arrive to help Parker, no reinforcements or nearby units. There was no reason for Mack not to take his time. He was no doubt out there, right now, planning his next move.

Parker held his breath and listened harder. What was the holdup, though? Taking your time was one thing, but the longer Mack took, the longer it gave his enemy to prepare. He should have been attacking by now.

"Hey," Cross hissed from over by the bakery. "D'you hear that?"

Parker did hear it. A far away humming, getting louder. A mechanical sound. Almost like a…

Parker hit the floor and shouted, "Get down!" The explosion rocked the store at its very foundations, and glass, debris, and bloody chunks from the piled-up corpses from the front of the store filled the air and landed with the pattering sound of hailstorms and rain.

"What the fuck!" shouted Cross.

"They rigged a goddamn car with explosives; rammed it into the barricades outside."

"*Explosives?* Where the hell did they get ordinance from?"

"Who knows," said Parker. "It's there for the taking for anyone who knows where to look. It doesn't matter. Just get ready to return fire."

Mack's men started firing their weapons before Parker even managed to spot one of them. The glass of the deli counter splinted but did not break – otherwise a bullet or two may have found its way into Parker's chest. He clambered across to the side of the counter and blind-fired into the supermarket, hoping to buy his own men the briefest chance to set themselves against their attackers.

Parker heard someone cry out at the front of the store and he couldn't tell if it was from a bullet or if they had trodden on one of Dennis's hidden nails. Dust filled the air and obscured vision beyond a few feet. Parker fired into the mist.

More rounds hit the deli counter and Parker ducked down. He

turned to his right to tell Cross to coordinate fire with him, to pin down the enemy.

But Cross was dead.

Cross sported a bullet wound in his forehead the size of a penny while the back of his head had exploded in a wound the size of a tennis ball.

Parker shook his head and cursed. "That motherfucking sniper."

Parker turned to his right and crawled beside the deli counter. Bullets seemed to hit all around him. Ahead of him, Anderson and Schumacher returned fire as best they could, keeping their heads down and hoping for the best. Beyond them, Dennis fired nails from his power tool wildly into the air, sending shards of iron death in a dozen directions.

There was a brief cessation in the firing and Parker knew that Mack's men were reloading. He shot up over the deli counter and screamed at his own men to, "Fire!" He took careful aim down his sights and scanned the area as time seemed to stand still. At the front of the store, the dust was clearing and Parker made out the briefest flash of green material. He squeezed the trigger and flinched as he heard his bullet hit soft flesh beneath the camouflaged uniform of his target. The man hit the ground screaming, landing on the cardboard-covered nails. His screams got louder.

"*Man down,*" one of Mack's men cried out, and Parker smiled as another body hit the ground in the aisles, slipping on the bleach and detergent and then taking a bullet from Anderson while he helplessly tried to keep his balance.

"Shit! Cooper's down!"

Parker's men seemed to be getting the upper hand, but that all depended on how many men Mack had with him. Parker's rifle ran dry and he crouched down to reload. He pulled a magazine from a pouch on his belt but frowned when he felt it was light. He'd forgotten that his current magazine was all he had left.

"Damn it." Staying low, he sprinted towards the barricade that protected Anderson and the others. They wouldn't have any spare ammo to give him, but he could act as a spotter for them and try to pick their targets.

As Parker neared the others, something struck the floor in front of him and rolled across the floor. His eyes went wide as he recognised what it was. "Get down!" he screamed. "Grenade!"

Parker skidded to the floor and began clambering backwards on his hands and rump. Anderson looked down at the grenade at her feet and froze. Just when Parker was sure he was about to watch her get blown limb from limb, her body lurched forward, with such force that she tumbled and skidded a clear ten feet across the floor towards Parker.

Parker shook his head in disbelief as Dennis threw aside his nail gun and leapt on top of the grenade. A muffled explosion erupted from beneath him and blood splatter hit the floor all around him. He was dead before even a full second passed.

Schumacher came running up and looked down at the mess. "Shit! I guess he wasn't willing to stand around and watch another woman die."

"We'll mourn him later," said Parker. "I promised we'd take out every last one of Mack's men and I intend on keeping my word."

Anderson fired off another couple rounds and then they all huddled down. "What's the plan?" she asked Parker.

"We need to fall back to the warehouse. There's only one entrance to focus on. We don't have the ammunition for anything else."

As one, they moved behind the deli counter and shuffled towards the warehouse entrance. Parker ushered everyone in before him and then slid in behind them. They immediately made for the nearest stack of pallets and aimed their rifles at the doors, except for Parker who was out of ammo.

"You fire on the first fucker that comes through that door," Parker ordered.

"You can count on it," said Anderson.

Sure enough, the first guy to come through the warehouse doors caught a fatal bullet to the chest. His body hit the floor already dead, and several more men spilled into the area spread out. Parker pulled out the chef's knife Anderson had given him earlier and threw it with all his strength at the doorway. It struck a man in the face and caused a bad gash, but that was it. "Knew that shit wouldn't work!"

Anderson and Schumacher kept firing their rifles, but never managed to land anther round successfully as the enemy took cover. Then the grim click of their rifles going empty caused them both to take cover themselves. All three of them were now out of ammo.

Through the doorway of the warehouse came Mack, red bandana soaked with sweat and covered in rubble dust. He had a military shotgun around his neck but was letting it hang loose with the muzzle pointed at the floor. He began to laugh.

"Come out, come out, wherever you are. If you had any more bullets you'd be firing 'em, so give up the ghost, my friends. We tried to take this place politely, but I'm afraid it has had to come to this."

"Who do you think you are?" Parker shouted out from behind a stack of Blu-Ray players. "You signed an oath to protect this country, not rape and pillage it."

Mack laughed. "Rape and Pillage. I like that. Like Vikings, yeah?"

"Like depraved animals, more like," said Anderson.

"Ooh, a lady with a smart mouth. Looks like it's our lucky day, boys."

"Not gonna happen," said Parker.

"Beg to differ." Mack fired his shotgun and took out a chunk of the DVD players. Parker flinched and kept low. He made eye-contact with both Anderson and Schumacher. Both of them looked back with fear, but also defiance.

"Look," said Mack. "Just get the hell out of here. We're not interested in you. We just want the food here. It's ours. You can go."

"Yeah, right," said Parker. "Is that the deal you made with all of the dead men and women at the front of this store?"

"They were just civvies, I have no respect for them. The world belongs to the strong now. I have respect for a serviceman such as yourself. You can go. You're man, too. Just not the woman you got with you."

Schumacher leapt from behind a stack of pallets and came at Mack from the side. While they had all been talking, he had managed to flank the man and was now lunging for him with a knife.

Mack spun around, the lowered shotgun too long and cumbersome to bring up in time to deflect the blow. Schumacher swung out with his blade.

The sound of gunfire in the cramped confines of the warehouse was deafening. Parker peeked around the corner in horror as Schumacher flew back against a stack of cardboard boxes and immediately started bleeding from what was left of his face. Beside him stood one of Mack's men, a smoking sidearm pistol in his hand.

"Who the hell are you guys with?" asked Parker, trying to stall for time. "All your weapons: shotguns, grenades?"

Mack laughed again. "Let's just say we were based out of Hereford when the shit hit the fan. We forgot to bring our beige berets with us."

Parker's eyes went wide and so did Anderson's. They were fucked. There were two of them facing off against a squad of SAS. The SAS were notoriously so tough that even if Parker had a fresh mag of ammo and emptied every round into Mack, the guy would probably just shake it off and keep coming. There was no way to win this.

Anderson spoke up. "If I come with you," she said. "Will you let my sergeant go? He's a good man and has helped a lot of people. If you let him leave I will come with you...*willingly.*"

"What the fuck are you doing?" said Parker in disbelief. "No way are you going with that psycho."

"It's the only way either of us will get through this alive. Besides, I'm already dead anyway."

Before Parker had chance to ask her what she meant, Mack answered the proposal. "You have my word. I'm not in the business of killing those who don't stand in my way. As long as they let me take what I want. And having a woman come *willingly* sounds like an interesting novelty. You have a deal. Come with us and your noble sergeant can go."

Parker was looking at Anderson and shaking his head. She looked right back at him with fear in her eyes, but it seemed to be fading, becoming something else; consternation. "Just let me say goodbye," she said. "Two minutes."

Mack huffed. "Fine."

Behind the stack of Blu-Ray players, Anderson moved up close to Parker. "Don't worry about me," she said.

"Are you crazy?" he said.

She pulled up one of her shirt sleeves to her elbow. "No, I'm not crazy. I'm sick. And I ain't getting better."

Anderson's arm was covered in a swath of pus-filled blisters. In the worst places they had come away to show weeping, raw flesh. She had it. She had The Peeling.

Parker felt sick, but managed to keep his voice low. "What the fuck? You have it! But there's been no new cases in weeks. The disease is supposed to be gone."

Anderson shrugged. "Guess it hasn't finished with us yet. It started yesterday evening. The rate it's spreading I don't even have a week left."

Parker's mouth dropped open. "I...I'm so sorry."

"Don't be. Those fuckers out there don't know I'm ill, so they'll take me as a fucking piece of meat and let you go."

"I still can't leave you," said Parker. "I can't leave you to live even one day with those monsters."

"You won't have to. As long as you do one last thing for me." She whispered into Parker's ear and he nodded. Then he smiled. It was a good plan.

"Okay," shouted Anderson. "I'm coming out, but Parker is going out the back and round the access road. You let him go peacefully and I'll be the best fuck you ever had. You try to chase him down and I'll struggle and bite until not one of you has a dick left. Deal?"

"Deal," said Mack impatiently. "Let's get it over with."

Anderson stepped out into the warehouse while Parker hurried for the back door. It felt wrong leaving her, against everything he stood for, but he had something he needed to do. As he fled the building, the sounds of Mack and his men tormenting Anderson turned his stomach. At least she wouldn't be suffering for long.

The fresh air of outside hit Parker like a slap in the cheeks. He hadn't realised how stifling the rotting atmosphere of the supermarket had been. He was glad to be out of there. What had at first seemed like a haven had instead turned out to be another sanctuary of nightmares.

He passed by the gate and soon realised that it was still padlocked. He looked around and quickly spotted a row of wheeled recycling bins. Parker grabbed the nearest one and yanked it with him towards the gate. Once it was in position, he hoisted himself up on top and managed to claw himself over the chain link, ignoring the pain of flesh grating from his palms.

Once his boots were back down on the tarmac, he sprinted across the car park, heading in front of the supermarket. The flaming remains of an old Volvo saloon stood in a blackened mess against the barricade trucks and Parker couldn't help but marvel at the amount of explosives Mack must have possessed. He kept on running, cutting between abandoned cars and trolleys, heading for where he and his men – all dead now – had left the Warrior. When bedding down on the night previous, they had covered the tank with a green canvas tarp. Luckily, Mack and his men had not noticed it up on the bank between the trees. As much as Parker had hated being tied to the rolling coffin the last several weeks, it now looked and felt like home. He was glad to return to it – he just felt great sorrow that he was returning alone.

Parker pulled back the tarp and leapt up onto the Warrior's flanks. He examined the vehicle's twin rocket launchers at its rear and was glad to see that they were all still primed and loaded: eight high-explosive rocket-propelled grenades.

Parker opened up the command hatch and slid himself down into the cockpit. He switched on the console and breathed a sigh of relief that the tank's battery was as healthy as when they had left it. The targeting readout flashed up and showed him a black and white picture of the trees in front of him. After tapping in a few commands, the display switched to display something else: the supermarket.

The large, square building in black and white seemed sinister, more like a prison or asylum. He would be glad to bring it to its knees. Parker tapped in the relevant commands, targeted the twin grenade launchers on the back of the building, where the warehouse was located, and then sent the orders.

With a fizz not unlike the sound of champagne being uncorked, eight rockets hurtled high into the air. Parker could not see them from within the cockpit, but he knew that they would be about to reach the apex of their climb, before tilting in mid-air and falling back down to earth; their unmoving target was a certainty.

Parker watched on the screen as the supermarket bloomed white in a violently shifting cloud. A split-second later, the tank shook and his ear drums popped as the air pressure became charged. With a grim smile, not of happiness but perhaps of satisfaction, Parker climbed out onto the roof of the tank and surveyed the chaos of the rubble that had once been a supermarket. The hollow building, lacking in central support had crumpled like a stack of cards, so flat that no one inside could possibly have lived. The area was decimated and all that now lived was a smattering of fires. Anderson was dead; so were Cross, Schumacher, Carp, and Dennis. But so were Mack and all of his men.

Parker didn't know if the sacrifice of his good men was enough to make the death of Mack's evil men worth it. He hoped it was. One thing was for sure, the nightmares of this world were not yet over. Anderson had proved that The Peeling was not yet finished, and, as Parker looked up at the dawn sky and saw unnatural lights filling it by the thousands, he started to understand that the disease that had destroyed the world was not the end of things to come, but just the beginning of something worse.

The lights in the sky were getting bigger.

THE PEELING: BOOK 4

PATIENT ZERO

The spacious minibus cut through the English countryside like a scalpel through flesh. From within its air-conditioned cocoon, it would be easy to forget the sweltering sun that beat down its summer rays. The tinted windows made the world outside seem dark.

Dr Gregory Penn watched the farms, fields and forests roll by and wondered how long it had been since he last saw a building. Being so far away from London gave him an unsettled feeling that he did not like. It was like he was somehow leaving civilisation behind.

I'm fleeing. Escaping my life so that I might find another.

But it was a choice he had made. Greg had finally sold out to the big money offer and was working for the Government. No more helping sick people in hospitals, no more saving lives; now he would spend his days researching whatever his new bosses told him to – whether it was a weapon of mass destruction or an anti-wrinkle cream.

The black-suited driver of the mini-bus turned down a wooded lane and reduced their speed. The vehicle began to bounce on its axels as the road became uneven and rocky.

"Are we nearly there?" Greg asked. The long drive was giving him too much time to think. He was getting anxious, doubting his decision.

Am I really cut out for this? Chief Virologist at the age of thirty-eight?

Well, I'm not cut out for anything else. Was never any good at being a friend, a husband…

"We will be there in less than ten minutes, sir," replied the driver.

Greg sighed. It was a relief to be close after so many hours of driving. With all of the back roads they'd taken, he wasn't even sure which part of the country he was in anymore. They could even have passed north into Scotland for all he knew. They'd certainly be driving long enough since Lewisham.

Up ahead, the minibus encountered a chain link fence. The driver slipped a mobile phone from his pocket and made a call. A few seconds later, a section of the fence slid aside on rails and the minibus passed through.

An automatic fence in the middle of nowhere... Very cloak and dagger.

A short while later, the muddy road opened up into a wide clearing. The area between the thick woods was almost a perfect circle – unnatural in its perfect curves. In the centre was a single building no bigger than a garden shed.

What the hell? This is the UK's finest Medical Research facility?

"Please exit the vehicle," said the driver. "Then proceed to the building ahead."

Greg didn't move.

"Sir, please do as I've instructed."

Greg cleared his throat and then unclasped his seatbelt. He pushed open the door and scooted along his seat. Twigs and dry leaves crunched beneath his feet as he stepped out of the minibus. The sounds seemed immense in the silence of the clearing. He slid the door closed behind him and headed up to the front of the vehicle. He leant towards the driver's window and tried to see through the tint.

"Excuse me," he said through the glass. "I think there must be some sort of mistake. This is-"

The minibus took off in reverse. The brakes squealed and the vehicle spun around to face the way from which they had come. Then it sped off into the woods, leaving Greg alone in the clearing.

Really not enjoying my first day so far.

He took a few tentative steps towards the small hut ahead of him and then stopped. He looked around, expecting someone to jump out of the trees laughing and saying that this was all one big joke. When it was clear that that would not happen, he carried on walking.

The building ahead had no windows. Just a single, metal door set into a concrete surround.

Greg reached the structure and placed himself in front of the entrance. The door did not appear to have a handle, or even a lock, and when he tried to push it open it held tight.

Great! What am I supposed to do?

A thought occurred to Greg and he banged on the door with his fist.

Anybody there?

The door opened, moving aside gently as if in the hands of some unseen butler. Beyond was a steep staircase that headed straight down into darkness. Greg stared in disbelief. It felt like he was looking down into the bowels of hell.

Despite his anxiety, Greg took the first step. Then the next. Then several more. He seemed to descend for ever.

It wasn't long before he was surrounded by shadows on all sides. The door at the top of the stairs had closed and with it, so too, the light from outside. The only thing preventing absolute darkness was a blinking green light lower down the staircase. Greg continued hoped it represented the end of his confusing journey.

Go towards the light, Gregory.

It turned out that that the green light was affixed to a security camera. Greg stared into its lens and imagined he could see someone at the other end watching him.

There was a hiss in the darkness up ahead and then a vertical sliver of golden light appeared. Slowly the sliver widened into a gap and a brightly lit hallway appeared beyond. Greg found it hard to breathe, but he managed to keep going and passed through the newly opened entrance.

He entered a featureless, white corridor. A voice from above startled him.

"WELCOME DR PENN. PLEASE ENTER THE SECOND DOOR ON YOUR RIGHT WHERE YOU WILL BE MET BY AN ADMINSTRATOR."

Greg noticed that the corridor was lined by dozens of doors on each side. The one he had been directed to was no different to any of the others. He did as instructed and opened the second door on the right.

Inside, a diminutive, bespectacled man sat behind a large, aluminium desk. He stood up immediately upon Greg's arrival.

"Dr Penn," the man said, heading out from behind the desk and offering his hand. "It's a pleasure to meet you. My name is Dr Matthews and I am one of the administrators here. I am also the site's physician, so I will be required to give you a health check tomorrow morning."

Greg shook the man's small hand and smiled. "A Pleasure. I have to say, I'm a little put out by all of this."

The man nodded and laughed as if he understood exactly what he meant. "We apologise for the clandestine nature of your arrival. I'm sure you understand that this facility is an extremely sensitive Government secret. Only the Americans know about it. The entire structure is erected beneath the ground and the lack of buildings up top is to avoid detection by satellites. Google Maps is the enemy."

Greg frowned at the man.

"That was a joke, Dr Penn. We may be secretive, but we still have a sense of humour."

"You keep saying *we*," Greg commented.

"We're a community down here, Dr Penn. It has to be that way with the nature of things. You understand that you will remain in this facility for the next three years?"

Greg nodded. He remembered signing the paperwork with a trembling. "I didn't realise I would be staying in a hole in the ground, though."

Dr Matthews stepped up to the Greg and placed a hand on his back. He began leading him back out into the corridor. "I think you will find that things are more than to your liking. But the only way for you to believe it is to see it with your own eyes. Come on."

Greg allowed himself to be ushered back into the corridor. Dr Matthews led him opposite, to a door on the other side of the corridor. Without word, he opened it and pushed Greg through.

Inside was a vast catacomb of wonders. A space the size of several football fields was laid out with numerous partitions, office cubicles, and blinking electronics. Hundreds of lab-coated personnel rushed about in a fever of hard work and commitment. Huge air conditioner units roared overhead.

"We just call this area, *The Floor*," Dr Matthews told him. "It's where we conduct most of our theoretical research and low-level experiments – blood work and the like."

Greg scanned the area with wonderment. He was aware that his jaw was hanging open but did nothing about it. "It's…It's…"

"Yep, it's something, alright. You probably won't spend too much time here, though. A scientist of your ability will no doubt be more at home in one of the private labs. Shall we?"

Greg did not speak as Dr Matthews continued with the tour. The man introduced him to the luxurious staff lounge, crammed with televisions, videogames, pool tables, and many other forms of entertainment. There was even a modest library crammed with mass market paperbacks.

Next was the canteen, which had a menu which would put most restaurants to shame. Dozens of people ate there, while some worked away on laptops and tablets.

"It's open twenty-four hours a day," Dr Matthews explains. "Most of our more committed researchers often work odd hours, so the cafeteria never closes."

Greg's stomach rumbled as he thought about eating. "Great. So what's next?"

"I suppose I should take you to your lab to meet your team. Then you can settle into your apartment."

Greg balked. "Apartment?"

Dr Matthews smiled. "Why of course. We don't expect you to spend three years in a bedsit. As a department supervisor, you will have one of the facility's larger suites. I think you'll like it."

"I…thank you. I would like to meet my team now." Greg was beginning to find the ground beneath his feet. He was here to do a job, to lead a team of scientists. Now that he had fallen down the rabbit hole, he was ready to get to work.

Dr Matthews led him back out into the main corridor and over to a steel door at the end marked RESEARCH LABORATORIES. B.S. lv 3, 4, 5.

Greg frowned. "Level 5? Bio Safety levels only go up to 4."

"Not here they don't."

"So…what is level 5?"

Dr Matthews looked at him like he was dumb. "More dangerous than level 4."

Greg sighed. "But what on earth is more dangerous than a level 4 containment facility?"

"Anything that can cause extinction."

Greg felt his jaw drop again.

"You see," said Dr Matthews. "There are other reasons we built this facility under the ground in the middle of nowhere. Very good reasons. And you, Dr Penn, are about to be placed in charge of several of them."

Greg's lab was deep underground. They had accessed it via an elevator ride that seemed to take forever. It turned out that all of the staff in the Level 5 labs had apartments nearby – Greg's included. It would allow him to roll out of bed and be at work within two minutes. He had a feeling, however, that the adjacency of their living quarters may well play into potential quarantine scenarios.

Keep us all bunched up together in case something gets inside us.

Dr Matthews led him down a sterile hallway and directed him into a large office. The long, walnut desk in the centre of the room already had a name plate with Greg's name and qualifications on it. He had worked at many of the UK's finest hospitals, but he had never had a desk like this. He went over and picked up the name plate. DR GREGORY J. PENN, BMSc, DSc.

"You like?" Dr Matthews asked him.

Greg placed the name plate back down and nodded. "I do. My team?"

"I'll send them right in. They can brief you from here." Dr Matthews stepped forward and shook Greg's hand. "A pleasure to meet you, Doctor. I'll see you in the morning for your medical."

"Good to meet you, too. See you soon."

Dr Matthews left the office and Greg headed behind his desk. He sat down on the plush leather chair and slid his legs into the foot pass of his new desk. He felt at home already. A little over five minutes later, three young doctors entered his office: two gangly males and a dowdy looking female. All three of them were pale and sickly looking.

Lack of sunlight? Or overworked? Will have to find out and see if I can do something to improve working conditions. That will make them loyal to me.

"Good to meet you all," he said to them. "While I intend to lead this team from the front, I will be relying on your for the next couple of days to help me get settled. I imagine you are three of the brightest minds this country has to offer. I look forward to working with you. In the meantime, would you please introduce yourselves briefly?"

The female of the trio stepped forwards. She had short brown hair and looked like a mousy librarian. "My name is Elizabeth Wilson. My speciality is infectious diseases. I've been at the facility for just under two years after transferring from a private research company."

One of the two men stepped forward. He was the taller of the two and had the beginnings of a blond goatee. "My name is Thomas Fenton.

My specialty is Allergy and Immunology. I have only been at the facility for eight months. It's a pleasure to meet you, sir."

Well, I know who the suck up is.

The last of the young doctors stepped forward. He had much darker features than the other man and seemed a few years older. He was plump and short, but had an air of authority about him. "My name is Dr James Button. My speciality is in Endocrinology, Haematology, and Internal Medicine. I have been at the facility for six years and have been running things recently since Dr Doherty moved up into senior management."

Greg whistled. "Very impressive. I can see why you were left in charge."

Greg caught a glint of resentment in Dr Button's eyes. Perhaps he felt that the supervisor role should have been his. He was certainly qualified for it.

Letters after your name doesn't always mean you're fit to lead, though. I'll have to make sure I stamp on any subordination the moment it happens.

Greg patted his fingertips together and nodded his head as he appraised his team. They were an impressive trio and he was lucky to have their skills at his disposal. "Okay, well, as you can see from the name on my desk, I am Dr Gregory Penn. My specialities are in Infectious Diseases and Neurology. I'd say that between us we have quite a broad spectrum of knowledge. My previous experience is mostly in emergency medicine and diagnostics. This is my first research post, but I intend to succeed in any and all tasks that we undertake. Every puzzle has a solution and every disease can be understood and controlled."

The three doctors nodded.

Greg stood up and clapped his hands together. "Okay, show me what you've been up to."

"THIS IS THE MAIN LAB," said Dr Button as he showed Greg around the most high-tech facilities he had ever seen. The main testing areas were in a separate space, behind thick layers of safety glass and accessed via a series of airlocks and containment areas. Inside, Greg could see row upon rows of biosafety cabinets. On Greg's side of the glass was a staging area with positive pressure suits and safety monitors.

"We keep strains of the Lassa Virus inside," Dr Button mentioned. "Along with all other known forms of Haemorrhagic Fever. We are also studying several yet-to-be classified pathogens and a new strain of Necrotizing Fasciitis that is unresponsive to all antibiotics in current use."

Greg raised an eyebrow. "Jesus! Where did it come from?"

Button cleared his throat. "That's…a complicated issue."

Greg folded his arms. "Okay, well, don't be shy. I'd like to know where the disease was found. It could help understand it."

Button turned to his colleagues, Fenton and Wilson, and then shrugged. They seemed to defer to him. "I was going to give you a few days to settle in before showing you," said Button. "But if you insist, follow me."

Greg followed his team to the back of the laboratory and through a door. Inside was another staging area, with a large steel door blocking entrance to the room beyond. Button tapped a code into a number pad on the wall and the door hissed and opened.

"After you," said Button, somewhat patronisingly.

Greg chewed at his bottom lip and then stepped through the open door. There was another identical door up ahead. Once the first door was closed, the second one opened. Greg's stomach turned a little as he anticipated what he was about to see.

But he never expected to find what he did.

In front of him was a large glass cage. Sitting right in the middle, watching a television, was a middle-aged man. He waved when he spotted them.

"You must be, Dr Penn," said the man in the glass cage. "I've been expecting you."

Greg turned to his team. "What the hell is this? Who is this man?" Wilson pursed her lips and looked nervous. Greg realised it was probably due to the tone of his voice having been so aggressive.

"This is Patient WC-00," Dr Button said. "The first and, currently, only carrier of Welshchild Necrotising Fasciitis."

Greg spun to face the younger doctor and gave him a stern stare. "There is no such disease."

"Yes, there is. And you are looking at it."

Greg looked at the man in the cage with great interest. He was about Greg's age, but seemed in better shape – like he exercised regularly. The television standing on the desk in front of the man flashed with images from a 24-hour news channel.

"I like to stay abreast of current events," said the man in the cage as he noticed Greg staring at the television. "Despite having never been a part of them."

Greg approached the glass. He saw an oxygen scrubber set against the ceiling and realised that the room was completely sterile.

It's a giant biohazard cabinet.

"How long have you been in there?" Greg asked the man.

"Since shortly after my birth."

Greg looked at his team and was astonished when they nodded to confirm it.

"Since you were a baby? Why? Why would they keep you here?"

The man stood up from his chair and shrugged. He came closer to the glass. "I have no ideas. Perhaps now that you're in charge you can finally let me out."

"Step back from the glass," Button said.

Greg shook his head. "I'm fine. I want to know why this man has been locked up his entire life."

Suddenly, the man in the cage leapt the three feet between them and smashed his hands against the reinforced glass.

Greg leapt back, startled.

The man in the cage smiled widely. His teeth were missing, his gums black. "They lock me up," he growled, "Because I am death itself. I am Plague."

Button put a hand on Greg's shoulder. "Come on," he said. "Let's go somewhere and I'll fill you in."

Back in the office, Greg was too wound-up to sit in his chair, so he perched on the edge of his desk while his team stood before him. As usual, Button was the one to do their talking.

"WC-00 was discovered on the 23rd January 1974 in the mountains of North Wales. An earthquake in the area, twinned with a nearby Army training exercise, led to the discovery. A small group of soldiers from the 1stBattalion Parachute Regiment were running fitness assessments for entry into the SAS. They found an abandoned child three-hundred feet above the ground on one of the foothills. The child was healthy, but crying."

Greg sniffed. "They found a baby just lying there?"

Button shrugged his shoulders. "That's what the files say. The child was totally abandoned. There was no one for miles around. The army could not explain it, but they took the child back to a base in Hereford. Within twelve hours, everyone that came into contact with the unidentified child was displaying flu-like symptoms. Twenty-four hours later and their bodies began to...*peel*."

Greg swallowed a lump in his throat, but then found himself laughing. "Peel? What on earth do you mean?"

Wilson cleared her throat. "There's a videotape in your desk drawer. You can play it on the console over there."

Greg looked left and saw a television and tape desk that he hadn't even realised was there. There was also hardware for DVD, Blu Ray, and a memory card reader. Greg slid open one of the slim, horizontal drawers at the back of his desk and did indeed find a tape. He went over and slid the cassette into the playback machine.

The television fizzed to life.

"What is this? What am I looking at?"

"This was recorded on the military base in Hereford," Dr Fenton explained. "When people started getting sick, one of the medical staff had the foresight to make a recording."

The image was grainy and spotted with noise. On a couple of occasions even the vert-hold went awry. What was clear, though, was that the images were coming from a handheld camera inside what appeared to be an infirmary.

A voice narrated from behind the scenes – the voice of the camera operator.

"*It has now been approximately eighteen hours since exposure to the Welsh child. Flu-like symptoms have now progressed to something more resembling the flesh-eating nightmares of science fiction. It is like nothing I have ever seen before. Specialists are en route from Porton Down but I fear that it is already too late for us.*"

The camera panned around the room and then zoomed in on a bedridden soldier.

As you can see, the flesh of this man's face is almost completely gone. His jawbone is exposed and his trigeminal nerve is apparent beneath the liquefying flesh. This man is melting alive. I pray that his pain is soon to end. I see no other outcome but to assume that it is.

Greg felt his stomach slosh as the cameraman continued showing scenes of biological devastation. He watched as at least a dozen servicemen lay in their beds, rotting from various parts of their body. One man even had his skeletal leg bones on display beneath his knees. The video ended with the camera man turning the focus on himself – displaying his own rotting face – and reciting the Lord's Prayer.

"Jesus Christ," said Greg, moving around and sitting behind his desk. The wooden barrier made him feel more secure. He realised, as he placed his hands out in front of him, that he was shaking.

"The base was immediately quarantined," said Button. "If it were not for the case the child was found by the military and taken immediately to a secure medical facility, the affects would have been far worse."

"Catastrophic," Fenton added. "The infection rate of exposure to the Welsh Child was 100%. survival rate: zero."

"No disease has a total kill rate. Not a single plague know to man."

"This one does," said Fenton. "But only with phase one exposure."

"What do you mean?"

"In tests, only subjects exposed to WC-00 directly displayed a 100% death rate. Of the test subjects exposed to infected patients, only 50% were symptomatic. They still contracted the virus and carried it, but it was dormant in their bodies – yet still highly infectious. On the other hand, those with symptoms, which eventually led to their deaths, were not at all symptomatic."

Greg rubbed a finger down the length of his nose and thought about what that meant. "So…those who were dying were not contagious, yet those who appeared healthy were? That would make it nearly impossible to contain if it entered the general population. There would be no way of telling who was passing it on to whom."

"Exactly," said Button. "Which is why WC-00 is probably the most dangerous human being on the planet. If he ever escaped…"

Greg nodded. He understood what it would mean. "So…this man, this WC-00, is one of the asymptomatic carriers?"

"No," said Button. "He is something else entirely."

"What do you mean?"

"He carries the virus, yes, and is extremely contagious, but he is not like the other carriers. The disease is present in his body on a genetic level. Almost as though he were engineered to carry the virus in his DNA."

Greg huffed. "You're talking about genetic engineering…in the 1970s? That's preposterous."

"Perhaps, but every test we have done on WC-00's tissue samples suggest that the virus is as much a part of his make-up as amino acids and mitochondria. He literally *is* the virus, in human form."

"I am plague," said Greg, remembering what the man had said to him.

"He says that a lot," said Wilson. She scratched at her forehead and let out a long sigh. "Since his isolation began, ongoing efforts have been made to socialise and enrich his existence, but in recent years he has begun to take on characteristics of-"

"Dementia," Greg guessed. "I'm not surprised. He's been locked in a glass cube his entire life. Has he ever even felt the touch of another human being?"

"Only when he was retrieved from the Welsh foothills," said Fenton. "The level 5 Bio Hazard protocols were created purely to house him. He's never left that room. Anyone that goes in must exercise extreme caution. Full safety measures."

"What about when he gets sick? How has he been kept healthy this whole time?"

"There has been no need," Button said. "His immune system is like nothing we have ever seen. He's never been sick a day in his life. Not even a cold."

Greg shook his head. "Well, I'm not surprised in an isolation chamber. He's probably never been exposed to anything. I was thinking more about internal disorders."

"You don't understand," said Button, somewhat condescendingly. "We have intentionally exposed him to all kinds of pathogens, from the common cold to smallpox. His immune system dismantled every single attack."

Greg's eyes went wide. The man was a miracle – if they could ever discover the reason for his total immunity…harness that knowledge in some way…

"Wait," said Greg. "What about his teeth. They were rotted and missing."

"Auto-immune response. The antibodies in his saliva are so aggressive that they attracted the bacteria growing on the surface of his teeth until there was nothing left but stumps. We serve him his nutrients in liquid-form now."

Greg sighed. "No human being should have to live like that."

"Many would agree with you," said Fenton, finding his voice, "but those in charge are just taking the only option available. The real blame should be with whatever terrorist created WC-00."

"You think terrorists are responsible?"

Fenton shrugged. "Some may have other opinions, but I see no other answers. Somebody was supposed to find WC-00 and contract the disease, before spreading it. It was only supremely good fortune that led to a safe quarantine."

"Three hundred and sixty-eight people were dead within thirty-six hours of the child being found. If the disease had gotten outside that base, you and I would not be standing here. We would all be dead, or not even born."

Greg leant back in his chair and held his breath. He concentrated on the pressure building within his chest and then finally let the air out. If WC-00 ever got out, then humanity would die out to the tune of 50%. *More than three billion people.* And he was now the man in charge of that never happening. Several hours ago, he had no idea that the destruction of mankind was being housed in a glass cage below the British countryside. Now that he knew, he envied the ignorance he would never again have the luxury of having.

I wonder what other secrets this chamber of horrors contains.

Guess I'll find out.

AFTER ONLY THREE DAYS, Greg had discovered all sorts of uncategorised biological nasties. The underground 'Level 5' lab housed methods of killing the world a hundred times over. It was a good thing that the facility was one of the most secure in the world. It would probably even put the American labs to shame.

Still, despite all that he had seen, Greg's mind kept wandering back to WC-00 – or Welshchild as his team referred to him sometimes. He couldn't believe that some unknown man of science had once engineered and condemned a new born child to a life of isolation – with the original intention being the semi-extinction of mankind. Welshchild's very existence was a tragedy. And it was something the world would never know

about. The man would spend every minute of the rest of his life inside a glass cage.

Greg lay back in the king-sized bed of his underground apartment and stared at the whizzing ceiling fan. It reminded him of the wheels on a speeding car; something he would not see again for the next three years.

After the breakup of his marriage, the chance to get away had seemed ideal, but now Greg felt like he was in a tomb and surrounded by agents of death. The only thing keeping him sane was the work – the thrill of being at the cutting edge of epidemiology. His efforts at the facility could directly influence the future of the world and its ongoing battle against infection. If he ever found a way to replicate WC-00's superior immune system, he would win a noble prize at the very least.

He's the priority here. He's a unique human being. The things he could teach us…

But in forty years no one has been able to do anything but contain him.

That's exactly why this could my chance to make a difference. Maybe I could even find a cure for the disease. I could allow that poor man to finally step outside and smell the fresh air.

Or am I just dreaming?

Greg hopped up off the bed and walked across the bedroom. He had no idea what time it was, but he wasn't feeling sleepy. He would go back to work until he was.

Being underground meant that time lost its importance. People worked when they were awake and rested when they needed to. It was a system that worked well. People were more productive when they could work to their natural rhythms. There were no early mornings and late nights, just work and rest entwined.

Greg threw on some clothes from the built in wardrobes and headed out of his apartment. The outside corridor led back to the labs and the air-locked areas. He could also get to WC-00's containment cell, which was his destination. He wanted to talk to the man, find out as much as he could.

Discover his secrets.

Inside the main lab, Button was working busily away. Out of the members of Greg's team, Button seemed the most resistant to downtime. The man ate at his desk and slept via short naps of only twenty or thirty minutes at a time. Greg both admired and pitied his dedication.

"Dr Penn, sir? Can I help you with anything?"

"No, I'm just off to see WC-00."

Button swivelled slightly on his chair and frowned at Greg. "There's nothing we can do for him, or with him."

"But to not try would be inhuman. The man deserves to have someone fighting to give him a normal life."

"He'll never have a normal life…and he's not human. No one raised in such an environment could be considered as such."

Greg nodded. "But that is our doing, not his."

Dr Button swivelled back around and faced his computer. With a weary voice, he said, "Just be careful. WC-00 has a way of getting inside your head. He's best left alone."

Greg didn't exactly understand what that meant, but he nodded and said, "I'll take it under advisement, Dr Button."

Greg headed through the lab and typed in the key code needed to enter the containment cell. The door hissed open and he stepped through into the airlock, before passing through into the next room.

WC-00 sat in the centre of his glass cage as he always did whenever he did not have company. When he saw Greg appear, he waved a hand dismissively and turned back to whatever he was watching.

Greg stepped up close to the glass and sat down on the chair he had placed there a day earlier. "Hello," he said as he got comfortable.

WC-00 kept his eyes on the television. "What do you want?"

"I just wanted to see how you were doing?"

"I woke up. Exercised for one hour. Ate breakfast. Switched the television on. Later I will have dinner and then go to sleep. Tomorrow I will do the exact same thing again. That will be my life until the moment I pass my final breath. I pray that it is sooner rather than later."

Greg raised an eyebrow. "You pray? You believe in God?"

"Yes, I believe in God. It is the only thing that keeps me going in here."

"That is good," said Greg.

WC-00 turned and grinned at him. "Yes, I have to believe in God, because the thought of standing before him one day and demanding answers for my pointless existence is the only thing with which I have to look forward."

Greg sighed. Religion could be a comfort to those who accepted it. It could also be fuel. Fuel for rage and hatred. His own belief was that a lack of religion in any way was the only way for society to occupy a rational middle-ground – but that was a conversation for another time and place.

"You're a well-spoken man, WC-00."

"Call me Welsh. I have never possessed a name, but that serves me better than an ID code."

Greg nodded. "Okay…Welsh. How did they educate you here?"

"Books, videos, interactions with men behind the glass. There is little else to do in here other than educate oneself. I like to know about the world that has been denied to me."

"Perhaps one day you will get to see it."

Welsh let out a long, bitter sigh. "That is a very cruel thing to suggest. Do not attempt to dangle impossibilities in front of me, Doctor. I have no time for hope."

"Everyone must have hope."

"Is that why you opted to spend your life three hundred feet below the ground? Despair lives beneath us and hope is in the clouds. It appears that you have gone the wrong way, Doctor."

Greg shifted in his seat. The man in the cage had a way of voicing things in an unsettling tone. His speech patterns were unusual – the product of having no native upbringing.

"I am here to do good," he said. "To give hope to others. *That* is my hope."

Welsh cackled. "There is no hope here. This is a factory of suffering. The only reason I live is so that men like you can try to understand me, to harness the invisible death that writhes across my skin. I am a weapon, Doctor Penn. Many things in this basement of monstrosities are weapons, but I am the most destructive. Yet, your thousands of blood tests, your endless experiments on me, have all been fruitless. My being is beyond your understanding. I am above anything you can achieve merely by existing. I am plague."

Greg considered Welsh's words and was disconcerted to recognise traits of self-aggrandisement. When there was no normal outlets to gain self-esteem, a person would turn their world-views inwards – convince themselves that they are above those around them. It was an unhealthy belief-system.

"You keep referring to yourself as *plague*? Why do you do that?"

Welsh shook his head and snickered, as if the answer was obvious. "Dr Penn, if you were to step inside this cell with me, your eyeballs would melt in your head. Your fingernails would shrivel and decay. Your blood would thicken in your veins and your skin would slide from your muscles like heated marzipan. To face me, man to man, would mean certain death. I make all other diseases quake in their boots. If I am not plague personified, then what am I? Should I ride a horse and carry a quiver on my back. Would that convince you of what I am?"

Greg rubbed at his eyes. The man before him should have been a wilting neurotic after so many years of isolation, but instead he viewed himself almost as a god. "You believe you are one of the four horsemen of the apocalypse?"

Welsh stood from his chair and headed over to the glass. "It was just a metaphor, Doctor, but my destiny was indeed great. If not for the actions of a squad of doomed servicemen on that grassy hilltop where they found me, I would not have been one of the four horsemen of the apocalypse...I would have been the apocalypse itself."

"And yet, here you are, impotent and alone. Your destiny is no longer yours to decide." The comment was mean spirited, but Greg could not help it. Hearing the arrogant and fatalistic words of the man in front of him made him angry. It almost sounded like Welsh wished he had spread his dreaded plague.

Come on, Greg. It's hardly surprising that he has a grudge against humankind. He's spent his entire life as a lab rat. What capacity of love would he ever have been given?

"Destiny takes a lifetime, Doctor. It is determined by a journey's ending, not by its beginning. Would you not agree?"

Greg thought about his own life. His beginnings had been bleak, yet bearable. His recent past had been even grimmer. He liked to think that his life's journey could get better. Maybe it really was only the end of one's life that counted.

"You are looking at me with great interest, Doctor," said Welsh. "But I assure you there are no secrets here...at least none that you could comprehend."

"I'd like to try," said Greg, more determined than ever. He had a desire to hear this man thank him. He wanted to show Welsh what gratitude was. The only way to do that would be by...

"I'm going to cure you," he said.

Welsh laughed, loud and hard. "Cure me from what? I am what I am. I need no cure. It is you who needs to evolve. I cannot be made sick by any organism or germ, and yet you seek to *cure* me? That is rich indeed, Doctor."

"I want to help you," said Greg, exasperated by the bitterness in Welsh's manner.

"Help yourself, Doctor. You need it more than I."

Greg stood up. "Suit yourself, but I assure you that one day you will get out of here and you'll thank me."

Welsh examined him carefully through the glass. "Well, if that ever does happen, Doctor, perhaps I *will* thank you…but you, on the other hand, will be *begging* me."

"HAS HE EVER TRIED TO ESCAPE?" Greg asked his team as they sat in his office together.

"No, never," said Wilson. "Which I suppose is strange. It would be impossible for him to get out, though."

"You're positive?"

"Aren't you, sir?" asked Button with a hint of accusation.

Greg shrugged. "I know that this is a very secure facility, but you think he would have at least tried to escape once during his forty years here. The way he talks about destiny and his superiority, I would think it drives him crazy being locked up."

Fenton folded his hands in his lap. "How do you drive a crazy person crazy? I'm sure a sane person would be beside themselves, but he is not a normal human being. Nothing about him is suspect to the normal rules of the human condition, from his personality right down to his very cells."

Greg cleared his throat and leant forward in his leather chair. "So what treatment have we tried?"

Dr Button answered. "We've tried mapping his genome, to try and identify where the virus is located and target it directly. That failed. We have tried every antibiotic in existence. They failed. We have tried full blood transfusions and organ transplants. Failure. We have tried radiation therapy and various chemical treatments. Fail-"

"Failure. I get it," said Greg. "So do any of you have any ideas how to proceed?"

"Yes," said Button. "We spend our times on projects with a future. You need to understand that in regards to WC-00 we are nothing more than glorified hospice nurses. No one has ever been able to make sense of him and, when he is dead, we should all just be grateful that the only known source of the Welshchild disease will die with him."

"What about his improved immune system? Has anyone come close to replicating it?"

Wilson shook her head. "We don't even understand it, let alone have any chance of replicating it. His white blood count is the same as anybody else's. We can't explain how he fights off infection. Previous Doctors have theorised that the Welshchild virus is hostile to other pathogens. It may be what fights off the illness."

Greg scratched his chin and stretched out his legs. He was feeling tired, but he was too excited to retire to his apartment. "This man is amazing. If only we could unlock his secrets."

"Just forget about it," said Dr Button. "He's a lost cause to all but those who created him."

Greg stood up and towered over his team. "Now listen here, Dr Button. I am in charge here. I will decide whether or not something is a lost cause. I want all three of your working on WC-00 for the foreseeable future. All other projects on hold."

Wilson objected. "Do you know how close this lab is to curing Malaria, HIV, even cancer? You want us to just…stop?"

"Do you not understand?" Greg shouted. "If we understand this man's immune system, there will be no need for a cure to malaria, or anything else for that matter. We will be the saviour of millions of people, billions for the years to come. This has to be our priority. Welsh Child Zero Zero is the key to a new, wonderful future for mankind."

Greg's team shifted in their seats and looked at him anxiously. They seemed unhappy at his request, but also a little buoyed by his enthusiasm.

Greg smiled at them all in turn. "We can be heroes," he said. "Heroes."

DAYS later and Greg was ready to get started. The planning stages were complete and it was time to start performing tests.

"There's no reason to go in there," Dr Button told Greg. "We have more tissue samples then we will ever need."

Greg pulled the positive pressure suit over his body from the feet upwards and started to fasten the seals. Dr Wilson helped him attach the gloves to the suit and lock the bracelets. "We're starting from scratch, Dr Button. I want fresh samples so I know that we are working with pure and up-to-date results. We shouldn't take anything for granted concerning this man."

Dr Button handed him the suit's helmet. "Fine. Just be quick and just be careful. Wilson and Fenton are both on lunch break. If something happens there's only me to help you."

Before Greg put the helmet on, he frowned at the doctor. "Careful?"

"Yes. It's been a while since anybody went inside, so be prepared. We don't know for sure how Welsh will react."

Greg fastened a utility belt around his waist and plugged it into the suit's input jack. "I can handle it," he said into the helmet's speaker.

Dr Button checked Greg's suit as he turned a full circle, checking for tears. When he was satisfied, they inflated the suite and Greg turned around, clomping towards the WC-00 airlock.

A vinyl tunnel had been erected inside to allow uncompromised entry into the glass cell. Welsh sat in the middle of the room, expectantly. Greg stopped in the tunnel midway and waited for the chemical shower to douse him. Once that was done, he proceeded to the glass cell. There was a key pad ahead and he quickly activated it. The door unlocked and slid sideways with a hiss.

He stepped inside.

Welsh observed him quietly, almost seeming uninterested.

"Dr Penn. How lovely for you to visit."

Greg laughed. "Less of the Hannibal Lector act. I'm here to help you."

Welsh looked confused. "Hannibal Hector?"

"Never mind. How are you feeling?"

"I can't get sick. I feel fine, as always."

"I meant in yourself, emotionally? Are you still feeling…*resentful?*"

"I do not resent," Welsh said. "I just hold people responsible for their actions."

Greg decided to ignore the evasive answers and just get on with things. He wasn't sure if Welsh even had the capacity to share on an emotional level. "I would like to take some tissue samples from you, if that is okay?"

"By all means. Did something happen to the other thousand samples that you already have?"

Greg opened up a pouch on his right arm and plucked out a syringe. "I'd just like to start fresh. It would ease my mind knowing that I have the very best samples available to me."

"So that you can use me to cure the world?"

Greg nodded. It was a clunky movement inside the helmet. "You are an amazing specimen, Welsh. You could be the key to a new future. A world without sickness and disease."

Welsh turned to the television and sighed. "And my reward for that is a lifetime of incarceration."

"If this works, you would be able to leave."

"I don't think so. By the time you even came close to understanding me, I would be an old old man. Many scientists have worked on me before you, Dr Penn. Better, smarter scientists."

The comment irritated Greg but he would not allow it to distract him. Whether Welsh believed it or not, he was trying to do good. The fact that success would effectively make him the saviour of the world was just a hefty bonus.

Welsh sat still while Greg took his blood. He placed the full syringe into an airtight rubber seal, which he then placed back into the pouch on his arm. Saliva swabs and even ear wax samples followed. Greg also took some of Welsh's hair and fingernail clipping.

Greg glanced at the television and saw that the news was on as usual. Riots in the Middle East were raging. He wondered if the region would finally find peace one day, and if maybe one day his work would help towards it.

Would people still fight in a world without disease?

With his first round of tests all complete, Greg prepared to leave the cell. Before he did, however, Welsh reached out and grabbed his wrist.

Greg looked down at Welsh's fingers around his arm and frowned. "What are you doing? Please let go of me."

Welsh looked him in the eye. "I just wanted to say thank you. I understand that you want to help."

Greg smiled. "I told you that one day you would thank me."

Welsh grinned right back. "And I told you that one day you would beg me."

Greg's heart skipped a beat. "I'm sorry?"

"You really should be more careful." He pointed at Greg's elbow.

Greg's eyes went so wide he thought they might fall out of their sockets. His heart pulsed and his lungs went stiff.

No, no, no....

The tear on the left elbow of his suit was minute. But it was there. He was compromised. The positive air pressure might be enough to save him, but...

"I...I..."

Welsh laughed. "How very unfortunate. You had such high hopes."

Greg staggered backwards and was surprised when somebody caught him. It was Dr Button. He was not wearing a suit at all.

"Button! Are you insane? Why the hell are you in here without a suit? We need to quarantine this whole level. I…I may be infected."

"Oh believe me, you are," said Dr Button. "You have no idea how contagious this disease is. A thimbleful is enough to infect a billion people. It truly is remarkable."

"Wh…what are you babbling about? We're going to die. We have to make sure nobody else does. You're insane exposing yourself like this."

Dr Button just laughed. "Don't worry, I was exposed a long time ago. I'm immune, Dr Penn. We all are."

Greg was struggling to breathe. The panic was like nothing he had ever felt before. He needed to get the hell out of the cell, away from the virus, but he couldn't. He could have the disease. "What do you mean, you *all* are?"

"The people I work for. The people who tried to release this virus to the world more than thirty years ago. We have been preparing. Billions will die, but we will go on. The world will be rebuilt. The world will be better. We are ready to see that change. It's been a long wait, but now it is finally here."

"You're insane. Fucking insane! Where are Wilson and Fenton?"

"I already told you," said Dr Button. "They're taking their break. Although, I think they may have eaten something that didn't agree with them. I'd imagine they're in quite an amount of discomfort right now. It won't last long, though, so don't worry. They will be dead long before the virus eats their flesh. They are the lucky ones."

Greg lashed out, went to grab a hold of Dr Button's neck. But Welsh leapt up and grabbed him in a chokehold. Greg grunted and heaved as his throat was restricted. "Pl….*please.* Don't do this. Don't…*please.*"

"Sounds like begging to me," Welsh whispered in his ear.

Dr Button shook his head pitifully as Greg began to fade. "You wanted so much to make the world better. Well, don't worry; you will have your wish granted. You just won't be around to see it."

Greg struggled with his last ounces of strength. "You'll never get out of here. They'll…stop you…"

Dr Button just smiled. "Once I release the virus into the entire facility, all I will have to do is wait a while. Welsh and I will walk right out of here. Then our true work begins. Of course I will disable all outgoing communications first. Wouldn't want the world getting warning."

Greg's vision was growing dark. The blood vessels in his forehead felt like they might pop. "Why…are…you…doing…this?"

Button opened his arms wide, like he was a preacher on a pedestal. "Because, Dr Penn, we…are…plague."

Forty-eight hours later and everybody was dead. Welsh and Button walked right on out of the facility and got into a car waiting for them nearby. Welsh wanted to see London first.

THE PEELING: BOOK 5

THE LIGHTS

The camp had been free of infection for almost two weeks, but the lights in the sky were making everybody nervous. The blinking green orbs had appeared only days before and had been hanging in the sky every time night fell. Every day when dusk approached, the members of the camp would wait with bated breath to see if the lights would still be there. Every evening it would become clear that the lights were not going away. If anything, they seemed to be getting closer – lower in the sky.

Gretchen looked out from her perch atop the roof of the ambulance and surveyed the rest of the camp. She and nineteen other survivors had gathered together inside a roadside hotel. The adjacent restaurant had provided them with some food supplies and ample amounts of beer and soft drinks. The hotel itself was newly constructed and gave them all the safety of communal living while also providing everyone with the privacy of their own room. They had blocked up the road to the hotel and kept a constant vigil for any other survivors that may have been lurking in the nearby area.

While Gretchen's group were not against welcoming other survivors, there was still the risk of infection. While The Peeling seemed to have abated somewhat, with new infections becoming more and more rare, there was still the old fashioned illnesses of influenza, dysentery, and pleurisy – and more importantly, there were no longer any doctors to treat them. While the movies always made sure that the group of desperate survivors had a medic amongst them, Gretchen's group had nothing of the sort. The members of the camp ranged from salesmen and factory workers to a professional dog walker – nobody who knew how to treat an illness.

Pritchett called up to Gretchen and told her that her turn to keep watch was over. He also had a piping hot cup of soup waiting for her. Gretchen hopped down off the ambulance and took the mug from the man.

He smiled at her warmly. "Everything A-okay?"

Gretchen nodded. "Haven't seen a thing. It's starting to get bloody cold though. We're going to have to find a way to keep ourselves warm once winter gets here."

Pritchett nodded. "I guess we could gather up all the spare duvets."

Gretchen nodded. "We'll work on it tomorrow."

She walked away, heading away from the roadside and back towards the restaurant where most of the group tended to congregate during the evening. Pritchett would keep watch for the next six hours, but other than him, nobody else would be busy.

As she suspected, almost every member of camp was situated in the eatery. Pendle and Groves had started a fire in a barrel in the centre of the room and had set up a couple of sea bass fillets on a makeshift spit. The smell of the fish made Gretchen's mouth water.

To prevent smoke, the group had opened up a skylight in the restaurant that seemed to do a good job of keeping the air circulating. Maybe in the winter they could set up more fires inside the buildings.

"Hey, Grets," said Pendle. He was a handsome young man with tanned skin passed down from his Spanish mother. His dark hair had grown out in recent weeks and the heat of the fire made beads of sweat form on the tips of his fringe.

"Hey, Pendle. Smells good. I'm surprised we still have fish that is good to eat."

"Groves smoked most of the meat and fish early on. We're just making a start on it all. The frozen sausages and burgers have all run out and the fries are running low. We're going to have to go out and start searching for canned food soon."

Gretchen nodded. "I'll start putting together a plan. There's a supermarket nearby. Hopefully it wasn't completely stripped clean in the early days."

Pendle sighed. They all remembered the early days. The chaotic time where rape and murder went unopposed and neighbours robbed one another with impunity. During the first tumultuous weeks of the infection, anarchy claimed as many lives as The Peeling itself. The Army had been called in to control the situation but, once the government fell, they soon became nothing more than a roving band of bullies, taking other people's supplies at gun point. Then, even the Army seemed to disappear and disband.

In the final few weeks, survivors had become more and more of a rarity. It had been several days since Gretchen's camp had accepted anybody new – a guy name Logan was the last, a man who claimed to have been a Physics teacher. They took him in for his expertise, but so far he had done nothing but keep to himself.

The survivors had all remained safe and well fed at the hotel since they'd gathered there four weeks ago, but a time was quickly coming where they would have to venture back out into the world – where rotting flesh lined the street and legions of rats tore holes in everything in sight. Gretchen shuddered at the thought.

She shuddered even more when she thought of her own family lying out there someplace.

When The Peeling had hit, Gretchen's husband had caught it almost right away. He had come home with a flu that quickly became a burning, tingling sensation all over his body. Then a scrap of skin came away on his ankle. It was quickly over from that point.

As the news report showed horrifying scenes of the flesh-eating virus, Gretchen was getting a first-hand view. Her husband was little more than a patchy skeleton by the time he died a week later. Gretchen's mother-in-law had the children, but in the chaos that ensued during the riots and looting, something had happened to them. When Gretchen reached her mother-in-law's home, they were all gone and there was no note. Gretchen had stayed there for days until somebody eventually set the neighbourhood on fire and forced everyone to flee. Gretchen had joined up with a roving group of ten survivors on the M4 motorway and eventually they had rested here at the hotel.

Gretchen sipped at her soup and shivered as it warmed her cold body. What she would give to have her husband's cuddling arms around her now. Had anybody been lucky enough to keep a hold of their spouse? Or their children?

She took a seat alone at one of the tables and looked around at her new family. Amongst the group was Shandi, an African American business women from Tulsa who had been visiting the UK for a meeting. The women knew nothing of her country back home, or the people she knew there. There was Bryan, who was perhaps their most handy member of the camp. He was a skilled carpenter and had helped them construct barricades over the windows and create makeshift weapons. Daniel was a salesman from Alcester and mostly kept to himself. Something suggested the young man was mourning on some great loss. A bubbly girl named Sally had worked at a Marks and Spencer department store in Redditch prior to the infection and was the cheeriest of the group. Her disposition seemed to be one where the glass was half full. Danny was an old factory worker from Longbridge, who had worked twenty years at the Rover car plant until the layoffs many years before. He had been working a metal press since then. There were a dozen other faces in the room, but Gretchen felt too tired to look upon them all. What she really needed was to go to bed, but she hated being alone in her cold, featureless hotel room.

"Why don't you just piss off," came an angry voice from the other side of the restaurant.

"We can't keep burying our heads in the sand. We need to have an open discussion about this."

"I don't see the point in freaking everybody out about something we don't even understand."

Gretchen sighed and got up. She went over to the two camp members who were fighting. It was Colin and David. Both were mid-forties men, but while Colin wore a dirty old suit and had once worked at a bank, David had been unemployed most of his life and was generally a lazy and abrasive chap.

"What is it?" Gretchen asked them.

Colin smiled at her, but it was clear that he was exasperated. "I'm just suggested that we bite the bullet and talk about those lights in the sky. They must mean something."

David rolled his eyes. "They could be a million different things. What's the point in stressing over them? They haven't done nothing since they showed up."

Colin rolled his eyes back at the other man. "It seems quite apparent to me that they are descending. They are much bigger than they were when they first appeared."

"No they ain't."

Gretchen waved a hand. "No, Colin is right. I think they are getting closer to us…to Earth or whatever."

David shook his head. "Fuck sake. There's nothing to worry about."

"I'm a bit worried," said Sally. "They have to mean something. What if they're missiles? Maybe another country doesn't want The Peeling spreading over to them and they're going to nuke us off the planet."

There was a frightened muttering as the others in the room listened in. The talk of being bombed was a fear many of them had and it had been discussed before.

Gretchen shook her head. "Missiles don't take days and days to fall; nor do they advertise their presence with great blinking lights."

"What then?" came a voice. "What do you think they are?"

"Probably just some environmental anomaly caused by all the methane."

"The *what*?" said David.

"The methane gas…from all of the bodies. There must be millions of dead just rotting in the streets. That amount of damage to the ozone layer…"

There was a collective sigh. Missiles, people couldn't deal with, but global warming… They hadn't cared about global warming before the world crumbled, so they most certainly didn't care about it now."

"She's right," said David. "I bet that's all it is. No need to worry about it."

Everybody filtered back to what they were doing. Colin approached Gretchen and spoke quietly. "Do you really believe that? About the methane gas?"

"Not really, but there's no point in speculating on anything worse."

"I suppose not. If you were to speculate, though; what would your guess be?"

Gretchen sighed, shrugged her shoulders. "The only thing that worries me is that those lights showing up right after the world's most devastating plague is too much to be a coincidence."

With that Gretchen decided that even the cold silence of her hotel room was better than the tense atmosphere of the restaurant. People were starting to get tetchy, and it would only get worse.

Back in her room, Gretchen picked up a paperback she had snatched from the hotel's lounge: *Going Postal* by Terry Pratchett. She had already read it twice and enjoyed the surreal Discworld and how it reminded her of the petty, care-free world she had once lived in.

After two pages she was fast asleep.

SHE AWOKE SOMETIME LATER to what felt and sounded like an earthquake. A glass of water fell off the room's desk and soaked the carpet. The empty hangers in the closet rattled.

Gretchen checked her watch: 3:13 AM.

She leapt off the bed and headed over to the window. She was on the second floor and could see clear across the car park. Pritchett was standing on top of the ambulance, still keeping watch. He had his hands on his head, obviously flustered by something.

"What the hell was that?" Gretchen asked herself. The rumbling had stopped almost as soon as it had started, but there was an electricity lingering in the air that put her right on edge.

She slipped out of her room and headed down the corridor. En route she met up with Pendle who was barefoot and hurrying in the same direction.

"What's going on, Gretchen?"

"Damned if I know."

The two of them headed down the carpeted staircase into the lobby below. There everybody was gathered. There everybody was demanding an explanation.

"Was it an earthquake?" Someone asked.

"In England? All we ever get here is farty little tremors."

"Maybe it's the global warming. Maybe our climate is changing."

"Earthquakes have nothing to do with the weather. It's about fault lines and plate tectonics," said Colin knowledgably.

"Let's just everybody calm down," said Gretchen. "We don't know anything yet, so let's just stay calm until we do."

Everybody muttered, but the shouting voices quietened down.

"So what do we do?" asked Colin.

"We go and check with Pritchett. He's the guy on watch. I'm sure he saw whatever happened."

"I ain't going out there," said David in his dirty boxer shorts.

"Stay here then," said Gretchen.

She started heading for the lobby's large entrance doors and found that a majority of the group were following her. She had learned weeks ago that people felt safest when they were acting as a herd. That was probably a rational reason for why the ordinary law-abiding citizens of the UK had taken to looting and rioting in the early days.

Outside in the courtyard, the cold immediately struck Gretchen. Even through her sweater, she felt it biting at her skin and nipples.

Up ahead, across the car park, was the ambulance they used as a lookout. Pritchett was still standing on top of it. He saw them approaching and waved his arms.

"You guys aren't going to believe this," he said, with both a twinge of excitement and fear in his voice.

"What is it? Do you see what caused the tremors?"

Pritchett nodded. "Hell, yes. And if you look up you will all get a great big clue as to what it was."

Gretchen, along with everybody else, craned their necks and glanced upwards.

The blinking green lights were gone. After days of looming over them all, they had disappeared.

Or maybe the opposite is true.

Pritchett spoke excitedly. "The lights just suddenly plummeted out of the sky as though somebody flipped a switch. All of them just shot right down to the earth and then...*boom!*"

"Did any of them land near us?" someone shouted.

Pritchett nodded. "One landed right over in the woods across the ring road."

People began to panic. "Oh, God. What the hell is it? It's something bad, isn't it?"

"A bomb, I reckon."

"Terrorists."

"Aliens."

Gretchen had to laugh at the last suggestion she heard shouted out. *Aliens.* It was absurd; yet somehow her laughter contained no mirth.

"We should check it out," said Colin. "We should know what we're up against."

"What do you mean?" asked David. "*What we're up against?*"

"I mean we should just take a look. Who knows maybe it could have even been a supply drop from the government."

One so heavy that it shook the earth. Somehow I don't think so, thought Gretchen.

Without any further consultation, Gretchen headed towards the edge of the car park, over the shrubs that bordered it, and onto the ring road. Cars lay crumpled up against each other in a long line, but it was easy to navigate around them, or even climb up over the bonnets when need be.

Pendle caught up with her; Pritchett and Colin were not far behind. Everybody else loitered in the car park; their herd mentality only going so far until they felt that it might endanger them.

"This can't be anything good, can it?" asked Pendle. "I mean, whatever it was shook me right out of my bed. What can hit the ground with that much force?"

"Guess we're going to find out."

As they crossed the ring road and headed for the woodland that bordered it on the far side, they passed by decaying bodies in abandoned cars. Most were bony corpses, stricken by The Peeling, but some were the victims of crime. They passed a man stabbed in the heart with a pair of scissors. Who had done it and why would be just another of the countless unknown stories that littered the landscape. Every corpse had a story to tell, but no way to tell it.

Gretchen closed her eyes as she walked past the carnage. Her nose still picked up the stench of old death but at least her eyes could shut off. She shuffled along, letting her feet find the way.

"Watch your step," said Pendle, seeming to know that she was walking with her eyes closed.

Gretchen opened her eyes in time to see the approaching curb and the embankment beyond. She stepped up and over it and began to descend down into the woodland.

"Where about did it hit?" Pendle asked Pritchett.

"Over there," the man pointed.

They headed east through the woods, following Pritchett's excited directions.

Gretchen couldn't be sure, but it seemed to be brighter up ahead, as if the moonlight were shining on something, or if something was shining by itself. The air also seemed lest crisp and chilly. The atmosphere was becoming muggy.

"I think I see something up ahead," said Colin. "Are you sure this is a good idea? Perhaps we should wait until morning."

Gretchen carried on walking. "If we're in danger now, we'll be in danger tomorrow. If we've learned anything these last few months, it's that waiting around with our heads buried in the sand doesn't work."

"I agree," said Pendle. "We need to know what the score is."

After several more yards, Gretchen became positive that there was light coming from up ahead. It was no brighter than the light from the full moon, but it was blinking and had a greenish hue.

"What is that?" asked Pritchett, his excitement had waned and he now spoke in a hushed whisper.

"I don't know." Gretchen stepped over a clump of weeds and sidled up beside an old oak tree. She flinched as something landed on her shoulder, but sighed with relief when she realised it was just a crisp autumn leaf falling from the branches above.

The sound of rustling made her flinch again. This time she looked to her left and saw a movement in the bushes.

Then an identical rustling spun her around to face the bushes in the opposite direction.

Pritchett was spinning around on the spot, looking everywhere. "What's going on?"

"Something's moving," said Colin.

"Not just one thing," Gretchen said. "I saw at least two things."

"Maybe just deer?"

"Maybe."

More movement in the bushes. This time from all around them.

"I think we should get out of here," said Pritchett. "I think we're surround-" Something seized Pritchett and dragged him back into the bushes. He disappeared so fast that it was as if his body had been attached to a bungee.

Gretchen shouted. "Run!"

Nobody argued and they all started sprinting back the way they had come. They leapt over roots and sidestepped tree trunks as they floundered in the darkness. Pritchett's screams rang out behind them but not for long.

Behind them the bushes rustled. A deep, ominous growl filled the forest.

"What the hell is happening?" Pendle shouted between huffs and puffs.

"I don't know," said Colin. "We need to get back to the hotel and put some thought into this."

"Let's just concentrate on not dying first," said Gretchen.

They spotted the road between the trees, several yards ahead.

"There's the road," said Pendle. "We can make it."

As soon as he said the words, Pendle caught his ankle on a half-buried tree root and went tumbling into the mud. Gretchen stopped to help him. But it was too late.

Something seized Pendle's foot and dragged him backwards through the mud. He screamed and reached out for Gretchen, but within a second he had disappeared into the trees.

Colin grabbed Gretchen by the arm and turned her around. "Come on, we have to get out of here now."

The two of them made it out of the trees and up the embankment. As soon as they hit the road they dodged behind cars and tried to mix up their escape route. The bellowing growls continued from within the woods.

The other survivors were still waiting in the hotel car par, and when they saw only two of the four explorers coming back, they began to panic and shout.

"Where the hell is Pritchett and Pendle?" David demanded. "Did you up and leave em?"

"There's something out there in those woods," said Colin, almost weeping. "We have to get inside."

Everybody panicked and the entire group of survivors began sprinting across the tarmac, heading for the hotel. Gretchen glanced behind at the woods across the road. Nothing seemed to be following them, but the glowing green light she had seen earlier had grown and now bathed the entire area in a putrid glow.

This is not going to work out well at all.

I think we may have just been attacked by aliens.

INSIDE THE HOTEL'S bar lounge, everyone stood around nervously, glancing out of the windows and jumping at every sound.

"We all need to just chill the fuck out," said David.

"Chill out?" said Colin. "Something abducted two of our members like something out of *Close Encounters*. We should all be in a very un-chilled out mood. In fact we should all be in quite a flap about things."

David smirked. "Perhaps I'm all 'flapped' out after what we've been through. Everyone here is a survivor. The whole world has ended but we're still here. I'm not about to panic now after surviving so much."

"We haven't survived whatever is out in those woods."

"Look," said Gretchen, raising a hand and gaining the floor. "Panic or no panic, I am telling you that something pretty damn dangerous is lurking in those woods and I'm pretty sure it came from whatever fell out of the sky. This isn't an infection or looters; this is something else."

"You're quite right," said a voice at the back of the room. It was the physics teacher, Logan.

Gretchen looked at the man. He was holding what looked like a triple scotch in his hand. "What do you know about it? Have you seen something?"

"Many things, my dear," replied Logan in a slurry mumble.

"Then stop being so fucking cryptic and speak," said David. "It's about time you did something useful around here."

Logan ignored David and kept his drunken focus on Gretchen. "We have visitors. Visitors whom made an appointment many many years ago."

"Visitors?"

Logan nodded. "You think that this is all a coin...coin...coincidence." The man belched. "There's hardly any of us left – probably less than one percent of the population. And believe me that it's this bad everywhere; every country. Every scrap of land."

"How do you know that?"

"Because I kept tabs, my dear. Ever since I stopped working for the Government and started teaching snot-nosed little kids about Hooke's law, I kept my eyes and ears open. The Peeling hit everywhere and there was no stopping it. The entire world was affected the same as us. We are the last of our kind – the last remnants of the human race."

"You're talking shit," said David. "There's still enough of us to get things going again. We'll have babies and repopulate. Sooner the better if you ask me."

"You said that you worked for the Government," said Gretchen. "In what capacity?"

"I was a researcher – part of the space program."

"Did we even have one? I thought space had become more the realm of private industry."

Logan nodded forlornly. "Unfortunately the times of putting boots on the moon were long behind us, but there were still many secrets to learn about the universe. We never stopped tracking the skies with our telescopes or sending up probes."

"So what are you saying? What do you know?"

"I know about the baby."

David snickered. "This guy has had a shit-tonne to drink."

Logan sneered at the lad, but continued. "Decades ago, a mysterious baby was found abandoned in the freezing cold hills of Wales. Everyone who came into contact with the child died. Guess how."

Gretchen narrowed her eyes. "The Peeling?"

"Indeed. Their skin rotted off in days, leaving them raving lunatics before their deaths. The child was isolated and kept that way until he was a grown man."

"Are you saying that this child was infected with The Peeling but lived like some kind of Typhoid Mary?"

Logan shook his head. "The child was a weapon – a dirty bomb.

One thing a human being can't resist is a baby. *They* knew that, which is why they used one as their dispersal method. What they didn't count on was the child being quarantined so effectively. Through a stroke of luck, the child was found by the Army who immediately took it back to base. The infection stayed within the rural outpost and stopped there. Their plan failed."

Gretchen shook her head. "Whose plan?"

"The aliens."

Gretchen laughed at that moment, but something about the seriousness in Logan's eyes – despite his drunkenness – told her to take him seriously.

"We'd picked up signs of life a few times. On our telescopes we spotted great blinking green lights that would disappear before we could pin them down. We would pick up strange radio chatter and radiation signatures that made no sense. We knew something was out there; we just didn't know *what.*

But when that baby arrived, we knew exactly what it was: a way to wipe us out."

Gretchen sighed. She went and poured herself a vodka from the optics. She wasn't usually a drinker, but right now she needed one.

"Why wipe us out?" asked Colin. "What would that achieve?"

Logan shrugged. "I never stayed at the project long enough to find out. When we learned about the child's make-up – how it was genetically infused with the deadliest virus in existence, I decided I'd seen enough. It was clear that humanity's days were drawing to an end. I wasn't about to waste what life I had left in a lab."

"So you what? Thought you'd waste time teaching kids stuff that they probably wouldn't live long enough to use."

Logan shrugged again. "Pay was okay and there was lots of holiday time."

Gretchen downed her vodka. "So what happened? You said the child was quarantined for decades."

"He was indeed. Then he escaped about six months ago. I know because an old colleague of mine died during his escape. I could tell by the way the Government were trying to cover it up, blocking any attempts at investigation, that the child – now a man – had escaped. I also knew what else that meant. That the End had arrived."

"But it didn't. We're still alive, and so are you."

"For now, yes. But the infection was only put on this earth to thin our numbers. For whatever reason, something wants our planet. For terraforming or mining, who knows? But they have thinned our number sufficiently, and now they are here to take their prize."

Gretchen hated to admit it, but it kind of made sense. If aliens ever arrived, it would make no sense to attack us with ships and guns. They would, by their very nature, be more advanced than humans. They would have far better means to destroy the planet's inhabitants – biological means. Humans didn't fight cockroaches with guns, they used gas; contaminated the very air they breathed.

"So what do we do?" asked Colin.

Logan laughed and took a sip from his whisky. "We wait to die, my friend. We wait to die."

NOBODY DARED to leave the building, or even go off alone to their rooms. The bellowing growls continued out in the woods and they all knew it would only be a matter of time before whatever was making them came closer.

Bryan, the carpenter, had assembled a team that was checking the existing barricades and trying to construct new ones. The chairs and tables from the lounge had been cannibalised for that purpose. By the time they were done, several hours later, dawn had arrived and the growling had stopped.

"Do you hear that?" asked Gretchen.

Colin shook his head. "No."

"Exactly. The growling has stopped."

"You think they're gone away."

Gretchen shook her head slowly. "Not at all, but perhaps we just discovered that they're nocturnal. Maybe on their planet it's always dark."

"How does that help us?" asked Bryan, hammer in hand.

Colin nodded and smiled, catching Gretchen's drift. "Because they would have evolved to suit their planet. They won't be anything like us – the odds are far too astronomical. If their planet is dark, then their eyes will be underdeveloped. We might be able to use light to our advantage."

Bryan sniffed. "I'll make sure we have fires ready to burn at a moment's notice." He walked off.

"You think we can fight back?" asked Colin. "If we really are facing something from another world."

Gretchen shook her head. "I think we're screwed. Something evolved enough to travel the universe and engineer a planet-killing virus will have no problem taking out a few stragglers."

"Oh dear."

"Doesn't mean I'm going to just lie down and take it, though. It's in our nature as human beings to fight, so that's just what we're going to do."

"You're damn right we are," said David, approaching with a pool cue in his hands. "Anything tries to zap me with a ray gun will get a cue full of chalk dust up their arses."

Colin giggled. "I'd like to see that."

David patted Colin on the back. "Let's find you a pool cue of your own and we can play doubles on their butt cracks."

Gretchen rubbed at her eyes. Since awakening last night, nobody had slept. It was beginning to take its toll and the back of her eyelids felt fuzzy and her mind kept spacing out for brief seconds. If they were about to be attacked by an alien clean-up crew, she felt in no fit state to fight them – but the situation was out of her control. As she looked around, she could see that everyone else was on the edge of their own sanity thresholds. Rather than strengthen them as human beings, the stress and hardships of the last few months had in fact weakened them to the point of emotional collapse. None of them could endure much more.

Perhaps the visitors know that. Maybe they've been hanging in the air waiting for just the right time to descend and finish us off.

She caught Groves, the resident chef, as he went to walk past. "Hey, Jamie. Can you go and get as much food as you can from the restaurant; I think we could all do with a big feast this afternoon."

Groves huffed. "You mean a last meal? Anyway, I'm not stepping outside with those things out there."

"It will be alright. We won't see them until dark."

"How can you be sure of that?"

"I can't, but if they are going to get us at daylight then we're screwed anyway as we're all standing around in a huddle waiting to be picked off."

Groves cleared his throat. "Okay, fine. I'll get what I can, but one sound I don't like and I'm straight back in here."

Gretchen smiled. "Of course. No one's asking you to endanger yourself."

"Yeah right." The man walked away, heading for the lobby and car park.

It was then that Gretchen realised that since Pritchett had died, no one had taken up watch on top of the ambulance. She knew that nobody would volunteer to go outside.

Guess it will have to be me then.

She checked in with a few more of the survivors and informed them that she was going to take watch. They all told her she was crazy, but they also seemed a little glad to have somebody out there keeping guard.

Not that I can do anything other than yell that we're all about to die.

Gretchen headed outside into the cold and this time welcome the crisp weather. It snapped her senses back into focus and stopped her mind from feeling so fuzzy. If there was a chance she might die soon, she wanted to take in every breath and enjoy it.

To her surprise, Logan came out after her, shouting for her to wait up. She turned to face him and was confused as to his presence.

He swished a bottle of Bell's whiskey about in his hand and then swigged directly from the bottle. "Need company?" he asked.

"From you? No thank you."

"Well, tough. I'm coming. I want to see the thing responsible for our deaths before one bites my head off. I'd rather face it head on."

"Seems like the only thing you like to face head on is a bottle of scotch."

Logan looked at the bottle and nodded. He threw it to the ground where it rolled beneath a parked car. "Guess I could use a break. Heavy thoughts make a heavy drinker, you know?"

Gretchen shook her head and carried on walking, tired of arguing. "I'm not surprised you're a drunk. You knew about this and told no one."

"Who would have believed me? The government would have shot me dead as soon as I made the mistake of walking down a dark alleyway. Just because I had the knowledge, didn't mean I could do anything with it."

"When this whole thing started people would have listened to you."

"By then it was already too late. The virus is unstoppable once it gets into the population. The only thing that saved any of us is that there seems to be some random percentage of immunity. I was as staggered as anyone to be included in that small percentage. I guess part of me hoped that the virus would be all there was too it, but deep down I knew there was more. Guess the drinking made it easier to kid myself."

Gretchen climbed the ladder set up against the ambulance and took to the roof. Logan followed.

"What were you doing before you came upon us, Logan? Where had you been for the weeks before?"

Logan shrugged. "Just wandering, really. I had a sister but she caught the Peeling. I had nobody else; not even a home I was proud of. Walking the roads seemed like the best thing to do. Keep moving, keep surviving. We're just like the nomadic tribes that made up the dawn of mankind now. All of our fineries are gone and all that's left is the animal underneath. The things I saw, Gretchen, on the road." He shook his head in disgust. "Maybe it's better if we're extinguished. Maybe that's the reason why. Our violent nature."

Gretchen chewed at her lip, watched the treeline across the road and saw birds. "Maybe you're right. The Peeling didn't affect any other species. Maybe whoever dumped the virus on us just want to restore the balance."

"Then that gives me a little hope; that at least the earth will go on, even without us."

Gretchen nodded. "Me too. But you know, it will only take two to survive. If this alien clean-up crew misses just one man and one woman, then the human race has as much chance as it ever did."

"From small acorns grow mighty oaks. That brings me hope to. Maybe somebody will make it – a new Adam and Eve."

"Let's just hope they do a better job of it than the last pair."

"Amen to that."

THE SUN RECEDED behind the horizon and the moon rose to take its place. Logan still shared the top of the ambulance with Gretchen but the old man had been sleeping for the last two hours. During that time, Gretchen had kept her eyes focused on the treeline. There had been no movement, no sound.

About an hour ago, Bryan came out to let her know that they were going to cook dinner and have the feast she had suggested. She had declined her invitation; she didn't feel like eating.

Now she sat silently, watching the sun disappear and knowing that she might never see it again.

The glowing green light appeared inside the forest again, illuminating the gloom of the canopy. Minutes later the bellowing growls resumed.

This time the growling seemed to be on the move. It was coming their way.

"Logan, wake up. Logan, wake the hell up."

Logan spluttered, opened his eyes. "W-what is it?"

"Shake off your hangover. I think they're coming."

Logan stared at her blearily for a second, before cottoning on to what she meant – and who *they* were. He shot bolt upright. "Where are they?"

Gretchen pointed. "Don't you hear them? They're coming through the woods."

Logan stared across the road at the trees. After a moment he took a big swallow and nodded. "Oh shit."

"That's putting it mildly. Come on, we have to get to the others."

Logan stood up, but made no attempt to leave the roof of the ambulance.

"Will you come on," Gretchen urged.

"I have to see them. I want to know what it is that's been watching us for so long."

"You're insane."

"Don't you understand? For millennia man has wondered if we are alone. We are about to set eyes upon a mystery that has kept humanity awake for its entire history. We are about to witness beings far superior to ourselves. We are about to transcend."

"You transcend all you want. I'm getting off this fucking ambulance."

Gretchen threw herself down the ladder and beat a hasty retreat towards the hotel. The growling from the woods continued getting louder. The moon rose higher in the sky.

The other survivors were all assembled in the lobby when Gretchen flew through the entrance doors. They had obviously heard the ominous growling and had been waiting to see what night would bring.

Colin shook his head, his eyes bloodshot. "They're coming, aren't they?"

Gretchen said nothing, just nodded.

Bryan, the carpenter, took the floor. "Everyone grab their weapons. We're safe inside this hotel, but let's be ready to defend ourselves against any unwanted attention. We've survived this long, no need for anyone to give up now."

Gretchen nodded at Bryan, a silent 'thank you' for keeping everybody focused.

He walked over to Gretchen. "Have you seen anything?"

"No, but I know they're coming. I could hear them moving through the woods in this direction."

"Any ideas? We need to take a stand."

"How do you take a stand against something you don't understand?"

Bryan shrugged. "By being ready for anything." He went over to the empty reception desk and took a golf club from the top of it. "Found this in one of the empty rooms. Hope you know how to swing it."

Gretchen took the graphite shaft. "I've been known to hit a few."

"Good. Let's hope they have soft heads."

There was the sound of crunching metal outside, from the car park. Gretchen and Bryan headed across the lobby and peered through the doors.

The ambulance had been tipped onto its side and had slid almost a dozen feet closer to the hotel. Its rear doors were open and the gurney from inside had spilled halfway out. Logan was nowhere to be seen.

Then he appeared at the doors, his bloody hands pressed up against the glass. Half his face was missing as if torn off by barbed wire.

"They're magnificent..." he moaned, before collapsing to the ground and dying.

Those still standing in the lobby screamed.

"Calm down," Bryan shouted. "We're all together and we're fine. No one panic."

"Don't panic?" someone said. "Logan has half of his face missing. What can do something like that?"

There was an almighty roar that shook the lobby's windows in their frames. There was movement in the shadows of the car park and the sounds of heavy footsteps – like a stomping elephant.

"It sounds like a herd of elephants out there," said Bryan. "Shouldn't they be little green men or something?"

Gretchen shrugged. "I think anything we imagined about aliens is very wrong. If they come from a planet with more gravity than us then they would be larger and heavier.

Groves raced down the main staircase, holding a flaming mop in his hands. He put the torch against a bin full of rubbish and set it alight. "We have fires set up all around. Hopefully the light will keep them away."

Gretchen nodded. "Good idea. Make sure they're all lit."

There were more sounds of the parked vehicles outside being pushed around by something monumentally strong.

Everyone regrouped at the bottom of the stairs, standing beside the bin full of flaming debris. The shadows continued to shift and swirl outside, something moving but unseen stalking the survivors.

Bryan returned with his flaming mop. The stench of faded bleach burning made Gretchen turn away. Once she was used to the smell, she took the torch from Bryan.

"What do you want with it?" said Bryan. "We have fires burning at all of the downstairs entrances as well as one in the lounge. We need to keep an eye on them all; last thing we want is to burn ourselves down."

Gretchen took the torch over to the entrance. The flames illuminated Logan's corpse. "I'm going to see if I can get a look at what's out there."

"That's crazy," said Bryan. "Stay away from the doors."

"I need to know what we're up against."

Gretchen didn't know why she was so determined to step outside, but something inside of her was tired of hiding. She wanted to face death head on; to finally say that she had had enough.

Gretchen shoved open one of the double doors of the entrance and slowly slid out into the courtyard. The roaring had stopped and no more vehicles were being shoved around. Something was still nearby, though; she could sense it.

Something flashed by in front of her, silvery scales peeking out of the darkness for a brief second. Gretchen tracked the movement with her torch, but it had been too quick.

Something else moved up ahead. Again she caught a glimpse of silvery scales beneath the moonlight. An important decision presented itself: whether to step back towards the hotel, or whether to venture forwards into the car park.

Despite what her thundering heartbeat suggested, Gretchen took a step forwards.

Something swopped past the back of her. She flinched and took another step forward. A low growl made the hair on the back of her neck stand up.

"Gretchen!" It was Bryan shouting. "Get back in here."

What the hell am I doing out here? Bryan's right, I need to get the hell back inside.

Gretchen turned around, holding the torch out in front of her.

As the cone of light around the flame moved, the darkness parted and illuminated the creature standing between Gretchen and the hotel.

Gretchen screamed. The thing in front of her blinked a reptilian eye the size of a basketball on a head the size of a Toyota.

An unseen appendage cut through the air and struck the torch from Gretchen's hands. She fell backwards on to her rump and dropped the golf club that she had forgotten she even had.

Surrounded by darkness, Gretchen could see nothing but the glint of moonlit scales as the huge beast towered over her. She felt its fetid breath beat down on her like an intermittent gale. She could sense the beat of its mighty heart within its cavernous chest.

The creature bellowed. Gretchen closed her eyes, frozen to the ground.

There was the sound of something being struck multiple times. Gretchen heard human voices followed by the inhuman growl of the beast.

Gretchen opened her eyes.

David and Bryan ran over to her and grabbed her under the arms. "Looks like you need a hand, you daft cow," said David.

The two men dragged her towards the hotel while a handful of other survivors – including Groves and Colin – proceeded to beat at the creature with a variety of make-shift weapons. The blows seemed to have little effect, but they at least distracted the enemy while David and Bryan got Gretchen out of there.

People held the doors open while Gretchen leapt through them and skidded to her knees on the tiles. David yanked her back up, before tuning and going back to the doorway. Groves and Colin were still outside.

The two men yelled outside in the courtyard as they continued fighting the monster. The monster replied with a rumbling growl so loud that it made Gretchen's head ache.

"We have to help them," she cried.

But it was too late. The ear-piercing scream that suddenly ripped through the air was proof enough that Groves and Colin were beyond help. Two seconds later, their screams halted and silence reigned.

Everyone left alive inside the lobby stood around in silence, glancing at one another nervously. The burning bin in the centre of the room cast dancing shadows across each of their stark white faces.

Gretchen felt her heart beating in her chest as she peered out into the darkness and saw nothing but a velvet sheet of black. If she didn't know otherwise she could claim that the courtyard and car park were completely deserted – but she knew that something unspeakable roamed the darkness out there, ready to extinguish them all.

"We have to get out of here," someone said.

"And go where?" said David. "Stepping outside is as good as committing suicide."

"Well, we can't just stay here."

"Nobody has been hurt staying inside. It's going out there that has gotten people killed."

The front doors of the lobby smashed into a thousand pieces as a shredded body came flying through the glass. The corpse hit the ground and lay on the tiles facing up with empty sockets where its eyes had once been.

Gretchen tried not to gag. "Jesus, Colin!"

"Not anymore," said David.

Everybody in the lobby scattered in all directions, some running up the staircase and others heading into the lounge. David got caught over by the doors by something that snatched in at him from the darkness. The brief flash of scales was all that Gretchen saw and then David was gone.

The hotel filled with the screams of terrified men and women, but Gretchen stayed rooted to the spot. The outside wall of the lobby crumpled as something huge began to force itself in. The creature was like nothing she had ever seen, nor even imagined.

Gretchen knew right then, as she stared at the beast from a place unknown, that humanity's days were over. There would be no last stands or intergalactic war. There would be nothing more than a frightened handful of people screaming for their lives.

In fact, the only victory she could achieve was not to scream at all as she faced extinction; so she just closed her eyes and waited; waited for it all to be over.

And within seconds it was.

SHORT STORY COLLECTION

To follow is a collection of short stories originally written for my Patrons (patreon/iainrobwright). They were written over several months in 2017. They are released for the first time in this book.

1. EHLLF

Chapter 1

"You promise Santa will come, Mummy?" Mia watched her mother's face closely, seeking out the truth in case her words lied.

Mummy smiled and nodded as she pulled the blankets over Mia's shoulders and kissed her forehead. "Santa will be here, I promise, but only if you go to sleep. The sooner you close your eyes, the sooner Christmas will be here."

From the bottom bunk, Tim cheered. Then: "Will Daddy come see us?"

Mia saw the flicker on Mummy's face that happened every time someone mentioned Daddy. She tried to hide it, and when she spoke she kept smiling. Mia wondered why she did that. "Daddy won't make it this year, sweetheart. Maybe next Christmas."

Mia missed her daddy lots, but she somehow knew she should forget about seeing him altogether, and give all of her hugs to Mummy. She thought Daddy had done something bad. "I love you, Mummy. I hope Santa brings something nice for you too."

Mummy's face quivered like she might cry, but she kissed Mia on the forehead, and did the same to Tim on the bottom bunk. Then she moved over to the light switch and left her hand hovering over it. "Goodnight, my babies."

A flick of Mummy's finger and the world went dark. Mia hated the dark, but her Hippo night light made most of it okay. Having Tim snoring beneath her always helped too. If there was anything nasty in the dark, it would get her little brother first. A horrible thought, but still one that gave her comfort—and anyway, she knew deep down that if something tried to hurt Tim, she'd do her best to protect him. Any monsters under the bed would have to eat them both. Then Mummy would be even sadder than she was now.

"Mia?" Tim said in the darkness beneath her.

"Yes?"

"Where's Daddy?"

Mia didn't have an answer. She rarely had answers to Tim's questions, and it frustrated her. He was five and she was seven, so she should know everything by now, but he always managed to find something to make her feel silly. Like now, she couldn't tell him where their daddy was, and that seemed stupid. Most little girls and boys knew where their daddy's were. "I don't now," she admitted. "I think he wanted to be on his own."

"Why?"

"Because he used to get angry and upset all the time. Like when you play on Mummy's tablet and don't want to share. He was like that all the time."

"I would share with Daddy," Tim muttered. "Why doesn't he want to share with me?"

"I don't know, Tim! He's just gone."

"Did Mummy send him away?"

Mia didn't know the answer to that one either, but she had a feeling about it. "I don't think Mummy did anything wrong. We should forget about Daddy because Mummy needs us more."

"I want Daddy."

Mia punched her pillow and tried to get comfy. "Well, boo hoo. Just go to sleep, Tim. Or do you want Santa to miss our house?"

"No. I want toys."

Mia sighed. Tim was still just a little kid. She had to remember that. "You'll get toys, I promise. Lots probably."

"And you will too, Mia."

"I'm too old for toys. I want clothes and make up."

Tim chuckled. "You still like toys too, Mia. I think Santa will bring you something fun to play with."

Mia's tummy burst with a sudden rush of excitement. She really did love Christmas, and the thought of it made her want to get up and wee. "Okay, maybe just a few toys for me too."

"If not," said Tim. "You can share mine. Goodnight, Mia."

"Goodnight, Tim."

Chapter 2

A bump in the night.

Mia opened her eyes. A noise.

Tim was awake too. "Mia? What was that?"

Mia blinked in the darkness, stretching her eyes wide and trying to see. All she saw were blotchy shapes though, black against black. She heard the ticking of the Mickey Mouse clock on the wall. At seven AM it would shout '*O tootles!*' and Christmas would arrive, but now its rhythmic ticking was scary. She wished it would stop, but she dreaded the silence even worse. What frightened her most was that Mummy had not come rushing into their room. If something was wrong, it was Mummy's job to take care of it. So where was she?

"Is it Santa?" Tim asked.

Santa? Mia felt another rush of excitement, but it wasn't enough to make her fear go away. Why was she scared? It was just a noise.

"I want to get up and see Santa," said Tim.

"No!" said Mia. "Just wait."

So they waited. The more time that passed, the more Mia doubted they'd heard anything.

More time passed.

The house was quiet. Mummy didn't come. Slowly, little by little, the darkness turned grey and Mia could make out the chest of drawers opposite her bed, and the Mickey Mouse clock on the wall above it. The mouse's white-gloved hand waved back and forth to her. It was three in the morning. Christmas was still far away. "We should go back to sleep, Tim. It was probably just the wind."

"There isn't any wind."

"Just go to sleep."

"Okay."

Tim was snoring again almost immediately. He had a skill for instant sleeping that Mia envied. She always took forever to drop off, staring at the ceiling and thinking about everything going on in her life—like what it would be like to not have a daddy anymore.

Cunk Cunk.

Tim was awake again. "Mia! What was that?"

Mia sprang up in bed, heart racing. "I don't know! Mummy! Mummy come in!"

Tim shouted too, and they didn't stop, even when they heard their mother stir and get out of bed. The only thing that quieted them was the eventual sound of a door creaking open. Mummy's door always creaked. She appeared in their room a moment later, switching on the light and blinking her droopy eyelids. "Kids, what is it? What are you shouting about?"

"We heard a noise," said Mia.

"It's Santa," said Tim hopefully. Mia thought he was wrong.

Mummy pulled an unhappy face and rubbed at her eyes. "Kids, it's not Santa. You need to go back to sleep."

"But we heard something!" Mia protested. "There's something downstairs."

"No, there's not! You're both worked up with excitement. It'll be Christmas soon, but not yet. Go back to sleep."

Tim gave in. "Okay, Mummy."

But Mia wasn't about to let it go. Mummy didn't believe her, fine, but there had definitely been a noise downstairs. "Mummy! There's something downstairs."

Mummy looked irritated and tired. She only ever got irritated when she was sleepy, like first thing in the morning or when Mia got up after she'd been put to bed. "Go back to sleep now, honey. Everything is fine, okay?"

Mia was about to argue more, but she didn't have to.

Cunk cunk cunk.

Mummy's face went all funny, and she froze like a statue. Mia felt a little sick in her tummy. "Mummy, what is it?

Mummy tilted her head like she was on the phone to Grandma. "Hold on, sweetheart. Just be quiet a sec."

Mia wanted to wee. She felt Tim shuffling in the bottom bunk. Having the light on in the middle of the night felt strange. Mickey Mouse's tick-tocking sounded louder than usual.

Tick Tock Tick Tock.

Cunk Cunk.

Mummy shivered like she was cold, but Mia knew it was the noise that made her do it. She was scared. "Mummy, I don't like it."

"It's just a noise, honey. I'll go take a quick look downstairs."

"No! No, stay here, Mummy."

"I want to come with you, Mummy," said Tim.

"No, both of you stay here. I'll bring you up some milk and we'll read a book before going back to sleep."

"Okay, Mummy," said Tim. He was always so happy to accept what she told him. Mia used to be that way, too, but now she needed more than words. She needed to see things for herself to accept what was real. Still, she was only a kid, and if Mummy wanted to go downstairs alone, there was no stopping her.

Mia pulled her blankets up under her chin as she watched her mother creep towards the door. She stopped for a few moments before going out into the hall, tilting her head to listen again. There were no more sounds. Whatever had been moving around downstairs seemed to have gone still. Mia reeled off the possibilities in her head. Her friend at school, Max, once said a fox got in through their back door one night and tore open a big bag of dog food in the garage. Maybe they had a fox downstairs. Foxes were cute.

Mummy told them to stay in their beds, and then disappeared, slipping through the doorway and entering the darkness of the landing. Mia and Tim did as they were told and sat in their beds quietly, the harsh glare of the bulb conflicting with the time of night. Mia's body clock was trying to drag her back to sleep, but her fear was making her want to do jumping jacks. A few minutes passed before they heard anything.

"Everything is okay, kids," Mummy shouted up. "It's just a lamp."

Tim got out of bed and Mia hissed at him. "What are you doing?"

"I want to see."

"We'll get told off."

"No we won't. I want to see what happened. I want to see if Santa has come."

Mia was about to order her little brother back to bed, but the thought of seeing whether there were presents under the tree was too tempting. She turned sideways on her bunk and slid down the ladder, landing beside Tim. She took his hand. "Come on then, but if we get told off you get the blame."

"Mummy won't tell us off. She said she would read us a book."

Mia pushed aside their door and stepped out onto the landing. It was dark, but the light from the lounge bled up the stairs and made it okay. All the same, Mia hurried with her brother towards the stairs, not wanting to wander the house in the middle of the night. The lounge was below, and the red tinsel attached to the skirting boards peeked up at her. She couldn't see Mummy.

Tim tugged at her arm and took the first step down. His fear was all gone, replaced by enthusiasm to find presents. Mummy heard them coming when the middle step creaked.

"What are you two doing out of bed?"

"We wanted to see what happened," Mia explained, hoping it wouldn't result in a telling off. Mummy didn't usually get angry, but when she did, it was scary. Ever since daddy left.

This time, though, Mummy just sighed and said, "Come on down then."

Mia's spirit lifted and she and her brother trotted down the final steps into the lounge. Christmas met them. The tree lights were off because Mummy said it wasn't safe to leave them on overnight, but the baubles and tinsel caught the shone all by themselves. Atop the tree sat the angel she and Tim had picked together at the supermarket. Beneath was an assortment of presents, wrapped and labeled in blues and reds—there were even a couple of green ones. Mia hopped and clapped her hands. "Santa came."

Mummy smiled. She was holding the lamp that lived next to the sofa. It must have fallen on the floor. "Yes, honey, but it's still too early to get up. Let me get some milk and we'll go up and read that story."

Tim moaned. "No fair. I want to stay up."

"Yeah," said Mia, eyeing up the presents piled beneath the tree. "I don't feel sleepy anymore."

"But Mummy does, and we're going to have a long day ahead, so we don't want to end up tired."

Mia sighed. "Okay, Mummy."

Mummy smiled and went into the kitchen. Tim dropped straight onto his knees and started fondling the presents. "You think I got an Xbox?"

"No," Mia snapped. "Mummy already told us we couldn't have anything too expensive."

"Why? James next door will get one, he already saw it in his dad's car."

Mia grunted. James next door got everything he asked for, but that was because his dad was a builder with lots of workers. "Mummy has to look after us all on her own, Tim. We have to be happy with what we get."

Tim crossed his arms and sulked. "Let's see how you feel if you don't get a mobile phone."

Mia had already eyed up a box that could have been a phone, but she dared not hope too much. She had wanted one for her birthday, but had only gotten some perfume. She'd thrown a fit and Mummy had cried, which left her feeling really bad. She didn't want the same thing to happen today, so she would smile and be thankful for whatever she got. But still, the box near the back of the tree was definitely the right size for a phone. And there was something else back there too. Something pushed right up against the skirting board next to the wires and the plug for the Christmas lights. It looked like a soft toy. Green and red…

"Okay, you two, let's get back up to bed."

Mummy's voice made Mia flinch. She turned, on her hands and knees. "Mummy, there's something behind the tree."

"We'll open the presents later, Mia, now take your glass of milk and go upstairs."

"No, Mummy, it's not a present. It looks like a dolly."

Mummy frowned, but didn't seem to care. "Okay, well, we'll look when the sun's up."

Mia turned back towards the tree and leant forwards. She pushed aside presents and reached out. There was definitely something back there, and it wasn't wrapped up like everything else.

"Mia! Do you hear me?"

"Just wait a second, Mummy. There's something back here."

"Mia!"

"Hold on!" Mia knew she would get a telling off for shouting, but she almost had the thing in her hand now. Green and red. Her fingers wrapped around it and she was surprised by heavy it was. Not too heavy to move, but not light like a soft toy should be. It made her even more intrigued, and she was barely aware of her mother's chiding voice behind her.

"Mia, I'm going to count to three, young lady!"

Mia yanked the thing out from behind the tree and spun around on her bum, facing her angry mother. "I've got it. Look!"

She'd not even had a chance to look at it properly herself yet, which was why they were all equally shocked when she held the thing out in front of her.

Tim was the first to speak. "It's an elf!"

Mia frowned. Her little brother was right. She held an elf in her hands, but not a fluffy Christmas decoration or soft toy. This was realistic. Its leggings were thick, red and green, and it wore a fuzzy green jacket with big white buttons.

Mummy looked confused. "What is that thing? I've never seen it before."

"Maybe Santa left it," said Tim. "I think it's for me."

Mia pulled the thing closer to her. "It's not yours! I found it."

"Give it here," said Mummy. "It's not anybody's."

It wasn't fair. Mia had spotted the elf under the tree and that must mean it was meant for her. But the look on Mummy's face told her it would be bad to argue. She removed the elf from against her chest and offered it out with both hands like a baby sleeping.

It opened its eyes.

The shock made Mia yelp, and she almost dropped the elf on the floor. She caught herself just in time and ended up lowering it clumsily to the ground. As soon as it was out of her hands, Mummy grabbed her by the arm and yanked her away.

"Ow! You hurt me."

Mummy didn't apologise. Instead, she shoved Mia and Tim behind her and stared down at the elf that was lying underneath the tree. Its eyes were once again closed, and it seemed to be sleeping. When Mia had dropped the elf, its hat had fallen off, revealing wavy brown hair and a patch at the side of his head that was covered in blood.

"It's hurt," said Tim.

"Just stay back," said Mummy. "It could be dangerous."

Tim giggled. "It's just a little elf. Santa must have left him behind."

Mia wanted a more sensible answer for what she was seeing, but Tim was right. She had found a real life elf under their tree. And it was hurt. "Mummy, we need to look after it."

"Until Santa comes back!" said Tim excitedly.

Mummy was clutching at herself like she was cold, and she didn't do anything but stare at the elf. Mia reached out and touched her. "It's okay, Mummy. Don't be scared."

Mummy snapped out of her daze and rubbed Mia's back. "I'm not scared, sweetheart. Just a little shocked. I think I should call someone."

"No!" said Tim. "They'll come take it away. We have to look after it until Santa comes back."

"Honey, Santa isn't..." She trailed off, and Mia thought she had been about to say Santa wasn't real. But he must be because there was an elf on their floor.

"Mummy, can we just make sure it's okay? It's bleeding."

Mummy rubbed at both of her eyes and then shuddered as if she had a chill. "This is not how I expected Christmas Day to begin. I'm going to need a drink after all this."

"I can get you some water if you'd like, Mummy," said Tim.

She rubbed his back and smiled. He looked tiny, standing beside her in his *Paw Patrol* pyjamas. "Mummy means a different kind of drink, but thank you, sweetheart."

"What are we going to do, Mummy?" Mia asked.

"I honestly have no idea. Just... let me deal with it, okay? Stay back."

Mia and Tim did as they were told and moved over towards the sofa. Mummy knelt next to the elf and shoveled her hands underneath it. She lifted it carefully, in the same way she got steaming pasta bake out the oven. Then she took it out of the lounge and into the dining space next to the kitchen. They all flinched when the sleeping creature gave a sudden *yip!* But it remained asleep.

Mummy lay the elf down on the table and stood with her hands on her hips. Outside, the leaves on the trees rus*t*led.

"Are you going to wake him up, Mummy?" Tim asked.

"How do you know it's a boy?" Mia didn't like the assumption. Why couldn't it be a girl?

Tim shrugged. "Pull down its trousers."

"We're not doing that!" snapped Mummy. She seemed angry about all this, and Mia couldn't understand why. Perhaps it was because Mummy didn't believe in elfs, and now she had been proven wrong. Mummy hated being wrong. She took her hands away from her hips now and used them to grip the edge of the dining room table. "I think we should put a blanket over it and switch the heating on. It's pretty chilly down here."

In just her pyjamas, Mia should have felt the cold too, but she was so excited that she felt like she might start sweating. "Yes, Mummy. I think a blanket would be nice."

"Can I get the blanket?" Tim begged.

Mummy nodded tiredly. "Yes, yes. Go into the kitchen and take your dad's smoking blanket from the broom closet."

Mia saw the sudden hurt in Mummy's eyes at the mention of their dad. She knew the blanket she was talking about--a tatty, multi-coloured thing daddy used to wrap around himself to smoke in the garden when it was cold. Mummy didn't allow smoking in the house. She was always very serious about that. Mia didn't understand why she had kept the blanket because Mummy didn't smoke.

Tim ran in and out of the kitchen in a flash, bringing with him the tatty old blanket that smelled of smoke and Daddy. Mummy took it and held it for a moment, like she'd forgotten what she'd wanted it for, but then she turned and lay it over the sleeping elf. She asked Mia to turn the dial up on the heating, and she whopped it all the way up to 35. That was much hotter than she was usually allowed to turn it. The radiators clonked like they always did.

Soon the house was warm, and the elf, underneath its blanket, was as snug as a bug in a rug. In fact, its cheeks were red, and it began to wriggle about.

"It's waking up, Mummy!" Tim hopped up and down.

Mia was excited too. She watched with wonder as the little elf clutched at the blanket and twisted and turned. In fact, it was thrashing about in the same way their goldfish did when Tim lifted it out of the water for a few seconds. It looked unhappy.

"I don't think it feels very well, Mummy," Mia said.

Mummy nodded and looked worried.

The little creature leapt up on the table and screamed.

Chapter 3

Mia covered her ears. "Mummy! Make it stop."

The elf's screaming was scary, and it made Mia want to run away. The little creature was up on its feet, racing around the dining room table and clutching at itself like it was on fire. Its fat little cheeks were bright red.

"It looks hot, Mummy," said Tim. "He didn't like the blanket."

Mummy moved both of them behind her again. The little elf stopped screaming and bent over huffing and puffing. Its pink tongue was hanging out.

Mia realised something. "Elves live at the North Pole. It doesn't like being hot. We shouldn't have put a blanket on it."

Mummy put her hands out to the elf. "We're not going to hurt you. It's okay."

The elf straightened up and stared at Mummy. It didn't look scared, it looked upset. Maybe it didn't know where it was. Mia had another thought and rushed off into the kitchen. Mummy shouted after her so she made it quick. She grabbed a glass and filled it with cold water from the sink. When she brought it back, she set it on the table as close to the hopping elf as she dared. When it clunked against the table, the elf flinched and hissed at her. Mia hurried back behind Mummy.

"I don't like it, Mummy," said Tim. "Make it leave."

"Shoo!" said Mummy, waving a hand at the elf. But it ignored her. It scurried over to the glass of water Mia had brought and peered into it. Mia held hope that the little elf was thirsty, and that her gift would be accepted, but the elf swatted the glass aside and sent water spilling all over the table.

"Bad elf!" Mia shouted.

Mummy moved them back another step. The elf was growling at them now, its eyes small and black.

"Elves are supposed to be friendly," Mia stomped her foot and wagged a finger in the air. "This is our house and we're just trying to help you."

The elf stopped growling. It tilted its head and stared at Mia. She was angry, but also worried, so she clung to Mummy's leg.

"Get away!" said Mummy, still waving her hand. The elf flinched and cowered. Mia felt like things were moving in slow motion. Even though Mummy didn't seem to see what was happening, Mia knew the elf was about to do something nasty. It crouched down like a cat and let out another angry snarl. Mummy waved her hands closer and closer to it, and she didn't listen when Mia told her to stop.

The elf jumped at Mummy and bit her finger. Blood squirted everywhere and the dining room filled with screams. The elf landed on the carpet with a thud and raced away. Mummy waved her hand about frantically, and Mia saw her finger was missing. Tim screamed.

In the lounge, the Christmas tree shook, shedding tinsel and plastic pine needles onto the tops of the presents piled beneath. At the back, against the wall, the elf hid away, munching on Mummy's finger. It must have been hungry, but that didn't mean it could eat people parts.

Mia hated the elf. "Santa will put you in jail!"

The elf peered out from beneath the tree. Blood stained its mouth, and it seemed to grin as it reached a tiny white hand into its coat and pulled something out. It looked like a Christmas tree decoration, a small metal shape, but it was black and sharp. The elf held it out on a string and made sounds that reminded Mia of a grumpy pig.

The black dangly spun on its string, twirling in a circle.

Then it flashed. Just once.

Mummy and Tim were still screaming in the dining room, but Mia heard one of them grab the phone from its cradle on the wall. Mia didn't want to take her eyes off the nasty elf in case it tried to bite Mummy again, so she looked around for something to shoo it off with. Her tummy sloshed, and she wanted to be sick, but Mummy needed her. It was a daddy's job to protect a family, but their Daddy was gone. So it was her job now.

She grabbed Tim's hobby horse—a giant unicorn head on a stick. Mummy said it used to be hers, but Mia didn't remember. She used the toy now to poke at the elf beneath the tree, trying to dislodge it. It hissed and spat at her like a cat, but she felt safe behind the long wooden stick. At one point, it lashed out and bit the unicorn's head, tugging at it and thrashing side to side, but Mia fought back, and flicked the elf into the air. It flew out from beneath the Christmas tree and crashed against the television. The panel tottered back and forth before tipping forwards off the cabinet and landing on top of the elf.

Mummy and Tim heard the noise and came rushing into the lounge. Mummy's arm was covered in blood, but she wasn't screaming anymore. Tim was trembling beside her.

"Mia, get back. It's feral!"

Mia's heart beat fast, and it made her fear go away. She wanted to chase the monster right out of their house, so she hit the back of the television with the hobby horse and tried to crush the thing beneath. "I hurt it, Mummy!"

"Get back!"

Mummy came and moved Mia away. Then, cautiously, she shoved at the overturned television with her foot. The elf was not underneath.

Tim screamed. "Mummy!"

The elf was hanging from the light shade, and it dropped onto Mummy's back and yanked at her hair. It tried to bite her. Mummy raced around the room, hitting herself in the head. as she tried to get the elf

Mia took charge again. She would not let this nasty little monster hurt Mummy again. She raised the hobby horse and swung it as hard as she could.

Mummy yelled in agony when the unicorn head smacked her in the face.

"Oops. Sorry, Mummy." She swung again, and this time managed to whack the elf. It flew again and landed on the shelf above the sofa. There it sat for a second, cross-legged and confused, before standing back up and preparing to leap back into the room. Before it did, something flashed in the middle of the room and distracted them all. Mia glanced and saw the metal dangly lying on the carpet. It was flashing over and over again, faster and faster. The elf stood on the shelf, grinning and chuckling. It even grabbed its fat little belly.

"Mummy, call the police," Tim begged. "I want the police. And Daddy."

Mummy snarled. She yelled at the elf and ran across the room, but before she could grab it, the lounge flooded with light. Mia had to cover both eyes. It was like the sun had come out in the middle of the lounge. Mummy lost her balance and fell backwards across the coffee table.

The sound of bells jingling rose among their frightened screams, and Mia had the strange sense of a crowd watching them. Shielding her eyes, she felt her way over to the window and fingered open the blinds. It was the middle of the night, but the road outside their house was lit up like a funfair. At first she thought she saw dozens of cats—pairs of golden eyes rowed up all the way to the end of their street—but then she realised what she was looking at. Hundreds of elves stood outside the house in a long line. In the middle was a pair of eyes set higher than all the other. A belt buckle glinted in the glaring lights.

Santa Claus had come.

Mia wanted to shout out to the fat, jolly looking figure in the road, but she knew, somehow, that this Santa was not the jolly man she'd read about in story books, or sang about on Christmas Day. He stood outside their house with an army of elves—and she already knew that elves were not friendly.

Mummy got up from the coffee table and sprung across the room again. This time she got her hands on the distracted elf and tossed it against the wall. It struck with a horrible thud and crumpled to the floor on its face. Mia thought it might be dead.

"Mummy, what have you done?"

Mummy was panting. She looked to Mia like a wild dog. "What?"

Mia pointed to the window. "Santa's here. He came for his elf."

Chapter 4

Once again, they found themselves with a sleeping elf. It wasn't dead, as Mia had feared, but it was hurt badly. The wound on its head had started bleeding again, and it was terribly still.

"Are they still out there?" Tim asked Mia.

Mia peered through the blinds. Santa and his elves were still lined up out there. "I think they're waiting."

"For what?"

"What do you think?"

Mummy was cradling the elf, even though it might wake up and bite her again. Her finger stump had stopped bleeding, but it looked horrible. The smell of the blood made Mia feel sick.

Mummy gave them both a weak smile. "It's okay, you two. Let me try the police again."

"I heard you try to call earlier," said Mia.

"The phone was crackling," she said. "Let me try again."

Mia shook her head. "No. The phones won't work. Santa won't let us call the police. He doesn't like people seeing him."

"We can see him," said Tim.

Mia nodded. She didn't want to think about what that could mean. "Mummy, we need to give Santa his elf."

Mummy laughed, but it was a horrible sound. She nodded at the injured elf in her arms. "I don't think he'll accept it like this."

"That's how it was when we found it," said Tim. "Just throw it out the window. Maybe Santa will leave. Why did it even come here? What does it want?"

"To bring us presents," said Mia. She had noticed the strange presents earlier, but now she wanted to investigate. Mummy's presents were all wrapped in red or blue, but two presents were wrapped in green. She picked up the one marked with her name and ripped it open.

The elf flinched in Mummy's arms.

Tim shook his head. "You're not supposed to open presents until Christmas morning."

"And elves aren't supposed to be nasty," Mia shot back. Her tone made her little brother cry, so she went over and hugged him. She still held the present in her hand, and she continued to unwrap it once Tim was okay.

"Huh," she said. "A Care Bear. I asked for one of these."

Mummy frowned. "No you didn't."

Mia nodded. "I wrote a letter at school. We all did. It was during lesson."

"I always ask you to write Santa a letter, but you never do."

Mia shrugged. Writing letters had always seemed silly to her. No way could Santa read them all. "I told you, it was for lesson. I had to do it."

Tim nodded. "I wrote one, too, for Mrs Tanner. We did a big one for the wall and we all wrote one Christmas wish on it."

Mia looked at the fluffy pink Care Bear. She didn't even really want the thing, but she had needed to think of something to ask for at the time. "What did you ask for, Tim?"

"A robot."

Mia went over to the tree and picked up the second green present. She unwrapped it, but already knew what she would find inside. She handed the toy robot to Tim, who took it with a smile, but then he pulled a face and threw it on the floor. "I don't want it."

Mia threw her Care Bear down and stamped on it. "I don't blame you, Tim."

The elf twitched in Mummy's arms. "Children, I want you to go upstairs. This animal is waking up again and I don't want you to get hurt."

Seeing Mummy so scared made Mia angry again, but it also made her think about something. "We won't get hurt, Mummy. Only you will."

Mummy frowned. "What do you mean?"

Mia couldn't be sure of what she was about to say, but it made sense. "Santa can't hurt children. And neither can his elves."

"Mia… what are you going on about? Please, just go upstairs."

Mia marched up to her Mummy, unsettled by the fact she felt like she was the one in charge. But this was no problem for an adult to take care of. When it came to Santa, it was a kid's area of expertise. "Give me the elf, Mummy."

"No! Mia, get away. It's waking up."

"It won't hurt me. I'm a kid. Every time it's attacked, it's gone for you, Mummy. Even when I was the one hitting it with Tim's hobby horse. The reason it was here was to leave us presents. Santa wants his elf back, but it has to be a kid who goes out and sees him. Mummy, I won't let you get hurt again. Give me the elf."

Mummy looked very old. Her eyes were locked on Mia and she stood completely still, but her arms moved in front of her. Slowly, she offered the elf to Mia.

Mia took it carefully. It stirred and whimpered and was cold as ice. They must have nearly killed it when they'd wrapped it in a blanket. Its head was still bleeding, but that wasn't their fault. How on earth it had ended up hurt beneath their tree, she did not know, but it was not their doing. Santa needed to know.

"Open the front door, Mummy."

"Mia…"

"Mummy, it's okay. Just do it. If anything happens, I'll run right inside."

Mummy opened the door and ice cold air blew in. In just her pyjamas, Mia was freezing, but there was no time to worry about that now. The blinding light outside was too painful to look at, so she had to squint at the ground. At the edge of her vision, she saw a line of shadows—elves lined up, watching her. She could be wrong about everything. They might attack her at any moment.

There was a frost on the grass and it crunched underfoot as she crept away from the house. The elf in her arms opened its eyes, confused again, but when it saw her it did not get angry. She clutched it over her shoulder like a baby and patted its back. "It's okay. I'm taking you back to Santa."

And to Santa she went. The lights were still too blinding to see properly, so she had to blink rapidly and steal brief glimpses of the giant man stood at the edge of their front garden. She heard quiet chattering all the way down the road—the elves were talking.

Looking down at the ground, Mia offered out the elf. "I'm sorry Mr Santa. We found your elf. He was hurt beneath our tree, but when we tried to help him he got very nasty. You should really be more careful about how your elves behave."

The elf squeaked in her hands, and sounded like a scared kitten now. Maybe Santa would be mad with it. She tried to look at Santa's face, but it was covered by shadow. All she could see was the giant, glinting belt buckle around his massive waist.

There was sudden movement, accompanied by bells jingling, and the elf was snatched out of her hands. A massive gust of wind blew a cloud of snow in her face, despite it not snowing at all this year. She spluttered and wiped her face, and when she could see again, the blinding light had gone. The road outside their house was empty. Overhead, the black sky was turning blue. Christmas morning would soon be here.

Mia turned and went back inside the house. There, her mother and little brother waited for her. They both gathered her into a hug. Mummy was crying.

As the sun rose, they gathered Santa's presents into a bin liner and threw them into the wheelie bin outside. Neither Mia nor Tim wanted them. Mummy made them hot chocolate, and they sat in front of the Christmas tree to open their presents to each other.

"Mummy," said Tim as he unwrapped his first gift.

"Yes, honey?"

"I don't like Santa."

Mummy laughed. "Me either. Maybe next year we don't write to him."

"Oh, I will write to him," said Mia. "I'm going to write him a complaint!"

They all laughed and spent Christmas together without another mention of Santa and his elves.

MERRY CHRISTMAS!

2. VLOG LIFE

Chapter 1

"Here's ten bucks, bro. Enjoy!"

The stinking vagrant peered at Lance in a confused squint. His cracked lips moved wordlessly, forming gobs of foul saliva at the corners of his mouth. A grey beard hung off his chin and seemed to move. Lice.

Lance waved the note in the hobo's face. "Take it, man. It's yours."

The vagrant glanced aside and stared right into the camera. Lance heard the mechanical buzz of the G7 X's lens as Tom zoomed in on the confused expression.

"You for real, kid?" Lance beamed. "Yeah, bro!" The hobo snatched the note and squirrelled it away into the folds of his rancid sweatshirt. He returned Lance's wide grin. "Thanks, kid! If only more people were-"

"Okay cut!" Lance turned away and quickly put a hand against his mouth to keep from gagging. "Come on, man, let's bounce. This fucker reeks of piss and who knows what."

Tom lowered the camera and nodded. "No kidding, bro. Think I'm gonna hurl."

The hobo frowned, then appraised himself as if he hadn't before noticed the crust covering his clothing. When he looked back at Lance, he was no longer smiling. "What are you kids up to?"

Lance could still smell piss, so he took another step away. "What's it look like we're doing, idiot? We're shooting a video."

The hobo rose up from his dirty stoop and stared at Lance. It wasn't an aggressive look, but he had become unfriendly—like a threatened dog. Lance wondered how you could live in the dirt and not feel threatened every second. Lance put a hand out to the hobo. "Back off, bro. You got your ten dollars so go get yourself a six pack on me."

The suggestion seemed to light the old man's fire. He stepped towards Lance, bringing the stink with him, and both of his hands clenched into fists. "Why give me money then insult me? You kids today make no sense. You take no responsibility for yourselves or your actions."

Lance smirked. "Coming from an old bum, that's pretty funny. We earn the big bucks, bro. That ten bucks I just gave you is less than I find stuffed down the side of my designer couch. Now take a hike before I kick your ass."

The hobo clenched his fists tighter like he was about to take things further, but then he seemed to deflate, and scurried off like a spineless worm. Fuckin' deadbeat.

"That was gold," said Tom, patting Lance on the back. "Subscribers will eat this shit up. The last 'feeding the homeless' video got eight-million views. This one could get ten. Fifteen gees, easy."

Lance fist bumped his camera man, making the thick gold bracelets on his wrist rattle. It almost covered the sound of his stomach rumbling. "My hunger is roaring fierce, bro. You wanna go get some *schwarma,* or a burrito or something?"

"I could go for a burrito, bro, but I got to go pay the meter if we're hanging."

Lance checked his watch—early evening. Cleveland's night scene would begin its tune any minute, and it was calling to him. Friday night and he was feeling pretty dope. This week alone, he and Tom had brought in twenty gees from ad revenue alone, and that didn't even include the t-shirt sales. New videos included a prank involving Trump supporters failing to help an old Mexican lady lying in the street (it was fake as shit, but the liberals ate it up), and a social experiment asking young sluts (actually paid actresses) if they would give Lance a blowjob in public for $1000—they all said yes. The channel was blowing up, yo.

"Okay, Tom, I'll meet you at the *Chub-n-Tuck* for some eats, then I wanna find a club and get laid."

Tom laughed. "Didn't you get laid last night?"

"And the night before. What's your point, bro?"

Tom shrugged. "Let me feed the meter and I'll meet you there. Get a Papa Bless Big Burrito for me."

CALORIE ALERT. Lance winced. "Those things are as big as my arm, bro. You gonna get fat."

"Long as we keep bringing in the cheddar, I don't give a shit."

"Word!"

Lance stood on the sidewalk for a while, watching his buddy disappear around the corner. It was a balmy night and life was awesome. Just breathing Cleveland's breeze was invigorating. He was alive tonight. Totally alive.

He was *Prankstar.*

Time to dab.

As Lance broke loose in the street, he heard a delightful sound. Two giggling girls strolled his way, and they squawked even louder when he gave them his trademark wink. They looked a little underage, so he'd have to give them a miss, but that didn't mean he couldn't have fun.

"Like my moves, ladies?"

Both girls were blonde, but one of them had dark eyeliner on, making her the sexier of the two. It was her who spoke. "What are you doing?"

"I'm just celebrating being rich and famous. Sometimes a playa got to dance!"

"You're famous?"

He nodded. "And rich. I'm *Prankstar*."

Both girls looked at each other and giggled again. Dark-eyes raised a thin eyebrow at Lance. That gesture alone made him want to screw her right there on the sidewalk. "Never heard of you," she said.

Lance smirked. "You will soon, baby. My YouTube channel is the 17th most viewed this year. I get three-million views a day. My shit is blowing up."

"And that makes you famous?"

"And rich."

Dark-eyes was going for it. The corners of her mouth narrowed as she pouted. "How rich?"

"Let's say I could go buy us a house to screw in with the spare cash in my bank account."

Both blondes gasped, but dark eyes was only feigning shock. "You're terrible."

"So make me behave. How old are you, sweetheart?"

"Seventeen." Bullshit. Lance would be surprised if she'd even hit sixteen. Still, girl had it going on, for sure. "Okay, fuck it. Meet me at the I-Dubz club at nine o'clock and we'll have some fun. I'll get us into VIP and have drinks sent to us all night. It's just across the river. You know it?"

Both blondes looked at each other and grinned. Dark eyes looked back at him. "Yeah, we know it. Are you for real?"

Lance took her chin between his finger and thumb and looked into her eyes. "Honey, you say you don't know who I am? After tonight, you'll never forget me. I'm fucking Prankstar."

Chapter 2

Lance gave the two blondes a twenty so they could get a taxi home and put on something appropriately slutty. Once he saw them off, he tried to check in with Tom, who had been gone a while, but got his voicemail. He crossed the road and headed for *Chub-n-Tucks, deciding that* Tom might already be there. The diner was a total dive, but the food was pretty dope. Six months ago, before YouTube pranks, a greasy burrito was all Lance could've afforded. His mom was a struggling waitress. His fuckwit father was down in Florida with his bitch girlfriend. It had been Lance and his mom on their own for six years now, living in a shit hole apartment and eating nothing but fast food. His mom had ridden him hard about the pranks at first, but she kept her mouth shut now that the cheddar was coming in. She had stayed out of his hair ever since that first YouTube check for twelve thousand dollars.

Your boy's a star, mom. Deal with it.

Cleveland's traffic was dying down, the everyday lull between the work day and evening play. That was what made him look to his right as he crossed the road and heard a revving engine. At the side of the street, a black van pulled off from the curb and headed in his direction. It was speeding up fast…

"What the Hell" Lance picked up pace, not wanting to get in the idiot's way. But the van veered towards him. Right fucking towards him. "Hey! Hey, what the Hell?" The van sped up. Its engine roared. Lance threw himself onto the sidewalk avoiding the screeching tyres by inches. As the van sped away, he lay there on the ground, wondering what the Hell had just happened. Lunatic tried to mow me down!

"Whoa, dude, are you okay?" a kid in a red beanie hat came hurrying down the sidewalk towards him. "That guy almost took you out!"

Lance patted himself down and winced when he realised he'd skinned his elbow. He cursed as he got back to his feet. "Motherfucker better hope I never see him again, or I'll sue him down to his shit-stained underwear."

The kid looked him up and down, a hand out but not quite touching him. "Wait, don't I know you?" He took off his beanie hat and unveiled a mess of brown hair, scratched at his scalp. "You're *Prankstar*?"

Lance rubbed his palms together, expelling the dirt from the sidewalk. He offered his right hand for a shake. "You a fan?"

The kid nodded profusely—that star-struck look in his eye that Lance loved so much. "Yeah, man. I love all that shit you do. That social experiment you did when you dressed up as a woman to see if transgendered people get hassled when they go into public toilets was dope, yo."

Lance smiled, remembering the skit well. It was one of his best, and he had looked hella good as a chick. "Thanks, bro."

The kid fiddled with his beanie hat, reaching a hand inside of it. "No problem. It's all fake as shit though, right?"

Lance frowned. It wasn't the first accusation he had received, but the kid hadn't seemed like a doubter. He was about to defend his content as real—the company line—when he saw the kid pluck something from inside his beanie hat. It was bright yellow and plastic. And it gave off a buzzing sound.

"Don't taze me, bro!" Lance's limbs turned to jelly, and he was suddenly falling towards the pavement. He was fully aware as he lay paralysed on his back, staring up at the darkening sky. He was fully aware of the black van returning and screeching up alongside the curb, the side door sliding open. He was fully aware as two men leapt out and bundled him into the back before driving away.

Lance was fully aware that he could be about to die.

Chapter 3

At first, Lance could not speak. Every time he tried, his lips quivered uncontrollably. But eventually, he could focus enough to get a few words out. "H-help! W-who are you?"

At the front of the van, both the driver and his companion glanced back at Lance. Both of them wore balaclavas. Both men said nothing.

Lance groaned. Pain in his testicles made him groan. Had he been tasered in the nuts? Screw that shit! "Just let me go, dawg. I have money."

The two men stayed silent. Lance tried to think. People were supposed to listen to the road for clues, or try to sense direction in situations like this, right? Okay, okay. Just stay calm and work this shit through. It felt as though the van had sped up, maybe on the freeway. Where were they taking him? Who were *they*?

He had no idea what direction they were travelling in. All he heard was the road beneath the tyres. "Please, just let me go. What did I do to you?"

He tried to give his question an answer. *Someone I pranked? It has to be.*

"Are you the guy we pretended to rob in the alleyway? The gun was fake, bro. You signed a disclaimer, remember? Is it money? You want to get paid? Fine. How's five-gees sound?"

The two men kept their attention on the road, ignoring Lance completely. They were both average build, but they had a menacing aura, like they would watch him bleed to death without an ounce of compassion. The man in the passenger seat looked like he had a beard tucked beneath his balaclava, but there was nothing else about either man he could identify.

Lance freaked out. He kicked both legs at the van's side panel. When that didn't work, he searched for a lock or handle, which led him to discover that the van's rear windows were thickly tinted, and that the interior handles, along with all the seats, had been removed. It was a full on rape wagon.

What the hell is going to happen to me?

With escape not an option, Lance's only choice was to attack. He got to his feet and rushed the two men up front, terror rising in him and escaping his lungs in an almighty yell. It was too cramped in the van's interior to throw a punch, so he grabbed the front passenger's neck and tried to throttle him. When the man reacted in surprise, Lance thought he had a good chance of fighting his way out of this, but then his face exploded in agony and he crumpled backwards into the van's rear. His vision turned a million different ways and liquid gushed down his shirt.

Blood. "You bwoke my dose! You bastard!"

The passenger turned to him and snarled through the holes in his balaclava. His voice was raspy, like a heavy drinker's. "Sit down before I break something else, kid!"

Lance swallowed his next words and made no more noise. Blood flowed down his face and his nose burned with agony. He was in big trouble here.

These guys mean business. *But at least they had their faces covered. No point doing that if they weren't going to let him go eventually, right? I'm just gonna get my ass handed to me, but I can take a beating. I'll come through this. Maybe I'll make the news and get even more views. Hell, the sympathy factor will be a goldmine if I play this right.*

What the fuck am I thinking about? I need to get the fuck out of here.

"Please let me go. I'm sorry. You're scaring me. Just let me go!"

The van screeched to a stop, so suddenly Lance tumbled head over heels towards the front.

"Okay," the passenger with the raspy voice barked. "Get the fuck out, kid!"

Lance swallowed, his throat thick with nose-blood. "W-what?"

There was an audible *click* as the driver reached forward and pulled something under the dashboard. Lance felt a draft behind him and realised the van's sliding door had fell ajar.

"Get the fuck out, kid!"

Lance didn't need telling again. He wrapped his fingers around the sliding door and threw it open so hard it almost bounced back and sliced him in two. Night had fallen and the balmy breeze met him. His feet hit the ground and he was running.

Running through the woods.

"Fuck fuck fuck fuck. Where the Hell am I?"

Lance didn't know of any woods in Cleveland, but he supposed the suburbs would have a few. If that was true, then there must be houses nearby—someone who could help.

Or I can call someone!

Still running as fast as he could, Lance yanked his cellphone from his jeans and dialled 911. The screen lit the darkness in front of him, but made it harder to see ahead. Several times, he stumbled to avoid going head over heels into a bush, or caving his skull open on a low hanging branch. Wherever he was, there was no well-walked trail he could see. Just wilderness. In fucking Cleveland?

Dead air filled his eardrums when his phone failed to connect. He glanced at the screen and saw he had no service. Where were all the houses? Where was he?

"HERE PIGGY PIGGY!" Lance looked back and saw only darkness behind him.

"THERE'S NOWHERE TO RUN, PIGGY!"

"SCREW YOU!" he shouted back. "I'm gonna brain you fuckers."

He tried his phone again, but it was still out of service. Eventually, he put it back in his pocket because it was slowing him down. Once the light from the screen was out of his face, his night vision returned and he could see ahead more clearly. He dodged between trees and picked up speed. The blood in his airways left him out of breath within seconds. But he had to keep going.

Something lay ahead.

A house!

No, a cabin.

Lance screamed. "HELP! SOMEBODY, PLEASE!"

A light came on in the cabin. Even though his heart was beating a mile a minute, the sudden hope of rescue sped it up to a flat out sprint. He knew the moment he stopped running he would keel over and vomit, but he kept going. Unable to slow down in time, he hurtled into the cabin's front door and shook the wood in its frame. The racket was so loud that there was no need to knock and announce his presence, so he turned around and faced the woods, waiting for someone to let him in. Were they still out there, following him?

Why had they abducted him just to let him go? It made no sense.

Had they changed their mind? Or were they just out to scare him? Were they done? Please let them be done.

The door at his back creaked and began to open. As he was leaning against it, Lance tumbled backwards through the doorway. He exited the darkness of the woods and entered the light of the cabin.

"Help me!" he begged, searching for whoever had let him in. But the cabin was empty, save for a single office chair in the middle of the main room. A single, naked bulb swung overhead casting shadows. Lance was shaking, he held back the vomit. He managed to control himself enough to cry out for someone. "Is... is anybody here?" Someone stepped out of the darkness at the back of the room, obscured by a blinding corona of light. Lance shielded his face. "I can't see you. Can you get that light out of my eyes?"

The figure did not move. The torch kept shining directly in Lance's face.

Lance glanced back out the doorway into the dark woods. "I need help. Do you have a phone?"

The stranger did not move.

"Please! Get that light out of my face. I need help, bro."

The light faded gradually, inch by inch. The corona coiled in on itself like an imploding star.

Then the stranger came into view.

Lance saw the balaclava covering the stranger's face before he saw anything else. His mouth realised what was going on before his brain did, and he spat out one word before it was too late. "Fuck!"

Hard and vicious, something struck the back of his skull and he was falling again. This time, he was asleep by the time he hit the floor.

Chapter 4

When Lance woke, he was smiling. Smiling because his mind had taken him to that big house with the indoor pool he'd been planning to buy. In his dream he was sunning himself with a beer. Now he returned to reality, and reality was grim.

He was sitting in that strange, out-of-place office chair. When he tried to move, he found, to his dismay, that duct tape bound his wrists to the arm rests. He could think of no scenario where that was not extremely bad.

At least his mouth wasn't taped. "What the fuck is your problem? Who the Hell are you guys?"

He saw no one in the room in front of him, but he knew his abductors must be near, and sure enough, a tall figure in a balaclava soon stepped into the space before him. Heavy boots clunked on the rotting floorboards and the stranger asked, "Are you comfortable?"

"No! I'm strapped to a goddamn chair. Let me go."

"Are you *Prankstar*?"

"W-what?"

"Are you *Prankstar?*"

"Yes!"

The stranger took another step closer to him, near enough to reach out and strike him if he chose to. It made Lance tingle with anticipation, fearful of a blow that might fall any second. The back of his head throbbed from the previous attack.

"Your YouTube video, *BLACK LIVES DON'T MATTER*, received 14 million views. In this video, you offered to sell cheap, illegal firearms to black men on the street. An overwhelming majority were seen accepting the offer. Your closing comments suggested gun violence is predominately caused by black people, and that they do not value their own lives. Do you disagree with what I have just said?"

Lance frowned, strained at his bonds. The stranger waited for his answer. "I… yes, I made that video."

"A social experiment?"

"Yes!"

"Was it fake?"

"What? No?"

The stranger pulled out a phone. It was Lance's phone. The contacts screen was open, centred on the C's. "Christopher Kazas is a stage actor. Why is his number on your phone?"

"I have hundreds of people on my phone, dawg."

The stranger nodded. "Yes, you do. Many are paid actors. Christoper Kazas was one of the black men in your video agreeing to purchase illegal firearms. Did you hire him? Was the video faked?"

"No way, bro."

There was a scuffle at the back of the room. Lance tried to turn around but his seat was secured to the floor. Several moments passed before a second stranger appeared at the front of the cabin. It was the man with a beard beneath his balaclava. He held a struggling body in front of him, applying a chokehold.

Lance fought his restraints, veins bulging in his forehead, when he recognised the person being thottled. "Tom! Tom, who are these guys, what do they want?"

The stranger shoved Tom onto his knees. His face was awash with tears and snot. Sobs competed with words as he spoke. "J-Just do what they tell you, Lance. They're fucking crazy."

Tom wailed as the handle of a knife struck him in the back of the head. The stranger without a beard now stood behind Tom and he turned his gaze to Lance. Dark brown eyes peered out from the twin holes in the thick black fabric. He asked a question. "Are you *Prankstar?*"

"Yes! You know I am."

"Do you make fake videos?"

Lance shook his head. "No way, bro."

The stranger nodded to his bearded colleague who pulled a dark cloth from the back of his trousers. He shook it out and revealed it to be a hood. He shoved it over Tom's screaming face. The stranger holding Tom down stared harder at Lance. "Do you make fake videos? Do you misrepresent black people? Do you exploit the homeless to make money? Are you creating false evidence with biased social experiments?"

"Just tell them!" Tom sobbed beneath the hood. "Lance, they're not kidding around."

Lance swallowed, but the lump in his throat remained. The fuck did these guys want? The more he stared at those dark brown eyes beneath the balaclava, the surer he became that his attacker was black. This was all just about hurt feelings. "I'm sorry," Lance spewed. "If I've done something you think is racist, I apologise. Let's talk about it. But it's not my fault if black people all want to carry guns. The videos are real, bro. I have nothing against black people. So fuck you!" Tom groaned. Lance was trembling. What the Hell was he doing? Why was he antagonising these psychos? Fuck them! I ain't some bitch they can scare. Except I'm about to piss myself.

Lance tried to redress his angry outburst. "This is crazy. You've made your point, but the videos are real. It sucks, I know." The stranger nodded slowly, like he was about to admit to this all being a giant misunderstanding.

He placed his knife against Tom's throat and pulled it hard like he was starting a mower.

Blood spatted the floorboards. Tom squirmed. A crimson jet arced into the air and ruined Lance's dirty white jeans. Lance gagged, but through his vomit choked vocal chords he yelled, "You fuckers! Tom! Tom! You crazy bastards!"

Tom fell face first against the rotting floorboards. His body twitched a few times, but then went still. The monster who had killed him stepped forward and wiped his bloody knife on Lance's shirt, looking him in the eye as he did so. Lance tried to move away, but the chair held him tight.

Yet one of his wrists seemed to move a little more.

His bonds were loosening. Just a little.

Have to get the fuck out of here. Just need a little time.

"What do you want? Why are you doing this?"

The man with the knife pointed the blade's tip at Lance's face, hovering above his right eye. "Are you *Prankstar*?"

"YES!"

"Do you post fake videos?"

Lance strained at his bonds, but tried not to show it on his face. He needed more time. "Yes, okay! The videos are all fake. It's all about the views, bro. People like hearing black people are criminals so I give 'em what they want. Welcome to the Internet, bro."

He rotated his wrists over and over, the adhesive tearing the fine hairs from his skin. Every twist made it a little further. The duct tape stretched and warped. He was almost free.

Just a little longer. "Thank you, *Prankstar*. You have admitted you are a fraud, a charlatan, a trickster. Your messages are toxic. Your influence is toxic. It is time for you to retire."

Holding the bloody knife in one hand, Tom's killer reached up with the other and clutched the top of his balaclava. He pulled it up over his face. Slowly, like a magician revealing a trick.

Lance's heart stopped. If the guy was ready to show his face, this would not end well. They'd already killed Tom. Lance was next.

No witnesses, bro.

Come on… He pulled harder at his restraints, no longer trying to disguise it. *Just a little more!*

The murderer in front of him was still steadily removing his balaclava. It was just up past his nose when Lance finally got his arms loose. The sudden jolt of excitement, the thrill of being free, launched Lance forward like a spring. He collided with Tom's killer while the balaclava was bunched over his eyes. He cried out in surprise when Lance's shoulder punched the air from his belly.

The two of them ended up on the floor in a pile.

Immediately, the murderer's bearded associate came for Lance, swearing beneath his own balaclava. Lance spotted the man out the corner of his eye and panicked. With both hands busy restraining Tom's killer, he had no way to fend off an attack.

Something glinted on the floorboards, lit by the swinging light bulb overhead.

Without thinking, Lance picked up the knife and swivelled around. He buried it right in the guts of his rushing attacker. The man made no sound, but he doubled over and changed direction, travelling backwards on his heels. Trembling hands went to his belly, and clumsy fingers wrapped around the knife handle jutting out of his middle. The eyes beneath the balaclava were wide and shocked and went even wider when he yanked the knife free with a sickening squelch.

Blood drenched the floor between the stabbed man's legs, like red waters breaking. He slumped to the ground in a position so awkward he could only be dead.

Tom's killer went still and stopped fighting. The balaclava still covered his eyes but his mouth sucked at the air. "W-what did you do? What's happening?"

Adrenaline-stoked fury in his veins, Lance landed a punch right in the guy's mouth. "Shut it!"

Then Lance leapt to his feet, empowered by the sudden role-reversal. Now these fucking clowns were the ones in trouble. He marched across the floorboards to retrieve the knife. When he saw what he had done, he took a moment. A man was dead because of him.

I was just defending myself.

Still just killed a man, though. Shit!

Shit!

The amount of blood on the floorboards could have filled a bathtub, and the body already smelt bad, like an open sewer. His stomach turned and his neck bulged. How had he not puked yet? "Shit, Lance, what did you do? You are so fucked."

At the sound of his friend's voice, Lance spun around in shock. That Tom was back on his feet was surprising enough, but that he gawped at Lance like he was the one who had done something wrong was even more bizarre.

"T-Tom? I…" Lance raced forward and held his friend tightly. "Shit, bro. I thought I'd lost you."

The remaining abductor removed his balaclava and backed off into the corner. He was a black dude, and his brown eyes fixed on his dead partner.

Lance left Tom and faced the other man down, backing him further into the corner. "Who the fuck are you? I swear I know you!"

The guy nodded hysterically. "Y-y-yeah, bro! I-I-I'm *PrankStorm.*"

More fury spiked Lance's veins, and a snarl took over his lips. "You fucker! This was all over YouTube? You want to take me on?"

The guy swallowed, wavered on the spot like he was about to fall down. "It was just a prank, bro. Just a prank."

"I'll fucking kill you!" Lance raised his fists, but Tom yanked him away. "Chill, dude. We got to figure this shit out."

PrankStorm laughed, a fraught, high-pitched sound. "We can't figure this shit out, bro. We're all fucked, yo!"

Lance looked at Tom, and at last noticed the slash across his friend's throat. The wound was peeling away at the corner and flapping. "Tom… what's happening? I don't understand. You were pretending to be dead? Why?"

"It was all fake, Lance. A set-up."

"But why? Why prank me?"

Tom raised an eyebrow as if the answer were obvious. "Because you're a fucking asshole."

Lance stumbled as if hit by a rock. "You don't mean that. We're bros! Partners!"

"Nah, bro. You keep most of the money and it's your face on camera most the time. I'm just your helper and you only see yourself as the star. I'm tired of your shit. *PrankStorm* wanted to take you down—expose your shit as fake and ruin you. Him and me are gonna start a new channel, yo. Better than any of the lame-ass bullshit you come up with. Now you screwed it all up. Screwed yourself more than we ever intended."

Lance frowned. His head threatened to split with the ache he had coming on. "What do you mean?"

"Don't you get it, Lance? We filmed all this shit. We got your confession on camera that all your videos are fake. Then you straight off killed a guy. You're fucked, Lance. Totally fucked."

Lance felt tears coming to his eyes, but he wouldn't let them spill. Fuck Tom. He had made Tom rich, and this was how he showed his appreciation? "They were *our* videos, bro. If our channel is a turd, then you stepped in it too."

PrankStorm spoke up from the corner. "We were just screwing around, Lance. You took it too far."

Lance stomped his foot, making both men flinch. "I thought I was gonna get whacked and dumped in the woods. I thought my best friend had just bled to death at my feet. They won't blame me for any of this shit, yo. It's you two who will fry. Manslaughter or whatever. Who the fuck did I kill, anyway?"

He marched across the floorboards and bent down next to the stinking corpse. He reached out and yanked the balaclava away. The astonishment knocked him back a full three feet. "The homeless dude? What the fuck?"

"It was him who told us about this place," explained Tom. "He and some of his buddies crash here sometimes."

Lance looked around at the cabin, saw that the rotting floorboards and moulding walls were only fit for the desperate. "Where is *here exactly*?"

"The woods behind the golf club. The cabin used to belong to a groundskeeper or something."

"I still don't get it. Why the Hell did this old hobo have a problem with me?"

Tom huffed. "Why you think, bro? You've been scamming the homeless for months. His name was Eric, by the way, and one of your pranks involved his girlfriend—or fuck buddy or whatever. I dunno if homeless people have girlfriends."

PrankStorm spoke up again, regaining some of his senses and now sounding far less rattled. "You gave her that fake money order for ten-thousand dollars."

Lance had almost forgotten the prank. The money order had been fake, of course, but his viewers didn't know that. They thought Lance was the most generous guy on the planet, and his subscriber count had shot up.

Tom continued. "The old girl tried to cash the cheque and got laughed right out of the bank. Eric said she overdosed after that. Guess it was the last bit of humiliation she could take. Eric tracked me down using the computers in the library. When he found out I was already planning on taking you down, we joined forces. Before Eric could go through with it though, he wanted to see one last time how much of an asshole you were. Needed to confirm it once and for all."

Lance groaned. "The prank earlier tonight?"

Tom nodded. "That was our go ahead. Eric raced off and met up with *PrankStorm* to tell him he was in, then they came and snatched you in the van. We paid some kid to taze you and I drove up to the woods in my van to meet everyone here."

"I thought you were my friend, Tom."

He shrugged. "Just business. Now Prankstar is finished. You're going to jail. This cabin is hooked up with six cameras."

Lance decided to verify the fact, and it didn't take him long to see the tiny lenses peeking out from the rafters. He also spotted one hidden below a pile of rotting cardboard in a corner of the floor. For a moment, he just stood there, struggling to understand quite what had happened. His best friend and biggest competitor had joined forces to take him down. They had only been intending to ruin him—expose him as a fake—but the fact he had murdered a hobo was down to them. The courts would probably make an example of them all though. Some judge would lump them all together and label them a bunch of privileged jackasses before throwing the book at them. Manslaughter charges all around. Tom and PrankStorm were right. He was screwed. They had screwed him.

Fuck you, both. This is nothing but jealousy. I made a success of myself. I don't need to be sorry. How dare they try to ruin me!

Lance ground his teeth, clenched his fists. Without a word, he knelt beside the dead hobo.

"Just get away from him, Lance," said Tom. "I'm calling the police, so just stay away from the body." Lance picked the knife up off the ground, but kept it close against himself as he rose again. He approached Tom, his former-friend now busy unlocking his phone, and shook his head. "Nobody is calling anybody."

PrankStorm stepped in front of Lance and held up a hand. "Just chill, bro. This shit got out of hand, but we need to end it now."

"I agree!" Lance slashed the air and two of *Prankstorm's* fingers clonked against the floorboards. The 3rd-rate vlogger screamed as blood spurted up in twin jets from his stumps. Nothing like the movies. So much more visceral. Almost enjoyable as he plunged the knife into his enemy's guts and twisted it hard both ways, burrowing the blade deeper. *PrankStorm* fell back against the cabin wall and slid down onto his butt, leaving behind a bloody slither like a diseased slug. Tom dropped his phone in shock. "Lance, stop!"

Lance was cackling like a chimp, and he didn't know why. He spoke through a manic grin. "Why, bro? I'm already on the hook for one murder, so what's the big deal?"

Tom had both hands up in front of him. He had gone white as a sheet and was shaking. "The first was an accident. You have to stop!"

"This is on you, dawg. You could have just spoken to me, Tom!"

"I know, I'm sorry."

Lance shrugged like it didn't matter. "Forget about it. At least now, you've got a chance to spill your guts."

Tom frowned. Lance buried the knife in his former-friend's guts, looking him in the eye as he slumped to his knees. "L-Lance…"

"Shut your mouth. I was gonna make you a millionaire, but instead you pull this shit. I'm fucking *PrankStar*, bro. I'm a video God.

Tom was swallowing hard and blinking rapidly. He held both hands on the handle of the blade, but didn't try to pull it out. "Y-you… you're on camera, bro."

Lance sneered. "So what? I'll find the cameras and wreck 'em. I'll burn this place down and nobody will ever know I was ever here. Tell the cops you and *PrankStorm* were off filming somewhere and that I haven't heard from you in a few days. It'll look like some kind of prank gone wrong, bro. Looks like the day you crossed Prankstar was your last."

Tom was shaking his head, but he almost seemed to smirk.

Lance booted his former-friend in the ribs. "The fuck you smiling at?"

"You're on film."

"I already told you I can deal with that shit."

Tom released a pained chuckle. "We're live streaming, bro. Give the fans a wave."

Lance's stomach fell to his knees. He looked up at the rafters, directly into one of the cameras and saw the cheap mobile router attached to it. Tom chuckled again weakly, but then expired, that annoying grin still on his face. Outside, the woods lit up as a dozen torches broke through the trees. Lance heard the shouts of police. Someone on the stream had alerted them. Murder was taking place live on the Internet.

Lance could only imagine the views he would get. At least he'd always be fam*ous.*

3. HEIRLOOMS

Chapter 1

"So, I think you'll agree, all things considered, this house is a bargain, yes?"

Tammy pinched a ceramic frog from the mahogany side table and fondled it. It was wearing yellow spectacles, and she liked it very much. Before she gave her reply, she glanced at her husband, Andy. From his subtle expression, she could tell he was thinking the same as her. She turned to the estate agent, Gizelle. "All this stuff is really included in the price? What if some of it's valuable? Isn't there family who want it?"

The estate agent shook her head, saddened. "The previous owner was a widow and had no children. A quiet lady according to neighbors. Much of this stuff is antique, but the charity the property went to said to sell it wholesale—cobwebs and all."

Andy swiped a hand at the mahogany stair rail, scooping tendrils of spider silk. "Good thing I don't mind spiders."

"Or spooky old paintings," added Tammy, nodding to an oil portrait halfway up the landing. It depicted a huntsman in traditional red jacket and black hat. The English gentleman stood beside his horse with a pack of foxhounds at his ankles. The dogs had bloody muzzles.

"So, are you interested in making an offer?" asked the estate agent. She had a pen in her hand but had made no notes during the entire viewing, nor did she carry any paper. Tammy wondered if Gizelle actually knew how to write.

Or how little she was charging for this house.

Tammy kept waiting for the penny to drop. The house itself was priced only moderately under market value, due to its rundown nature. The decor needed updating and a new kitchen was sorely needed, but the property sat within their price range, and could one day be worth a lot more. What made it a true bargain was the sheer amount of furniture included. While none of the knick knacks were particularly of Tammy's taste, the imposing dining room table alone must have been worth a grand. It was pure mahogany and heavier than her car! What they wouldn't keep they could sell. The place had character, perhaps a little too much, but one day they would make it their own. She knew it. The house had an atmosphere she couldn't describe, but it made her tummy warm. Maybe it was the feeling of home. Stupid to shop with her heart, but the way a house made you feel when you walked through the front door was important. Andy would agree.

"Can we have a minute?" Andy asked Gizelle who seemed more predatory by the second, growing an inch as she leant towards them and showing more teeth in her fixed grin.

"Of course," she said. "I shall wait in the dining room, but I'll need to rush you as we have other viewings later."

Tammy rolled her eyes. "Sure."

Once Gizelle walked out of earshot, Andy smiled at Tammy. "You like this place, huh?"

She shrugged, not wanting to seem overeager, even to her husband who might prod her playfully about it. "It has everything we want," she said. "Three beds, big garden, garage and driveway. Plus it's different. All the other houses we looked at were thrown up like Lego. This house has everything we've been looking for."

"Including the ghost of Widow Twanky."

She bopped him on the arm. "You like it too, I can tell."

"Are you kidding me?" he raised one of his bushy, copper eyebrows. "I freaking love it. There's a four-poster bed in the master. I can finally be a princess!"

"And that dining room table; I think it was built in the Dark Ages. The whole downstairs has real wood floors too, no laminate rubbish."

"Original thatched roof as well," Gizelle's voice piped out from the dining room.

Andy frowned and smirked at Tammy. "Okay, I think we've made our minds up now, thank you."

"Excellent!" Gizelle was back in the room. "Asking price?"

"Let's try five below," said Tammy. "Unless you're willing to clean out all the cobwebs."

"I'll put forward your offer and try to give you an answer today. This house will be a real gem once polished."

Tammy glanced up the stairwell at the portrait oil painting and shuddered, the only thing about the house she didn't like. And the first thing she would sell.

Those blood soaked muzzles.

"Which charity?" said Andy.

Gizelle frowned. "Sorry?"

"You said the property was left to a charity. Which charity?"

"Oh, erm, yes… I believe the late owner left everything to a battered women's shelter. Your purchase will go to a very worthy course."

Tammy's stomach grew hot, and she fingered the knot over her bottom left rib where the bone had thickened and healed. As she walked towards the front door, she leant into Andy and whispered. "I want this house."

Chapter 2

Tammy flopped on the kingsize mattress and winced. "Ouchy! This bed isn't as comfy as it looks."

Andy approached the four-poster bed and clambered on top of her. "Maybe it needs activity to soften it up."

Tammy shifted, trying to avoid the painful lumps and knots. "I think the springs are gone. We'll have to change it. No point having an antique four-poster bed if it feels like lying on potatoes."

"I'm trying to come on to you here and you're talking about potatoes."

"Don't potatoes turn you on?"

He kissed her mouth. "You turn me on!"

As he bared down on Tammy, a sharp pain stabbed her side. "Ooh. Argh. Get off me. Off off off!"

Andy leapt up. "You okay? What is it?"

She pushed herself up to sit on the edge of the bed. "My rib is playing me up. We really do need to get a new mattress. It's too firm for me."

"Okay, Tam. I'll sort it out. You want me to get you some pain pills?"

She rubbed at the bottom of her ribcage and winced again. Odd that her old injury was nagging her. For so long, the broken rib had faded from memory. Now it flared so badly she could feel the knuckles shattering it all over again. "No, it's okay. I took some pills earlier. They didn't help."

Andy stood there, arms folded, face concerned—no longer horny. She knew the sight of her pain upset him—it was part of the reason she loved this gentle and caring man—but neither of them knew a way to discuss the past without it ruining their future, or at the very least their day. Andy wasn't jealous in an overt, controlling way. He was jealous in a pained, silent way. Talk of her ex, Jay, was uncomfortable for him, as talk of his past dalliances was painful to her. That was why they both tried to pretend the past did not exist. That was just fine by her.

Pain subsiding, Tammy got up and gave Andy a hug. "Come on! This is our first night in our new house. Let's go crack open the wine."

They descended the creaking stairs, hand in hand. Tammy made an admission. "I really hate that painting."

Andy stopped halfway down and faced the portrait, nose to nose with the smug fox hunter and his pack of bloody hounds. "Yeah, I think I hate it too. I understand the idea of culling animals and hunting and all that, but still… you have to be some kind of asshole to make a sport out of tearing apart terrified animals."

"Will you take it down?"

He placed his hands around either side of the frame. "Right this second."

There was a tearing sound like what Tammy imagined the sound of a scab being ripped free would sound like. As the frame pulled away from the wall, cracked, yellowing wallpaper came with it. A large square of bare, dusty wall remained. And a fist-sized hole.

Andy teetering on the stairs and staring around one size of the large frame in his hands. "Sorry!"

Tammy stared at the black hole, and a strange feeling descended upon here, like it might suddenly suck her in. "Yeah... It's a real mess."

"I'll get some filler tomorrow and sort it. Right after I order a new mattress, change a dozen lightbulbs, and mow the lawn. Bugger, moving into a house is stressful, huh?"

The lights flickered on and off for a second, but Tammy still focused on the hole. "I think it was there before you moved the portrait."

"The painting was put there to cover the hole? Makes sense. Maybe I should put it back?"

Tammy snapped. "No! I hate it."

"Okay okay. I'll put it outside with the rest of the rubbish. I hope we don't find any more damage. Last thing we need is a money pit."

Tammy blinked and pulled herself away from the hole. "It's not a pit, honey. I'll start Ebaying stuff tomorrow. We'll make a fortune, I'm sure of it."

The painting's weight seemed to increase in Andy's arms, because he stumbled down the last steps and quickly lowered it to the wooden floor of the hallway. His hands were dusty, and when he wiped them on his t-shirt, he left gray smears against the pastel blue cotton. "You sure you want to sell it all?" He picked up a jar with a brass horse head on the lid. When he yanked the lid up, the jar spat out metal spikes in a circle. "This thing is pretty cool, whatever it is."

Tammy smiled. "It's a cigarette dispenser. You put a cigarette in each of the spokes and pull up the handle when you want one. My dad used to have one."

"Okay, so where do you put your spare vape canisters?"

"Don't be a doofus. Put it down. Might be worth a few quid."

Andy placed it back on the side table next to the ceramic frog she had fondled when she'd first viewed the house. The bespectacled frog could stay, but the horse dispenser was an ugly, archaic thing that made her think of yellowing wallpaper and ash covered coffee tables. Her childhood wasn't bad, but the smoky atmosphere of her family's living room wasn't something she missed at all. Even the memory was acrid and stung the back of her throat.

Andy hoisted the oil painting again and heaved as though it weighed a tonne. Her husband was handy, but not strong. "I'll go stick this outside," he said, "so we don't have to look at it. You pour the wine."

"That I can do." She smiled, but as the lights flickered again, she raised an eyebrow at her husband.

"Yeah, yeah, faulty electrics. I'll add it to the list. Money pit, I'm telling you."

"Our beautiful family home, I'm telling *you.*"

He gave her a cheeky wink. "Maybe later, we can start on the family bit."

She kicked him up the butt as he stomped down the hallway. "Maybe you can fix the holes in the wall before you go poking around mine!"

"I've got filler for both," he said as he went out the front door.

Chapter 3

By nine o'clock Tammy had drunk enough wine to feel dizzy, but it was the nice kind of dizzy. They were sitting on a dead lady's sofa, watching a documentary on a bulky 32inch television one of Andy's friend had given them, and now had a mortgage to pay every month, but it really felt like the start of something new. Their life together had begun this day. That alone was dizzying. The wine just expedited matters.

"I think I need to go to bed," Tammy admitted a little shamefully. It was very early in the evening to admit defeat.

Andy sipped the last of the wine in his glass and nodded. "Me too. I have a long list of stuff to do tomorrow, and I can do without a bad head."

"Gonna fix that hole?"

"After I fix yours."

Tammy laughed. "I know I started this hole reference thing, but it's actually pretty unsexy."

"Okay, what if I call it your-"

She put her hand over his mouth. "Let's just go upstairs."

Both a tad unsteady on their feet, they clambered up the creaking stairs, bumping into both wall and bannister. Eventually, they found their way to the bed where Andy eagerly threw Tammy down.

"Ouchy! This bloody mattress is digging into me again."

Andy smirked. "Just deal with it while I dig into you."

"We really need to work on our dirty talk."

"I'll add it to my list."

They tore at each other's clothes, and before long they were making love. And it was love, for in that moment, Tammy felt so close to this man who would never hurt her, that she knew in here heart she would grow old by his side. This man with whom she now owned a house. A home. A future. Once upon a time, the days ahead were dark and occluded. Jay had stomped away her future and replaced it with fear. That she was now free and happy was enough to make her cry. Coming out the other end of darkness and stepping naked into the light was like a rebirth, and it only made her appreciate her new life even more.

After they were done writhing around, they lay on their backs, panting and staring up at the ceiling through the gap in the four poster bed.

Her post-sex daze faded and thoughts began to refill her head. "How do you think her husband died?"

Andy turned his head to look at her. "What?"

"The widow who owned this house. How you think her husband died?"

"How on earth am I supposed to know?"

Tammy let out a sigh, running her fingertips over her own naked tummy. "I think he was abusive."

"Why do you think that?"

"She left the house to a battered woman's shelter. Why else would she do that?"

"Doesn't mean her husband abused her. Could have been a previous relationship, like with you."

Tammy closed her eyes and missed a breath.

Andy turned onto his side and lay his head against her shoulder. "Sorry, I didn't mean to-"

"No, it's okay. Jayne made my life a living hell, but it's over now. It finally feels over. This house… When I heard our money would go to a battered woman's charity, it just felt… I dunno."

"Right?" Andy ventured.

"Yes! Almost like my life had gone full circle and I could finally get closure. I don't know why, but I think the woman who lived in this house survived abuse too. I know what it's like to be with someone who thinks they own you, who treats you like love is an unbreakable obligation that can't be broken even if you act like shit. I know what it's like to be terrified of the person you love beating you senseless."

"She's probably glad this place went to you," Andy said softly.

"I think so. That's what I feel."

"Doesn't mean her husband abused her though. You're just a man-hating ex-lesbian."

She punched him on the arm, but then climbed on top of him, straddling him cowgirl. "Maybe I'm still a lesbian, and the only think keeping me straight is your cock."

"Which is ironic seeing as it bends to the left."

She slid his hardening member back inside her. "It hits the spot."

Andy ran his hands over her stomach to her breasts. Her lower rib flared with pain again, but it only reminded her of how much her life had changed. And how much she loved this man between her thighs. They made love again and fell to sleep

Chapter 4

Tammy awoke in pain. Her rib roared like a chainsaw and for a moment she had no idea where she was. She sat bolt upright, naked and sweating. Andy was right up beside her.

"Honey, what's wrong?"

She looked around. "I… nothing. Just didn't know where I was for a moment."

Andy rubbed the sleep from his eyes and hugged her. "You're dripping, honey! Everything is okay. This is home."

She kissed him on the mouth and smiled. "I know. It's fine. Gonna take a shower."

"That would be wise, honey. You feel like a slice of cod."

"Gee, thanks!"

She climbed stiffly out of bed and padded across the threadbare carpet—another thing they would need to replace—then went into the bathroom across the landing. The suite was old, but not in the plastic avocado style you sometimes saw in dated houses. This bathroom was classical. The wash basin balanced on a delicate ceramic pedestal, and the toilet was large and round. Most modern toilets were barely big enough to contain a decent-sized shit. Andy had proven that to her time and time again over the years. The stuff you forgave when you were in love.

She laughed at her own gross thoughts and was smiling as she splashed water on her face from the cold tap. It felt good to cleanse the sweat from her forehead. Why had she got so hot? She didn't feel ill. Perhaps she'd had a nightmare, although she felt no after-effects of one.

Just getting used to a new environment, she decided. I don't think I slept well. Noises and smells I'm not familiar with.

The shower danced against its fixing as it summoned water from the depths of the house, and it was several seconds before a stream burst forth from the large brass head. It came out hot—too hot—and Tammy swore as it burnt the backs of her shoulders. Slowly, she and the water negotiated and found a lower temperature to agree on. Then heaven.

Despite the house—and therefore its pipework—being old, the water came out fierce and fresh. It slapped at her skin and pulled away the sweat and dirt. The heat found its way inside of her and made her entire body refreshed. It was a great way to start the day.

Andy made it better by slipping in beside her.

"What do you think you're doing, mister?"

"Just checking on you."

"What do you think needs checking down there?"

"Think I left my car keys somewhere."

She laughed, almost slipping in the shower. Andy caught her and they kissed. But they never got to finish.

The shower clunked and rattled, so violently that it risked coming loose from the wall. Andy turned off the water urgently, and they both stood there looking at one another, wet and wide-eyed.

"Money pit!" said Andy.

She shook her head, but didn't smile. "It's all just character. We knew what we were getting into."

"My list is getting really long, honey."

"Like another part of you, I see. Let's not waste it."

They finished making love in the shower, with the water turned off.

Chapter 5

After breakfast, Andy got to work fixing the hole above the staircase. Tammy brought him a cup of tea. "How's it going?"

Andy took a sip, despite the brew being hot. He always did that. "I found some filler in a box of our stuff so I should be able to sort it out. Will need painting afterwards though."

Tammy peered into the hole again, but this time felt no bizarre pull. It was just a hole. "How deep does it go?"

"It's not a rabbit hole. It's just a hole in the plasterboard." He put his tea down on the step and mimed pulling a rubber glove onto his hand.

Tammy giggled. "Are you about to give our house a prostrate exam?"

"Take a deep breath and hold it," Andy whispered to the wall, then delved his hand into the hole and rooted around. "Hmm, I seem to see the problem here, Mr House. You seem to have developed a—Fuck it!"

Andy yanked his hand back and grasped it against his chest. The tea on the step went flying, but the carpet was so old it barely mattered. Tammy saw blood and grabbed Andy's arm. "What happened? Yikes, that's a nasty cut, honey!"

Andy growled, like the house had bitten him on purpose. "There's something sharp in there."

"What?"

ANDY PUT his hand back inside the hole.

"What are you doing? Don't hurt yourself worse."

"It's okay, probably just a nail, but I thought I felt something else."

Tammy's guts stiffened while she watched her husband root around in the hole again. She waited for him to cry out in more pain again as the nail scratched him a second time, but he was careful this time, knew what to expect.

"I feel it again."

Tammy bent down to pick up the fallen tea mug, but she kept her eyes on her husband. "What do you feel?"

Andy shook his head, then pressed it flat against the wall so he could get his arm deeper into the hole. "Something plastic. I think, maybe…"

Slowly, he removed his arm from the wall. His hand clutched a dusty old sandwich bag, and inside were several items. A scrap of paper, an old watch, a knife.

Tammy squinted and tried to make sense of it. "What is all that?"

Andy scrunched up his face. "Dunno. Let's take a look."

He took the baggie into the kitchen and Tammy followed. They sat at the widow's dining table and put their elbows up on its thick surface. Andy upended the baggie and released a cloud of dust and insulation fibres, making them both cover their mouths and cough.

Andy slid out the contents. The knife had pierced the baggie and must be what cut his hand. The wound on his middle knuckle still bled, but he didn't seem to notice. The first thing he examined was the watch. It looked expensive.

"It's a Cartier," said Andy.

"Is that good?"

He shrugged. "Dunno. There's an inscription on the back. Says, *For the Newcrombie Master of the Hunt. James Gibbs. 21.12.1989.*"

Tammy shuddered. "That horrible oil painting must have been a self-portrait."

"Why do you hate him so much?"

"I don't know."

He unravelled the scrap of paper, yellowing and crisp. Old.Tammy waited while he read it silently himself.

"Well, what is it?"

Andy spun the paper on the table so she could read it. It was a newspaper clipping.

SADISTIC HUNTSMAN ON THE RUN/POSSIBLE SUICIDE.

"Jesus! What the hell!" She read on.

Local Master of the Hunt, James Gibbs (54), has fled his wife and home after evidence was discovered linking him to an international pedophile ring involving several members of the British gentry. His wife, Edith Gibbs (52), denies all knowledge of her husband's activities and claims to have found a suicide note in her husband's belongings. The couple were childless.

"This article is fifteen years old. What was it doing in the wall?"

Andy chewed at his lip and gave no answer.

Tammy felt a lump in her throat, and for a moment she had to breathe through a bout of nausea. Eventually, she spoke. "Do you think his wife knew he was a pedophile?"

Andy laced his hands together in front of him and looked a little ill. "Don't they always? I mean, if I was out gathering up children and taking them to my secret lair, you would know something was up, right?"

"I don't know. Do you see, though? I knew her husband was a bad man. Who has a painting of themselves like that?"

"Covering a hole..." said Andy. "Hiding a knife... And the newspaper clipping was from after the guy disappeared, so Edith must have been the one who put it there."

"Doesn't mean she did anything wrong."

"Come on, Tam. Why would she hide a knife and her husband's watch?"

A joyless smirk found its way to Tammy's face, and she slunk back in her chair away from the table. Folding her arms, she said, "Maybe she killed him after finding out what he was. Maybe this is evidence of his murder. Good for her."

Andy cleared his throat and hissed through his teeth. "Jeez, Tam, that's pretty cold. If it is evidence, we should hand it in to the police."

"Yeah," she said. "I mean no!"

Andy frowned.

She explained what she was thinking. "We hand this stuff over to the police and this house becomes a crime scene. You want to get kicked out the day after we move in?"

"What are you talking about? They won't do that."

She reached across and took the knife off the table, then held it up to examine the tip. Either blood or rust covered it, ancient now, part of the steel. "Edith hid this in the wall. Who knows what else she might have hidden. The police will dig the ground out from under us and keep us from moving in for months. Then we'll be left with the repair bill. Our life will be ruined."

"But we can't cover it up. We could get in real trouble."

"Cover what up, Andy? Like you said, we know nothing for sure. Maybe the watch and the knife were just her husband's belongings, and she wanted to hold on to them."

Andy nodded. "And then hid them in the wall. Right, yeah, normal behaviour. Look, I see your point, Tam. Just let me think about it."

She put the knife back down and sighed. "I was happier when this place was just a money pit."

"What is it now?" Andy asked.

"A murder house."

Chapter 6

Andy came out of the bathroom and saw Tammy sitting on the bed with her laptop open. He rubbed the back of his neck with a towel, todger swinging freely, and then rolled his eyes. "Will you give it a rest?"

She shifted against the headboard, lumpy mattress digging into her. "Just five more minutes. Just listen to this first. I found an article that says Edith Gibbs donated her entire fortune to child abuse charity—almost three million—and admitted that her husband was always a violent and spiteful man. She hoped that by emptying their accounts, she would force her husband out of hiding. This is from a magazine article."

"She sounds like a good woman," said Andy, pulling on a pair of briefs. His brown hair was still wet, and would dampen his pillow.

"Or maybe it was all just a story to make her look innocent. I think she did it." She closed the lid on her laptop. "After he went on the run, nobody ever saw or heard from James Gibbs again. He had no money and no help. Edith even sold the mansion they lived at."

"Maybe his pedophile ring buddies helped him."

"I doubt it. They were all rounded up and arrested in a sting operation. They would have taken James, too, but he caught wind of it and fled."

"How did he know?"

Tammy put her head back against the headboard. "The police tried to take James at a country club he was staying at, but he left the scene before they found him. A friend admitted to warning him that the police had arrived and were asking for him. He felt sick after finding out what he'd done."

James sat on the bed and put his hand on Tammy's knee. He stroked her shin up and down. "And that was the last time he was seen?"

"Yeah."

"If the police came for me, I know where I would run."

Tammy looked at him. "Where?"

"Home."

"That's stupid. That's the first place the police would look."

Andy nodded. "I know. But I would want to see you before they got me. Maybe James ran home and confessed all to his wife. Then she killed him."

Tammy felt her guts roll over. "I can't imagine what I would do if you came home and told me something like that. That you were a child abuser. That our entire marriage was a lie. It would just…"

"Make you want to kill me?"

She turned to him with tears in her eyes. Through imagination alone, she felt the betrayal Edith must have felt. Andy was her whole world because she loved him with her whole heart. When you trusted a person fully, you gave them the power to end you. Your fates became entwined. "I could never kill you, Andy. I think I'd kill myself first."

"Don't talk like that."

"No, I mean it. I was so miserable when I met you. You saved me. I never thought I could be happy like this. I didn't know people like you existed. You make me feel safe with a simple look. When I've had a bad day, it doesn't matter because I know it ends with you on my side against the world. How can I ever feel alone knowing that?"

Andy scooted up on the bed beside her. He reached out and took one of her hands. "You're pretty great too, you know? You talk like everything you have is down to me, but the reason I fell in love with you in the first place is because you're amazing. On our first date you made us watch Grease and eat ice cream. You didn't want to do anything fancy or play the usual fucked up dating game. You just wanted to relax and be yourself from the get go. I've always known where I stand with you, and that's rare, Tam. It's rare to find someone who isn't trying to be somebody else all the time. That… that Jay ever hurt you, I just can't understand it. If I thought I had caused you one ounce of pain, I would… shit, it would kill me."

She kissed his cheek and put her head on his shoulder. "I know. I love you, Andy. You would never hurt me. You're not a monster like Jay or James Gibbs. If Edith killed her husband, I don't care. I know what she went through. She found a way out for herself. I want you to put the knife and everything else back inside the wall before you seal it up. Let James Gibbs remain missing. She bought this home for herself and put the stuff in the wall to remind herself never to be a victim again. She took back her life with that knife, I know it."

Andy sighed. "Maybe James really did go on the run. What could she have done with the body if she killed him? She was just a little old lady, right?"

Tammy huffed. "She was in her fifties, and women are stronger than you think."

"Sounds like you really hope she did it."

"Better than a pedophile escaping into the unknown, isn't it?"

"I guess. Don't think I really want to think much more about it. I agree we should just put the stuff back where we found it and move on. Can we be done with this now and live our lives?"

"Yes. I'm sorry. I know I've taken up the whole day with this. Just got to me is all."

He kissed her mouth and scooted beneath the covers. "I know honey. Edith brought back a lot of hard stuff for you, but she lived a long time and filled this house with the things she loved. We have no reason to believe she wasn't happy by the end."

Tammy turned off the bedside light and moved under the covers, tried to get comfortable on the wretched mattress. "I'd like to think so."

"Sweet dreams, honey."

"Yeah, you too, although I don't think that's possible on this mattress. How did Edith sleep on it?"

Andy pulled her close and spooned her. The heat of his tummy against her back was soothing. "It's probably taken Edith's shape. Won't fit anybody else but its original master. I ordered a new one."

"You did?"

"Yeah, it should be here soon."

"Great. Good night."

"Good night."

Chapter 7

"The hole is all filled," Andy shouted from the hallway. Tammy headed out of the kitchen, eating cereal from a bowl. The hole above the stairs was now pure white against the yellowing wallpaper. Soon, they would tear the old paper down and paint it all to match.

"You did a great job, honey. Thank you!"

"At least now this place is a little less of a money pit."

"You put the… you know… the *stuff* inside?"

Andy nodded. "Let the past remain buried and the future run free."

"That's beautiful. You make that up yourself?"

"No, I think it was a line in a porno movie."

Tammy shook her head and then slurped more cereal. She was about to speak when the doorbell rang.

"Huh," said Andy. "I didn't even know we had a doorbell."

"I'll get it." Tammy hurried down the hallway and placed her cereal on the old mahogany side table she knew would end up being home for her car keys. When she opened the door, she faced a man dressed all in blue.

"Delivery."

Tammy frowned. "Delivery of what?"

"A new mattress, sweetheart."

Andy hopped from the bottom steps and joined Tammy at the door. "Wow, that was quick."

The man in the uniform was blank-faced. "Where you want it, mate?"

"Upstairs, please. I paid for the old one to be taken away, too."

The delivery man frowned. "I'll have to check that with the boss."

"Whatever you need to do, mate."

Tammy turned to hi and grinned. "Thank God you got it delivered so fast. I had another awful night on that old mattress again. It's nice we got a lot of things included with the house, but second hand mattresses are not something I'm a fan of, I've realised."

"I had another surprise for you, too," he said. "Come look."

She followed Andy back over to the stairs where he bent down to pick something up of the step. He raised it up and positioned it over the patch of wall filler. When he stepped back, he revealed it to be a large print taken from their wedding photos. In it, they were side by side, cheek to cheek, and smiling at the camera. It was her favourite picture from the album.

"I was going to put it in our bedroom, but I think it looks good here."

Tammy nodded. "Me too. It makes this our home now."

They stood there enjoying a cuddle for almost a full minute, letting the two delivery men struggle by with the mattress. It was a scream from the bedroom that eventually broke them out of their perfect little moment.

Tammy bolted upstairs with Andy behind her. She found both delivery men cowering up against the wall like they had seen a mouse.

"What is it?" she demanded. "What is it?"

One of the two burly men pointed a trembling finger at the bed. Tammy turned slowly to see what had frightened him, and at first didn't know what she was looking at. Andy understood straight away, because he covered his mouth in horror. She had to take another two steps before she could work it out.

"No! Are they... are they bones?"

Amongst a length of fading red cloth, buried in the recesses of the box springs was a collection of grey and yellow mottled bones. It looked like the carcass of a corn-fed chicken, but the pieces were too large—and in the shape of a human.

"It's James," said Andy. "The bones are wrapped in a huntsman coat."

Tammy nodded. Even without the coat, she would know for sure that this was James. These were the bones of a child abuser. "Edith spent every night sleeping on top of his corpse."

Andy swallowed, covering his mouth still. "She was a monster."

Tammy shook her head. "Only the monster he made her be."

"I'm calling the police," said one of the delivery men. "There's a goddamn corpse in your bed."

Andy looked like he was about to throw up. "We've been sleeping with a body all week. Oh God!"

As Tammy stared at the bones of James Gibbs, she couldn't help but imagine the anger that must have exploded from his wife. Part of her was glad Edith got her revenge. The other part of her joined Andy in revulsion and vomited on the floor. Once she was done, though, she tried to make light of it. "Don't people usually leave their skeletons in their closets?"

James looked at her, speechless.

4. THE EAGLE & THE WOLF

Chapter 1

Manius Furia placed down his sword and scabbard, placing it with his *scutum*. He propped the entire bundle against the thick bark of an elderly oak tree. Dawn crawled towards them, a few hours distant, and his scouts needed rest. The thick forests of Northern Gaul had fought Manius's men every step of the way since leaving their brothers of Legio IV Gallica back at the main camp outside Vesontio.

Manius's *optiones*, second-in-command, came strolling over in the heavy-footed way that betrayed his Remi heritage. Members of the Remi tribe were notoriously 'big boned,' yet despite his girth, Carigo was a woodsman down to his marrow. Manius relied on the big man all too much. Their *centuria* was named the Cloaked Eagles, but only Manius was born of Rome. The only man shaven and clean amongst six-dozen wild men.

"Centurion, would you have us camp?"

"I would, Optiones. Four sentries in three rotations. We shall break camp in exactly six hours."

Carigo stomped away to see it done. The *optiones* organised his men with ruthless efficiency, whacking any man dawdling in the head with the flat of his *hasta.* That he used spear over sword gave away his Remi preferences. The other scouts were Gabali, loyal to Rome as a Gaul could be, but still Gauls. Manius had commanded the auxiliary *centuria* for eight weeks now, and so far, the tribesmen impressed him. Hailing from the mountains, the Gabali were strong and hearty, and complained little, but then few in Caesar's legions had cause to complain. The Great Man treated his soldiers well, even named them his son.

Manius loved Caesar no less than any other. The Great Man was truly a father as much as a general.

That didn't mean Manius enjoyed the task he'd been given. Scouting the unkempt lands of the Belgae was an awkwardly achieved task. The forests grew thick, and it rained without end. Manius's men carried their armour rather than wear it, preferring the freedom of loose fitting shirts and short trousers. The only thing in the Cloaked Eagles favour was the abundance of wildlife in the forest through which they travelled. The men filled their bellies to bursting every night, boding well for Carigo who ate twice as much as most men.

In absence of a proper camp—they had neither the space or equipment to lay stakes—they spent most nights and early mornings beneath cow-hide tents disguised with branches and leaves. Sentries hid in the treetops, but the scouting party's encounters thus far had been few. That could change at any moment.

Carigo approached again, palming a handful of berries into the space inside his scraggly brown beard. He grinned with bright red lips. "Tar berries. A good find. Would you like some, Centurion?"

"Perhaps later. I would wish to go over our route for tomorrow's journey."

"As you are, Centurion. We're nearing the river Sambre, and should be able to cross if we look for a place narrow enough. The Bellovaci dwell nearby," he spat berry juice on the ground. "A bunch of unclean brutes, but not to be trifled with. Your man Caesar is right to worry. Last village we travelled through gave me a feeling we were most unwelcome there. Our presence is only going to get less wanted."

"Did you hear anything about the Bellovaci's disposition towards Rome?"

"Not fond." Carigo wiped his wet mouth with the back of a meaty fist. "If Gaul gives your man problems, it will be amongst the Nervii and the neighbouring tribes. We're treading into hot water."

Manius grunted. "Caesar is not my man, he is our man. You have pledged allegiance to Rome."

"Aye, but that don't mean I have to love it. You Romans are decent enough, I suppose, but you can't change a man's heart by enslaving him."

Manius felt a shiver and tried to disguise it by folding his arms. "Can I count on your loyalty, *Optiones*?"

Carigo grinned. "Don't worry, Centurion, I won't put my spear in your back. You should be more worried about the Bellovaci doing it."

"We are only here to observe. Caesar wants an accounting for every tribe in the region not yet allied with Rome. When we spot the Bellovaci, we observe, and then we move on."

"To the Nervii," said Carigo. "About as fierce as they come. They've never had a man turn his back on a fight."

Manius nodded. "Again, we are not here to fight, Optiones. Each man here was picked and trained to stay hidden, to disappear into the landscape itself if pursued. I am not a blood-lusting fool seeking glory."

Carigo lifted the corner of his mouth, as if amused, but after a moment's thought he nodded. "Good to know. Worst men are the men out to prove themselves."

"I shall be brave when bravery is required, as I would expect of us all."

Carigo smirked again, but turned and trotted off. Commanding auxiliaries was difficult. No way of knowing their little quirks and habits. What looked like rudeness to a Roman might be something else entirely to the Remi. While he trusted Carigo enough to sleep at night, an unassailable palisade existed between them. They were different species of the same animal.

A pair of Gabali prepared Manius's tent, and he crawled beneath it. Already stripped of armour, he stayed as he was in shirt and trousers. There would be a chance to undress and wash at the river. With no horses in their party, the only sound was the quiet chit chat of the Gabali settling down to bed. Their tongue was foreign, but the tone light-hearted and relaxed. When soldiers stopped laughing, that was the time for an officer to worry. Manius closed his eyes and thought of home. Did Aemilia miss him as much as he did her? Was their new daughter well? That he had not yet laid eyes on little Tarentia burdened him so. If he died in battle, he would never see her even once. What would become of her then? No name or dowry to speak of, she would be married off to some socially stagnant knight or worse.

Damn you, Sulla, and your proscriptions.

Manius's father, Titus Furia, had been one of Gaius Marius's men and, as such, took the Marian side in the civil war against Cornelius Sulla. When Marius lost his mind, and then the war, Sulla took great offence at the Marian supporters. The Proscriptions had been dark days. Days when men such as Titus Manius could wake up one morning and see their names pinned up against the *Rostra*, marked for death. The rewards for proscribing were so high that two of Titus's very own slaves had bludgeoned him to death in the street. Titus's full wealth was seized by the state, and the two murderous slaves received their freedom. Dark days indeed. But what made Sulla's revenge viler was a caveat that all descendants of the proscribed be stripped of their birth-right and status. Manius was the son of Titus, a wealthy patrician, but by the time he donned the Toga Viriis at fifteen, he stood lower than a pauper with a name meaning nothing.

At least Caesar's ascendancy put Sulla's memory in the past where it belonged. Caesar was not a petty man like Sulla had been. He would sooner see an enemy toss aside their enmity than die on his sword. It was Caesar who recognised Manius's name in the role calls and immediately elevated him to Centurion, with promise of one day fully restoring his name and station. If Manius retained The Great Man's favour, little Tarentia would grow into a woman of wealth and means. It was because of her, his daughter, that Manius vowed to make it back home to Rome, and become a senator.

With thoughts of his baby girl drifting through his head Manius fell sound asleep.

Chapter 2

Manius awoke to shouts. That they sounded more angry than afraid, eased his mind. But the sudden shock from sleep still left him reeling in the dark. Carigo appeared and steadied him, the man's spear equipped but held casually by his side.

"What is it, *Optiones*?"

"Bloody wolves. Got into our supplies and took all the venison. Tell your man that once he takes Gaul, he needs to take care of the pests once and for all."

Manius blinked and adjusted to the dark. Most of the eighty Gabali were up and about, but only a handful were active. The panic was over before it had begun. "How did a pack of wild mongrels get past our sentries, Carigo?"

"The sentries were watching for men, not creatures of the night. A wolf can crawl up through the bushes until it's right on top of a man. And forget the 'mongrel' talk. The wolves around here can grow bigger than a man. In fact, some Bellovaci pray to the Great White Wolf of the Ancient Groves."

"Jupiter's cock! You *cunni* will believe in anything. In Rome, wolves are to be kicked and shunned, not feared."

"And in Rome, you stay indoors whenever an eagle takes a shit on the forum. We all believe different things, Centurion."

Manius realised he had belittled the Remi man's beliefs, and so chose not to take offence at the man's counter-remark against Rome. He dropped his shoulders and allowed himself a laugh. "I suppose Rome's auspices might seem odd to an outsider, as fear of wolves seems odd to me. Nonetheless, the sentries failed in their duties. Have them on half-rations for three days."

Carigo nodded. "Long as you don't include me in that, fair enough. Can I have their rations?"

Manius realised the man was joking. "Let's hope we encounter nothing as dangerous as your wit. How long have we been encamped?"

"About five hours, I'd say. Sun will be up before you can take a shit and wipe your arse."

"Then there's no point going back to sleep. Assemble the centuria."

"Aye, Centurion."

Ten minutes later, they were once again on the move. Just as Carigo had said, the sun came up to meet them almost immediately. Their camp had been near the edge of the woods so they soon broke free onto a grassy plain. The river shone ahead of them like a slow-moving snake of the brightest silver. Gaul had moments of splendour when it wasn't raining.

Being so close to the river, the area made prime farming land, which presented them with a grave problem. A young Gaul was leading a steer across a paddock beside a small homestead. When the farmer saw the line of scouts approaching, he panicked. It looked like he would run, but fear made him freeze and he stood there in place, eyes brimming with tears. The Gaul saw his own death approach.

"We must slaughter him," said Carigo, although he did so without relish.

Manius said nothing, for he knew the obvious thing to do. If they did not kill this young farmer, he would run and tell the Bellovaci of their presence. "Seize him."

A group of Gabali broke from the group and grabbed the startled Gaul. He kicked out at them and begged, but he did not dishonour himself by screaming.

"What is he saying?" Manius asked Carigo.

"He says, 'Love Rome. Love Rome. No hurt.' Should I kill him now?"

Manius put a hand up to keep his *optiones* from doing anything. "Hold on. First ask this man what he knows about the Bellovaci."

Carigo nodded, then spoke in that uncouth language all the men shared. After chatting with the farmer for a minute, the Remi man turned to Manius and said, "He says there's a Bellovaci village called Carlei right across the river, but you can't cross here."

"Why not?"

Carigo asked the man and relayed the reply. "The mud in this section of river will suck a man down and drown him. The only safe place to cross is further North-East, but that would take us right into the heart of the Nervii."

"What about taking the river further West?" asked Manius.

Carigo relayed the message. The farmer went pale and glanced around sheepishly. When he spoke, he did so rapidly and alarmed.

"What did the man say?" Manius asked.

Carigo shrugged, as if he didn't quite understand it. "He said no one crosses the river West."

"Why not?"

"It is a sacred place, he says. Only the Lacuscii can go there and any who trespass in their groves will meet a bloody end."

Manius rolled his eyes again. He needed the Gabali on board with whatever he decided, and now he worried. Would they share the Bellovaci farmer's delusions? "What do you make of this, *Optiones*?"

Carigo chewed at the side of his mouth as if desperately hungry. He let out a laboured breath and then threw his arms out in a shrug. "The Lacuscii are a myth even I don't believe. Most Remi men probably haven't even heard the tales, they're so old. The Lacuscii are a tribe of men who mated with the creatures of the forest when history first began. Over time, they became as much beast as man, and their druids gained power over nature itself. It's a children's tale. Truth is, this unwashed bugger is trying to divert us north where his bastard Nervii will cut us to ribbons."

Manius tapped on the wooden pommel of his Gladius—the one thing of his father he had managed to retain. "I'm inclined to agree. The man's expression when I suggested going West was untrustworthy. He'd hiding something"

Carigo sighed, then pulled the spear off his back and placed the tip under the farmer's trembling chin. "I'll kill the bugger."

"No wait!" Manius held his hand up again, but wasn't sure why. Why did it pain him to slaughter this tribesman? One day, he would likely take up arms against Rome. Letting him live was a betrayal against Rome. If he let the Gaul go, and he made it to the tribal leaders, he would give up the Cloaked Eagle's location.

But killing the farmer seemed unjust. Not like something Caesar would do at all.

Then Manius saw the woman and child. They stood near the homestead, anxiously looking on. The little boy in the mother's arms was pointing and cooing at the Gabali. The mother tried to shush he child.

"He comes with us," said Manius.

Carigo frowned. "He's Bellovaci scum, and you want to bring him along, feed him, guard him? What about his woman and child? You want a squawking infant along?"

"We'll butcher the man's steer for extra meat, and once we're out of Bellovaci territory, we'll release him. Tell his woman that if the enemy finds us, we shall slay her husband the moment we unsheathe our swords. If she remains at her home, and alerts nobody, she will see her man return safe and sound."

Carigo glanced at the Gabali who seemed as little enamoured by the idea as he was. While they were not natural enemies of the Bellovaci, like Carigo's Remi were, they were still not friendly. Carigo couldn't wipe the frown off his face. "I don't understand your thinking, Centurion. We are a scouting party. Having a prisoner will compromise us. How will we stay silent if this lad cries out to the nearest enemy we see?"

"If he makes one sound intended to give us away, you may kill him, *Optiones.* Until then, he has done nothing deserving of his death."

"Being Bellovaci is enough," Carigo muttered.

Manius locked his jaw and stared daggers at his second-in-command. "*Optiones!*"

"Yes, okay, all right. Your will, my hand, and all that. I'll inform the lad he is now an honoured prisoner of Rome. Best tell his woman too."

After receiving the news, the young Gaul bowed and muttered enthusiastically.

"He says 'thanks'," said Carigo.

"I gathered, thank you. Okay, men, form up. We're heading West."

The men butchered the steer and collected the choicest meat, leaving the rest to the woman and her child. Then they resumed their journey across the plain. Reaching the river, they headed West. That was when the young Gaul started hopping, long blond locks flapping in the breeze. "Ester ester!"

Carigo translated, not that it was necessary. "He means East."

"Tell him we are going East, and that we will cross away from the Nervii realm."

Carigo said so, but the Gaul kept arguing, on the edge of panic. "Ester ester!"

Manius groaned. Thank Jupiter there were no other tribesmen in the area to hear them. "Tell that man we are a scouting party and that no harm will come to him or his kin so long as he shuts his damned mouth, right this instant."

Carigo seemed at a loss, not something the big man wore well. "He knows that, Centurion. The bugger keeps insisting we're heading into danger. I think he truly believes it."

Manius stopped marching and approached the troublesome prisoner. The Bellovaci farmer begged him in foreign tongue, waving his arms madly. He was making it very difficult to justify not killing him. With a sigh, Manius threw a stiff punch. The Gaul slumped to the silty mud beside the river. "Pick him up. We shall carry him the rest of the way."

Carigo grunted. "Still think we should kill him."

"Such actions are growing more favourable, Optiones."

DESPITE HIS ARGUMENT, Carigo was the one to carry the young farmer. As the strongest amongst them, he still managed to keep pace, as if carrying nothing more than a sackful of figs. The Cloaked Eagles made good time and soon stopped amongst the nearby hills to wash in a stream running toward the river.

Manius waded up to his knees, but the water ran no deeper. It felt good to rinse the stink off him, and he sat down in the current and allowed the stream to rush around his torso. He'd lost a little weight, despite eating well, but these were the best years of his life physically. He was strong and lean, with stamina to march a whole day through. While scouting duty lacked the finer pleasures of Roman life, like wine and whores, it hardened a man's body better than being at camp. He hated it out here in the wild most times, but he knew he would miss it when it was over. Few Romans got to explore beyond the main roads laid by their forefathers.

Carigo, however, looked a man who would spend the rest of his days away from civilisation. The Remi were a well-fed sedentary people, but his *Optiones* had a nomad's spirit, more Germanic than Gaul. But the Gabali making up the bulk of the party were most adaptable of all. Wiry men with vulpine eyes, they saw everything and hid themselves with preternatural ease. Manius had learned much during the short time he had commingled with them. Far more enlightening than being surrounded by a bunch of bickering legionaries. Romans had too many opinions. These Gabali men got on with the job at hand.

As Manius continued washing himself in the stream, laying back on his elbows so that his entire body sunk beneath the surface, he thought once again about his daughter. That Tarentia was black of hair like he, was understood from his wife's letters, but he knew not yet of her eye colour and complexion. Was she pale, like her mother? Did her eyes shine green as finest jewels? Or smoulder like burnt, brown mahogany? He could not wait to see her, yet the prospect of arriving home was daunting. So much time and distance to draw in, and all while surrounded by Gauls.

Something bumped against Manius's tricep, but he kept his gaze on the grey-blue sky above him. One of the men had merely struck him as they waded by. But then something else bumped against his other arm, causing him to lower his gaze upstream. He frowned at what he did not understand. Dark shapes moved in the water, floating past on their way downhill towards the river.

Some of the Gabali in the water chattered, calling out to one another.

Men splashed. Others on the riverbank cried out.

Manius leapt to his feet. His stomach clenched. Objects bumped against his shins.

Corpses.

The stream was full of corpses. Nothing too large—rats, squirrels, and maybe a half-dozen fox cubs—but the bloody flotsam came in an endless wave. The water was red with animal blood.

Manius rushed to the water's edge and climbed the bank, almost slipping in the silt. A dozen Gabali did the same, a tide of shouting men.

Once on dry land, Manius demanded an explanation. "What could cause such an ungodly thing?"

Carigo held a hand against his chin, watching the stream as more corpses floated by. It didn't seem shocking to the Remi man, but instead profoundly interesting. While others screwed their faces in disgust, Carigo seemed only thoughtful. Manius approached his *optiones* and demanded answers again, even though it was not his fault. The big man gave no reply, kept on standing there with a thoughtful expression.

The Bellovaci farmer roused from his unconsciousness at the water's edge, now fully awake. He muttered and mumbled at first, his fear slowly rising in the tone of his voice. The last thing Manius needed. "Quiet that man before I gut him myself. I will have no more noise from him."

One of the Gabali grabbed the young Gaul by the scruff of the neck and shoved him away from the stream. The roughness was enough to shut him up for now.

Finally having enough of Carigo's silence, Manius demanded his input a final time. Carigo moved his hand away from his chin and looked at the Centurion. "If you were to ask the Bellovaci lad, he'd tell you this was the work of the Ancient Grove. A warning that we step into a land not ours. But we are all servants of Rome now, ay? And Romans tread wherever they please."

Manius frowned. "Do you hold stock in the farmer's warnings?"

"Do I believe in gods and monsters? No, Centurion, I do not. The only monsters I know are men, and the only Gods are kings. Both commit foul deeds."

"Glad to hear you have sense. We continue onwards then, but what of this odd occurrence? It is a poor omen surely?"

Carigo gave his characteristic half-smirk. "Omens are for Rome. This is not Rome. The only thing here is the known and the unknown. Do I know what would cause a stream to carry corpses of a hundred dead animals? No, I do not. But if we continue onwards, then perhaps we shall learn."

Manius studied the Gabali men. They were unnerved by the occurrence, but it left them pugnacious rather than afraid. These were men who did not tolerate the bizarre. In that way, they were as Romans. Rome also did not tolerate ignorance.

"Let's move, Optiones. I want to cross the river as soon as possible so we may find safe camp on the other side."

So, the Cloaked Eagles marched on, ascending the largest hill that would lead them back towards the river on the other side.

Chapter 3

Atop the hill, Manius watched the sun slip behind the clouds. A light drizzle had started, which he feared would turn ferocious. The river lay North-West, two miles distant, and a mile further than that, it narrowed by two-thirds. That was the place to cross. But to make camp early here and cross tomorrow, or try to make it across the river first… which was wisest?

Manius decided to make camp on this side of the river. They could sleep knowing their backs were safe whereas on the other side of the river they could be attacked and pinned against the water's edge. Better to have a full day's march on the other side so they could take time to scout a safe spot. They'd lose time overall, but keeping to this side of the river until tomorrow made most sense.

"*Optiones*, we will descend the hill, and camp in that forest beside the river. We shall cross tomorrow."

The young Bellovaci acted up again, and this time tried to make a run for it. A Gabali kicked his legs from under him and sent him sprawling into jagged rocks. Carigo winced and then laughed.

Manius, however, did not laugh. "What is that *cunni* shouting about now?"

"Says thatthere forest is the sacred grove he spoke of. The hunting grounds of the Lacuscii."

"You mean the tribe you say is a myth and most have never heard of?

A tribe that has no reason to oppose a centuria of Roman scouts just passing through?"

Carigo shrugged his wide shoulders. "Even if they are real, we should have enough men for them to keep their distance. No point picking a fight for the thrill of it. If they do exist, they are surely a shy people, more likely to hide than confront. If I'm wrong, then at least we'll have a good fight on our hands. I'm not a fan of dying, but killing… well, that thickens the blood. Makes me hungry."

"Everything makes you hungry, Carigo."

"Aye, which is why I'm all for making camp early. The forest will shield us from any Bellovaci on the other side of the river, so the Gabali can use the extra hours to hunt and relax. Nothing better to settle a tribesman's nerves than a big hunt."

Manius cleared his throat and briefly watched the men. "You think the Gabali are anxious?"

"In a way, Centurion, yes. They think the scene back at the stream was some kind of threat. Set their minds to a useful task and they will relax themselves ready for bed."

"So be it, Optiones. Have the men strike camp inside the forest first, then they may hunt until two hours past nightfall. I wish to cross the river as early as possible come the new day."

"Ay, Centurion."

Manius remained on the hill's summit as the Gabali filtered down its side. He wanted to keep his view of the land as long as possible, so not to be caught unawares. Would they truly find a lost tribe inside the forest? The thick expanse of trees went on for miles, so much so they might not even see any tribesmen, even if they existed.

And what of the grove itself? The young Bellovaci seemed to think the place was touched by death, a dangerous place.

Pah, primitive superstition. Even Rome once held unsavoury beliefs, human sacrifice for one. Something intolerable to today's Romans. These Gauls just needed to catch up with the rest of the civilised world.

Once the Gabali disappeared into the woods, Manius went in after them, but he kept his hand on the hilt of his Gladius as he descended the hill.

ONCE CAMP HAD BEEN STRUCK, in a small clearing between trees, that

Carigo informed were Silver Firs, all was peaceful and quiet. Thoughts of unexplained danger went away. Even the young Bellovaci farmer had calmed, sitting cross-legged on the floor and staying quiet. A good thing too, because Manius had reached the conclusion that the man must be killed, but if he remained calm, he might still get to see his woman and child again. Manius would like that very much. The boy deserved a father.

And may the young farmer pass on my clemency to the Bellovaci and show them Rome does not wish to fight. Rome wishes only to uplift the whole of Gaul and bring it into the great tapestry of nations.

Roughly half the Gabali had gone deeper into the forest to hunt deer and rabbit, which left the camp quieter than usual. Manius tried to enjoy it, but hustle and bustle was the background to a soldier's life, and it was unsettling to hear so little. In fact, the forest itself was more silent than he would have expected. Where were the birds, the squirrels, the insects?

Carigo came and sat beside Manius on the ground. He chomped on salted fish and offered a part. Manius took it and thanked him. "No problem, Centurion. Got to enjoy these little moments. Superstition might have kept the Bellovaci away from this place, but it means we get to enjoy it in peace. It's an honour. We are nature's guests here. You may wish to sacrifice a fatted boar to Camulos. Let him know your gratitude."

"If we find a boar, you may do so, yet I see none here."

"Ay. Well, let's see what the Gabali bring back. Those mountain men were made for hunting."

"Living in the mountains leaves little option not to be, I'd expect. Do you never yearn for a permanent home, Carigo? After your campaigning is through, will you take a wife?"

The big Remi man seemed to think on this, as if it were a real consideration. Eventually, he shrugged, as if any answer he gave could not be certain. "Why stick to one place with one woman when the whole world is on offer? Men are like wolves, Centurion. It's in our blood to roam. Your Romans identify yourself by a city, instead of the people you are. You expand throughout the world, yet you always go running home every time. Why? All of your problems lie in Rome—your politics, your wars. Men are not meant to rot in place. Move on and your problems fade to dust. Stay in one place and they gather like flies."

Rather than object, Manius allowed the man's words to gestate. "There's wisdom in which you speak, yet I would not give up my wife or daughter for anything."

"You've been with whores?"

"I… of course."

Carigo chuckled. "Romans want it all. To roam and war, fuck and steal, but return home at the end of the day to the bosoms of your wives and the comfort of your villas. The Germans have it right. They take what they want and never stay in place—they have no illusions of civility like the Romans."

"Careful, *Optiones.* You are a loyal subject of Rome, yet you speak like a traitor."

"Is it treachery to speak one's mind? If I were the great weakling, Cicero, I could slander all and sundry under the guise of satire."

"I hold no great love for Tulius Cicero, for the man holds enough for himself, yet he is a Roman citizen. A Consular."

Carigo smirked. "And so, we get to the crux of the argument. You label me a Roman in ways only that suit you. I am less than you, yet must act even more Roman than a true Roman. I do not love your glorious Republic, Manius Furia, and I never will. If you wish to execute me for that, then do so now."

Manius realised his fists had clenched, yet it felt more instinct than actual offence. As much as the Remi man's words were anathema, he couldn't help but like the man. "I ask only one thing of you, Carigo."

"Yes, Centurion?"

"Do not speak your mind in front of any other Roman but I."

"Long as I can speak my full mind to you, Manius Furia, then I will keep it in your care."

Manius nodded and the two of them grabbed forearms, an ironically Roman gesture.

"It's getting dark, Centurion. I'll have the Gabali still in camp get some rest, so they may keep watch tonight while the hunters sleep."

"I shall join them," said Manius. "I have a feeling tomorrow will ask more of us than days prior."

Carigo patted him on the arm and smiled, fish bits dotting his scraggly brown beard. "Long as the Lacuscii don't come slaughter us in the night, aye?"

Manius swallowed, but felt stupid once Carigo released a belly laugh so loud it shook the leaves from the trees.

Chapter 4

That night, Manius wasn't awoken by shouting, but by the sound of breathing. As soon as he opened his eyes, he sensed a presence right beside him. Hot, fishy air on his face. Before he could cry out an alert, a meaty hand clamped over his mouth. He tried to struggle, but another hand held him down.

"*Quiet, Centurion!*"

Manius blinked twice and Carigo's face revealed itself in the darkness. He was lying on his belly and leaning over Manius, but his eyes were pointed elsewhere. When he removed his hand from Manius's mouth, he did so slowly.

Manius understood enough to keep quiet and whisper. "What is happening?"

"Something's in the camp. I thought I noticed something in the trees when night first fell, but when I went into the forest, there was nothing there. Whatever it was I saw in the trees, it's back. It's in the camp."

"Then raise the alarm."

Carigo shook his head. "Wait! Let's see what we're up against."

Manius rolled onto his side, looking where Carigo did. Sure enough, a shadow moved through camp, slinking between tents. It made no sound, or so little it was covered by Gabali snores. The shadow belonged to no man, that Manius could imagine, for it was large and low to the ground. A beast.

"It's a wolf," whispered Carigo.

Someone in camp got up in the darkness. They did not scream at the shadow nor alert others in the camp. In fact, Manius didn't think they were even aware of the shadow's presence. Was one of the Gabali getting up to take a piss?

When the man's slender frame finally took shape, it became clear who it was. "It's the Bellovaci farmer," said Manius. "He's planning on making a run for it."

"Blasted imbecile," said Carigo.

"We have to get to him."

Carigo nodded, then started shuffling towards the centre of camp on his belly. Manius grabbed his sword and started after his Optiones, both men in the dirt like slugs. The young Bellovaci crept between sleeping Gabali, careful not to step on any of them and ruin his chance at escape.

The shadow moved towards the unaware farmer.

Faced with the need of urgency, Carigo heaved from his belly into a crouch. He hissed a warning to the young Bellovaci, but it only succeeded in startling him. Realising his silent escape had been foiled, he turned and ran.

Right into the shadow.

The beast leapt up and devoured the young Bellovaci, tearing into him on the ground. His screams woke the camp and eighty Gabali leapt from their bedrolls. Chaos erupted.

Manius leapt up and raced towards the centre of camp. The young Bellovaci's screams ceased, replaced by the shouts of confused Gabali. The shadow flitted between tents, somehow avoiding the reach of the men. Swords swung at empty darkness and Gallic curse words filled the forest. Carigo yelled to the men, trying to keep them from doing anything stupid like stabbing each other. The man had his spear in front of him and used it to slap any man making too much noise. Meanwhile, Manius kept his eyes on the shadow. Slowly, taking each step carefully, he crept towards the beast.

Could it be a mere wolf?

The thing was as large as a man. Larger.

The first Gabali fell. The shadow rose three feet and came down on top of the man as he looked in the opposite direction. His screams lasted seconds. One of his brothers came to aid but became the shadow's next victim. Once both men were dead, the beast dashed between tents, vanishing from the spot where the panicked Gabali converged. Manius still had the shadow in his sights though, and he continued towards it.

He told himself to stay back, to let his men confront this thing, but he could not. Why?

Because these were his men, and they were dying.

He would gut the bloody wolf himself and use its pelt as a coat.

The shadow took down another man, forcing Manius to move faster. He almost tripped over a sinewy rope attached to a tent, and his stumble announced his presence to the enemy. The shadow focused on him.

It slunk towards him, a living part of the darkness.

Mars, help me slay this beast.

Manius gripped his sword tightly and wished he had grabbed his *scutum*.

The shadow rose in front of him, two feet taller than he.

Manius did not flee. To turn his back now would be his end. Instead, he held his sword in front of him.

As the shadow edged closer, its odour filled his nostrils—an earthy stink. Its features came into view.

POINTED EARS, bristle of fur, yellow, lupine eyes.

And a human face.

Manius felt his heart stop, and in that instant the beast pounced. It felt like the forest itself was falling down on him, and all he could do was thrust his sword out in front of him. The weight that collided with him was too much to bare. He fell backwards into the mud. The huge beast crushed the life out of him.

Manius lay there in agony, waiting to be torn asunder.

The moment never came.

Hotness covered his chest. Blood, or something else?

Carigo's shouts filled the forest, and the Gabali fell silent. Manius tried to call for help, but he could not breathe, the weight on his chest too great. Seconds passed and the pressure in his lungs grew until he saw stars. His life ebbed away. Oh, Jupiter, take what you will for a single, glorious breath. Just one more breath to fight off the darkness.

Chest threatening to explode, Manius felt lightheaded and then dizzy. Suffocation was not the way he thought to die. Where was the honour? Was this Mars' plan for him?

Then the weight shifted and Manius seized half a breath. When the weight fell away completely, he sucked at the air wildly, gasping and coughing, wailing and choking. A meaty hand clamped his shoulder. "That's it, Centurion, get your fill. You're all right. Get some air. It's right there."

Manius nodded his head to let his *Optiones* know he was hearing him, but he concentrated only on the glorious air filling his lungs. It took some time before he finally got a hold of himself. He sat there on the ground, covered in blood, and pawed at his shirt while wondering where it had all come from. A wound crossed his belly, a thick scratch, but not enough to account for all of the blood.

"You gutted the bastard," said Carigo, pointing at the shadow on the ground. Manius's sword stuck up out of its middle. "Not bad for a Roman."

Manius was too beaten to laugh. He shook his head in confusion. "That thing. It's not a wolf. It's a man."

"You get a bonk on the head, Centurion. It's a wolf. I told you the things run big in these parts. No wonder there's no game in these woods. I couldn't believe it when the hunters came back empty handed. It nearly made me wake you."

"I'm telling you, Carigo! Look at that wretched thing. I swear it by Jupiter and Mars both."

Carigo tutted and sighed, clearly humouring him, but when he turned his head towards the shadow, he froze.

The Gabali mumbled amongst themselves.

"The stories are true," said Carigo, more to himself than any other. "No!"

Manius had recovered enough to get off his back, yet he didn't try standing. He dragged himself along on his side until he was right beside the beast he had slain.

Yet it was a beast no longer.

Lying in the mud on a bed of broken twigs and leaves was a naked man, the likes of which Manius had never seen. His skin was white as purest marble and he lacked a single hair anywhere on his body. His dead eyes were yellow suns, clear even in darkness, and his ears curled up into points. Inside his open mouth were sharper fangs than a man had any right to own. This creature had been of the forest, a beast as much as a man.

Carigo shook his head in disbelief. “The Lacuscii… The Lacuscii are real.”

Manius was shaking his head too. “You didn’t tell me everything, did you, *Optiones*? So, tell me now.”

Chapter 5

"The stories about the Lacuscii are told to scare children and keep them from wandering too far into the woods," explained Carigo. "Parents warn their sprogs about wolf men in the trees that will eat them. No one believes it's true."

"I believe it," said Manius, the Gabali stood in a huddle behind him. His slaying of the beast had elevated him in their eyes. "Tell me the stories in full."

Carigo looked at the dead tribesman lying on the ground and nodded. "They are changers. Men by day and monsters by night. They descend from a human male named Luscus and the great white she-wolf Vuluptra. For generations, they have preyed on those entering their forests, breeding carefully to keep their numbers down. They are a quiet people, knowing the world would hunt them down if they were deemed a threat. I never believed the stories, Centurion, but I think we may have entered their grove. If that's the case, we need to leave right now. There's a reason no game exists in this forest. The Lucuscii hunt here."

Manius hated to admit it, but he believed it all, Jupiter forgive him. Yet, he was on a mission for Caesar himself. "We are soldiers, *Optiones.* These Lucuscii might have the taint of the wolf in them, but they can be killed. What would you do if we were bested by Bellovaci?"

"I would say give me a sword and a place to stick it."

"Exactly. Men fear the unknown, but with your explanation, the

Lacuscii are not unknown. They are a tribe in hiding, but tonight they killed subjects of Rome. It is not something that may go unanswered."

Carigo looked at him through narrowed eyes. "Where's the man who promised not to lead us to pointless deaths in the name of Rome?"

"You would have us flee like children?"

"I would have us live. Rome does not know all, Manius Furia. Some things no civilised man can understand. This grove is of the Gauls, and it does not care about the glory of Rome."

Manius looked at the Gabali. Their fearlessness had evaporated, and they now looked like frail senators surrounded on the steps of the Forum by torch wielding plebs. These men had families they wanted to get back to. That poor Bellovaci farmer had a wife and child waiting for him back at the homestead, trusting in the word of a Roman. Manius's word was already broken, and the glory of Rome had been diminished. Were the losses worth the risk? Was punishing a forgotten tribe for crimes against the Republic more important than completing the mission Caesar gave them?

Manius stood gingerly, ribs aching. With a shaking right hand, he clutched his gladius and yanked it out of the Lacuscii warrior's chest. A gout of blood spewed forth and pattered the leaves on the ground. With a snarl on his face, he turned to his men with the bloody sword raised high. "I am a centurion of Rome, and a son of Caesar. You are the Cloaked Eagles, tough men and servants of Rome. Tonight, we have been beset by a foul enemy. An enemy who attacks sleeping men in the night without warning. Gabali men litter this forest, their lives cut short by abominations born of man and beast. Yet, I would ask no man here to risk his life for something not tasked of him by Rome itself. I lack Imperium, and such cannot speak for Rome. Caesar has asked us to scout the tribes of Gaul, and this is one of them. He did not ask us to fight them. That will come later. Therefore, our report will include the Lacuscii as a tribe hostile to Rome. We will return of a day to raze this wretched forest to the ground, and every beast within it. But not tonight. Tonight, we flee, for not to would be foolhardy. Let us pack up, Eagles. We are leaving."

He had never seen the Gabali move so fast. They swept through the clearing like hunted hares, gathering up their bedrolls and abandoning any belongings that rolled away from them. Carigo studied Manius and, when caught looking, gave a respectful nod. Then he left to gather up his own belongings.

Manius gathered his *scutum* and moved over to the fallen Bellovaci.

The young, blond Gaul wore a woven braid around his neck, a thing made with a woman's delicate craft. Manius plucked it free and placed it inside his belt. Little would stem his woman's grief, but she deserved back what was hers. He would also see she received payment from Rome, if she accepted such an offer.

"We lost five men," Carigo reported moments later. "Plus the Bellovaci lad. One Lacuscii did that. You're a wise man, Manius Furia."

Manius nodded, although some part of him still nagged that his 'rational decision' to leave was really cowardice and fear. "We still need to cross the river, Optiones. We still need to scout the Bellovaci and the Nervii. If we return to Caesar without..."

"By day," said Carigo. "Once we're back on the hill we need only wait for daylight. The Lacuscii are only men in the glare of sunlight. We can cross the river at dawn while the beast inside of them sleeps."

Manius nodded.

The Gabali formed up, carrying their dead amongst them. Manius had no intention of keeping them for a single second, so he led the way back out of the forest, sword unsheathed and *scutum* held firm in front of him. The wound on his stomach burned, but the pain only made him move faster, a reminder of what he was leaving behind. The darkness seemed to have blackened further and the trees, both ahead and behind them, swayed with renewed life. Several times, Manius thought he saw shadows move from one place to another. Several times he thought he saw something watching.

"How deep did we travel into the forest?" Manius asked Carigo.

"We came in about half a mile, I'd say, but I'm not positive we're heading in the exact same direction. Either way, we'll be out soon enough. Just keep moving."

Twigs broke as the men hurried through the trees, but when twigs broke up ahead, Manius called a halt.

"What do you hear, Centurion?"

"We're being watched. Something has looped around in front of us. They want to keep us from leaving. But why?"

Carigo readied his spear. "Because we're meat."

Manius groaned as he thought about the lack of game in the forest. "We're the largest prey they've had in years. Men! Form a shield wall. Leave our fallen behind, lest we join them."

Such a manoeuvre was difficult in the cramped forest, but the Gabali did a decent enough job of clumping together and raising their shields.

Some wielded spears, like Carigo, but most adopted the gladius given to them by Rome. It made the shield wall unbalanced and awkward. Fighting this way was not why the Cloaked Eagles existed.

Carigo tilted his head and whispered. "Centurion, shadows, up ahead."

Manius nodded. He had already seen the shapes flittering in the darkness, twenty yards ahead. "Men! Forward march, half-time. Those *cunni* want to dash themselves against our shields then we shall let them."

The Gabali moved forward, feet tangling the weeds and roots that tripped them constantly and made the whole formation waver. Shields on the flanks moved forward, pointing towards the enemy.

The shadows remained ahead, multiplying in number.

"I count at least a dozen," said Carigo.

Manius nodded silently, focusing on where he was putting his feet. A man beside him tripped, and he had to reach out and steady him.

Step, step, step.

The formation moved forwards, keeping as tight as it could, shields locked together.

The shadows remained in place, ready to meet them. Within seconds, the two groups would clash.

"Shields forward," Manius shouted.

Any shields still facing the flanks now turned to clink against their neighbours, forming an impenetrable shield in front of them. The Lacuscii could not break through, Manius was sure of it. His men would cut their way out of this forest and gain revenge for their fallen brothers.

"Ready!"

The men breathed heavily, steeling themselves for battle. Swords and spears slid through the gaps in the wall.

Manius locked his jaw. Clenched his sword.

Something caught the corner of his eye.

Shadows to the left, sliding out from between the trees.

The enemy had sprung a trap.

Carigo realised it too. A smirk crossed his face, visible even in the darkness. "Clever boys!"

The shadows leapt out from the forest and attacked on two fronts, one group striking the shield wall and locking the formation in place while the second group pounced upon their undefended left flank. The men there were not unprotected, their shields locked in front of them.

They fell quickly, sides torn open by sharp claws glinting in the moonlight.

For the second time that night, Gabali screams pierced the air.

Manius growled. Jupiter fuck this grove.

He wheeled to his left and leapt amongst his men, screaming for them to kill, kill, kill. To their credit, they rallied, and managed to unthread their weapons from the shield wall and turn them on the enemy. Carigo killed the first beast himself, driving his spear right through its groin, so deeply that the weapon was nearly lost to him. He had to place his foot on the creature to yank the hasta back out. The dead beast turned back into a man, pale fleshed and tainted by the wolf.

More beasts fell to spears and sword, but the shield wall broke as men stumbled and tripped in the dark. Each time a man fell, another would try to fill the gap, but slowly the Lacuscii pushed them back and forced them to fall over their own feet. Shields got wrenched away and tossed aside.

More men screamed.

Manius leapt up in the air and plunged his sword into the neck of the nearest beast, grinning as its arterial blood spurted into his face. He felt the blood drip down his face and it sent him wild, made him a force of nature. He twirled, in a most un-Roman fashion, and impaled another foe. Leaping and kicking, he fought like the gladiators of Capua he had watched as a boy. His enemy was primal. So he became primal, and he matched their ferocity.

Carigo bellowed. A creature grappled with him, and bit into his neck. He pulled his spear around and slid it up beneath the beast's ribs. On its back legs, it looked as much a bear as a wolf, and even mortally wounded, it continued to attack. Carigo roared and shouted in Gallic, no doubt cursing the thing biting into his neck.

Manius ducked under a swiping claw and made his way to his struggling *Optiones.* A few steps and he was there, thrusting his sword into the beast's back and pulling it right out again. Then stabbing again. Over and over. Blood was everywhere. He breathed it in the air.

His attacker now dead on its feet, Carigo shoved the beast aside. His spearhead had snapped off and his neck bled profusely. He clamped a hand against the wound and grinned at Manius. "Looks like you led me to my death, after all, Centurion."

Manius took hold of the fading Remi man. "My apologies, *Optiones.*"

"Fuck it, I'm not dead yet." He shoved Manius aside and threw himself at the nearest attacker, tackling it to the ground despite it being bigger. He pummelled the creature's head until its skull cracked open then let out a belly laugh as loud as thunder. "Years from now," he shouted, "the Lacuscii will be scaring *their* children with stories about *me*!"

More shadows emerged and fell on top of the Remi man, but before they could envelop him, he grabbed the broken shaft of his spear and rammed it into his own eye socket, killing himself instantly. He remained there on his knees, dead but not fallen.

The Gabali closed ranks. Those still holding shields did their best to form a wall. But it was no use. The shadows filled the forest and surrounded them on all sides. Every second, a beast leapt out to take a man, and the formation grew smaller, tighter. More vulnerable.

Before long, Manius realised, with absolute horror, that only three Gabali still lived. Eighty men slaughtered in a single night.

"I am sorry, Caesar. I have failed you."

Two of the three Gabali men fell, their deaths sickening and painful.

Manius wished he could speak Gallic. Wished he could tell the lone soldier fighting beside him that he was sorry. But it would mean nothing. Within seconds, the Gabali warrior was yanked away into the night, screaming as he died.

So Manius stood there alone, surrounded by an enemy not even the mighty Rome knew existed. A myth made real. Wolf men of the forest.

A children's story.

Jupiter, forgive me. I ask you to look over my daughter. Provide Tarentia with a man greater than I.

Tarentia! Oh, how I wish to gaze upon you before my death.

The shadows moved in, took up space around Manius. But they did not attack. He could hear their breathing, smell their stench, yet they did not tear him apart. "What are you waiting for, you cunnis? You stink of shit and piss, so get it over with."

Still, they did not attack.

Instead, they backed away. Why?

It wasn't until the first thin shaft of light pierced the canopy of the trees that Manius realised the source of their retreat. Jupiter had sent the dawn. True daylight was still an hour away, but its impending arrival was enough to send these creatures back to their nests.

Like a protective mother, the forest seemed to swallow up the Lacuscii until Manius was standing there alone. For a second, he wondered if they had even been there. Perhaps he suffered malaise, and this was all a fever dream. He certainly felt lightheaded. Would he wake up soon? Or die in his sleep?

The sight of six dozen dead Gabali told him he was not dreaming.

Manius staggered over to Carigo, a part of him needing confirmation that the big man could actually be killed. Of course, it was no surprise to find the man dead. The Remi was no Roman, but he had served with honour. Even in the face of his own death, he had fought for his brothers. Bravery was a most Roman virtue. Manius removed the broken spear shaft and lay his Optiones down beside a thick oak tree that matched the man himself. "I am sorry, Carigo, to leave you in such a cursed place. I shall return and find what remains of you, I give my word as a Roman."

With more daylight breaking through the trees, Manius made his way out of the forest. He felt nauseous and dizzy, the wound on his chest burning, but he was able to keep going by stopping at every tree to take a breath. An hour later, the small shafts of sunlight turned to great beams, and he was free.

The grassy hill lay ahead, a place he had recently stood and watched for threats. He had found none, but how wrong he had been. Now the hill mocked him, not least because he lacked the energy to climb it. He ended up dragging himself on his belly, not knowing if he would ever make it to the modest summit. His head spun and his chest burned. Death lay behind him in the forest, but he wasn't so sure it didn't lay ahead of him too. He was a failure to Rome, crawling on his belly like a worm. But one thing kept him going.

Tarentia.

Manius opened his eyes beneath a wooden roof. That there were no screams to wake him was a comfort, yet his heart beat with fear. His body burned and his mind spun. Death all around him. Monsters. Blood. And shadows. He had taken himself to the underworld and left eighty good men behind.

So where was he now? What Hell greeted him as just deserts?

A familiar face watched over him. A woman.

He spoke the answer the moment it came to him. "The farmer's wife. The Bellovaci."

"No, I am Helvetii. My husband was Bellovaci. The Nervii slaughtered my family when I was a child and I was taken in by the Bellovaci.

My husband was a good man, but I was given to him as trade when my village went hungry and was unable to pay for his meat. He was a good man. He is dead?"

Manius nodded. "Not at my hand."

"You went into the forest?"

"I am sorry."

The woman nodded. She seemed upset by the news, but not broken as a good wife should be. "He always said that forest was cursed, that I must never let my boy enter."

"The boy was not his?"

"No. Part of the reason I was traded as chattel. Nobody desires a woman with an unwanted child. Who will provide for him now, I wonder?"

"I shall see that Rome pays its debt to you. Your husband's death was in service to the Republic. How… if I may ask, do you know Latin?"

"I not speak it so well, but I try. My father was a mercenary who fought with Quintus Sertorius in Hispania. He was recruited when great Roman pass across the Alps. My father make it back alive to raise me till I was eight, then Helvetii clashed with Nervii and he was slaughtered with the rest. A waste. My father was a good man. A servant of Rome."

Manius kept nodding his head. He realised it was a tremor in his neck and fought to stop it. Shivers wracked his entire body.

"You are ill, Roman. The fever may yet kill you. I have done what I can, but wound on your chest festers."

He coughed and cleared mucus from his throat. "T-thank you. If I perish, send word to Rome that a centuria lies dead in the forest. They will reward you for your loyalty. Keep my body and they shall pay you handsomely for it too. I am a centurion."

She nodded. "You are lucky I found you, Centurion. Your body was at the top of the hill. The shield you carried caught the sunlight like a beacon. I saw it from a mile away while I was out playing with my boy."

"W-where is your boy now?"

"Asleep. As you should be. It is getting late."

"A whole day has passed?"

She nodded with a little grin. "The sun went down just before you awoke. I shall check on you in the night, but you must sleep again until morning."

Manius tried to agree, but his throat was thick and sore. His body shook harder and his fingertips itched like they were being bitten by ants. His head pounded like a drumbeat.

"Be still," the woman said, a mixture of worry and pity on her pretty face.

Manius coughed, spluttered. His mind whirled with horrifying images. His vision turned red. "The… the… the wolves!"

She frowned at him. "Wolves? Where wolves?"

"The wolves. The wolves."

"Where? Where wolves?"

The itching in his fingertips turned to pain and he felt the nails split open. A tingling in his mouth alerted him to teeth lengthening and his jaw widening. Something was happening to him. He was changing.

He was a changer.

Chest burning, Manius fought for breath. Bolt upright in bed, he turned to the woman and threw out an arm. When he saw the prickly hairs popping up along his forearm he almost gagged. The woman saw them too and her mouth fell open. "L-l-leave," he roared. "Get your boy and run. RUN!"

Eyes still wide, the woman nodded, and, thank Jupiter, she turned and fled. Manius held himself in place as long as he could until he heard her gather her crying child and flee into the night.

The night. It calls to me.

What am I now?

A beast in the night.

A Roman by day.

His body continued changing, but he kept his mind. He knew to show himself as a monster would mean death. Rome did not abide monsters. Yet, he could not abandon his life. He had a home, a wife, a daughter.

Tarentia!

Manius spilled from the homestead and entered the freezing air of the Gallic night. He smelt everything around him and sensed the heartbeat of every creature within a mile. The hunger inside of him was primal, and the strength he felt…

The change in him was glorious. He was more than a mere man now.

Yet he kept his mind. The only way he would ever see his daughter was by being smart. He would travel by day and hunt by night. The enemies of Rome would become his prey as he made his way back to the civilised world.

As he made his way back to his life in Rome. He would live a life of secrecy and shadow, as all of the most powerful men in Rome did. Sulla had had his perversions. Caesar too. This would be his.

Yes, he would make this work. The Lacuscii were primitive Gauls, but he was a Roman. He would use this curse as the gift it was. By day he would live as a man and by night he would be something great and powerful. Nothing would hold him back. Nothing would stop him.

And once he was home, he would pass on this great gift to his wife and child, and future grandchildren. Their bloodline would last until the end of time, purer than the purest patrician. Wolves in sheep's clothing. It was all so clear to him in his animalistic mind. He was a predator now. Smart and strong. Devious and sly. A wolf.

And his only place now was home. Back to his wolfpack.

Back to Rome.

Every night, the streets of the great city would fill with frightened whispers. "Where's the wolf? Where's the wolf?"

5. CHICKEN BOY

Author's Note: Chicken Boy

So this is for you, my readers, a glimpse into the chaos that is my life. Obviously, the characters in this story are caricatures and the plot almost nonsensical, but some of the dynamics and interplay between the fictional Wright family are truthful and intimate. A piece of ourselves that we give to you in gratitude for all that you give us.

I willingly give this candid glimpse of my life, and poke fun at myself, because I love and trust my readers, you Patrons most of all. I also love —*nay* adore—my family, and I truly hope that comes through in the story you just read. I hope my wife forgives me for allocating her mildly nagging tendencies, because the truth is that she is perfect. If anyone has flaws, it is me. The beauty of our relationship is that she does such a good job of making my good points overwhelm the bad. Jack and Molly, I also love with all my heart and in a way I never understood before I was a parent. Just looking at them can give me butterflies and the thought of them being in pain reduces me to tears.

I would also like to make it clear that I love my mother-in-law, but nonetheless, sometimes I find Grandma a bit scary. Her wraith like presence in the story is just me having fun. Honest. Grandma, if you are reading this then I am sorry.

The events in the story are in no way truthful, but they do emulate the absolute nightmare we had with illness during our 2017 trip to Portugal. Sal and I had terrible colds, which in my case developed into sinusitis that I am still suffering with today, 3 weeks later. Jack got over his Chicken Pox as if they were nothing, a real trooper as he always is. Many of you have watched him grow up, and I feel like you went through his ordeal with us. Thank you.

Molly, however, currently asleep in her room beside my office, is taking her turn with the Chicken Pox now. Compared to Jack's outbreak, it's scary. She is suffering far worse, and her porcelain skin seems ill equipped to deal with the blisters currently ravishing her beautiful little body. Although Chicken Pox isn't serious, I got a little teary today seeing her suffer. Again, that's what being a parent does to you.

I'll end this note with a quick FYI to my American, Australian, and Canadian fans. The UK does not vaccinate for Chicken Pox, and that's cool. I do not know a single person who caught it as an adult, and most of us only know that we even had it as kids by asking our parents. If Jack is anything to go by, it's good to just catch it young and be done with it. You may not agree, but ultimately, it is merely a difference between our country's health care decisions.

And as always, thank you for giving me this life. It's so much fun to do what I do.

Love you.

Iain

Best selling author!

Chapter 1

"Iain, get out the queue, we don't have time."

"But I want to get a burger. They have a McWhopbanger XXXXL, look! It has bacon, beef, shrimp, and gummy bears on it."

Sally glanced up at the menu board and groaned. "You eat that and you'll die. Remember what happened when you ate that steak in Florida? The flight leaves in thirty minutes, babe, and we're not even at the gate. You can eat on the plane."

Iain huffed, but he stepped out of line, banging an elderly lady with his backpack. "Probably for the best," he admitted, "they charge twenty-eight quid for fries."

Sally tugged at his arm. "Come on, we have to go. Portugal awaits."

They hurried out of the burger joint and rejoined Grandma and the kids. Jack was tugging at Molly's arm, making her laugh even as her little tendons stretched to their limits.

Sal pointed her finger. "Jack, don't pull on your sister!"

"Sorry, mommy."

Iain watched as a few more hairs on his wife's head turned grey. If she got any tenser, she would spin away like a top. He patted her on the back. "We'll make it."

"Only if we run."

Grandma stared at them both, clutching her pearls and perspiring slightly as she shouldered an oversized carry-on.

"I know I know, mum," said Sal. "We're heading to the gate now."

Grandma turned and got going.

The rest of them hurried after her. Little Jack's feet rotated like pinwheels keeping up with the adults, but he seemed to enjoy the urgency. The more stressed mommy and daddy were, the more fun things would usually be. Sal clutched Molly to her hip, who chuckled with each bumping stride. Halfway to the gate, Iain decided to keep shit real by leaping up onto a strip of empty seats and running across the top of them.

"Iain, get down!" Sal shouted.

Jack laughed and redirected his run, heading over to the chairs where he climbed up after his daddy. Smoke erupted from Sal's ears as he tried to corral them onwards. Grandma kept going, leaving them to their fates.

Iain saw his wife's glare and winced. He stopped messing around before he got in real trouble. Grabbing Jack, he chased after Grandma at full speed. Sod's law had meant their gate was at the very end of the terminal, so by the time they got there, the airline staff looked royally pissed off. A few people in wheelchairs were still yet to be boarded, but all the fully mobile people were all onboard.

"Passports, please?"

Sally had all of their passports in a wallet and handed them over to the scowling woman.

"Real airplane," said Jack to the woman, dropping down from his father's arms. "Swimming pool. Airplane." It had been Jack's mantra for the last three weeks since they told him about the holiday. He was going on an airplane to a real swimming pool, he would tell all who would listen.

The passport-checking-scowly woman ignored Jack's cuteness and got on with her taxing job. She did, however, stare in Iain's direction. After a few moments, he smiled at her. "Trying to work out where you know me from?"

The woman blushed. "Yes, I… I was just looking at your passport. Are you Iain Rob Wright, the famous author?"

He gave her his best wink. Sally groaned. "Guilty as charged."

The passport-checking-scowly woman almost toppled as her knees buckled in an actual swoon. "Oh wow," she gushed. "I'm such a huge fan. The Final Winter is the greatest horror novel of our time. You're so handsome too. Would it be okay if-"

"Iain!"

He blinked, shook his head, and realised everyone was looking at him. The passport-checking-scowly woman glared at him. "Please board now, sir. You are holding up the other passengers."

Sal prodding her husband in the back. "Will you pay attention, Iain? You can daydream on the plane. Help Jack, please."

Iain located Jack lying on his belly pretending to swim. He scooped him up and entered the corridor quickly. Grandma was already at the lifts about to go down without them. When they stepped inside the claustrophobic vestibule, Sally handed Molly to Grandma and examined the floor-buttons. To save time, Iain reached out and jammed his palm against them all.

The doors closed.

Sal folded her arms and glared at him. "Babe! You don't even know which floor we need."

"The plane is on the tarmac. We just need to go down."

And down they went. All the way to floor -1. The doors slid open and revealed an empty corridor.

"This doesn't look right," said Sally.

"Let's just take a look." Iain stepped out, leaving them no choice but to follow. The corridor snaked to the left, bringing them into some kind of storage area. Cages were stacked up on either side.

"Jail," shouted Jack, seeing the metal bars. "Naughty!"

"Yeah," said Iain. "Jail is where the naughty people go."

Sal turned back towards the lift. "This isn't the right floor, Iain. We're going to get bloody left behind."

Grandma was already heading back to the lift.

"Just chill, Sal. We'll make it in-"

Jack screamed. When both parents spun around to see what had happened, Jack was stamping his feet in a dance of pain. He waved his hand in front of him. "Chicken hurt my hand."

Iain hurried forward. "What?"

Sal shoved him aside and picked Jack up, holding him close. "Oh dear, did you hurt your hand?"

"Chicken."

"A chicken? Oh dear."

Iain pointed, confused by what he was seeing. "Sal, he ain't kidding. There's a chicken in this cage."

"What?"

He waited while Sal marched over to where he was standing. Sure enough, a bedraggled chicken pushed up against the bars of one of the cages like it was trying to get out. Its feathers were jet black and puffed up. The only colour was on its head—red.

Sal's eyes bulged in her head. "Let me look at your hand, Jack." A tiny scratch lined the space above his little thumb. Sal looked looked at Iain. "Can you catch anything from chickens?"

"Only chicken AIDS."

"Not funny. I'm worried."

Iain put his arm around them both. "It's just a scratch. Come on, Grandma is trying to leave without us."

They raced back to the lift just as the doors were closing again. Grandma could have kept them open, but she said nothing about it. This time, Sal kept Iain away from the buttons until she knew the right one. Floor 1 was marked as BOARDING, and when the door opened on that floor, the outside world met them along with a wide bodied bus that seemed to list to one side. A light drizzle fell on their heads, which caused Sal to snatch Molly from Grandma and shield the baby girl's strawberry blonde hair with her arm. Everyone was already on the bus and they stared out at the Wright family like vengeful ghosts. Even the people in wheelchairs were waiting.

"Sorry," said Iain, stepping up in the massed huddle. "Sorry, sorry. It's okay, I'm an author. Sorry."

The bus took off the moment they were all aboard, almost throwing Sal and Molly right back off the step. Somehow, Grandma had found a seat at the back and was nattering to another woman.

Sal was moist from the rain, but had kept Molly bone dry. The little, ginger haired baby was looking over her mother's shoulder at all the sweating strangers with fascination. An old woman waved at her and she giggled. Molly giggled at everything. Iain wished he was a baby.

EVENTUALLY, they came to their plane, and it was concerning to see its left wing was a different colour to the rest of its body, like some banged up motor. Still, what could you expect from *Big Budget Super Duper Airlines Direct Discounts Plus*? It would at least get them to Portugal alive, right? Like, that was the minimum criteria for an airline. They weren't allowed to kill you.

Yeah, it would definitely be fine.

As last to board the bus, the Wright family were the first to disembark, much to the chagrin of the other travellers. A smiling air hostess-slash-steward-slash-whatever the most up-to-date PC term for an airplane waitress stood at the bottom of a staircase. Jack immediately ran to her, pointing and shouting. "Airplane swimming pool."

"Oh, okay," said the woman, not understanding two-year-old. "That's lovely."

Iain nodded to the woman and wondering if the glint in her eye was because of the tight t-shirt he was wearing. Probably not. More likely she just recognised him from the back of his latest, semi-autobiographical book — Living with a giant penis: The real truth.

Grandma was already halfway up the stairs.

"Hold daddy's hand, Jack," said Sal.

Daddy threw out a paw and initiated locking procedure with his son. Their hands came together, and they proceeded up the stairs. The cabin crew met them at the top, along with the pilot who he couldn't help but notice was cross-eyed. Sure it's fine, he told himself. You don't need great eyesight to fly a plan nowadays, right?

The cabin's centre aisle was about the width of a baguette turned sideways, which meant Iain had to force his hips forward like he was shoving dough through a pair of tights. Sal was behind him and helped with a friendly shove between his shoulder blades.

"Marmar," said Jack, pointing to Grandma who was already in her seat and reading a magazine. He leapt up into the chair beside her, while Sal hustled her way into the end seat, holding Molly on her lap.

"Where should I sit?" asked Iain.

"Your seat is behind me," said Sal.

He stood for a moment, trying to understand what was happening. Was she saying that for the next three hours he could actually sit in peace, alone, with no kids or other so-called 'loved-ones' bugging him for anything?

Sally shoved Molly back at him. "Can you take her, please?"

The flame headed infant smiled so wide that a line of drool spilled out onto his shoe. "Sure… Come here, sweetheart. Are you beautiful? Yes, you are beautiful!"

Molly belched. It smelt like Steak Tartar.

He remained standing a while longer until the two people sharing his row had seated themselves. Once sat down himself, the hostess-slash-stewardess-slash-air warrior showed him how to strap a baby to his torso.

"It's so nice to see such a loving father," she said to him. "I hope your wife appreciates you."

"Well, you know, it never hurts to hear it once in a while. I just do my best, you know? I want to be there for my family. Be a good man."

The smiling woman leant over his lap, lips touching his ear as she purred, "I wish all men were like you. Your wife probably worships you."

"Excuse me, sir?"

Iain blinked and shook his head. "Huh?"

The stewardess was staring at him with a thick, painted-on eyebrow raised. "Are you comfortable with what I've shown you? You seemed to drift off."

"Oh, er, yes. I can handle a seatbelt. I'm a best selling author."

She cleared her throat. "How nice. Enjoy your flight, sir."

"Thank you." He eased back in his seat. Molly stretched out and kicked him in the crotch, but his ball sack had long ago turned to pink tree bark. He just absorbed that shit now. He had a headache, but that was normal. During the last three years, a low-level headache was the most he could hope for.

"Chicken hurt my hand, Marmar," said Jack from the row in front.

Sal mentioned it too. "It looks bad, mom. What if he gets tetanus?"

"I WOULDN'T WORRY," said Iain through the gap in the seats. "I'd imagine that tetanus vaccination he had when he was young should stop him getting tetanus."

"He hasn't had tetanus jabs."

"Yes, he has. It was in that 5-in-1-with-no-added-autism jab he got. Molly had it too."

"Are you sure?"

Iain shrugged. "Not completely."

"Great, thanks honey."

"You're welcs, babe."

The pilot came through the intercom, but spoke no words that made any sense. Whatever he was saying, it led the stewardesses-slash-cloud explorers to leap up and start enacting some sort of improv dance routine involving plastic gimp masks and disembodied seat belts.

Then they were off, plane surging forward along the runway with its different coloured wings. Jack cried out for a few seconds, but then decided he liked it and laughed. Sal pointed out the window and pointed out all the things that were quickly fading away beneath them, much to his amazement. Iain glanced over his row companion's laps and saw inner city Birmingham give way to farmland and country estates.

Molly spent the next hour reaffirming her love of kicking daddy in the crotch, and eventually he had no choice but to switch seats with Sally for a while. She had Molly while he had Jack. Infuriatingly, the baby went straight to sleep on Mommy, while Jack, on the other hand, was wired. Currently, he played with Itsy, a huge lifelike bird eating spider that was his best friend during the day (it was Bear during the night). Every time he shoved it in his dad's face, Iain shuddered. He did not like spiders. Or the Bachelor. God, he hated that show.

"How's your hand, little man?" he asked his son.

"Chicken in jail. Naughty."

"Yeah, that chicken was naughty. Sometimes you can't rehabilitate offenders. They're just fowl."

As Jack was only two, the pun was lost on him, but he seemed amused enough that the focus was on him. He held out his chicken scratch proudly. "See doctor?"

Iain frowned when he saw the injury again. He could swear it wasn't so bad when it had happened. The narrow scratch was now inflamed, red on both sides. A strange little zit had also appeared on a patch of skin nearby. "You okay, darlin'?"

Jack nodded. "Chicken hurt."

"Yeah, it's your chicken hurt." He put his arm around his son and gave him a love. The heat coming off his little shoulders was concerning. Iain glanced over at Grandma, but she was lost in Sudoku, so he turned instead to look through the gap back at Sal. First, though, he made eye-contact with the older gentleman in the centre seat—"Hey!"—but eventually got his wife's attention. Molly had woken up and was now kicking her in the crotch, which was pleasing to him, but then his mind turned back to Jack's injury.

"You okay, honey?" asked Sal, calmer now that there was nothing for her to be in charge of until they landed in Portugal.

"Yeah, it's just… this scratch on Jack's arm looks pretty bad."

She sat forward, but only slightly because of the crimson-headed beast on her chest. "What do you mean?"

"I think it's infected."

"Already? Can you get an infection that fast?"

"I'm not sure. Let me check my medical dictionary."

Sal rolled her eyes. "Is he okay?"

"Yeah, I think so."

"Maybe we should take him the doctors when we land."

"Doctor make better."

Iain turned back to smile at his son. "Yeah, the doctor will make your better, panda cheeks."

"Chicken hurt."

He looked back at Sal. "It obviously isn't bothering him. Maybe it's nothing."

Sal relaxed back into her seat, but her expression remained taut. "Keep an eye on it."

"Roger that."

He turned back to face front and was immediately met with the bulbous back end of Itsy against his nose. The scream he let out startled several passengers, so he decided the spider needed a nap. He pulled out his phone and loaded up some games to play with instead.

Jack grinned. "Animal game."

Iain smiled back. "Alright, animal game it is."

GET YOUR COPY HERE: https://play.google.com/store/apps/details?id=com.kidsgamesprojects.zooforkids&h

Chapter 2

The plane landed on time, and when the doors opened, they were all met by that wonderful blast of heat that let you know you had arrived somewhere hotter than where you'd left. Crazy to think a mere three hours could take you from the rain and cold to the scorching heat.

Sal made sure that Jack said 'thank you' to every member of the cabin crew on his way off the plane which delighted those passengers waiting behind. Grandma had reached the bottom of the staircase, but was kind enough to wait. Together, the Wright family hustled onto another wide-bodied bus that, not being British, appeared clean and well-maintained. The trip along the tarmac to Faro airport wasn't at all unpleasant. The late afternoon sun did a lot to improve their moods.

"We're here," said Sal, beaming.

"Where?" asked Iain, confused.

"Portugal."

"Swimming pool," said Jack.

Sal held Molly in her arms, the little girl's hair brighter than the scorching sun above them, but she was still able to wrap a spare arm around Jack. "Yes, we will see the swimming pool later at the villa. You're hot, sweetheart. Are you okay?"

"Yes, mommy."

"Okay, then."

THE BUS HALTED, and Grandma leapt off and headed into the terminal, forcing them to hurry after her. Faro was a far smaller airport than Birmingham, so the whole vibe was far more laid back. The staff here actually smiled. Back in Birmingham, Iain had witnessed an old lady drop her spectacles in front of a custom's officer, who stood there and watched while she bent her poor back searching for them. Then he told her off for holding up the line.

Sal had the passports out again and shoved them towards a smiling woman in a booth. Iain was pretty sure the woman didn't live there, but that's what he told Jack who then stared at the woman confused for the next three minutes. Being from a nation of happy people, the customs officer smiled at Jack and asked him to identify himself as the young man in the passport. "What is your name, young man?"

"Jack!"

"And what are you doing in Portugal?"

"Swimming pool."

"Ah, official swimming pool business. You may enter."

Sal prodded Jack forward gently. "Say 'thank you.'"

"Thank you."

The Wright family and Grandma passed through Security and headed out into Baggage Claim. It was there that Iain noticed another couple of zits on Jack's arm, although these were nowhere near the site of the chicken scratch.

"Babe! Look at Jack's arm."

Jack overheard and examined his own bicep.

Sal frowned.

Iain pointed. "He has spots."

Sal passed him Molly, the baby girl blinding him with the intensity of her amber locks, and knelt down next to Jack. She pushed up the cuff of his T-shirt sleeve and examined his arm in full. More spots revealed themselves.

Iain readjusted his grip on Molly, making her giggle. "What do you think it is?"

Sal rolled down Jack's sleeve and stood up. "Chicken Pox."

"What? How do you know that?"

"Because there was an outbreak at his nursery last week. He must have caught it. We're lucky because they wouldn't have let us on the plane if we'd known."

Iain kissed the top of Molly's bright red head. "Seriously?"

"Yes, it's really contagious, and dangerous to infants and old people."

He sighed. "Always with the infants and old people. Are there any illnesses that aren't life threatening to them?"

Grandma grabbed her luggage off the carousel and started for the exit. Iain had to act fast to grab their other bags while Jack and Sally collected the pushchair from the back. It felt good to put Molly down as the little angel weighed a tonne. Once the baby was strapped in, they all took off after Grandma before they lost her all together.

They found her outside, sitting on a bench. They had hired a car, so Sal read the instructions from page 17 of her self-printed 'travel pack' and led them across a grey ocean of car park until they reached a small booth half a mile away. A swarm of Portuguese people set upon them, but Sal held her ground until one of them relented and produced a set of car keys. The swarthy man told them to follow.

The car allocated to them was a cross between a van and a tank, but, piling inside, they found it comfortably large. Iain wedged his hips between the two child's seats like he was pushing monkey faeces into a purse, but once settled he had more room than he expected. Grandma had her legs stretched fully in the front passenger seat.

Sal sat in the driver's seat for a short while, staring at the dashboard. Not only would she need to get used to driving on the right-hand side, but the van-tank was also an automatic and not the manual she was used to. Sal had offered to be designated holiday driver because Iain could barely avoid crashing on British roads, let alone European ones.

Pulling onto the main road, Sal immediately veered to the left, forcing Grandma to yank the wheel back to the right. Once she joined other traffic, though, she was fine, playing follow the leader with a banged up Toyota Corolla. There was a inflatable banana poking out its rear window, but Iain decided it better not to ask questions he didn't want to know the answers to.

"How's Jack?" Sal asked him by way of the rearview mirror.

Iain studied Jack, who had quickly entered his travelling fugue state that meant he would fall asleep at some point in the near future. It was thirty minutes from his usual bed time back in the UK, and it had been a long day. "He's got more spots. They're like little blisters."

"That's Chicken Pox," she said. "We'll have to book him to see a local doctor. What a wonderful start to the holiday. We won't be able to go anywhere."

Iain frowned. "For how long?"

"I'm not sure. A week maybe."

Iain pulled a face. "So most the holiday. You promised you'd take me to the zoo."

"Swimming pool," said Jack drowsily.

"There's a pool at the villa, honey," Sal said. "We can spend all week swimming, I promise." She switched her focus back to Iain. "At least it's hot all week. Imagine if we'd booked a hotel room."

"Yeah, that would suck. Are we nearly at the villa?"

"I think so. Grandma has the map, but it's not making a lot of sense."

"Hold on, I'll sat nav it." He took out his phone, which led to Molly making a grab for it, but he avoided her deadly sharp nails and opened Google Maps. Typing the address of the resort, he waited for the GPS to kick in. "Okay, turn left here."

"What? I'm on the highway, Iain. The only way to go is straight or come off on the right."

"Well, it says to go left, what do you want me to say?"

Sal turned to glare at him, steering blind for a moment. Grandma grabbed the wheel. "Did you put the right address in?"

"No, I put in Narnia. Of course I put the right address in—Oh, wait, sorry. I had it set to pedestrian mode. One sec… there! Yeah, you should just keep going straight on the highway, honey."

"Daddy, chicken hurt."

Iain looked away from his phone and at his son. "I know, honey. That naughty chick—Whoa!"

Sal yanked the wheel in fright and the van-tank swerved across lanes. "Iain! What's wrong?"

Jack was smiling happily enough, but spots now covered his entire face. Little blisters that looked like the might suddenly pop, like that infected dude on the bus in the X Files. "He's got more… pox."

Grandma glanced back, and when she saw Jack there was a slight hint of shock on her face, but she didn't express it. Instead, she just gazed at Jack lovingly. Jack blushed. Molly squealed. The kids loved Marmar.

"Just let me get us to the villa," said Sal, sounding stressed. "I can't concentrate on driving."

Iain kept his mouth shut, glancing sidelong at his increasingly disfigured son. Chicken Pox was no big deal, right? That's why they let kids catch it in the UK. He had it himself as a kid, and couldn't even remember it now. It was one of those conditions that looked worse than it was. Like leprosy. Or being Donald Trump.

The sat nav took them off the highway and over what seemed like a dozen mini-roundabouts. Either side of them, paradise rolled by. Golf courses merged with undulating hills and sweeping lakes. The sun was setting, which added a warm orange glow to the lush greens, and palm trees grew in an orderly fashion, never imposing, always complimenting the view. For a moment, it was enough to make Iain smile and relax. Then jack coughed and broke the serenity.

"You want some juice, dolphin lips?"

"Orange juice."

Iain reached into the footwell and rummaged in a bag Sal had stashed there. Inside, was everything one could possible need for a toddler, including a freshly prepared juice bottle. He handed it to Jack who promptly downed the entire contents, letting out a gasp afterwards. "More orange juice."

"I don't have any more, darlin', but we'll be at the villa soon."

"Swimming pool?"

"Yes, and the swimming pool. It's late, though, so we might only get to look at it tonight. You can swim tomorrow."

"In a minute?"

"No, tomorrow."

"Later?"

"Yes, later."

Jack nodded, satisfied that an agreement had been reached. The spots on his face were fluid-filled, but they didn't seem to bother him. He gazed sleepily out of the window at the beautiful scenery, but only lit up if he saw a digger or workman on one the many building sites. People often cried out about the worldwide housing shortage, but the amount of open space here in the Algarve made it clear that it wasn't an issue of land-mass, other than that the rich owned too much of it. Down here on the coast, ten millionaires could provide enough ground to comfortably house a thousand people apiece.

"Okay, here it is," said Sal, pulling off the final mini-roundabout and driving up to a barrier. A resort employee came out of a hut and approached the van-tank. Jack waved, and it was a good thing the rear windows were tinted because he might have sent the poor man running in fear. Little Jack now resembled some kind of cheery, waving alien.

Grandma spoke to the employee and procured a key and directions. Sal followed a narrow one-way system that took them in a loop around the resort. They passed by a pool hangout and some shops, but Iain tried not to get too excited, for it sounded like they would be spending the next week confined to the villa. Still, the weather would be glorious and they had their own swimming pool, so it wouldn't be all bad. His fans were eagerly awaiting his next book, but he was only human and he needed a break. It would give him time to think about how he was going to break it to his mailing list that he was planning to switch to writing hardcore erotica. Horror was his first love, but whips and butt plugs were where his heart truly lay. That one story he wrote secretly, under the name Karma Leigh… Damn!

No thinking about work, he told himself. You're turning grey with all the strain you put yourself under. You have a wonderful wife and two beautiful children to enjoy… He looked at Jack. *Well, one of my kids is still beautiful, even if she has hair hot enough to light a stove.*

As if sensing his love, Molly grinned at him, her little rabbit chompers peeking out from under her top lip. There was a small amount of food on her forehead, but he had learned months ago that trying to keep her clean was a losing battle. Girl loved to eat. And when you were serious about eating, you sometimes ended up with crap on your face. You just had to own it. Thug life.

Sal steered them into a cramped carport better suited to a Smart Car than their van-tank. She turned off the engine, and for a few moments, they all sat there in silence, tired and sweaty from the journey. Then Grandma got out and headed for villa's front door.

Iain reached forwards and squeezed his wife's shoulder. "Thanks for getting us here. I couldn't have done it."

"Thank you, mommy," said Jack, not knowing what he was saying it for, but sensing it was appropriate. The kid had got so smart lately. He'd even stopped shitting himself.

"You're welcome," said Sal, turning to face him with a weary smile. When she spotted Jack's face, her mouth fell open. "Jesus."

Iain nodded. "I know, right? He looks like pizza."

"Let's get him inside."

They disembarked and assembled on the driveway outside the villa. Grandma had taken the key, so had already let herself inside. The front door hung open, awaiting them. Iain opened Jack's door and Sal came and unbuckled him. She pulled him out and carried him into the villa. "Can you lock the car, babe?" she shouted back over her shoulder.

"Yep, sure thing." He took the keys out the ignition and closed all the doors, then pressed the fob to lock the vehicle. Trotting down a couple of stone steps, he entered the villa. Sal and Jack met him in the large entrance hall, but Grandma was outside, sat beside the pool. She was visible through the French doors.

Sal stroked Jack's sweaty head as he stood beside her leg and glanced around at the giant house. When she looked at Iain, she seemed to expect something from him.

Iain shrugged. "What's up?"

"Where's Molly?"

"Oh shit! I left her in the car. I... wait right here."

He ran back outside before Sal had time to hurt him.

Chapter 3

After a copious amount of Google searches, and with it being two hours past Jack's bedtime, Iain and Sal put the lad to bed. He was still fine in himself, and the images they saw online more-suggested he had the good ol' Chicken Pox. No big thing. Most kids got it, and it was better to do so young. The nursery warning had not been a hoax. They had been keeping shit real.

After Jack and Molly were both soundly asleep in adjacent rooms upstairs, the adults made themselves a cup of tea and took in the delights of the villa. The pool was unheated—something Iain was deeply unhappy about—but it was well lit and surrounded by a lovely patio. The sides of the villa sported grass, with plenty of room for Jack to stretch his legs come morning. Being house-bound for a week might not be so bad.

"Wish we had a bottle of wine," said Sal, as they sat beside the pool. In the last hour, she had been bitten six times, and now had swollen ankles and a weird bump on her neck. Iain was staring at the wall where a pair of lizards were crawling over one another. When he heard his wife talk, he frowned.

"Huh?"

"Wine," said Sal. "I want wine."

"I think I have some in my other pants."

She sighed. "I suppose we should just turn in. We won't be able to get breakfast at the resort in the morning, so mum and I will have to find a supermarket while you have the kids.

Iain groaned. Raising kids was supposed to be a group activity. "Great. Looking forward to it."

Grandma went to bed. They watched her go, then Iain patted his knees and got up too. "Okay, I'm going up then. Where's my Kindle?"

"In your ass!" Sal chuckled.

Iain didn't joke about his Kindle, so he stood there waiting for a proper answer to a serious question.

Sal sighed when she realised he would not be laughing at her joke. "It's in the side pocket of my suitcase."

"Okay, I'll see in bed."

"Yeah, sure. I'll lock up down here, babe, don't worry. I'll bring some water up too. Anything else you would like, honey?"

"Do we have any muffins?"

"No."

"Then water is fine." He went to leave, but caught sight of the two lizards again, competing over a mosquito hovering around a wall lamp. He couldn't not look. Sal turned her chair so she was facing him a little more and scratched at her thigh as another bite mark appeared. "Maybe I'll bring you up something extra special, big boy."

"R-really?"

"Yeah," she purred. "You're such a magnificent husband, and a perfect man. I can't believe I'm married to a best selling author."

Iain smiled. "You deserve it, honey. You really do."

"Deserve what? Iain, what are you muttering about?"

Iain blinked and shook his head. "What, oh nothing. See you upstairs."

She frowned at him, then turned back towards the pool. His mind was always running away with him. Part of running a business-of-one was constantly being in work-mode. He often found it hard to just clear his mind and think of nothing. Over the last few years, as his success and workload had grown, he'd found himself getting too easily distracted. It was vital he shut off and relaxed this holiday. He risked burning out otherwise. If he wasn't careful, he'd end up a hare-brained lunatic like his old colleague, Matt Shaw. It had been ages since the care home let the poor misfit out in public. Last Iain heard, Matt spent all his time in a padded room stitching teddy bears together.

Iain headed up the stone steps in the entrance hall and climbed up onto the balcony. He couldn't help but check in on the kids before her retired for the night. He always loved their peaceful snoring, and he still had that horrible, irrational fear they might pass away in their sleep. When Jack had been first born, and he had learned about Cot Death, he hadn't slept for six months. That fear had lingered, and even with Molly eight months old and Jack three years, he still woke up in the night panicked sometimes. He had no idea being a parent could be so terrifying.

When he opened Molly's door she immediately turned over and farted, making him chuckle. *Just like her mother.*

When he tried the next door, he heard only silence. He lingered, head tilted and listening. Every passing second without sound made his heart beat a little faster. Then, a moment away from rushing into the room and shaking Jack awake, he heard a grunt followed by the whistle of a blocked nose. Poor little guy was unwell. Best to leave him be.

"Love you, Jack," he whispered as he closed the door.

Cluck!

Confusion halted Iain just as he was about to pull the door against the jam. As it was, a shadowy black slither still remained. Had he disturbed Jack? Or was the strange noise just his son clearing his throat. Was he bunged up, feverish? Sal was the expert on the various Pox of the world. He ended up standing there, motionless, not wanting to disturb his son any further, but also not convinced that Jack was okay.

Cluck!

Iain opened the door wider again. "Okay, what the heck?"

Stepping from the light, he was blind in the dark, but Jack's silhouette disturbed the shadows above the bed. What was we doing awake? Had they been noisy downstairs?

Something brushed against his foot and made him flinch—although that wasn't really the truth. What actually happened was he leapt back three feet like a startled cat. When he realised nothing alive was scuttling around his feet, he swept about with his foot, trying to find whatever had touched him. He found something with his toes and, like a monkey, picked it up so he could grab it with his hands. The manoeuvre beat bending over any day. He'd left that shit behind in his twenties. God bless the monkey foot pick up.

The thing he held in his hands surprised him, not something he expected to find in the bedroom of a luxury Portuguese villa. A huge goddamn feather the size of his own penis—eleven inches at least.

Cluck!

Okay, this was getting ridiculous. What was going on? "Jack, are you okay, sweetheart?"

Bwakirrrrk!

He fumbled for the light switch on the wall.

The lights blinked on.

Jack was gone.

A chicken perched on the bed. A chicken the size of a frikkin' Dalmatian.

"Arrrrrrrgh! Shit! Sal, Sal!"

There was a voice echoing from below, one that got louder as it rose up the stairs. "What? What? What?"

"Sal Sal Sal."

"What? Iain, did you shit the bed again? Because if you did—"

"Just come in here!"

She entered the doorway behind him and shut the heck up. Her bottom lip wobbled. "W-w-w…"

"Yeah," said Iain. "You see?"

"That… that…"

Iain nodded. "I know."

"Are you playing a trick on me?"

"Yes, honey. I genetically engineered a giant chicken over the last ten years so I could prank you one night on a future a holiday. Bazinga!"

"Where's Jack?"

He felt his own lower lip tremble. "I think… I think this thing ate him. It's revenge of the KFC. Fox News warned us this would happen. They said if Obama got in, genetically altered poultry would rise up and take over the world. They warned us and we didn't listen."

Sal didn't respond, just nodded slowly. "If that thing ate Jack, then why is it wearing his Paw Patrol pyjamas?"

Iain covered his mouth at the sight of the little green shorts covering the chicken's ass. "Oh my God. It ate our son and then stole his jammys. Noooooo!"

"Cluck! Swimming Pool. Airplane. Cluck!"

Sal and Iain stared at each other. Iain opened his mouth to speak, but no words came out.

"Did that chicken just say what I think it said?" asked Sal.

"I… I think it just..."

The chicken flapped about on the bed, spinning a circle and bobbing its head. "Jack play now. Armbands. Swimming pool."

Sal ran forward and threw her arms around the huge bird. "Oh, Jack. It's you. I thought we'd lost you."

"Eh… honey? I still think this qualifies as 'losing him'. He's a chicken."

She whirled on him. "He's our *son*!"

"Granted. But our son is a chicken. I'm not sure I signed on for that."

Sal covered her mouth and gasped. "I can't believe you just said that!"

Shame washed over him. They always said they would love their kids no matter what, that if Jack or Molly had been born with Downs or Autism or whatever, it wouldn't matter. This… this was no different, right? So Jack was a chicken. He was still their precious little boy.

He shook his head. "Christ, I'm going to have to become a vegetarian, aren't I?"

Chapter 4

Grandma agreed they needed to call a doctor, so after speaking to reception on the phone, the resort manager arranged for a local English doctor to come over. The middle-aged ex-pat now stood in the villa's sitting room, watching with interest as Jack pecked at a cushion on the sofa. Ironically, goose feathers spilled out.

"Has anything like this ever happened before?" asked the doctor.

They shook their heads.

"Any family history?"

Iain frowned. "Of turning into chickens?"

"Yes."

"No."

"There's been an outbreak of Chicken Pox at his nursery," said Sal. "He broke out in spots earlier today."

The doctor tapped his stethoscope against his chin and seemed to think. Jack clucked periodically and tried several times to squeeze through the French doors to get to the swimming pool. At one point he laid an egg, which confused all of them as it made sense that Jack would be a male chicken—a rooster or whatever.

"I think we should all sit down," said the doctor, still watching Jack with interest and tapping his chin.

"Okay," said Sal. "Should we… feed him or anything? There's some cereal in the kitchen."

"I saw that," said Iain. "That was pretty cool of the resort."

"Please, sit down," the doctor urged.

They did as they were asked, except for Grandma who went over to Jack and stroked his feathery back. The doctor leant forward so that both parents could hear him well. "I think what has happened is that your son has turned into a chicken."

Iain and Sal looked at each other. Sal spoke up. "We know! What can we do about it?"

"Have either of you ever kept chickens before?"

"What? No. We want our son back to normal. You must know how to treat this."

"I'm just a semi-retired doctor. I came to Portugal to play golf, not cure Chicken Disease."

Iain put his arm around his wife who was in danger of taking off. Her voice had altered, and she was assuming the identity she always did before she kicked ass. Once he had seen her chase a builder down the street for blocking their driveway. He made it two miles before she caught him and tore an apology from him. Now, Iain looked at the doctor pleadingly. "Kids don't just turn into chickens."

"Not normally, no."

"Not ever. Doctor, please, what should we do?"

The doctor straightened up and sighed. "I will arrange for a specialist team to visit, but in the meantime, you must confine yourself to this house. If this thing is contagious… Did you ever see that Fox News report?"

Iain looked at his wife. "I told you!"

"Just leave," said Sal to the doctor. "Send your specialist team or anybody else who will actually help, but I would like you to leave right now."

The doctor stood up, glancing sideways at Jack one last time, then nodded. It seemed like leaving was all he wanted to do. It was just 2AM, but he stifled yawns as if he'd been up for days. Playing golf all day must be exhausting.

The doctor scooted out the door and Sal slammed it behind him. Then she looked at Iain and let her mask slip. He held her as she sobbed into his shoulder. "We'll figure this out, honey."

"What if we can't?"

"We'll cross that road if we come to it." He chuckled. "Like the chicken, yeah? You get it? I said cross the road-"

"Shut up, honey."

"Okay."

Grandma appeared with two cups of tea, handed them over, and went back to Jack who was in the process of pooping up the curtains. Iain wondered if that was the chicken or the three-year-old in him. The resort would charge them for that.

"*Cluck! Telly.*"

Sal wiped her eyes and smiled at her chicken boy. "You want to watch TV, honey?"

Jack flapped his wings and almost took off. Iain retrieved the remote from the table and switched on the modest flat screen on the wall. He knew his son would demand YouTube be on, so he quickly switched it on and selected some weird ass crap where people dressed up like Spiderman and Elsa. It was Jack's favourite. The video he selected was about Spiderman pooping out jelly beans. Oscar worthy stuff.

Jack hopped up on the sofa and nestled down, tucking his spindly legs beneath him and pulling in his feathery wings. For the first time since they had led Jack downstairs, he finally settled still, as mesmerised by the TV as a chicken as he was as a boy.

With things straightforwarda little calmer, Iain and Sal joined Grandma in the kitchen. They sipped their tea and stared at the ground for a while.

"What if Molly gets it?" asked Sal.

Iain rubbed at his eyes. "We checked on her. She's fine, sleeping, and Grandma has the baby monitor if anything happens. I think it has something to do with that chicken that scratched Jack back at Birmingham airport."

"You think it was infected with something?"

"What was it even doing alone in that corridor?"

"Maybe it was terrorists?"

"You think they want to turn us all into chickens?"

Sal chewed at her lip, then said, "Maybe we should check the news. You have your phone?"

"Hell yes. Stephen King is going to hit me up any day now and I can't afford to miss his call." He reached into his pocket and pulled out his Samsung Galaxy Pro 9-3x4 Edge+S and handed it to his wife. She placed her thumb against the reader and unlocked it. Then she rolled her eyes and grunted.

"What is it?" he asked.

"You have a message. Guillermo Del Toro wants you to let him make a movie of one of your books again."

"Jeez, that guy doesn't take no for an answer. I already told him he can offer me all the millions in the world, but I won't sell out the integrity of my work. I'm a serious author. I won't let the Final Winter be butchered by an avaricious filmmaker. Can you believe he wants to relocate the story to Hong Kong, and instead of a pub he wants to set it in a noodle bar. Hollywood, man…"

"Honey, I love you, but I really don't care. How do I get to Google?"

"Sorry, yeah. You just press that icon there that says Google."

He waited while his wife did a quick search. Whatever she found engrossed her because she scrolled quickly with the phone right in front of her nose. Her skin turned alabaster, and she tilted the phone so he could see it.

"Oh fuck!" Iain swallowed a lump in his throat as he read the article's headline.

BBC NEWS: Birmingham International Airport locked down after attempted terrorist plot. Former author and escape mental patient Matt Shaw held for questioning.

"They don't mention what the attack was," added Sal, but people are saying the whole thing is being suppressed. Whatever it is, they don't want anybody knowing.

Iain took back his phone and had a thought. Bringing up his contacts, he scrolled through the list until he reached the Ms:

Matthew McConaughey

Matt Shaw

Michal Bray

Mike Myers (don't answer!)

Mitch Pileggi

He hit 'Matt Shaw' and waited for it to connect. The roaming charges would hurt, but he could always beg his Patrons for more money to pay the bill if he had to.

Somebody answered. It wasn't Matt. "Who is this?"

"Iain Rob Wright."

"Who?"

"The best selling author…"

"Sir, the phone you are calling has been seized in connection to a crime. How do you know the owner?"

"He used to be a colleague, but a few years ago he broke in and stole all my clothes, so I teamed up with his wife, Marie, and had him committed. Is Matt okay? I mean, like his normal level of okay?"

"I cannot discuss an ongoing investigation. Have you had any recent contact with Matt Shaw?"

"He sends me love letters now and then, but I haven't seen him in person in years. Did he… Did he turn anyone into a chicken?"

The man on the other end paused for several seconds, then: "Sir, I need you meet with you right away. If you have information-"

Iain ended the call. He looked at Sal and shook his head. "I think Matt went full Tyler Durden."

Sal frowned at the reference. "What?"

"I think he released a chicken virus."

"He wouldn't."

"Come on, Sal. We both know the guy is capable of anything. He's an evil genius, and after he won that Bram Stoke award he went right off the deep end."

"You think he was targeting us specifically?"

Iain shrugged. "He sent me a pair of his underwear last month, so I'm obviously on his mind. I bet he has a crazy fan at the airport that helped him. All that guy's fans are whackos. Anyone with an ounce of sanity reads my books over his."

Sal shook her head. "No, I met Matt before. He's a little odd, and strangely handsome, but I don't think he would want to hurt us. In his own weird way, I think he loves you, Iain."

Iain sighed, but had to agree. "You're right. I've always known he had feelings for me ever since he snuck into my bed in Cardiff, but I tried to play it off as a joke. Maybe he didn't mean to turn Jack into a chicken. Maybe it was just one of his pranks."

"Either way," said Sal. "If he is behind this, I'll kill him."

"Me too."

Grandma left the kitchen, but returned soon after, clutching her pearls anxiously. She motioned for them to follow her, and they did so quickly, tea sloshing in their unsteady mugs. It was now 3AM and Iain's eyes were getting fuzzy, but he was pretty clear about what he saw in the sitting room. Jack still nestled on the sofa, a giant chicken in Paw Patrol shorts, but there was something different this time.

"His feet!" said Sal.

Grandma nodded.

Iain grinned. Jack was still a chicken, but tucked beneath his plump breast were the beautiful little feet they were all used to.

Sal turned to Iain and matched his grin. "It's wearing off."

"It's his immune system, honey. I always told you the men in my family have superior genes."

"Iain, I've seen you try to eat a prawn with the shell on. And a chestnut. And you left the wax on a cheese wheel once before eating the whole thing. In fact, you have a problem with all foods that aren't straightforward. Superior genes might be a bit of an exaggeration."

He opened his mouth to argue, but nodded. "Okay, fair enough. Still, I think Jack is fighting whatever made him ill. My mom always said it's best to catch these things young."

"They say that about Chicken Pox, not…" she grunted. "Not being an actual chicken."

Iain pointed to Jack's pink, human feet. "Looks like it still applies."

"What should we do?" Sal asked. "Wait it out?"

Iain looked at the TV at a man dressed as the Joker farting on a man wearing a Hulk mask. "I guess we sit and enjoy some fine YouTube entertainment."

Jack *clucked* and wafted his wings. It seemed to be an invitation to come sit with him, and so they did. Grandma didn't scoot up to make space, so only Sal could sit on the sofa with her and Jack. Iain took the armchair nearby. They tried to watch the weird superhero mash up videos for as long as they could, but eventually Iain noticed his wife falling asleep. As his own eyes drooped, he knew he would be joining her soon.

Chapter 5

Iain awoke with a headache. The sun streaming through the French doors didn't help. He squinted until his eyes adjusted and then looked around the room. Sal was snoring on the sofa, legs up on the cushions where Jack and Grandma had been. She raised one leg and farted, but remained sleeping.

Iain waved a hand in front of his nose. "Shit, honey, what did you eat?"

Sal's eyes snapped open and she bolted upright. Rubbing at her face, she struggled to come to. "Wh-where's Jack? Did I have a nightmare?"

Iain sniffed. "About Jack being a chicken?"

"Yes!"

"It wasn't a dream, honey."

With a leap, she got to her feet. She pulled a face and pinched her nose. "Iain, you're disgusting! What did you eat?"

Iain sighed. "Yeah, sorry, honey. I thought you were asleep."

"Where is Jack?"

Iain didn't know, so he listened. Sounds came from outside, and he noticed that the French doors were ajar. "I think somebody is outside."

Sal grabbed his arm and yanked him up. They headed over to the doors and Iain slide them open fully. Grandma was sitting at the edge of the pool, legs dangling in the water. When she saw Iain and Sal, she smiled, then nodded her head to the side.

They both had to take a couple of steps to the side to get a good look at what Grandma was indictating, but once they did, they both put their hands to their mouths in shock. Sal started sobbing.

Iain felt tears coming too.

Little Jack sat next to Grandma with his legs in the water, kicking and splashing happily. He saw his parents watching him and grinned. "Swimming pool!"

Sal nodded. "I know honey, it's a swimming pool."

Jack was covered in spots, but there were no signs of him being a chicken. In fact, it now looked like he had the regular old Chicken Pox. Their son was back. It had been a overnight bug. Nothing serious.

"Come give mummy and daddy a hug," said Iain, beaming.

Jack leapt up and ran over to his parents, throwing his arms around them both. "Chicken better now."

"Yes, honey," said Sal. "Chicken better now."

Something whooshed overhead and made them all duck. Iain glanced up to see a black helicopter hovering close enough to throw water out of the pool. Jack pointed up at it like it was amazing. "Birdy!"

Two black-clad men rappelled out of the helicopter and landed right on the patio. One of them had an MP5 pointed at them. "Get down now!"

Iain frowned. "No thanks. Who are you?"

"We are the Police and you've been ordered to get down. We have reports of a contagious disease here. We are here to contain it."

Sal bit her lip, pulled Jack close.

Iain shrugged. "It's just Chicken Pox."

The man lowered his gun slightly and frowned. "What?"

Iain moved Jack away from his mother so that they could see the spots on his arms and face. "Just Chicken Pox, dude. We called a doctor last night, but he was a bit out of it. Think he was drunk, to be honest. Anyway, he told us to stay put until it cleared up. No problem"

The soldier was shaking his head. "No he called is... we... we had reports of a... Drunk, you say? But he gave us a report!"

Sal lifted her chin and shot the man a glance. "Of what? What would make you point a gun at an innocent English family trying to enjoy the hospitality of your country? My husband is a bestselling author and he will write about this."

Iain nodded to his wife. "Thanks, honey."

"Shut up."

The man's colleague whispered something into his ear, and he put the gun away. "I'm sorry. There seems to be some confusion. I must investigate the house, and have a quick look at your son, but if this is all a misunderstanding then I can't apologise enough. This is not how Portugal treats its guests."

Grandma got up, shoving the officer out of her way. Iain apologised to the man. "I think she's off to make a cuppa. Do you drink tea?"

"No thank you. I shall not keep you long."

And he didn't. After a brief examination of Jack, the two police officers declared a simple case of Chicken Pox. After giving the villa a cursory inspection, they eventually hurried towards the front door. Their last words were a promise to cover the cost of accommodation by way of an apology, which was nice. The man with the gun waved goodbye to Jack before he left, who thought he was wonderful, if a little scary.

The men gone, Sal collapsed into Iain's arms. "How did you know to lie?"

"It's what I do for a living. I make shit up. If we admitted Jack had been a chicken they would have carted him off some place. You saw how they arrived. They came to fuck shit up."

Sal glared at him. "Will you watch your language in front of Jack?"

"Sorry. I'm sure this isn't over, in the long run. Our old friend, Matt, has done something crazy back home it seems, but let's just cross that… *bridge* when we come to it."

Sal kissed him on the cheek. "This has been a crazy start to a holiday."

"I know. My fans will be so worried. I haven't posted on Facebook for a whole day. You know how they get if they don't hear from me."

"Yeah… Anyway, I could kill a cuppa. Where's Grandma got to?"

"I think she's in the kitchen."

Iain knelt down to Jack, who was fiddling with the sandals they'd made him put on. "Hey, darling, you want to go find Grandma?"

Always loving a task—like 'Jack, can you pass mommy's phone?' and 'Jack, can you go downstairs and get daddy a coke?'—he went racing off to find his favourite person in the whole world, shouting the whole time, "Marmar?"

Sal and Iain looked into each other's eyes, both of them sharing the relief, the appreciation, and utmost love that they were both feeling. They shared a brief kiss and then followed their little boy into the kitchen.

"I think you have a good idea for your next book, honey."

Iain huffed. "A story about Jack turning into a chicken? Who would enjoy something that stupid?"

"Yeah, you're right. It's not something a serious author would right about, is it? Besides, I know you didn't want to think about work this week."

"Right, I've had enough stress, thank you very much. I'm just glad we can finally start relaxing."

"Me too."

Cluck!

Sal and Iain froze in the hallway, right outside the kitchen door.

Iain swallowed. "Did I just hear that?"

Cluck!

Sal nodded, her face turning white.

The urge to vomit assaulted his guts, but he took his wife's hand and pulled her with him into the kitchen. They couldn't believe what they saw.

"Chicken," said Jack happily. "Chicken Grandma." He was sat on the floor and giggled at the giant chicken sat beside him. The chicken wore Grandma's pearls.

Iain looked at his wife, eyes bulging and a vein throbbing in his head. "I think it's contagious."

Sal rubbing at her eyes as if she couldn't believe what she was seeing. "Mom, are you okay?"

Cluck!

The baby monitor hissed and came to life on the counter. *Cluck cluck, wah!*

Oh no! Molly had it too.

Iain didn't panic, though. Instead he just shrugged and opened the fridge to get some orange juice. "Ah, at least we know they'll get over it. Breakfast?"

Sal sighed. "Yeah, I'll go get breakfast. You stay with the kids and Grandma."

"Great. Just leave me with to look after the chicken family."

"I told you it would be hard work when you married me."

"Yeah you did, but you never said it would be fowl!"

"Iain, I want a divorce."

"That's fair."

7. THE WITNESS

Soon I will take her, not because I want to but because I must. It is what I am. It is what I do. I am the Witness.

I've been watching her for a while now, studying her, enjoying her. She is playing with her little boy in the park. He seems to love her very much. The way he reaches out his hands whenever he passes by, as if she is somehow magnetic to him. Several times, she has grabbed his wrists and swung him around gleefully, but now she is shooing him away, ordering him to go and play with the other children. She loves her boy, but does not want him all to herself. She wants him to socialise. The girl is a good mother. A young mother that expects to live a long and happy life.

Sometimes, we don't get what we expect.

Sometimes pain and suffering replaces the joy we hope for. I am a being without joy, but I enjoy seeing it in others. It is interesting, and I enjoy it all the more when it is due to be snuffed out. In these cases, the joy is ethereal and all the more delicate. I wonder if my delight in torment makes me wicked.

The woman's name is Donna Fawcett. She is unmarried and raises her son alone. I know this because I am the Witness. I watch before I take. Maybe I shouldn't. Perhaps my voyeurism makes me sick, but it seems important to know who I am taking. Their deaths are always so beautiful, spectacular even, but it is only in view of their lives that their ends can truly be enjoyed. How many have I taken now? How often has my head filled with screams, my mouth with blood? I feel, taste, and see all. It is my curse, but a blessing also to be so connected. Still, sometimes I mourn for the lives I take. I mourn for the simplicity of them. Few victims know the things I do.

I begin my slow journey towards Donna, stalking her in my own casual way. It is nearly time. Time for her to lay eyes upon him. It will be a frightening experience for her, but it shall not last long. At least she will have that. Her son is on the swing now, kicking his legs to try and get himself going. Donna can't help but give him a helpful push. Nearby, other mothers play with their own children, as well as a father with a small girl. He keeps glancing at Donna, and I can tell he desires her. But is he a married cheater, or a divorced father? Is either of interest to Donna? Perhaps. I am not intelligent when it comes to reading social cues, even after so many years watching. Witnessing. Donna is an object of affection for many men, I assume, with her long blonde hair and slender figure. She does not work out, that I have seen, but she eats little. Money is tight and she spends it on her son. The father is never mentioned nor seen. Sad for the boy. About to get sadder.

I take a seat at the edge of the park. Perhaps I should not be so close. To be around children with none of your own is a warning flag in today's society. I am not a child molester, but it is, perhaps, a good thing I am so unnoticeable. Most give me no more than a cursory glance, and few remember my face. The only person that needs to see me is Donna. I am here for her. Mine will be the last face she sees. That is just how it is. I cannot help who I come for. I cannot help what I am. Many would call me a monster. Truly, I see myself as an angel.

Still, I sometimes yearn to be something else. Something that does not put such fear in people's eyes.

To speak with someone as a friend...

Such silliness, to even be thinking that someone like me could have a friend. I may be an angel, but that doesn't change the fact I am still seen as a monster by all who meet me. The newspapers will write about me taking Donna with horror and sadness, like they always do. They love to write about me. I sell their papers for them. People are obsessed with me. Terrified by me. I am the Witness.

This close to her, I can see the blue in Donna's eyes, and the green in her son's. Are his father's eyes that colour, or do they originate from more distant relations? They are undeniably related, though, despite their physical differences, and I wonder if the boy's hair smells the same as hers. Do they use the same apple-scented shampoo?

Will I be able to get one last inhalation of Donna's scent before she slips away?

I almost feel bad.

The boy will be left an orphan, unless the wayward father returns, and what kind of man might he be? The kind that walks out on his responsibilities, obviously. Maybe if he hadn't left, I wouldn't be here. Maybe Donna would not be on my list. It is beyond us both now.

Donna must die.

That is why I am here.

It's time to go, so Donna gathers her son from the swing and holds his hand. He comes willingly, as all good boys do. They make quite a pair, mother and son, an oil painting made real. They leave the park and cross the road together, the lights turning green just as they reach the middle. A young man in a loud car comes speeding around the corner, heading right towards Donna and her son.

People in the park look up, jolted by the noisy engine and screeching tyres.

Donna has to drag her son out of the way to avoid being run over, but she does not shout or swear--not in front of him. She simply kneels down at the side of the road and explains that there's a reason roads are so dangerous, and they just saw a good example. Being the good boy he is, her son promises always to look both ways. I can see the jolt of fear that still lingers on Donna's face though. For a moment, a mother's fear was in her. Her child had been in danger. I saw the change come over her, almost supernatural, ready to leap in front of the speeding vehicle and save her son if need be. A subtle change that probably even she was unaware of.

It seemed in this world, children were always in danger.

So were adults.

I am the death that stalks you, Donna, the misery that whispers in the night, turning your smiles to tears. I am the Witness.

And it pains me so.

And yet it pleases me more.

Soon.

But not yet.

Donna heads down the pavement for a while, and when she pulls her boy off the street into a McDonald's, he squealed. The boy did not get

Happy Meals as often as other children. His mother was poor. That didn't affect how much he loved her, though, and I can see how the mild adversity is building character in him. He is a kind boy, yet tough enough to face the subtle horrors of life.

He is not tough enough to face me, which is why I hang back. I only want his mother.

Let him continue being strong once she is gone.

The poor child.

I stand in the doorway of the restaurant, peeking from the corner of my eye. An old man passes me in the doorway, the sadness of being the surviving spouse of a long marriage evident in his face. He nods politely, but I see the fear. The fear that exists in all old people, asking themselves the question: will this be the day I die? Will it be violent, or quick? Embarrassing or peaceful? The shadow of death looms over them like a low hanging cloud.

As it does Donna today.

Her cloud should come later, but it is here early.

Donna sits down with a tray filled with food for her son. There is only a water for herself. I know she will eat pasta or bread later, whatever she finds in the cupboard. I imagine her stomach rumbling while she watches her son gorge on chicken nuggets. Yet she never stops smiling, looking at her boy as if he is brand new. Several times, she reaches across the table just to stroke his cheek. There are many other children in the restaurant, and many more parents, but none look at one another the way this mother looks at her son. He is her world. The only good thing in her life.

Soon I will separate them.

Donna pulls apart a plastic bag and reveals the toy from her son's Happy Meal. It is a small racing car, and she has fun pushing it back and forwards across the table with him. They chat and laugh for a while longer, not rushing the moment, until Donna helps him take the tray to the clean-up station. He empties his litter dutifully and then asks to be picked up. He is still young, but too old to need picking up, yet Donna reaches down and heaves him up anyway, struggling with her first few steps until she gets some momentum. The boy is tired. He wraps his arms around his mother's neck and puts his cheek against her shoulder.

I follow them down the street to the row of flats where they live. The building is near the town's busy centre, a noisy and unpretty place, but inside they have made it a home. I have seen it several times. Donna does not lock her door until bedtime.

Now she is typing in the code to enter the building. I stand back, moving behind a nearby bus shelter. The old woman sitting here studies me. I ignore her. My eyes are only on Donna. Through the glass of the stairwell door, I see her climb the stairs. She lives with her son on the first floor, Flat 3. There is one neighbour opposite in Flat 4, but the young man who lives there is asleep all day and stoned all night. Donna does not like him. Nor does her son.

Once I am sure Donna is safely inside her flat, I approach the building. I know the code, so I step inside quickly. As I climb the stairs, I look upwards, ensuring no one sees me. Not that it matters. No one ever remembers me.

No witnesses ever describe the Witness. The Witness is unknown.

The hour is getting late, the sky turning a subtle shade of grey that will eventually fall to black. I see this through the cracked window on the upper stairwell. I am standing outside Donna's door. Last night, standing in the shadows of her hallway, I watched her bathe her son and put him to bed. I try her front door and find it unlocked, as I do every night. She is too trusting. For her, danger comes in a speeding car or a meningitis scare at her son's school. What is going to happen to her will come as quite a shock. Hopefully it will be quick. Sometimes it is. Not always.

I sneak inside, moving into the space beside the coat rack. I am good at hiding, naturally attuned to the shadows but washed out by the light. I am ordinary and unnoticeable, a part of nature. A force that cannot be seen, only felt.

I hear the sound of running water, a bath being run. I salivate.

Donna and her son briefly appear in the hallway, chasing after one another, but they do not look my way. Her son has no pants on, and she is fighting him to get off his shirt. It is all a game, as it always is with these two kindred spirits. Sometimes I wish I had a mother like her, and not just a father. Would it have shaped me differently? Perhaps.

The bath is not quick, a little longer than usual in fact, for tonight they are washing hair. The boy complains. The mother sings. Then the bath is over and I am tingling in anticipation. I have looked forward to Donna's death for what feels like an eternity. The more I have gotten to know her, the more I have wanted to meet her face to face. Is it wrong to take pleasure in my work? I can't help it, it is how I am made. It is what I am for. I am the Witness.

Donna reads to her son before bed always, and tonight it is the

Gruffalo. A modern tale and not one I have heard before. Strangely, I find myself listening and enjoying it too.

Eventually, I tire of standing in the hallway and creep into the living room. There, I wait. Always waiting. My patience is my virtue. I must never rush. That would dishonour my role in this world. I do not care about honour, but it is part of me all the same.

Donna says goodnight, but she does not come into the living room. She goes into the kitchen. Some nights she has a single glass of wine, but tonight she fills a beaker from the sink and drinks water. I watch her through the open doorway--there are hinges and a frame, but no door. Odd. Part of being poor, I suppose. Also part of being poor is the threadbare carpet in the living room. The crisscrossed backing-fibre are showing in several places, and next to the sofa is a large flap of underlay sticking up like a flap of sliced skin. A clean ashtray sits on the scratched glass coffee table in the centre of the room, but it is full of pennies. Perhaps Donna's son is saving for a new toy. He probably wouldn't get it now.

Donna enters the living room and is finally in my presence.

I pick up the scent of her hair and sigh. Delightful.

As always, she picks up the TV remote and switches on the set. She pays no attention to what is on yet, and instead goes over to the windows and closes the curtains. Then she goes out into the hallway and locks the front door. Locks herself inside with me.

Her end is here.

Stepping back into the living room she sees me. She sees me just as her foot snags against the torn flap of carpet beside the sofa. Sees me all the way down as she trips and falls awkwardly. She looks right into my eyes as the side of her head smashes against the cold hard corner of the glass coffee table.

Then she sees nothing at all.

Donna is dead.

I wait, as I always do. I have fulfilled my role. I have Witnessed. Now I must move on.

Not just yet though.

Donna reappeared, staring down at her own dead body. I always find human disbelief fascinating. A species that prides itself on reason, yet only accepts reason when it suits what they already hold to be true. Staring at their own death is not enough to convince them they are dead, yet they might look up at the moon and know that it moves around the earth. An odd animal, human beings.

When I step to my right, Donna startles.

"Who are you!"

"I am your Witness. For all those who die alone, a Witness must be present."

"Why?"

"Because God does not want anyone to die alone. I am here to see your last moments so that your death does not go unnoticed."

She looked down at her body again. "I'm not dead."

"But you are."

"No."

I sigh. It is a conversation I have had many times. "Poverty killed you, it would seem. Money would have had that carpet replaced."

"I asked the landlord twice."

"He did not listen. Now, I imagine, he will."

She shakes her head at me, this time with tears in her eyes. "I am not dead."

"You are. You know it. It is... distressing, I imagine, but you know it for sure."

"What are you?"

"A creature just like you. What do you think I am?"

She stares hard at me, one eye squinting. "Death? Except you look like an old teacher of mine, one who I used to really like."

I nod understandingly. "I appear as I need to appear. Most people see their parents."

She sneers slightly at that, but there's no time for me to question her. Nor is it my place. "We must go."

"Where? Are you a demon?"

"Perhaps."

"I can't go. My son needs me."

I look towards the door across the hallway, behind which a sweet little boy sleeps. "I am sorry."

"No you're not. You're a monster."

There was that word again. The one they always used. "I am no monster."

She folded her arms. "I'm not going anywhere."

"There is no choice involved here for either of us. You are dead. This place is for the living."

Tears now stream down her face, but they do not move me. I like this woman, but I am not capable of further feeling. I would like to spend more time with her, but I am not permitted. Perhaps, with time, I could come to care about her tears. It would please me to find out.

The way she looked at him should probably have made him feel more than the mild pity he was used to. "I'm all he has. What can I do to stay?"

"Nothing. It is done. Your son no longer has a mother."

"You bastard!"

"I am sorry. Truth is the only speech permitted to me. You are dead, your son is not. One day you will be reunited."

Her face lit up at that. He could not tell the future, but if the statement was untrue he would not have been able to say it. Therefore, it was indeed God's plan that this mother would one day be reunited with her son.

Not this day though.

She wipes her nose with the back of his arm and tries to catch her breath. After a loud swallow, she stares at me hard. "I'll really see him again?"

"Of course. You may even get to watch him live his life."

"Am I... going to Heaven?"

I wish that was a question I could answer, for all the times I have been asked it, but it is not my place in things to know. I am a Witness. No more. "Heaven is a word. All I know is that there is a place for all things. You are a good woman, a good mother, a good person. Those things are virtues above most others. Wherever you are going, you should not fear it. Not at all."

She nods slightly to herself and I can see her coming to terms with her death. Humans seemed equipped with a filter to help them through the transition. They are not quite the same after death as they are in life. Not so hysterical. And that is a good thing for me.

"Are you ready?" I ask her.

She is about to answer when a noise cuts her off.

"Mummy? I heard a noise."

Her eyes go wide and she stares at her son's bedroom door. The tears start afresh. Her bottom lip quivers.

"Mummy? Mummy, are you there?"

She attempts to go to him, but I take her arm and freeze her in place. "You won't be able to reach him. You are dead."

She looks down at her limp corpse and speaks in a voice more full of pain than any I have ever known. "W-W-What is going to happen to him? What is going to happen to my boy?"

"I do not know."

"He's all alone. He has no family. Who will look after him?"

"I do not know."

"He's just a little boy."

I sigh. "I know. It is time."

She tries to fight me, but once I hold her, there is no escape. You cannot escape a Witness. We are a force.

"Let me go. I'm not leaving. I'm not! Fuck you!"

"Mummy! I'm scared! Can you come cuddle me?"

She screams in pain, anguish beyond my understanding. Her eyes fixate on her son's bedroom door as it begins to slowly open. Soon the boy will step into the living room and find his mother's cooling body. Donna does not need to see that. Even I understand enough to know what torture is.

Before she can take another full breath, Donna is gone, sent to whatever place it is people go to once I have Witnessed them. Perhaps her pain will fade away there, or perhaps it will be all she is left with. Those questions are not for me to answer. I am only here to Witness.

I look across the hall and see the bedroom door now fully open. The little boy steps out in his pale blue sailboat pyjamas. He has not yet seen his mother, but he will any moment now. It will no doubt be terrible for him, and part of me wishes I could do something to help. But I cannot. It is not my place.

So I step past the boy into the hallway, no longer visible with my work now being at an end. Before I leave to Witness the next soul, however, I turn and watch the boy cross the hallway, padding on his little bare feet. I don't know why, but I can't leave without first saying something. The words I choose are, "Good luck, child, and God bless."

Perhaps I do care.

8. THE BOB SAGA

The following is inspired by true events. Part one has been told before in the AZ of Horror. Part two is being recounted here for the very first time…

PART 1: M IS FOR MATTY-BOB

"How did you sleep last night?" Iain asked his wife, Sally, as he came downstairs at 8AM.

Sally, holding their ten-month old baby, Jack, in her arms, blinked slowly. "Like shit."

"What time did he wake up?"

"Half-five, but I left him babbling 'til six."

Jack reached out to Daddy and Sally thrust him away gladly. She sat down on the sofa and sipped her coffee while Jack proceeded to pull his daddy's hair.

Iain took a seat beside Sally, Jack on his lap, and reached out for the mug of tea waiting for him on the side table – Sally was so good to him, so good to Jack. The television was on, playing a loop of *Timmy Time* that she had found on Youtube.

"What time you going to your mum's today?" Iain asked.

"After Jack's nap. You starting a new story today?"

"No, I'm still editing at the moment. Waiting on Stephen for a cover, too. Did you hear something in the night?"

Sally frowned at him. "Like what?"

He shrugged. "Not sure. I thought I heard something in the garden. Probably just cats."

"God, Iain. Don't tell me that! I'll be seeing strange men in the dark now."

Iain adjusted his struggling son on his lap and chuckled. "Sorry. It wasn't anything like that. Just wondering if our cat got into a fight or something."

"No, Jess was in last night. It was raining."

Iain sniffed and then pulled a face. "I think there's a poop in the poopy pants."

Sally sighed, but then put on a great big smile and tickled Jack's ribs. Looking into his face, she said in a silly voice, "Is there a poop in the poopy pants? Do you have a poop in your poopy pants?"

Jack giggled deliriously as his mother picked him up and took him away to change him in the spare room that now possessed the constant odour of 'poopy pants'.

Iain picked up his laptop from the side table and started checking emails. He deleted the spam that had resulted from a month-long hobby of entering online competitions and sorted out any messages of import. There were the usual sales reports and promo responses, along with a few fan emails, but one message in particular stood out. It read:

"YOU ARE MY LIFE."

Iain frowned and clicked the email to open it. What popped up on his screen was a photograph of a smiling ginger man in glasses. He was topless and held a finger to each nipple. Written across his round tummy, presumably in lipstick, were the bright red words: Iain Rob Wright for the Win!

Iain felt a knot in his stomach. As his popularity as a horror author had increased, there had been several occasions when fans had made him feel uncomfortable. Some had demanded his time more than he was able to give them, while others had confided strange stories about their lives or asked him for personal details about his own. As much as Iain adored each and every one of his fans, he had a wife and child that took priority. It was situations like this man now that Iain found so hard to deal with. This man was obviously a supporter of his work, but possibly a little unstable also. What was the best thing to do? How to let someone down gently without being an asshole about it?

Iain checked the sender's name and identified the man as MATTY BOB. Strange name for sure.

"Iain!"

Iain flinched and almost dropped his laptop. From the panic in his wife's voice, it was clear that his presence was required. He hopped up from the sofa and hurried into the spare room where the stench of fresh poopy pants hit him in the face like a wet kipper.

"Woah!" he said, waving a hand in front of his nose, then looked at his obviously upset wife. "What's wrong, babe?"

"There's a man in our garden."

Iain felt that knot in his stomach again. "What?"

"In the garden there is a man, look!"

Iain slid around the room's bed and went to the window. Sure enough, sitting on the lawn, plucking at blades of grass was a man in a bright red cape like Superman's.

"What the hell?"

Sally picked Jack up from the changing mat on the bed and held him against her chest. He immediately gave her a right hook and then started pulling at her necklace. "Should I call the police?"

Iain was stuck staring at the strange man in his garden. He couldn't be sure, but it might have been the man who had emailed him. He spotted a crop of gingery-blond hair and a pair of glasses.

"I… just hold off on calling the police. I'll go and talk with him."

"Iain, you shouldn't go out there. He could be crazy."

"That doesn't make him dangerous. He might need help."

"Iain, you surely are the kindest man alive. I hope that all your fans know that."

Iain smiled. "I'm sure they do. God bless them all."

"Iain?"

Iain snapped out of his daze and looked at his wife. "Sorry, what? I was daydreaming."

"How can you be daydreaming? I said, should I call the police?"

"What? No, I'll deal with it."

"Be careful."

Iain nodded. "Just stay up here."

He went down to the lower floor and into the kitchen. Sure enough, the man was still sitting in the garden. When he saw Iain through the French doors, he leapt up and began waving.

Iain swallowed the lump in his throat and stepped outside. "Can I help you?" he said. "You're in my garden."

"I know, I know," the man gushed. "You're Iain Rob Wright. You call your fans Wrighters. Well, I'm your biggest Wrighter. I love you.

"How did you know where I live?"

"Your address is listed at Companies House. Your business is registered here."

Iain sighed. He was no businessman and left those kinds of things to his accountants. His office was at home, which was why his business's head office was listed as the same. Damn it!

"What do you want?"

"To meet you, of course. Did you get my email, my picture?"

"I did. Thank you… I guess. You really can't be here. This is my home."

The man took a step towards him.

Iain held his ground, wanting to appear in charge. Now that the other man was standing, it was disturbingly apparent that he was mentally unwell. He wore only muddy boots, stained white y-fronts, and that bright red cape.

"I had to see you," he said excitedly. "I had to tell you that your novel The Last Winter is the best horror novel of all time."

"The *Final* Winter."

"What?"

Iain cleared his throat and said it again. "It's the *Final* Winter, not the *Last* Winter."

"Oh, yeah, right, I knew that. Well, anyway, it changed my life. Harry is me. Do you understand?"

"Not really. You need to leave. I will chat to you happily via email, but you can't come to my home. My family deserve privacy."

"How is little Jack, and Sally, too, of course? Where is she?"

"Out," Iain lied. "If you don't leave, I will have to call the police."

"Like in ASBO?"

Iain sighed. "Yes, like in ASBO. It's been lovely to meet you – Matty, is it? – but you have to go."

"It's Matty-Bob."

"Okay, Matty-Bob. Time to go."

"Can't I come in and have a cup of tea?"

"No, you cannot."

"Okay. Well, I'll see you soon."

Iain tilted his head, narrowed his eyes. "What do you mean?"

"Nothing. Keep writing, Iain. You da man."

With that, the unhinged fan swept up his cape and ran towards the back fence. He leapt up and tried to climb over it, but ended up dangling foolishly.

Iain rolled his eyes and groaned. "Jesus, man, let me open the back gate for you."

-2-

"If he turns up again, I'll call the police," Iain told his wife as he spread Marmite on his toast. "He's a bloody nutcase."

Sally nodded understandingly. "Well, we all knew this could happen when people started calling you 'the next Stephen King'. With your remarkable talent and skill, people were always going to fall hopelessly in love with you. The other horror writers have barely had a chance since you came along."

"I know, I know. Sometimes I think about retiring just to make it fair, but it just wouldn't be right, would it? Everything I have to offer the world…"

"Iain?"

Iain shook his head and snapped out of his daze. "Sorry, what?"

Sally shot him a scornful glance. "Were you even listening to me? I said that I'm leaving with Jack now, but you need to call the police if that crazy man comes back. I don't want to come home and find you tied to a chair."

Iain frowned. "Did you see the guy? I could take him easily if I have to."

Sally groaned. "You're not on a council estate anymore, darling. My husband is a man who watches cartoons with his son; whose favourite show is Nashville; and who cried when Buffy's mum died. So no more talk about fighting crazy men in our garden, okay?"

Iain nodded and watched his wife and son go out the front door. He sat down at the kitchen table and ate his toast in silence. He had work to do today, but was completely unmotivated. The man in the garden had distracted his thoughts for the day, which meant he probably wouldn't get into a good flow until Noon.

Maybe he would take a bath to snap out of his fugue. Do a bit of reading and get his head in the game? Yeah, that was what he would do. He'd soon forget about that crazy man who had invaded his privacy.

Unless he came back.

-3-

In a funny mood, Iain had spent the last thirty minutes taking bathtub selfies of his scrunched up face and chin, then uploading them to Facebook. His fans were horrified, but also amused, so it had been worth it.

He turned the tap on with his foot and shuddered as the hot water brought the temperature up.

His phone pinged for an email.

It was from Matty-Bob.

So grate to meet you earlier, Ian. I felt we really connect and I'm just sorry you aske me to leave. I understand what I did wrong, thou, and I am on my way to correct its.

Iain sat up in the bath, alert. Was that psychopath coming back to the house?

"I brought pizza!"

Iain leapt up out of the bath so quickly that he slipped over the side and fell to the ground headfirst; his naked arse left pointing in the air. The pain didn't register as much as the panic, though, so he was up on his feet quickly.

Matty-Bob stood in the doorway to the bathroom, this time wearing a scruffy brown tuxedo that looked like it had been dragged out of an antique chest.

"Wow, fella!" Matty-Bob pointed to Iain's uncovered genitals. "Did you get that thing from an elephant? Your wife is a lucky girl."

"I… I am blessed."

"Hey, Iain?"

Iain shook his head and snapped out of the daze caused by the blow to his head.

"You okay there?" Matty-Bob asked. "That was quite the fall you took and you went a bit fuzzy on me there for a moment."

Iain looked at the lunatic holding a pizza and was utterly shocked, and very very angry. "What the fuck are you doing in my house?"

"I brought pizza!"

"Fuck your pizza."

Matty-Bob looked confused, but then he shrugged. "Okay." He proceeded to pull his penis out of his pants and shoved it into the cheesy pizza.

"Jesus Christ!" Iain shouted. "I didn't mean literally. Get the hell out of my house. I'm going to have you arrested, you maniac."

Matty-Bob looked confused. "But you love your fans. You say so all the time. That's why I'm here, to be with you."

"To be with me?"

"Yes. You say you love your fans, well here I am – your very biggest. Or is that all bullshit? Do you just pretend to be a nice guy? Is it lies? Please don't tell me it's lies."

Iain realised he was debating this man while standing completely in the nude. He grabbed a towel off the rail and wrapped it around himself. "Of course I don't pretend, but that doesn't mean you can just break into my home. If you wanted to meet me, you should email me like any normal person."

"You don't meet fans, though."

"I do sometimes."

"Not really."

"I have a ten month old son. Meeting people is not something I have a lot of time for. That doesn't mean I don't care, though."

"I know," said Matty-Bob. "That's why I came to you. Come here, big fella."

The man went to hug Iain, but Iain shot out a leg and kept him at bay. "What? No, not 'come here, big guy'. More like, 'get out of my house, you goddamn freak'."

Matty-Bob froze on the spot, his embracing arms stuck open like pincers. "It's all lies, isn't it? You don't love your fans."

"I do," Iain growled. "Just not the ones who stick their dicks in pizzas."

Iain turned around to look for his phone, but was dismayed when he saw it at the bottom of the bath beneath the water. "I'm calling the police," he said, "So you'd better-"

Something struck him in the back of the head, sending him sprawling back into the bathtub. He thrashed in the water and turned himself around to face his attacker.

"Eat it!" Matty-Bob screamed, shoving a slice of pizza into Iain's mouth. "Eat my cock pizza, you liar."

Iain managed to right himself in the bath and kick out with his legs. Matty-Bob went flying backwards into the wall, giving Iain the chance to leap up out of the bathtub and make a break for it.

Matty-Bob grabbed out at Iain's shoulder as he passed, long dirty nails digging a furrow in his flesh.

"Ow!" Iain yelled. "That really hurt."

Matty-Bob snarled. "Not as much as it's going to."

Iain had lost his towel and was naked again, but he couldn't worry about that now. He ran down the stairs, testicles slapping against his leg while Matty-Bob was right behind him, screeching and hollering like the madman that he was.

"I just want to be friends," he kept shouting. "You always say how you consider your fans to be your friends, your family. Liar!"

Iain crossed the middle-floor landing and wheeled towards the next set of steps. With no regard for his own safety, Matty-Bob threw himself down the stairs and collided with Iain's back. The two of them went tumbling down the stairs, hitting the cat litter tray at the bottom.

Matty reached out and grabbed a pile of cat shit that had fallen out and immediately started thrusting it at Iain's face. "Eat it, you lying son-of-a-bitch. You lying ol' dirty bird!"

Iain threw a punch and caught Matty-Bob under the chin just as the cat shit was about to meet his lips. Matty-Bob fell sideways to the floor, while Iain clambered back to his feet and ran into the hallway.

Matty-Bob was right behind him again, continuing the chase. "I just wanna hang out," he shouted. "NO BIG DEAL!"

Iain reached the front door and grabbed the handle, ecstatic that Sally hadn't locked it on her way out. But before he could pull open the door, Matty-Bob flew into the back of him and started licking his ear.

"Get off me, you freak."

Matty-Bob smacked his lips. "Taste like chicken."

"I just had a bath."

Matty-Bob leapt forwards and this time bit Iain in the shoulder, clamping down hard like a zombie from one of his books. Iain managed to shove the maniac away from him before any blood was shed.

"You're insane."

"Remember when Shawcross died at the end of Ravage? This is just like that, don't you think?"

Iain shook his head. "Shawcross was the bad guy. Bad guys lose." He wound up a punch and let it fly, but Matty-Bob ducked and punched him in the gut.

Iain dropped to his knees, wheezing.

"Just calm down, Iain. Put the kettle on. We can talk about what book you're going to write next. Maybe you can put me in it. You do that sometimes for your fans, right? Like you named the boat in Sea Sick after some woman. Well, I can promise you that whoever that woman was she doesn't love you as much as I do. Write a book about me. Make me a dashing hero. I love you, did I tell you that?"

Iain tried to catch his breath. "If you love me… then leave me… alone."

Matty-Bob pulled a knife from his tuxedo pocket and held it up in front of him. "Not until I have something to remember you by."

Iain groaned. "Won't a simple autograph do?"

"Anybody can get your autograph. I want something nobody else has."

Iain yelled in terror as Matty-Bob lunged at him with the knife. His eyes closed instinctively, but no pain arrived – just a tugging at his hair.

Iain opened his eyes again to see that Matty-Bob had cut a lock of his hair off and was smelling it. "Some of your fans think you're going bald, but I think it gives you an air of distinction. What does Sally think? I can't wait to meet her. Is she really as sweet as she seems? Do you think she would let me be Jack's Godfather?"

The thought of having his family subjected to this maniac's fantasies brought Iain's mind back into focus. He climbed to his feet, leaning against the wall for support.

"Matty-Bob?" he asked, once his balance had returned.

"Yes?"

"You know I grew up on a council estate, right?"

"Yes, you grew up poor and managed to make something of yourself. It's such a wonderful story."

Iain nodded. "Then allow me to give you something from my past."

Matty-Bob grinned, but the smile was soon wiped off his face when Iain booted him between the legs like Pele kicking a football. He fell over backwards like an ironing board, groaning all the way.

Iain was straight out the front door and yelling for help.

Three kids playing cards at the side of the road screamed when they saw him running towards them naked.

One little girl pointed a finger at him and shouted. "You won't fiddle me, you pervert."

Then the three of them took off, screaming for their parents.

Iain looked around, seeing no adults to help him and wondering what the hell people would think of him standing there in the buff. His penis had shrunk to a raisin and his fat belly was heaving in and out. If this ended up on Facebook, he was ruined.

Matt-Bob came staggering out the door behind him. "Why won't you just love me," he pleaded. "All I've done is support you. I have all of your books. Even that shitty one, Thrillobytes, that you took off sale. When I heard Amazon banned D is for Degenerate, I sent them my own shit in the post. Everything I do, I do for you, Iain."

Iain backed off, gravel biting his heels and making him wince. "Just... just wait until the next time I do a convention. We can hang out all day then. You have my hair, what more do you want?"

"I want you in me?"

Iain pulled a face. "I don't even know what that means, but it doesn't sound like something I would agree to."

"You're so wonderful, Iain. So much better than that talentless hack, Matt Shaw. You and me should take a trip together. I know it's hard work being a father, so let's go to Vegas!"

Iain kept on backing away. In the distance he noticed the children were returning with their furious looking parents. They were looking to beat up a pedophile, but it was not what it seemed. Iain was the one who needed help.

"You know," Iain said, trying to stall. "Disney is really more my thing."

Matty-Bob gritted his teeth and started beating his own head with his fists, over and over again. "Damn it! I knew that, I knew that. So dumb, so dumb!"

-3-

Iain put a hand out. "It's fine, Matty. Just calm down."

Matty pulled his fists away from his head and glared at Iain. A line of blood formed from his hairline down to his nose. "My name... is... Matty-*Bob*!"

Matty-Bob rushed towards Iain, the knife held out in front of him once again. But this time it didn't look like he was coming for hair.

Iain turned and ran, arms flailing in the air. "Jesus, God, oh bloody 'ell. Help me, somebody. Oh bloody 'ell."

Matty-Bob yelled strange obscenities. "You mother-humping ass-butt!"

Iain looked at the children and their arriving parents, cried out to them for help, but he only made them confused.

They would never make it over to him in time.

Matty-Bob closed the distance between them. Raised his knife. Snarled.

The screech of tyres.

A maroon Nissan Qashqai squealed around the corner, almost going up on two wheels.

Matty-Bob froze, looked confused at what he saw coming towards him.

Then the large family car thumped into him, sent him toppling into the air, over the panoramic sunroof, and back down to the unforgiving road.

There the man lay now, panting in the street, his antique tuxedo torn and wet with blood.

Sally pulled on the handbrake and leapt out of the car. She approached her naked, panicked husband with caution. "Iain, what the hell is going on?"

He shrugged. "You know, just work."

Sally grabbed Jack out of his car seat and moved Iain away from the injured maniac on the road. The neighbours arrived and tried to understand what they were seeing. Pretty soon they seemed to get a grasp on the situation and didn't seem to mind the fact that Iain was naked at all. In fact, both the men and women in the crowd seemed delighted by what they saw. They couldn't help themselves but wink and purr in his direction.

One of the members of the crowd stepped forward to speak with Iain. "I'm sorry we weren't here to help, Mr Rob Wright. A man as talented and handsome as you should always have someone watching out for him. Rest assured that from now on, no one in this street will ever fail you. We are forming an Iain Rob Wright Protection Society and will never again allow you to come to harm."

Iain nodded and shook hands with the man. "Thank you, thank you."

"Iain?"

Iain opened his eyes and saw his wife staring at him. "Sally?"

"Yes, I just said the police are on the way. Come on, we need to go inside and get you covered up. You're freaking everybody out. I think you messed yourself a little at the back."

Iain looked down at the shit on the back of his thigh and realised he must have done it when he was running in terror. He was usually due a toilet break around now – he'd missed it. He looked over at Matty-Bob who was still down on the ground, semi-concious. "Is this the price of fame?" he asked his wife.

"No," she said. "This is the price of you being a dope. Now come on, inside."

Later on his official blog, Iain Rob Wright wrote concerning the incident:

"I don't know if I can ever get over something like that… It's weird. Even though I know Matty-Bob is institutionalised, I still think about him once in a while."

Following the blog post was a single comment, left by a fan named Brian Stone. He simply stated: *Didn't you steal that from Misery?*

END.

THE REAL LIFE MATTY-BOB

I AN
ROB
WRIGHT

PART 2: REVENGE OF THE BOB

"Why is it that as soon as you move into a new house, you find the walls are made from papier mâché and the carpets are actually sixty percent insect carcasses? This place looked lovely when we viewed it."

Sal stared at me like I was a child—the default setting for how my wife looked at me. "Iain, we've changed the carpets and they're lovely now. The walls are being re-plastered and painted next week. Cheer up, you miserable bugger."

"I'm not a miserable bugger," I mumbled. "You're a miserable bugger." I heaved a wooden side table into the skip and watched it splinter. It seemed roughly half of our belongings were damaged in the move, causing me to bleed even more money replacing everything. I vowed never to move house again. Sal was glaring at me, daring me not to snap out of my mood. "I know, I know," I said. "I'm just stressed. The dishwasher door is still missing. When are the builders coming?" I looked at a white van across the road, wishing it was them, but it wasn't.

"Tomorrow, so stop bloody moaning. Will you go round the back and see if you can find the water meter? I need to sort all the utilities out before Christmas."

I nodded. Then left her on the driveway to get the kid's out of the car. Jack was singing Christmas songs and Molly was crying because she was hungry. The normal soundtrack to my life lately. In fact, it was a relaxing break going to the side of my house all by myself.

The electricity and gas had meters sat in boxes on the wall, but the water readout had so remained elusive. The builders had said to look for a manhole cover in the garden so that was where I looked. The previous owners left a lot of debris—plant pots and such—and I had to kick it aside as I cut a path along the patio. I could see no manhole covers anywhere, but I did spot an opening at the base of the retaining wall between the elevated lawn and the sunken patio. It looked like a drain—a wide, narrow hole cut horizontally into the bottom of the brick wall. Inside, it was pitch-black. A shiver danced along my spine. I looked back to see where Sal was, but the driveway was quiet. She'd taken the kids inside.

I stared into the drain. Could it be where the water meter was hiding? It seemed a strange thing to have in a garden, but I wasn't much of an expert about plumbing. I got down on my hands and knees to take a closer look, and cold air wafted in my face, along with the smell of…

Gingerbread?

Something shone in the darkness. The glint of an eye.

"Hiya, Iain!"

I froze, an icicle stabbing right into my heart. I knew that voice.

Two familiar eyes glared back at me from the drain. My lower lip trembled. "W-what are you doing here?" I asked.

"I came to play," purred the voice in the sewer. "Do you want to play a game?"

I shook my head. "No."

"Too bad!"

An arm shot out of the drain and grabbed my wrist. I struggled to get free, but the weight pulling me down was too much. My hand disappeared into the shadows and I couldn't retrieve it.

I felt teeth against my flesh.

"Ouch! Shit, why are you biting me?"

"Mmmph… Because I… mmph… heard horror authors taste like… mmph… Bovril."

The revulsion helped me to yank my hand back, and I scrambled away from the drain, screaming at the top of my lungs. "SAL! SAL, COME QUICK!"

Sal came rushing out into the garden, ready to vape. This time I smelt aniseed. "What? What is it?"

I pointed at the sewer. "It's Matty-Bob! He's back."

Her eyes widened, and she stared at the drain. Then she surprised me by taking a hit on her vape and calmly strolling over to me. She placed her hands on my shoulders and blew smoke over my shoulder. Definitely aniseed. "Honey, Matty-Bob can't hurt you anymore. He's been locked, and he's never getting out. Not after they caught him eating that squirrel."

"But…" I pointed at the drain again, but there was only a slab of darkness there. "He was there, I swear it! The bugger bit me."

Sal looked at the back of my hand as I waved it in front of her face like I was bloody John Cena. Sure enough, a circle of teeth marks pitted my flesh. It wasn't enough to convince her, though, because she pulled me into a hug. "Just calm down. I know you're upset about that review you got calling your work 'school-boy drivel', and that one last week saying you were the literary equivalent of herpes." She started to chuckle. "Or that classic one last year that said you write like a baboon with a hangover—"

"What's your point?" I snapped.

"That you're under a lot of stress, honey, what with the move and everything."

I nodded. Of course I was feeling overwhelmed. "And Molly never stops eating," I said. "I tried to eat a peanut the other day and she went mental. I had to hand it over. Sal, I'm scared to go in the kitchen. She's always there… looking at me."

"Honey, she's not even eighteen months old. You two will have to learn to get along."

"I know. Just... can tell her she can't have my peanuts."

Sal frowned at me just as Jack stepped out into the garden. He looked around with a smile on his face and, as he ran towards me, he almost tripped and landed on his face twice. He stayed upright long enough to collide headfirst with my genitals. I doubled over and gave him a cuddle while I bit down on my pain. "Hiya... sweetheart. You... ah, Jesus Wept, that hurts... okay?"

Jack grabbed the back of my neck and hung from me like a baboon. "This our new garden?"

"Yep. You like in?"

"Bigger than old garden?"

"I haven't measured yet, but I'm quite sure it is, yes. Mummy and Daddy got it for you and Molly."

Jack smiled and covered his mouth dramatically. "Oh, thank you, Daddy. Thank you very much for my new garden!"

I got free of his grasp and grimaced. To Sal, I whispered. "I swear he's going to end up in theatre. He's so dramatic."

Sal chuckled. "Fine by me. Maybe he'll be able to get us tickets to Shrek."

Jack spotted an old football amongst the debris and went and kicked it. From the kitchen, I heard screams of agonised, burning hunger."

Sal nodded at me. "Go get Mol a biscuit."

"She's already had about ten," I argued.

"Then she's only about halfway done. Go on! She'll make you pay for it if you leave her waiting."

So, somewhat shakily, I went into the kitchen while wondering if I was losing my mind. I swear Matty-Bob had been in the drain, but thinking about it now made it seem absurd. Just stress, I thought. Yep, that was all.

Molly glared at me as I entered the kitchen. Chocolate covered her chomping maw, and she held one last, smushed-up biscuit in her clenched fist, which she thrust at me balefully. The message was clear. GIVE. ME. *MORE!*

I hurried to the cupboard and grabbed the snack box. When I found the cookie tube empty, I panicked. Hands shaking, I frantically searched the new kitchen. I found bread sticks next to some plates and hoped they would suffice. I got them to my growing daughter just as she readied herself for another onslaught of barbaric screams. She snatched the bread sticks from my hand and shoved them into her mouth, eyeballing me the entire time she chewed. *LEAVE!*

So I left her sat in her highchair and went into the lounge. My big TV hung on the wall, and just looking at it reduced my stress. A flat screen television, even when switched off, was a thing of beauty. So shiny and sleek. My own reflection smiled back at me.

Something behind me moved—a shifting blur in the glass panel. I spun around to catch sight of it and found the hallway door slowly closing. Must have been the dog, I told myself, but then I saw Oscar asleep on the sofa.

"Oscar! Get on your bloody bed."

The dog looked at me with stroke-face, upper lip curled inside out and one floppy ear folded on top of his head. All the same, he knew the jig was up, and retired to his rarely used bed. Jack came into the room and tossed a plastic apple at me. It hit my genitals and doubled me over. I gave him another cuddle. "What you up to... oh God, I'm gonna puke... darling?"

"Making a picnic for you and mummy, Molly, Oscar, Granma, Nanny, Grandad, Auntie Siobhan, Uncle Leigh, Uncle Andy, Lily, Aunt—"

"So basically everyone we know?" I said. "Okay, got it. You want me to help you?"

"No, Mummy help."

I stood. "Okay dokay. Should I just leave?"

Jack cuddled my leg, then nodded his head. "Yes, Daddy, you leave. Go have lie down."

I frowned. "S-seriously? A nap would be really nice."

"Yes! Go nap!"

Sal came in, holding Molly in her arms. The baby had a breadstick in each hand, plus a third sticking out of her mouth. "You're not going for a lie down and leaving me with the kids, matey."

"B-but Jack said I could."

"Jack is three."

Jack looked at Mommy earnestly. "Daddy want to go for lie down."

I stared imploringly at Sal. "Daddy does!"

She shook her head and laughed. "You'd spend your whole life asleep if I let you. Can you take Molly for a minute? I need a wee."

WIth little choice, I took Molly and ducked as she tried to take out left my eye with a bread stick. I sat on the sofa with her and switched on the TV. I got a shock by what I saw. A pair of nipples came up on screen. Nipples I would recognise anywhere.

For the last two years, Matty-Bob had been sending me naked pictures from the institution. I reported it several times, but he kept posting them out somehow. The words he had once written in lipstick on his torso, were now etched in prison-ink. IAIN ROB WRIGHT FTW. The mantra that had first led the crazy misfit to my doorstep. Being a writer came with certain dangers. Being a horror writer attracted oddballs left and right. And Matty-Bob was the oddball king.

Three years since the last time he'd invaded my family's lives by turning up at our home and trying to kill me. Now he'd found my new home. I placed Molly on the floor, ignoring her angry cries, and ran to the television. I put my head against the wall and peered behind the set, searching between wires and fixings.

And there it was, sticking out the side of the panel—a little red USB stick I'd never seen before. I yanked it out and examined it in my palm. PROPERTY OF BRAYSHAW SECURE HEALTH INSTITUTE.

There was a crusty white stain on the end that was either saliva, or something else.

"SAL! SAL, COME QUICK!"

She came rushing into the room, impatience written on her face. I knew when she'd mentioned needing a wee, what she'd actually meant was a poo. And that poo had been interrupted. A marriage faux pas.

"What is it now, Iain?"

"Matty-Bob is here. Look!"

I handed her the USB stick, and she examined it. The frown on her face hung around a long time before she finally looked at me with a modicum of acceptance. "Did you get this in the post?"

I shook my head. "I found it sticking out the television. He's been in our house."

"That's impossible." She yanked her phone out of her pocket and I saw her hand shaking. She selected the Institutes' number from her phone book and dialled it. It wasn't the first time we'd called them—or even the hundredth. From a few feet away, I could hear the line ringing, but nobody was picking up. Sal looked at me and tapped her foot while she waited. Molly whacked me in the ankle with a plastic tea pot and I hissed in pain, but I didn't take my focus off my wife's face, or the sound of that unbroken ringing. Why wouldn't they pick up?

Then I heard a voice and saw Sal react. I couldn't make out what was being said, but when my wife replied, I was hopeful.

"Oh, hi. This is Sally Wright. Could you call me back as soon as you get this please? It's regarding your patient, Matty-Bob. It's urgent. Thank you."

Deflated, I asked the obvious. "Voicemail? When has it ever gone to voicemail before?"

Sal tapped the phone against her chin, thinking. Then she turned and scooped Molly up in her arms. "Get Jack. We're leaving."

"Good idea." I scooped Jack up in my arms, leading him to giggle and beg me to spin him. Together, as a family, we hurried for the front door. Even Oscar got the hint and left his bed.

Sal threw open the door to the porch.

And stopped in her tracks.

Me and Jack bumped into the back of her. "What is it? What-"

Our porch was filled by a massive parcel wrapped in Christmas paper and it was blocking the front door. "We need to move it."

"Just leave it, Iain! We'll go out the back."

I took a step towards the box. "No, that's where I saw Matty-Bob hiding. He was in the drain."

"Iain, he obviously left this here for you. Don't touch it."

But I couldn't help it. I was a writer, and a writer must explore and experience the world to feed his unquenchable thirst for knowledge. A writer's unique spirit and thriving libido must never be suppressed. Although few, we are a gift unto the world that must, at all times, be allowed to fly free.

Sally prodded me in the back. "Iain! What are you stood there for, daydreaming when we should be getting out of here? If you have to look inside the bloody box, then just get it over with."

"I'm sorry!" I snapped out of my daze and went into the porch. The box was well wrapped, and must have cost a fortune in paper. I wondered how it got here and then spotted the white van parked across the street. It said BSHI on the side and it now made perfect sense. BRAWSHAW SECURE HEALTH INSTITUTE. Matty-Bob had stolen a van and escaped. My hands were shaking as I carefully pushed aside the lid and peered inside. It was packed full of something—lots of somethings.

I reached inside.

"Careful," Sal warned me.

Hands still shaking, I retrieved one of the items from the box. It was a head. Gwyneth Paltrow's head.

Sal cleared her throat. "Is that… is that a dummy's head?"

I turned the thing around in my hands, marvelling at the detail. "I think it's wax. Maybe it's how Matty-Bob spends his time at the Institute."

"Okay, I'm calling the police," she said, and started dialling.

"You can't call the police," said a voice from inside the living room. I've cut the power."

I span around and finally saw him, standing there in the nude next to our sofa. His flaccid penis was stuck against his leg.

Sal groaned and rolled her eyes. "Oh no, you cut the power? Good for you, idiot. I'm making the call on my mobile. Oh, yes, hello, can I speak with the police, please? We have a dangerous intruder who's been prosecuted for stalking my family already. Yes, thank you, I would really appreciate you being quick."

Matty-Bob's eyes went wide as he realised his mistake. He searched around frantically, grabbing one of Molly's toys. It was a fluffy unicorn, and he launched it across the room. It struck Sal on the top of her head and bounced off harmlessly. She sighed and took Molly out into the hallway while she spoke with the police. I sent Jack after her.

I stood alone with a psychopath.

"You can't be here, Matty-Bob. You know that!"

"Why? Because The Man said so?"

"Because a court-appointed judge and a team of licensed therapists said so. You're scaring my family. You're scaring me."

Matty-Bob smiled. "Good! I am here to kill you, Mr Rob Wright." He reached behind his back and produced a knife.

I moaned. "Did you have that clenched between your butt cheeks?"

He shrugged. "I didn't have any pockets."

"You might have had if you were wearing clothes. Why the hell are you naked?"

Matty-Bob put the knife to his nose and sniffed it. From his reaction, it didn't smell nice. "I can't exactly walk down the street in my nut-house uniform, can I? Would draw attention to myself."

"But walking around naked with an IAIN ROB WRIGHT FTW tattoo on your belly is an everyday sight?"

He started breathing quickly. He clutched his temples and grunted. "Stop confusing me with your logic. I don't do well with logic."

"Evidently," I said. "Look, Matty-Bob. I appreciate you being a fan of my books, but you can't keep invading my life like this. The police will be here soon, so just hand over the knife and take a seat. Not on the leather though—I'll get you a newspaper or something."

The knife lowered towards the floor, and Matty-Bob gave a long sigh before padding across the new carpet towards me.

"That's it," I said soothingly. "There we go. Nice and slowly."

Matty-Bob made it over to me, but stopped a single step short. There were tears in his eyes. "I thought I could be the Bachman to your King."

I frowned. "They're the same person, Matty-Bob."

Matty-Bob sneered. "Exactly."

The blade came at me too fast to react. My cheek felt cold, and then hot, and then wet. I fell to my knees, clutched my face and howled. "Not my face, not my beautiful, perfect, unforgettable face. What have you done? Damn it, man, what have you done?"

Sal came rushing back into the room without the kids. "What have you done? Oh, God, no, not his face. Not his beautiful, perfect, incomparable face."

I staggered over to my wife and let her hold me. "Thanks, honey."

She looked at me. "Thanks for what?"

"For what you just said about my face."

"I never said anything. Are you okay? What's happening?"

I showed her my wound and wept against her chest. "He's disfigured me."

"No, he hasn't. It's barely a scratch."

Buoyed by the news that my face had escaped ruin, I turned back to face my attacker. How dare he try to kill me. How dare he try to deprive the world of one of its few great artists.

But Matty-Bob was gone.

My eyes narrowed. "What are you up to now, you cock knocker!"

I hurried into the kitchen and found him rooting around my fridge. When he turned to face me, he had this evening's frozen pizza in his hands. Slowly he began to lower it towards his waist.

I thrust my finger at him. "Matty-Bob... Don't. You. DARE!"

Matty-Bob looked me in the eye defiantly. He kept on lowering the pizza until it was down at his middle. With a slight hop of his heels, he brought his swollen, red testicles down on top of the pizza. The grin on his face was maniacal. "Eat my cock-pizza, bitch."

I snarled. "Never."

He flew at me with the frozen pizza, swinging it at my head. It caught me above the left eyebrow and suddenly I had blood flooding into my eyes. I shoved out blindly and struck Matty-Bob's soft flabby chest. He lunged at me again, and I grabbed the nearest thing I could find, which was the mid-height oven. I yanked open the door just as he came at me, which caused him to smash right into it. The crack of the door against his ribs was sickening. He bounced back and doubled over the island worktop.

I heard police sirens. "It's over Matty-Bob. This time they'll lock you away for good this time."

Matty-Bob was still face-down on the island, but he reached out with both arms, rooting around blindly. His fingers found the Matt Shaw novel I'd been reading with my breakfast every morning. He bolted upright and flung the paperback at my head. It hit me right in the gob, and I tasted blood.

"You sick bastard!" I mumbled, then lost my temper. I leapt across the kitchen and grabbed Matty-Bob by his ginger hair. I shoved his face down onto the hob in the center of the island and switched it on. "Damn you to Hell. Damn you all to Hell!"

Matty-Bob squirmed and yelled, but I was waiting for screams. But none came. It was several moments before I realised the hob was an induction model, and wouldn't come on without an appropriate pot or pan.

Matty-Bob fought back and managed to headbutt me in the nose with the back of his head. He threw me backwards against the sink and prodded the button for the waste disposal. It growled angrily, with no water or food to sate its metal teeth. Matty-Bob punched me in the stomach and grabbed my wrist, forcing my hand towards the sink.

"No!" I begged. "Not my typing hand."

"Don't you type with both hands?" Matty-Bob asked.

"Depends what I'm doing!"

We struggled against one another. Matty-Bob was winning, my hand inching closer and closer to the rubber baffle over the hole of death. The waste disposal whined hungrily, begging to taste my flesh. "What do you mean, it depends what you're doing?" Matty Bob asked.

"It means…" I said, through gritted teeth. "That sometimes an author gotta wank."

I sprang up with all my strength and forced my wrist free. I punched Matty-Bob in the face with lefts and rights. I was like Rocky Balboa avenging Apollo's death, smashing Mr T with relentless blows. I was poetry in motion, the God of pugilists everywhere. Adonis reincarnated.

"What are you doing?" Matty-Bob asked.

I realised I was punching the air like a madman, not connecting with any of my blows. Matty-Bob had picked up a knife from the counter and now held it in front of him.

Outside, the police sirens were close. I heard voices outside.

"My doctor said the only way I will ever be sane again is if I murder you."

I raised an eyebrow. "I really doubt your doctor said that."

Matty-Bob shrugged. "Not those exact words, but I read between the lines."

He came at me with the knife. I had only a split second to decide what to do to save my own life. I did the only thing I could think of. I asked myself, *What would Jesus do?*

Kick him in the balls, my son.

Kick him in the balls.

I nodded, knowing what I needed to do. I punted Matty-Bob right between the legs, crushing his testicles against his undercarriage and lifting him right off his feet.

He crumpled backwards onto the island and let out a tremendous bellow. His cheeks turned red as he went into labour, huffing and puffing through the pain.

Police piled into the kitchen from the hallway and from the garden, surrounding me on all sides.

"What happened, Mr Wright?" A female officer asked.

"I kicked him in the balls."

She frowned at me. "Jeez, was that really necessary? He's just a nutjob."

I growled. "Now, he's a nut job with no nuts."

She shook her head at me in disgust. Another officer mumbled under his breath, *"What an asshole."*

Sal walked in with the kids. When she saw me, she looked a little surprised. I was, after all, covered in blood. "You're still alive then?"

"You know me," I said, shrugging. "I may be a gentle author at heart, but I'm all man where it counts."

She sighed. "Yes, honey, of course you are. The kids are outside with the neighbours. We've caused quite the scene. They're already mad at you for shaving their cat, so this isn't going to help.

I huffed. "I told you before. I need to shave cats. It's just who I am."

She patted me on the shoulder. "I know, honey. I know."

I looked at her. "Do you have a cat I can shave right now?"

"No!"

"Shame. I could do with one to calm my nerves."

"Matty-Bob was still groaning, even as the police officers got him to his feet. He looked at me differently now, defeated—sad. "Do you know what it's like to be me?" he asked. "To not know what's real or what's normal? To me, authors are not just people. They are gods. They create worlds as gods do, and they can change people's lives like gods do."

"But we're just human," I said holding out my palms. "I know it's hard to believe, but we bleed like the rest of you."

"Oh, brother! Sal muttered in the corner. "Can we just get this over with, please? I need to put some turkey dinosaurs in to cook and you're all blocking my oven."

The police officers nodded their apologies to my wife and took

Matty-Bob out of the house. As they took him down the hallway, he twisted his neck all the way around to look at me, like an owl. I shuddered.

"You haven't seen the last of me," he swore. Then he winced. "Jesus, can someone help me get my neck straight. This really hurts."

And then he was gone from my life once more, a fleeting impact that would forever change the landscape of my life, like an asteroid hitting the earth. Perhaps this tortured soul was the Ying to my own tortured Yang. Whereas I turned my darker thoughts to magic on the page, Matty-Bob found himself unable to find such a valuable outlet and invariably-

"Iain!"

I spun to face my wife. "Yes, honey?"

"Can you go to the neighbours and get the kids, please? They just text me to say Molly has a poo in her nappy and they are not happy to deal with it. Also, make sure you apply lotion to her bum because she's been getting very sore lately. Ask Jack if he needs a poo as well, as it's about that time."

I sighed and headed for the front door. *The life of an author*, I thought to myself ruefully. *Both a blessing and a curse.*

DEDICATED TO ALL MY FANS, BOTH TWISTED AND SANE.

Plea From the Author

Hey, Reader. So you got to the end of my book. I hope that means you enjoyed it. Whether or not you did, I would just like to thank you for giving me your valuable time to try and entertain you. I am truly blessed to have such a fulfilling job, but I only have that job because of people like you; people kind enough to give my books a chance and spend their hard-earned money buying them. For that I am eternally grateful.

If you would like to find out more about my other books then please visit my website for full details. You can find it at:

www.iainrobwright.com.

Also feel free to contact me on Facebook, Twitter, or email (all details on the website), as I would love to hear from you.

If you enjoyed this book and would like to help, then you could think about leaving a review. The most important part of how well a book sells is how many positive reviews it has, so if you leave me one then you are directly helping me to continue on this journey as a fulltime writer. Thanks in advance to anyone who does. It means a lot.

WANT FREE BOOKS?

Don't miss out on your complimentary Iain Rob Wright horror starter pack. Five bestselling horror novels sent straight to your inbox. No strings attached.

For more information just visit this page:
www.iainrobwright.com/free-starter-pack/

Also by Iain Rob Wright

- **AZ of Horror**
- **Animal Kingdom**
- **2389**
- **Holes in the Ground (with J.A.Konrath)**
- **Sam**
- **ASBO**
- **The Final Winter**
- **The Housemates**
- **Sea Sick** (FREE)
- **Ravage**
- **Savage**
- **The Picture Frame**
- **Wings of Sorrow**
- **The Gates**
- **Legion**
- **Extinction**
- **Tar**

Sarah Stone Thriller Series

- **Soft Target** (FREE)
- **Hot Zone**
- **END PLAY**